THE
ANGRY
WOMEN'S
CHOIR

Also by Meg Bignell
The Sparkle Pages
Welcome to Nowhere River

THE
ANGRY
WOMEN'S
CHOIR

MEG
BIGNELL

MICHAEL JOSEPH
an imprint of
PENGUIN BOOKS

MICHAEL JOSEPH

UK | USA | Canada | Ireland | Australia
India | New Zealand | South Africa | China

Michael Joseph is part of the Penguin Random House group of companies
whose addresses can be found at global.penguinrandomhouse.com

Penguin
Random House
Australia

First published by Michael Joseph in 2022

Cover design by Christabella Designs
Typeset in 12.25/17.5 pt Adobe Garamond Pro by Midland Typesetters, Australia
Printed and bound in Australia by Griffin Press, part of Ovato, an accredited
ISO AS/NZS 14001 Environmental Management Systems printer

A catalogue record for this
book is available from the
National Library of Australia

ISBN 978 1 76104 671 1

penguin.com.au

MIX
Paper from
responsible sources
FSC® C009448

For Ed, Bess and Lucie. Stay kind. Brush your teeth.

'I get the greatest feeling when I'm singing. Your feet are anchored into the earth and into this energy force that comes up through your feet and goes up to the top of your head and maybe you're holding hands with the angels or the stars, I have no idea.' Cyndi Lauper

𝄢

'Come sister, melt the city, twist a rhythm to the streets. The long winter has withered if you lit a spark.' Tap Dance, NY Wages for Housework Committee, 1984

Prologue

WEST MOONAH WOMEN'S CHOIR DISHES UP MORE COMFORT TUNES

Review by M.A.B., 28 July 2019

Last week's performance by the West Moonah Women's Choir at the Festival of Voices offered up generous serves of the 'singalong, sway and smile' repertoire the choir's audiences have come to rely on. Flamboyant choir director Bizzy Nancarrow took no risks in what has otherwise been a vibrant, thought-provoking festival. Longtime fans of the choir would not have been disappointed.

A heartfelt, skilfully arranged rendition of Ben E. King's 'Stand By Me' never goes astray. Kyrie Kalbfel's soprano was as exquisite as ever and solos by Kyrie's daughter-in-law Rosanna Kalbfel and emerging talent Avni Sasani were remarkable as always. But I, for one, would like this choir to step out of their parlour-tunes happy place and into something that better reflects the choir's unusual history.

The West Moonah Women's Choir first met on 2 July 1984, the day Cyndi Lauper released 'She Bop', her controversial song about female masturbation. Bizzy Nancarrow adored Cyndi

Lauper with such vehemence that she changed her hair colour to match Cyndi's hectic orange.

Founding member Irene Hawke informed me that four women attended that first meeting at Moonah's iconic Laetare Gardens Function Centre ($17.99 evening hire with hall, dance floor, 'enchanted' interior garden and stereo system). All the women reportedly experienced varying degrees of bewilderment in the face of Nancarrow's unusual appearance and clamorous voice.

'She has this loud, zigzagging Irish accent,' Hawke said, 'and she was saying things that raised an eyebrow or two. She also said, "The choir shall be a place where we can breathe, where we can share, a place where we need not leave our troubles at the door but bring them in, hand them about and sing them away." I loved that most of all, it really got me. I imagined my troubles floating away on the music.'

Bizzy Nancarrow elaborated. 'I've always said that our weekly sings are not about worship or reverence. They're not even about music. They are about voices. *Our* voices, coming all the way from here'—she thumped her chest—'and here'—she tapped her head—'and here.' At this juncture she placed her hand between her legs, letting it linger there a moment. Her choir members simply laughed and nodded in agreement, unsurprised. Their eyebrows did not rise.

On that first gathering, though, two of the women excused themselves on the spot. Irene Hawke and Kyrie Kalbfel stayed, then couldn't help but return the following week, thereby securing their place in history as founding members of arguably the state's most popular choir. Bizzy Nancarrow credits the choir's longevity to the quality of friendship on offer and the satisfying side effects of singing: a strengthening of the diaphragm that she says helps to sustain tenacity.

This tenacity has fuelled the choir's focus on activism and secured its reputation as a women's group with modest influence. It has lent its melodious voice to many a worthy cause over the years, including Aboriginal reconciliation, citizens against domestic violence, breast cancer research, child protection, migrant resources and climate change action.

Bizzy Nancarrow is well known for her long-term community and environmental activism, and for being the muse for the eighties chart-topping feminist wake-up song 'Liniment Girl' by Barbara Takes a Trip.

But it is Nancarrow's 'sideline' business enterprise, Very Cross Stitches™, that has brought her world acclaim. Her ever-growing series of counted cross-stitch designs depicting social justice and feminist slogans have captured the world's imagination, sparked fierce conversations and brought her unexpected fortune. A Bizzy Nancarrow Very Cross Stitch once hung in the office of Julia Gillard, Australia's first female prime minister.

The rest of the choir bring just as much colour to the show, if not in their hair then in their backgrounds. Avni Sasani, for instance, is making waves in the national music scene with her singer-songwriter career. Dr Sally Cartwright, known for her ground-breaking work in the Royal Hobart Hospital burns unit, is also a longtime member. Infamous murderess Eleanor Flynn, having done her time for murdering her husband, reportedly sings with the choir after she completes her work as a cleaner in their rehearsal venue.

Kyrie Kalbfel's daughter-in-law, Rosanna Kalbfel, was diagnosed with terminal cancer in 2017 and has evidently faced her illness with courage and candour. She has been composing a list of tips and advice for her husband and four children.

'It's called *La Lista*. A catalogue of important things she might not be around to tell them,' explained Kyrie. 'She takes it with her everywhere. It's inspiring and funny and unseemly and completely heartbreaking.'

'It's a guidebook to living,' added Bizzy.

Rosanna herself waves away these compliments and adds that the words of advice are 'just little *sassolina*. Stepping stones'.

When I said that I would like to read such a field guide myself, Rosanna laughed, handed me a thick blue notebook and said, 'Go ahead. It is boring-boring but at least it will get the children to sleep.'

All this considered, my challenge to this most talented choir is to refresh their repertoire into one as fascinating, inspiring, funny, unseemly and heartbreaking as themselves. Or perhaps they can ponder the title of Cyndi Lauper's hit album *She's So Unusual* without churning out the same old eighties covers *time after time*.

I wonder whether they might act upon a word of advice from Rosanna Kalbfel's La Lista, which is this: 'If you want to serve pudding, serve pudding. But make it something glorious. Tiramisu or bombe alaska. Don't waste your treats on vanilla pudding.'

I mean, we all like vanilla pudding, just not at every meal.

Chapter 1

In the Ordinary

On a gloomy Tuesday morning in early August, Freycinet Barnes wakes with a potent and unaccountable sense of dread.

Her feet and legs ache. No, it's not an ache. It's a heaviness. They seem unwilling to move into the day. She blinks at the ceiling, presses her thighs with her hands and tries to coax them into action.

'Come on,' she whispers ten minutes later when she's still lying in the same position. 'Get up.' Recalling a favourite expression of her father's, she adds, 'You can't fly so you have to stand.'

She finally hoists herself to a sitting position and searches her memorised weekly schedule for events out of the ordinary that might be causing this weighted apprehension. There are none. It occurs to her that the events *in* the ordinary could be to blame. The drear of repeated activity. Another round of school lunches. Another Tasmanian August in which the days get longer but also colder and the hints at deliverance from winter are just cruel teasings.

'I'll put something different in today,' she whispers to her feet. 'I promise.'

She moves gingerly to the bathroom and stands before the mirror, gathering human intelligence from the evidence before her.

Swollen eyes. Otherwise known as eye-bags. Freycinet wonders what she might unpack from them. Two glasses of wine and a restless sleep are likely to be the most immediate items. Three, actually. Three glasses of wine on a school night. Associated shame. Other items muddled into the restless sleep are the forgotten name of a schoolteacher, a missing birth certificate, a misplaced spare key, the dog's constant licking of his left paw, Year Ten maths and the rising unease that comes with buying an expensive green rug when perhaps it should have been blue. Layered in with those is the self-contempt that comes with worrying about rugs when there are people sleeping in the streets with no rugs, plastic floating in the oceans, and other things far more deserving of worry. The cycle of privileged disquietude.

Frey's heart is beating oddly. Too fast, tripping on itself at intervals. There is no adrenaline to explain it, no adventure. Just another Tuesday with its ordinary ticks and ordered tocks. Scheduling, marshalling and logistics have become Frey's thing. Her craft. She stares at her reflection and thinks back to a time when her days never knew what might come. A time that seems like a faded storybook.

The doorbell rings.

'Once upon a chime,' she says to her reflection.

It rings again. 'Can someone get that?' she calls. 'God, who's this early?'

There is a squabble in the hallway and a 'Fuck off, Tom'.

'Hey!' Frey calls.

The doorbell rings again.

'Someone?' Frey takes a jade face-roller to her puffy eyes and says, 'You can't answer the door looking like that. You are the Minister for Home Affairs and Social Services.'

This is her husband Gil's favourite title for his wife. 'Ah, here comes the Honourable Minister for Home Affairs and Social

Services,' he will declare when she joins him at a work function. 'My wife, Frey.'

Lately the title has begun to grate. She wonders whether all the things that grate on a person eventually leave the skin fragile and thin.

The management of the household, with its labyrinthine intricacies, has begun to rankle too. Its immaculate timings and smooth runnings have got a bit wobbly in the wheels. *If the wheels were to fall off*, Frey wonders, *would the minister be forced to resign?*

There is a sudden and urgent knock on the bathroom door.

'Mum?'

Frey jumps.

'Mum? MUM? Tom took my sushi.' The whine in the child's voice makes Frey think of blackboards and fingernails. And wine, frankly. She holds her breath, squeezes her eyes shut and wonders how she might disappear. *And she vanished in the puff of an eye.*

'MUU-UUM. He took it out of my lunchbox. Tell him to GIVE IT BACK.'

Frey opens her eyes and whispers to the lines on her forehead, 'Tom, give Lily's sushi back.'

'NOOO! Now he's EATING IT!' Lily's voice sirens through the walls. 'MUU-UUUM.' She pounds on the bathroom door.

Frey, fearing collateral damage, opens it a little way, puts a finger to her lips and pulls Lily into the bathroom.

'Okay, you're right, we have to do something about this. Let's call the police.'

Lily blinks up at her mother, her pale eyes suspicious, then furious. 'Mu-um.'

'Theft is a crime. Sushi theft is especially heinous. I'd better get dressed first. Don't let on, he might make a run for it.'

'I'm serious, Mum. He's such a dickhead, I wish he'd just die.'

'Oh, that's even easier. Let's kill him.'

'Mum.' Lily begins to cry. 'You're being a dickhead too.'

'Actually, *you're* being the dickhead. You haven't thought of the fact that if Tom ate your sushi for breakfast, then you get *his* sushi, and he gets breakfast in his lunchbox.'

Lily sniffs. 'You called me a dickhead.'

'Yes. You called me one too. And I'm in my pyjamas, which make my bottom look huge and me especially vulnerable.'

'I don't like egg sushi.'

'But it will be worth taking the egg sushi in exchange for seeing Tom go to school with porridge in his lunchbox.'

Lily giggles.

'Now, can you let me get dressed in peace? And I mean peace. Don't go anywhere near Tom. Or Grace. Morning Grace is a very deadly monster.'

'You can't have a *very* deadly monster. It's either deadly or it's not.'

'A brain like that and it still didn't think of porridge revenge? Be off with you.'

Frey pushes Lily back out the door and returns to her reflection. She turns side-on and runs a hand over the curve of her bottom.

The doorbell rings again, three times in grumpy, quick succession.

'Shit,' she says to her reflection. 'Shit. I've lost the spare key. Lily?' she calls. 'That'll be Dad, I haven't left a key out. Can you let him in?'

Gil clatters in from his morning bike ride a minute later and booms, 'Jeez, don't rush, you lot. Where's the spare key?'

Something flutters in Freycinet's stomach. She marvels at how closely anxiety can mimic adoration. She also notes the time.

'Right,' she whispers. 'You're behind. You are fine. You're just a bit sluggish. Hurry up.' She pulls on her shapewear knickers and bra, then slips into a green silk shirt and black pants, an outfit carefully selected for a Tuesday comprising a school association meeting, a vet visit, lunch with Gil, an afternoon assembly with Tom presenting as sports prefect, an hour waiting at Grace's dance class and no adventures. She smooths her already smooth blonde hair (the weekly schedule includes a Monday wash and blow dry) and applies a subtle coating of makeup to her face, some shimmer to her cheekbones and a delicate swish of mascara to each eye.

'Frey?' calls Gil.

'I'm just coming,' Frey replies, hoping that no one mentions the sushi in front of Gil. Sushi is clear evidence that the school lunches are not homemade.

'The spare key's gone.' Gil is right outside the bathroom door.

'Yeah, sorry. I'll get another one cut.'

'And I can't meet you for lunch today after all. Clients want to talk cute Tassie niche assets.'

Frey opens the door to see Gil, lycra-clad, rippling with handsome health.

'Morning!' she says. 'You were quick today. I didn't think you could get any fitter.' She plants a kiss on his lips and breezes past, turning her face away (*Don't look at my eye puffs*). 'Don't worry about lunch. I'll go and see Dad instead.'

'That okay?' asks Gil, following to be sure. 'I tried to get out of it but it's interstate investors and they're only here until tonight.'

'No worries. Really.'

'I'll make next week's happen, I promise.' He catches her arm, pulls her to him.

Frey kisses him so he can't focus on her eye-bags. He kisses her back, gives a little 'mmm' of desire.

Tom, their seventeen-year-old, turns into the hallway. 'Gross,' he says without looking up from his phone. 'Old people kissing.'

'Hey, Tom,' says Gil, releasing Frey and following his son towards the kitchen. 'I shaved ten whole minutes off my best time this morning.'

'Yeah, massive tailwind, Dad,' says Tom.

'Not 'round at Taroona.'

Frey watches the swagger in Tom's shoulders as he walks to the pantry. *He is perpetually pleased with himself,* she thinks.

'You should get yourself into something, Frey,' says Gil, who, Frey realises, walks with the same gait as his son. 'Keep yourself fit.' He unwraps the newspaper.

Frey clenches her bottom. She gets the milk from the fridge and remembers the time she'd broached the idea of a horse-riding trip away on her own, back when Lily was a toddler and Frey had felt at her most confounded.

'How'll we manage that?' Gil had asked, and Frey hadn't known how to answer. Tom was still having to do complicated physio exercises back then, no one but Frey knew how to put Grace's hair into a perfect ballet bun, and who would manage lunches and bedtime stories? How would indispensable Gil Barnes find time away from Barnes and Rutherford Property Development? And there was the question of the inevitable mother-guilt. Frey couldn't be sure that even solitude, horses and exhilaration could salve such guilt. So, the idea was filed as 'all too hard', then shelved. The Minister for Home Affairs remained in her seat. Around the same time, Gil had told Frey she was selfish for not sharing her pineapple juice. Again, she believed him.

Frey flicks the kettle on and tries to relax her clenched jaw. She hasn't yet made the beds or got last night's pyjamas in the washing machine.

She can't bring herself to fill Tom's lunchbox up with porridge. There's a particular brand of scorn Tom reserves for his mother, which is starting to burn. She makes him a chicken sandwich, pops an extra chocolate ball (homemade) in with Lily's egg sushi, then applies an extra layer of makeup under her eyes in time to drop all three children at their respective school gates and get to the vet with Acorn the labrador, to see about his licking.

𝄢

Eight hours later, Frey pulls into the carpark of Derwent Dance Academy and wonders

1. *How could I have possibly fit in lunch with Gil?* and
2. *Where has another day gone?*

There had been the time spent working out a new diet for her itchy-footed, processed-food-fed labrador. Then a long visit to her father, Roger, who did a crossword and used up most of his customarily sparse conversation on the dog. Then she had Barnes and Rutherford work to do, the school association meeting, chopping and stacking wood, grocery shopping, the chemist and school assembly and hello, three o'clock. Time to pick up Grace for her dance class. She hopes no one asks what she's been doing all day, the way they usually don't.

Grace is out of the car before it's fully stationary, inside the academy building before Frey can wish her goodbye. *Of course*, thinks Frey. *She's sixteen, not twelve. What a difference a few years makes.* Frey remembers the earnest little girl with the pale ringleted hair and the huge smile, now thoroughly lost to womanly beauty and cool self-confidence.

Frey locks the car and follows Grace inside, where the waiting room is warm and she can comfortably catch up on her emails. She has just tapped the inbox icon on her phone when someone to her right giggles, then says, 'Hi, Frey?'

Frey turns to see a small, yellow-blonde woman with bad posture and a face she's seen before. 'Yes, hi.'

The woman giggles again and Frey feels prickles of irritation then shame. She wishes it wasn't the hair and the posture she'd noticed first. The woman's smile is warm beneath its shyness. Frey tries to remember her name.

'Tammy,' says Tammy, evidently noticing Frey's memory lapse. 'My Diana is in Grace's class at school.'

'Yes, of course. Hi Tammy.' Frey looks for eye-bags, but sees none.

'They used to be in the same dance class, too, but Grace is miles ahead now. You have such a talented daughter; you must be so proud.'

'Thank you.' Frey turns back to her emails.

Tammy clears her throat. 'And Diana adores your Tom.'

Frey has a sinking feeling. 'Does she?'

'He's quite the heartbreaker, isn't he.' More giggles.

Frey wants to say, 'Actually, he's a right arsehole. Lock Diana up immediately.' But instead she says, 'He's really just a big kid. I don't think he wants all the attention.'

'That's not what he indicated to Diana.' Tammy smiles again, but the warmth has faded. 'Before he stopped talking to her altogether.'

'Oh.'

'Yep. The full ghost treatment.'

'I'm so sorry.'

'No, no.' Tammy puts a hand on Frey's arm. It feels weighted. The heaviness of Frey's morning returns. 'I'm just saying because I was worried Diana might have done something to hurt him. She can be thoughtless sometimes. Not nasty-thoughtless, never nasty, just vague.' Frey watches Tammy's right hand clench as her arms fold. The index finger of the left hand taps the upper arm. *Animosity*, Frey thinks, and ponders how Tammy managed the initial warmth in her smile. *This woman does passive aggression quite well.*

'I'm sure Diana didn't do anything wrong,' Frey says. 'I've heard how lovely she is.'

'Yeah,' says Tammy. 'People take advantage of her kindness.'

'To be honest,' says Frey, eyeing Tammy's right foot as it taps the ground, 'Tom doesn't say much. He's a typical seventeen-year-old boy.'

'He didn't mention Diana? They were dating for quite a while.'

'Um, well, he did. I think. Sorry. He's having an arrogant phase. I'll talk to him.'

Tammy's smile returns. A hand briefly grasps Frey's arm. 'Oh no, please don't. Diana will kill me for saying anything. And don't be sorry. She was probably way too keen. Not cool, you know.'

'Grace says she's lovely.' Frey wishes she could spontaneously shape-shift into a different person entirely. *I need a disguise.*

'Thanks,' says Tammy. 'She doesn't hang out with Grace much, really. Diana loves to dance but she's not really part of the group. Big boned, two left feet, if I'm honest. Not like Grace. I'll let you go.' Tammy touches Frey's arm again.

'Yes, I have to be . . .' Frey hasn't realised she's been edging away. She gestures vaguely with her thumb in the direction of the exit. Tammy nods a bit of thinly veiled understanding and walks towards a group of parents, hugs one of them. Frey follows the stern direction of her thumb out of the building, through the carpark and onto the street.

'Shit,' she says to herself. 'What do you think you're doing out here?'

She curses Tom and walks on, turns into a side street, away from passing traffic. There's an old-time milk bar feel to the New Town neighbourhood. Frey is automatically fond of it. In her faraway, coastal town childhood the streets were like this. Hot bitumen, sleepy, modest houses, distant ice-cream truck music. She suddenly craves a bag of Samboy chips and a strawberry ice cream.

She passes an open window, through the smell of casserole and the sound of someone hammering. Industry. Other people doing their things.

Her thoughts turn to dinner. She wonders whether she should try offering up casserole to her family, whose tastes favour a trendy Mediterranean diet. Her stomach rumbles. She is cold, wishes she could just surrender to the requisite Tasmanian puffer jacket, for warmth and for the possible relief of assigned identity or, failing that, camouflage. *Who am I trying to be if not a mother waiting for her children?*

In the tinted windows of a car, Frey catches sight of her carefully set face. The palsy of decorum. She unclenches her jaw (again) and walks on, a small smile tacked onto her lips. It settles in, the smile, because on the next corner is a pretty blue-and-white house with frilled shutters like eyelashes. Frey imagines them fluttering. She walks on, up a rise, past a tiny flower shop and down again. The afternoon begins to feel less cold. *It's always a good idea to move out of your usual beat*, she thinks. *You start to see things again.*

And that's when it happens. That's when Frey, just recalling her promise to put something new into Tuesday, steps right into the path of an oncoming car.

The discordant squeal of tyres drowns out everything, but her body is primed and switched on. It sees the car just before impact and jumps, turns counter-clockwise, tucks and rolls across the bonnet, hits the windscreen, then slides back the way it came. With time lagging now, she registers the comical appearance of the little car and its rounded, lemon-yellow bonnet with its funny, surprised headlights.

Spotto, she thinks, recalling a game her children used to play involving spotting yellow vehicles. *We haven't played that for years.* She rolls across the bitumen and comes to rest in a pile of green silk and fine black wool.

$$\flat$$

Stepping Stone Number 104, from *La Lista* by R.K.:
Make the effort to find out people's names, remember them, use them. It will make people you meet feel worthwhile, and more likely to remember you. It isn't nice to be forgotten.

Chapter 2
Another Realm Entirely

Kyrie and Rosanna Kalbfel sit in Kyrie's Fiat 500 in astonished, horrified silence.

It's a ticking sort of silence, the sort that follows a series of hideous clunks, then makes the world whirl around with heartbeats and horror and thoughts of terrible consequences.

Rosanna, never one for silence, is the first to react. 'Oh my God,' she shouts, rattling the troublesome passenger-side door. 'We have killed a woman, Kyrie. What on the earth?' She flaps her hands above her head. 'What is next?'

But the shouting has triggered Kyrie into action, and she has opened her driver's-side door and is already out on the street. Rosanna, still exclaiming, yanks on the handle. 'Come on, stupid door.' She pushes and heaves but it doesn't relent. Rosanna curses her weak arms. 'Idiot muscles.' She shimmies over into the driver's seat and is halfway out Kyrie's door when she pauses to breathe and make an instinctual sign of the cross before hurrying out to where a green-shirted woman lies elegantly on the road. Kyrie, measured and gentle, is by her side.

'No, no, *I'm* sorry,' the prone woman is saying. 'My fault. Please don't worry. I don't think I'm hurt.'

'Don't move, though,' says Kyrie. 'We need to get you properly checked. What's your name?'

'Frey. Freycinet. I'm really okay.' She moves her arm, grimaces, then smiles.

'Oh my goshes, Freycinet,' says Rosanna. 'I will call the ambulance.' She pulls out her phone.

'No,' says Frey. 'Please, that's not necessary. I'm fine. You weren't going fast, and look at your tiny car.' She waves at the Fiat. 'It's probably come off second best.'

'You were all tumbling,' says Rosanna. 'Like a stunts woman in the movies. Your body was all over the shops, who knows what is broken in you.'

'It was pretty impressive to watch, actually,' says Kyrie, and is pleased to see a healthy blush rise into Freycinet's face.

'I'm sorry,' Frey says again.

'Well, I am Rosanna,' says Rosanna. 'This is Kyrie. No more sorry.'

'It was an accident,' says Kyrie.

Frey attempts a smile. 'I was in such a . . . I promise I haven't hurt my neck or my back. I'm going to sit up.'

'Just take it slowly,' says Kyrie.

'The internal injuries can be creeping up on you, Freycinet,' says Rosanna. 'And we should not be making a fly out of an elephant.'

'I don't have much pain at all,' Frey insists. 'Just a bump on my arm. I protected my head.'

'It looked quite dramatic,' says Kyrie.

'It was amazing,' Rosanna exclaims. 'You must be in the shock. I am in the shock too, my God. I thought you were a dead woman and I could meet you in heaven. It is very lucky that Kyrie is such a grandmother driver. She just *noo-ne-noo* along everywhere. If I had been the driver, you would be dead for sure.'

'You have a rip in your blouse.' Kyrie clucks. 'And what a lovely blouse it is.' She touches one of the tiny green buttons at Frey's wrist.

'Not to worry,' says Frey. 'I need something to verify my story about being hit by a car.' She tries to laugh. 'I feel okay. I might just have a few bruises, but nothing that'll earn me much attention at home.'

Rosanna nods. 'We could drive right over your legs so you could have some time with your feet up? Give a break from the chores?'

Frey laughs. 'Sounds blissful.'

'You young women are so busy,' says Kyrie. 'Always needing to rush. It's a wonder there aren't more of you being hit by cars. I'll help you up, Freycinet. Rosanna, can you get the tissues from the glove box?'

'Oh, don't worry,' says Frey, inspecting a graze on her elbow. 'There's no blood to mop up.'

'For your tears,' says Kyrie, putting a hand lightly to Frey's face.

It is the first time Freycinet Barnes has cried in years. She shed a tear or two at her mother's funeral but before that she can't be sure. She lets Kyrie wipe her tears away and knows that the sheer kindness of her is sure to bring more.

Ten minutes later, Frey is standing and certain that her injuries don't extend beyond a few grazes, a bruised shoulder, a tender area on her left buttock and that same heaviness in her chest. She is equal parts pissed off with herself for such a lapse in concentration, and proud of herself for avoiding a more serious injury. She is also extremely surprised and a bit embarrassed about her tears, which are still coming. The achingly gentle hands of Kyrie and the vast, interested eyes of Rosanna are like a mother's long-lost voice.

'You might be stiff and sore tomorrow, yes?' says Rosanna.

'Definitely,' agrees Frey. 'It's been a while since some of those muscles have been disturbed.'

'I cannot believe that you went all flying and tumbling and there is not even any blood. It was a proper trauma, yes?' Rosanna searches Frey's face.

Frey brushes away such care, but also wants to take it in her hands. 'I'm well padded,' she says, with a hint of sob in her voice.

'But you are not okay, I think,' says Rosanna. 'You are feeling not right, yes?'

Freycinet considers the question. She can't seem to fix upon any feeling. She searches for facts, instead, which are easier to grasp. That Rosanna's headscarf is the colour of a blue cichlid fish she'd once seen at the Oceanarium in Moscow. *Only the males are electric blue. The females are grey*, she thinks. More facts: some women are able to read air and deliver affirmations with a touch of the hand. Grey hair doesn't have to age a person. Tumbling skills are a prefrontal-cortex skill that can be learnt and retained in muscle memory.

'I feel okay,' she replies in the end. 'No pain anywhere. I'm sorry that I ran into your dear little Fiat.'

'Not a worry,' says Kyrie.

'Do you know,' says Rosanna, 'that Isadora Duncan the dancer was injured in cars two times? And that her two children drowned in a car that fell into the Seine? Then, finally, her long scarf got caught in the wheels of a convertible and it choked her to the death.'

'God,' says Freycinet.

'You are lucky not to be Isadora Duncan.'

'Rosanna rather enjoys a bit of tragedy,' says Kyrie. 'She's Italian. Can we drive you somewhere, Freycinet? Where did you come from?'

Frey surveys the unfamiliar street and thinks, *Another realm entirely.* She dabs her cheek with the heel of her hand, where another tear has fallen. 'I'll be fine. I must be a bit hormonal.'

'Doesn't make trauma any less real,' Kyrie says.

'If we can't be taking you to the hospital then I think we should be watching you for an hour or so,' announces Rosanna. 'You could be unstable.'

'Yes, please let me drive you somewhere,' says Kyrie. 'It's cold and you're in shock.'

'Let us *take you* somewhere,' says Rosanna, her face breaking into a huge smile. 'Somewhere that will cheery you up.'

'I need to get back to dancing,' says Frey.

'You don't look like you're dressed for the dancing,' Rosanna observes.

'It's my daughter's class.'

'Do you have her dance shoes?'

'No.'

'Are you the teacher?'

'No.'

'Then you do not need to get back to the dancing.'

'Rosanna,' says Kyrie, 'we should let her get back to the dancing.'

'No, we should be bringing her with us. We cannot be watching her hobble away. She needs our observations.' Rosanna puts her night-sky eyes on Frey's dazed ones. 'You don't have to get in the car in case you think we are kidnappers. We'll park it here and we can walk just there, that place there.' She points along the street to a large, disgruntled-looking building, brown, fronted by a row of tall, scraggly conifers. 'We are on our way there, come with us for a little bit and we can make sure everything is in the right places.'

Frey insists again she needs no observation, although she is not entirely sure everything is in the right places. Kyrie presses a card into her hand. Frey looks at it. *Kyrie Kalbfel*, it says. *Family Law Barrister*.

'Please call if you have any injuries that we can help with,' Kyrie says. 'I mean it.'

Frey thanks them, apologises again and hurries away before Rosanna's beseeching eyes turn her around and take her with them.

𝄢

Frey walks on with only mild discomfort in her hip and elbow. Her mood is strangely elevated, animated by adrenaline and the absurdity of what has just happened. She almost laughs, pondering how to relay the incident's details to her family, and decides before she has even made it a block away that she need not tell them at all. *It was an incident*, she thinks. *Incidental.*

She turns a corner to take a longer way back to Derwent Dance Academy, hoping that an extended walk might restore a semblance of normality. A section of footpath on the next block is shadowed by a thick cypress hedge with a scent that reminds Frey of primary school. Many times she led her friends into the depths of the school oval's boundary hedge, an activity that was strictly forbidden. And every time she led them out again, undetected. She continued to spend the occasional lunch hour in the hedge long after the friends lost their nerve. Frey slows and lets this hedge tousle the top of her head, a comforting sensation that makes her smile.

At a driveway, the hedge breaks and Frey's smile broadens at the sight of a couple standing about six metres away, beside a pale-green weatherboard house. They stand close, his hands caressing her upper arms. Frey admires the woman's blue coat, the man's shapely physique, his well-cut suit and the tender way he touches her. She sees the man laugh, put a hand in his pocket and extract a set of keys. And then without warning, Frey's body flings her forward towards the next section of hedge and presses her out of sight.

Gil. That's Gil. She feels momentarily ridiculous. *It can't be.* She tries to stand, to walk, to be normal, but her body keeps her flat against the hedge, then moving swiftly to the waist-high wall of the neighbouring house. She scales it cleanly, then follows the dividing fence at a crouched run, until she is just metres from the couple, concealed behind the palings.

'Oh, do you now?' The woman's voice is teasing and light, brimming with laughter. 'I can't imagine why.'

The man replies, but his words are muffled. He laughs. His keys jangle.

It can't be Gil. But that's his laugh. Frey moves to a nearby tree with branches weighed down by enormous, pale-yellow grapefruit.

The woman laughs and says, 'I wish!'

Frey straightens up beneath the tree until she can see over the fence. From this angle the man's face is in profile. She is only partially concealed but that doesn't matter, his eyes are fixed on the woman's. She counts four full seconds and lets her mind find purchase amid a cloud of racing thoughts. *It's him. That's my husband. Is it?*

She crouches again, out of sight, and moves silently, taking a grapefruit with her. The neighbour's back yard is L-shaped, so she slips around the dog-legged corner, following the fence until she finds a missing paling. There she pauses and sneaks another look. She can see the back of the woman now. The man's face is concealed, but the shoes are Gil's shoes, the hair is Gil's hair.

It can't be.

From her crouched position, Frey braces her body, aims and pitches the grapefruit directly at an upper-floor window at the back of the house.

Glass shatters and falls.

'Fuck!' says the man,

The woman shrieks.

Both faces turn in shock.

Shick. Frey takes a photograph with her phone, but she doesn't need it to verify that her husband has been standing beside this house, his hands on another woman as she gives him wishes. The startled man who turned towards the sound of broken glass is, without question, Gil Barnes. There is something different about the familiar terrain of his face – as if someone has applied a filter to remove shadows – but it's most definitely him.

I can't meet you for lunch today after all.

Frey runs.

She scales the fence at the back of the neighbouring block, and two more beyond that, then sprints the length of a laneway, across a street and into the next. The breaths tear through her, heartbeats pound into her ears and she listens as her body thrills and exhilarates and tells her what to do. Does its thing. It scares her. She feels pain in her lungs, thinks of Gil's hands on the blue coat, the woman saying, 'I can't imagine why' and 'I wish'.

She stops running outside the open door of the brown building where Kyrie and Rosanna had said they were going. Its scruffy trees beckon cheerily, as her mind catches up with her body and says, *Hide*.

𝄐

Stepping Stone Number 16, from *La Lista* by R.K.:
You have an inner knowing in you that will knock on your ribcage and twang your stomach lining when you are being (or about to be) a dickhead. You are also likely to feel it when someone near you is being a dickhead. Don't ignore it.

Chapter 3
Heraldry

The interior of the brown building is Frey's next shock of the day. The foyer's carpet is so floral and swirly it makes Frey feel seasick. Its wallpaper is gold, striped with pink. In the corner is a huge purple urn filled with metallic blue flowers and from the ceiling hangs an enormous shard-glass chandelier. It appears to Frey like the decorator has raided a jumble sale specialising in bad taste and kitsch.

Frey looks back at the open door, the prosaic street outside. Beyond that, somewhere, Gil and the woman in the blue coat are puzzling over a broken window. Frey walks further into the building, past printed pictures of flowers and fairies and misty, tizzy gardens, to a second interior door. There, she listens.

It's difficult at first to place what she hears. She might remember it one day as a sort of heraldry, a declaration of something that can't be put into words, but beautifully articulated all the same. There are lyrics but she can't hear them for the sound. There are notes, but she can't hear them for the music. Voices. A little bit of piano but mostly voices, with the sort of perfect harmony that can fill your chest cavity, swell hearts and thoughts and spill from your tear ducts. Frey closes her eyes on the sound, so it can't escape. *What is this feeling?* she thinks. *Flying?*

She sees golden things and grand places, and from that distance she wonders whether she might have been killed by the yellow Fiat, and this is the bit of life after life. *No wonder I've felt so strange since I woke up this morning*, she thinks. *It's my death day.*

The voices spiral downwards and diminish. Frey feels a catch in her heart and is disappointed to find it still firing. She might have just slipped quietly into the end of things. *Happily ever hereafter.*

There is silence then, but for the tiny *plop* of a tear onto the carpet at Frey's feet. Shortly after that comes a woman's harsh voice shouting, 'That bloody Benedictus. It's made me need another wee.'

There is a waft of laughter and another voice that says, 'Thank you, Quin. That could explain why the alto was a little tense.'

The door swings open and a young woman bursts out. She is short, stocky, with cropped, dyed blonde hair. Her T-shirt says 'Don't fuck with Alice'.

'Won't be a tick!' she shouts. She stops when she sees Frey. Her thin eyebrows rise.

'Hi,' says Frey. 'Sorry, I was . . . that sounded amazing. I'm, um . . .' She thinks. *What am I doing?* 'I was hoping to see Rosanna and Kyrie.'

'Rosanna! Kyrie!' shouts the woman without taking her eyes off Frey. 'There's a woman here to see youse.' She sends Frey a lopsided smile, says, 'Gotta pee,' and keeps walking.

Rosanna is the first to the foyer. 'Freycinet!' she says. 'Oh goodness, do you need the hospital?'

'No, no, I just . . .' Freycinet gazes at Rosanna. On her head, over her blue scarf, is a gold paper crown. 'You're singers.'

'Yes,' says Kyrie, who has arrived in the foyer, also in a crown. 'Are you all right? Do you need us?'

I think I do, thinks Frey.

'Come in, come in,' bellows Rosanna. 'You can be our tiny audience. You're in time for the Furies.'

'You definitely don't have to,' says Kyrie. 'I can take you to the dancing school. Or to your family.'

Frey thinks about her family. 'No, thank you,' she says. 'I'd like to hear more singing. Will there be more of it?'

'Yes, of course. This is a choir,' says Rosanna.

'Singing is the best medicine I know,' says Kyrie. 'And if it doesn't work, we have a doctor here.'

Rosanna grasps Frey's hand and pulls her through the door to where the voices are rising again, this time in a cadence of chatter.

Once through the door, Frey has further reason to believe that she's making the final steps into the afterlife. She finds herself in a large hall, lined with sheer pink curtains, through which shines a virtual luminescence of tiny lights. The ceiling, which she looks up at with mouth ajar, is draped with the same sheer material, layered on top of itself in a fancy, spiralled star and intertwined with silver-sequinned ribbons. At the centre is a giant, rotating mirror ball, which throws the fairy-lit walls right back at their blushing selves.

And that's not the half of it. Beneath the ceiling and amid the shimmer is a small group of women standing in two perfect lines in the centre of the room. They are all wearing identical gold paper crowns. To the left of the front row, a miniature dachshund sits so perfectly still that Frey wonders whether it might be another decoration. And standing before them all, her crown perched atop a head of sculpted hair in a shade of pink that matches the curtains, is a woman with the most incredible cheekbones Frey has ever seen. *Okay, now I know I'm dead. This must be my Judgement and that fabulous creature must be God.*

'Everyone,' says Rosanna, 'this is Freycinet. She is the one we hit with the car and threw into the sky and could have killed.'

Kyrie winces.

'She is alive,' Rosanna continues, 'and she wants to hear some music!'

'It's Irene's birthday,' says Kyrie. 'We don't always wear crowns.'

'Happy birthday, Irene,' says Freycinet to the group.

'Thanking you,' says a small, older woman. 'I clean forgot until Bizzy picked me up for choir.'

Rosanna laughs. 'Happy Irene's birthday, Freycinet.'

Freycinet smiles. 'Thank you.' She sees all the curious eyes on her. But not the eyes of the God-woman. She feels those.

'You really should have popped into an ambulance,' says a tall, muscular woman with a straight grey bob and red glasses.

'We tried to tell her,' says Rosanna. 'She wouldn't have a bar of it.'

'I'm okay,' says Frey. 'It was nothing, really.' She thinks of the injury that came after the accident, the one involving her husband and her heart, and decides that the Fiat incident was a mere hiccup in comparison.

'It was spectacular,' says Rosanna. 'She went *wheeee* up onto the car and then rolling on the road. You should have seen it.'

'Holy shit,' says a young blonde woman who is sitting at the piano.

Another young woman – this one perhaps still a girl – asks in a soft voice, 'Do you need a doctor? Sally's one.' She gestures towards the woman in the red glasses.

'Sounds nasty,' says Sally. 'I'm long retired but can do a quick examination if you like.'

'No, really,' says Frey. 'I'm fine.'

'But you should sit down,' says the God-woman with the cheek-bones, who speaks with an Irish accent. 'We'll sing you a little bit of medicine. We can hold off on the Furies for a moment.'

Frey does as she is told, because she's been rendered eleven years old and very shy. And because she wants to know what 'the Furies' could possibly be. Kyrie takes the third place in the back row. Rosanna stands in the centre of the front row. Quin returns and moves to the end nearest the piano. The little dachshund remains motionless. All so orderly.

'"Amazing Grace", please everyone,' says the director. 'Extended version. A cappella, thank you, Mary.'

Mary is the young woman at the piano. Not required to play accompaniment, she moves into the back row. She is extraordinarily tall, and her legs get her into place in what seems like a couple of giant strides.

The director raises her hands and there is a moment of silence so pure Frey wants to drink it. But then comes a rising, single soprano voice, gradual enough for it to be felt before it is heard. It isn't clear who is the owner of the voice, and then it is swallowed up by a flourish of other voices so that Frey finds herself lost among those for a moment before the solo voice returns. Frey sees that it is Kyrie. *Of course it is.* The voice matches the kind face, the long silver hair so perfectly. This version of 'Amazing Grace' seems to be a call-and-response arrangement. Frey feels herself wanting to sing too. She can't remember anyone calling her to action so sweetly.

In stark, jarring contrast, Frey's phone rings. An insulting, manufactured marimba sound. She scrabbles around in her pocket, grasps the offending phone and in haste, drops it. It clatters to the floor. With everything sinking, Frey looks fearfully at the director, but there doesn't appear to be a beat missed. There doesn't even appear to be a beat. Just an unbroken flow of exquisite sound. The dachshund blinks. Rosanna sends Frey a sympathetic smile and a hint of a wink, in the middle of another celestial bar of Kyrie's singing. Frey sends a smile back, mustering it from somewhere beneath her mortification. A distant, disembodied squawking alerts her to the phone on the floor. It's Lily, bleating indignantly from somewhere in a real eleven-year-old world. Frey swiftly presses the end-call button, suppresses a painful twinge of guilt and switches the phone to silent. She is relieved to witness the return of her usual efficiency.

The music draws her in again and builds slightly, drowning out embarrassments and the echoes of Lily's protests. It keeps her safe until it drifts to its end a few minutes later.

'Oh gosh,' she says after a little respectful pause. 'Thank you. How beautiful. I don't think I should even clap. One person clapping seems sort of wrong. Thank you. And I'm so sorry for the phone, God. I mean, gosh.' She laughs. 'I feel I should pray or something, after that.'

'You just did,' says the director. '"Amazing Grace" is a prayer. We're not a religious choir, though some of us are frequent God-botherers, but that's an old favourite of ours. It's a good re-set song.' She smiles at Freycinet in a way that makes Frey wonder whether there's a riddle hidden in her words.

'Well, it was simply beautiful. Your voice is panpipes in the mist, Kyrie. You're all amazing. I'd die to sing like that.'

The women, who are moving out of their lines and over towards a circle of chairs, laugh bashfully.

'That's so lovely of you to say,' says Kyrie. 'We've had a few disappointing reviews lately.'

'We got likened to vanilla pudding,' adds Mary.

Sally nods. 'They called us "parlour-tune" singers.'

'Ouch,' says Frey.

'Ouch is right,' says Irene.

'Frey,' says Kyrie, 'meet Mary, Eleanor, Quin, Sally, Avni. And this is Bizzy.' She pats the arm of the luminous conductor, who turns her cheekbones towards Frey. 'Bizzy is our director.'

'Hello there, Freycinet,' says Bizzy, holding out a manicured hand.

'Hello, Bizzy,' says Frey, looking into Bizzy's amber eyes and feeling every bit eleven again. 'Very pleased to meet you. And thank you for letting me intrude on your choir practice. I've loved listening, but I really have to go. Dancing will be over soon.'

'You should stay for the Furies, though,' says Bizzy as she settles into a chair, 'It's strictly thirty minutes. And our most vivifying vocal exercise. Join the circle.'

'Perfect for days when you've been hit by a car,' says Mary.

'The Furies?' asks Frey.

'Every week we each say what's really annoyed the shit from us,' says Rosanna.

'In under thirty words,' Bizzy adds.

'Each,' says Sally.

'And then we sing it all out, give it to poor old Laetare Gardens,' says Bizzy, gesturing to the walls of the building. 'It's our rage repertoire.'

'Don't be fooled by the sickly sweet decor,' says Quin. 'These walls have soaked up so much of our anger they'll probably fucken explode one day.'

'The rage repertoire was Rosanna's idea,' continues Bizzy, 'back in 2003.'

'My mother had just then suggested I hire an exorcist to rid myself of the evil spirit I have within me,' says Rosanna.

'Oh,' says Freycinet.

'She has a very oppressive god,' Rosanna adds by way of explanation.

'We decided it was time to give in to our anger,' says Bizzy. 'It really helps us with our feeling-singing, as opposed to thinking-singing. Thinking-singing can sound a bit didactic.'

'We were way ahead of our time,' says Mary. 'Everyone's getting on the rage wagon these days.'

'Except for our Eleanor,' adds Rosanna. 'She hasn't felt angry for years because she is dead on the inside.'

A solemn-looking woman in a ballgown nods and says, 'It's true, I'm dead on the inside.'

'She's a work in progress,' says Quin. 'Like me.'

Frey's eyes widen. The little dog rests its head on Eleanor's feet. Eleanor glances down at her and says, 'That's Penelope.'

'Hello, Penelope,' Frey says, but Penelope doesn't stir.

'So we're the West Moonah Women's Choir,' says Bizzy. 'But occasionally we're the Angry Women's Choir. But that part is strictly confidential. We don't perform the Furies publicly, and anything we say doesn't go beyond this room.'

'Of course,' says Frey. She wonders whether she should offer to leave, but her curiosity is deepening.

'We're all trying to convince Bizzy to let us perform the rage stuff,' says Mary. 'It's our best thing.'

'Not on anyone's nelly,' says Bizzy with a shake of her head. 'I'm all for stirring things up but the West Moonah Women's Choir manages that perfectly well in its steady, peaceful way. The Angry Women's Choir would burn down the world.'

𝄡

Stepping Stone Number 25, from *La Lista* by R.K.:
Home is one thing, but only when you step out of it and see other places and other worlds will you know that home is everything.

Chapter 4

Shouty Sneezes

Rosanna is first to make her offering to the Furies. 'I am cross,' she declares, 'because my *miracle medical trial* is not proving to be such a miracle medical trial. My cancer has not had a response. Yet. So I might be using up everybody's hope and losing my hair again for nothing. Also some *bastardo* stole Ilaria's wheelbarrow.'

Frey wants to cry out but swallows it down. *Oh my God,* she thinks. *She's terminally ill? How can those eyes not live to old, old age?*

'Oh, and it was new at Christmas that barrow,' says Mary. 'Bastards.'

'No time for comments, please,' says Bizzy. 'Sally?'

'A woman at the council called me cute the other day,' says Sally. 'I think I preferred being fifty and invisible.'

'My boyfriend,' says the softly spoken young woman named Avni, 'shouts his sneezes and it drives me crazy. One of his sneezes scared a child the other day.'

Irene is next. 'I'm so angry with Harvey for being dead,' she says. 'Sometimes I throw snails into his veggie garden. And then of course I have to fish them out again, because I do like an iceberg lettuce. Is that too many words?'

'No, that's perfect, Irene,' says Bizzy. She nods at Quin.

Quin moves herself forward in her seat and says, 'I'm not even forty and I think I'm hitting the menopause. I'm grumpy as fuck and my periods are all over the place. Also I'm bloated as hell. Could I be lactose intolerant, Sal? I've had a thing for milkshakes lately.'

'Possibly,' says Sally.

'You're always grumpy as fuck,' says Mary.

'But!' Quin continues. 'I met a bloke. At uni. He's actually nice. Like *nice* nice. Kind and that. Shy.'

There is a rise and fall of pleased exclamations.

'Good cock too,' adds Quin. 'Nice shape.'

Frey laughs.

'Excellent,' says Bizzy.

'Your go, Bizz,' says Quin. 'What's bum-steering your wheelhouse this week?'

'Would you like to add your own, Freycinet?' asks Bizzy, because Frey is next to Quin.

'No, thank you,' Frey says quickly. Another image of Gil scrolls into her thoughts. The woman in the blue coat saying, 'I wish'. The little pleased buzz she felt when the grapefruit met the window in a direct hit. She wonders whether these are all hallucinations as a result of being hit by a small car.

Bizzy's amber eyes study her for a moment before she smiles. 'Okay. Eleanor?'

The broad-shouldered woman in the ballgown shakes her head.

'Well,' says Bizzy. 'I am furious with Small Smellypants. He has sent a lawyer's letter proclaiming that we must pay the extortionate new rent. He actually wants us to pay the two hundred per cent increase each month. He really wants us out. Can we do anything, Kyrie?'

Rosanna looks at Frey. 'Small Smellypants is the owner of Laetare Gardens.'

'Small Smellypants?' asks Frey.

'Paul Bellavance,' says Eleanor.

'Paul Bellavance?' echoes Frey. 'As in, the politician Paul Bellavance? Famous footy player?'

'Let us guess,' says Sally. 'You've had a crush on him since he kicked seven goals for St Kilda against Geelong in 1993?'

Frey laughs. 'Every girl I knew had a crush on Paul Bellavance, even before he left Tassie and became a sports star. He was very charismatic, and so good looking. And now every woman I know is just so grateful to him for how he spoke up for those victims of sexual assault. I see him and his wife occasionally because their daughter goes to the same dance school as mine. He's still gorgeous, everyone's really—'

'Keen to give his dick a little rub?' suggests Quin. 'Give him a bit of a blowie? He'd love that, wouldn't he, Bizzy?'

Frey isn't sure how to respond.

Kyrie steps in to help. 'Paul Bellavance's very public stance against sexual misconduct against women is, well . . .'

'A pile of steaming cockamamie,' says Eleanor.

'And she'd know,' says Irene. 'Eleanor cleans his house twice a week.'

'And he was very quick to tell the prison reformists how much he trusts a murderess to clean his home,' says Mary.

'He's a proper knob-shiner,' says Eleanor. 'Never even puts his cotton-buds in the bin. I'd feel sorry for his wife, if I could feel. She's not a bad person. Lonely in her enormous house.'

'Wow,' says Frey. 'I know he has a kind of high-gloss polish, like a lot of politicians, but I didn't think he would be . . .'

'A complete fake?' offers Sally. 'It's all part of his life-long campaign of self-promotion. It's not even to do with politics. He wants to be seen to be standing up to the straight white men but he's one of the worst. He thinks women are idiots. Particularly us. He hates us.'

Kyrie nods. 'He's had it in for us since Bizzy refused to be charmed by the rubbing of his penis on her in 1992.'

'I mean, men were always getting their penises out in the nineties,' says Bizzy. 'One couldn't possibly be impressed by them all.'

'Let's just say,' says Mary with a smile, 'there's more to Paul Bellavance than the handsome saviour that meets the eye. I know. I literally study men of his type. There are knobs like him wokefishing all over the place.'

'Wokefishing?' Frey asks.

'Men who pretend to be feminists so they can satisfy their egos and their penises. They usually make a big song and dance of their liberal views but have the full kit of assorted microaggressions on hand at all times. Bellavance is a particularly performative wokefish. He'll be the keynote speaker, mansplaining feminism at the Mother's Day breakfast.'

Sally chimes in. 'Mary's doing her thesis on women's creative resilience. That's why she's hanging around with us old feeblies. We're her thesis.'

'Yep,' says Mary. 'I'm researching the Betty Friedan idea that creative pursuits can turn struggle into growth and lead women closer to self-actualisation and contentment. I'm delving back into feminist theory before it got all dressed up in power suits and threw its rage at glass ceilings. When it could sing and dance and laugh and make stuff.'

Rosanna beams at Frey. 'Aren't you so glad you bumped into us?'

'We're running behind, my loves,' says Bizzy. 'And I want to move on to the good news.'

'Small Smellypants has terminal syphilis?' asks Quin.

'Almost as exciting,' says Bizzy. 'No, in actual fact, we're going to hold a rally.'

'Stop the press,' says Mary flatly. 'The West Moonah Women's Choir go to a rally.'

Kyrie frowns. 'Bizzy, we do up to ten rallies a year. I'm still recovering from the RSPCA one. We have Pride Month coming up . . .'

'No, we won't be *going to* a rally,' explains Bizzy. 'We'll be hosting one. We've never done that. This will be our very own.'

'Yes, yes, yes!' shouts Rosanna, clapping her hands. 'This is just what we need. Drive our own revolution.'

'Let's not get too ahead of ourselves,' says Kyrie, eyeing Bizzy with suspicion. 'I know that look. What's brewing, Fizzy Wheelbarrow?'

On the floor at Eleanor's feet, Penelope whines.

Frey watches with interest as Bizzy's poise shifts slightly and her hands fidget. *She's unsure*, Frey thinks. *Maybe even nervous.*

'Well,' Bizzy says, 'I'm thinking it's time for us to create a few more feminist ripples. We don't want the fifth wave of feminism to be all sparkle and no substance.'

'We don't even want it to be a wave of feminism,' adds Mary. 'More like a river of humanism.'

'Bizzy,' says Kyrie. 'Does this have anything to do with being likened to a vanilla pudding?'

Frey watches Bizzy perform a classic evade-the-question. 'I just think now is the time,' she says. 'My Very Cross Stitches has built quite a following. Everyone listens when Dr Sally speaks and Avni is set to take the world by storm. We should capitalise on our respective platforms and get up on a world stage, pull out all stops and—'

'Hijack Valentine's Day and turn it into Vagina Day?' suggests Quin.

'Well,' replies Bizzy. 'There's an idea.'

'Which aspect of feminism?' asks Sally. 'People need a solid, distinct reason to leave their busy routines and wave a placard.'

'Domestic violence could use a bit more world stage,' says Kyrie.

'Can everyone please stop saying "world stage"?' asks Avni. 'The idea makes me feel sick.'

'You're going to be on one, one day, Avni,' says Mary. 'You'll have to get over those poor nerves of yours.'

'I agree we should have a focus,' says Bizzy. 'We can brainstorm that. But mostly I think feminism needs to be properly rousing again. I mean really rousing, aspirational, enchanting.'

'Explosive,' adds Mary.

'We need to be mindful of Irene's weak heart,' says Sally.

'Nah, I'll be right,' says Irene. 'It'd take more than that to get me worked up. I learnt to master this old ticker years ago. Harvey walked into the kitchen the other day and I still didn't up the beats.' She looks at Frey. 'And Harvey's been dead ten years.'

'I think it's almost twenty years, Irene,' says Mary.

'Good Lord,' says Irene with a chuckle. 'No wonder the car's had the Richard.'

Frey wonders again where on earth she has found herself.

'I could sing a murder ballad,' says Eleanor. 'That'd get some attention.'

Mary gasps. 'We could debut the Furies! Go as the Angry Women's Choir!'

'Absolutely not,' says Bizzy. 'The Furies are for our personal nourishment and motivation. But we do need to shake up our repertoire, which is partly why I'm giving us a focus. But mostly I'm just concerned that everyone gets cross about something for a bit, does a bit of shouting, then goes back to their busy lives until the next woman is felt up in the workplace, or raped, or murdered.'

'Perhaps women just have far too much on their plate, and they only have limited time to give,' says Freycinet.

Mary snorts. 'Of course,' she says. 'One must leave time for blow-waves and manicures.'

Frey wishes she hadn't spoken.

'Maybe they're putting the wrong fucken things on their plate,' says Quin. 'Lining it up and snorting it up their noses.'

'Someone has to stay on the home front,' says Rosanna, sending Freycinet a kind nod. 'We can't all be on the front line.'

'I like the idea of re-enchanting feminism,' says Kyrie. 'In between the high-profile uproars, it has been a bit sequestered by academia – no offence, Mary.'

'None taken,' says Mary. 'I agree. It's the point of my thesis. Feminism in the too-hard basket for so many in the mainstream.'

'See, we're brainstorming already,' says Bizzy. 'I think late summer for this rally. We don't have any big engagements in February next year.'

'Sounds good,' says Mary.

'It needs more thought,' says Sally.

'Okay, well, could you all put it on your plates and give it lots of your thoughts, please?' asks Bizzy. 'Quite soon? The second half of this year is already whizzing by.'

Frey's phone buzzes in her hand. She jumps out of her chair. 'Sorry,' she says. 'God, I really have to go.' She checks her phone for the time and sees that there have been four missed calls and a text from Grace that shouts, 'WHAT THE HELL? I GOT A LIFT HOME WITH DIANA'S MUM.'

I was killed by a small car, Frey imagines replying. *And in the after-life I saw your father with another woman, then met some fascinating angels.*

Another text message silently pops up. This one from Gil. 'If you're passing Officeworks can you get ink cartridges pls?'

'You sure you're not vexing on anything, Freycinet?' asks Irene.

'No,' says Frey. The word rushes out with too much urgency and Frey is not quick enough to catch it.

'Okay then,' says Quin. 'And my pop's a preacher man.'

'I, um . . .' Frey looks at Rosanna's waiting eyes and almost pours out the story about the man who is her husband, the woman in the blue coat and whatever it was she was wishing for. She diverts her thoughts, improvises. 'I really hate being called Frey. And everyone calls me Frey. It makes me feel like a bit of chewed ribbon. It's, um, just a quibble, really. And "Freycinet" is pretty silly, I know . . .'

'Well, my actual name's Byzantine Nancarrow,' says Bizzy, 'So I take your silly and raise it with my ridiculous.' She smiles so kindly that Frey almost sits down again.

'Take very good care of yourself, Freycinet,' says Kyrie. 'And be our audience anytime.'

'Yes,' Rosanna says, moving to press her hand onto Frey's shoulder. 'Come back and assure us that you have no car-hitting injuries.'

'I will.' Frey edges towards the door. 'Sorry again, Kyrie and Rosanna. And thank you all for having me.' She is almost out of the heavenly gates when she adds, 'I don't think you're anything like vanilla pudding.'

In the foyer, Frey pauses for only a moment to send Grace a quick text message ('Home soon, I'll bring dinner, sorry!'), and is almost back in the real outside world when the singing of the Furies begins. And for the fourth time that day, Frey is stopped in her tracks.

It is not the jarring sort of stoppage brought about by an adulterous husband, the impact of a small car or the angelic sounds of a very good choir. This is a reaching of strong hands, a harnessing, an arrest. The sound is no more than a vibration at first, but it rises and swells until it is a presence, even in the inside-outside air of the open foyer. A solid line of sound that contains multiple voices and layers of notes pressed so perfectly into harmony that the seams are imperceptible. The line thickens, the sound grows louder, then retracts, leaving behind a single, muscular voice. It rises and falls, this voice, but stays in a husky low key, drawing wisps of other higher ones along with it. Frey can't make out any words, but has a sense that this is not English, that perhaps it's not any recognised language at all.

Frey had vaguely imagined an angry repertoire – their Furies – to contain the traditional songs of rage and resilience. 'Hit Me With

Your Best Shot' or 'These Boots Were Made For Walking', but the idea seems insulting now. This euphony, that voice with its rugged depths, is otherworldly and inclusive. It dissolves knots in her muscles and ideas in her head and tells her that rage doesn't have to be ugly. It can be measured and exquisite and captivating. She realises that perhaps anger is a skill you can practise until it's perfect.

A few minutes in, the music changes key and gives her a little shove. She moves with assurance from the foyer into the night, only pausing on the street corner to look back and check that the building isn't on fire.

𝄡

Stepping Stone Number 12, from *La Lista* by R.K.:
Be a good listener. Don't join a conversation merely to wait for your turn to speak or to offer advice. Join to listen.

Chapter 5

It's a Lot

Freycinet returns home at twenty-nine minutes past seven, more than two hours later than her usual Tuesday homecoming. She brings with her a family-sized chicken-and-leek pie, a tub of pre-made salad, a bag of grapes and no printer cartridges. She slips into the house through a side door and steals into the bathroom for a moment with her reflection.

A wild-eyed, messy-haired woman faces her. 'I told you I'd put something different in today,' she whispers. She touches her faintly tear-marked cheek and laughs.

Lily, who has evidently heard the car in the driveway, or spotted the shopping bag outside the bathroom, calls out, 'Mum!' And then, 'Guys, she's here, I think. MUM?' She is clearly scandalised.

Freycinet once longed to hear her babies say 'Mum'. Now it's bandied about so much it has lost all meaning.

'I'll be out in a minute! Sorry!' She removes the torn silk blouse and replaces it with a plain white T-shirt.

'Where have you been?' asks Lily on the other side of the door.

'I lost track of time, I'm, hang on . . .' Frey studies her reflection. 'Is Dad home?' She smooths her hair.

'No! We've been all alone all this time. You didn't answer your phone.'

Frey fixes where she's cried away her makeup then opens the door to Lily's incredulous face. 'I'm sorry, darling, I got hit by a car.'

There is the briefest of pauses before Lily says, 'You did not.'

Frey walks to the kitchen with Lily in tow. 'I did, actually. I had to spend a couple of hours in observation.'

'Not funny, Mum. Grace had to get a lift home with a stranger. She could have been kidnapped.'

'Grace got a lift home with Diana's mum Tammy,' says Frey. 'She was fine.'

Tom is standing at the bench eating a bowl of two-minute noodles, so Frey adds, 'Is Diana a friend of yours, Tom?'

'Diana who?' he replies, heading for the couch.

'Diana in Grace's class. Diana from dancing.'

'I don't do dancing.'

'He did Diana, though,' says Grace, walking in from the study, phone in hand, disdain on face. 'Where did you go, Mum? It was dark and frigging freezing.'

'I'm sorry, darling,' Frey says, 'I got . . . waylaid and, er, had to go to a meeting. What do you mean he *did* Diana?'

'Nothing,' says Tom. 'Shut up, Grace.'

Grace rolls her eyes. 'You went to a *meeting*?'

'Well,' says Frey, 'it's kind of a long story. I've had a really odd day, actually. I was just going for a bit of a walk and—'

'Acorn shat in here,' calls Lily from the pantry.

'What?' Frey responds. 'Oh, for goodness sake. Did you not let him out?'

No one answers.

'Could you clean it up, please, Lily? There are some bags in the laundry.'

'No way!' Lily runs from the pantry and out of the kitchen.

'I have homework,' says Grace, moving swiftly back to the study.

Frey looks at Tom. He is on the phone. She gathers up the memory of the music she heard in the foyer of Laetare Gardens, holds it to her and takes a roll of paper towel and some disinfectant to the pantry. Her body is beginning to ache, which pleases her. Physical pain is manageable.

13

Gil arrives home just as Frey is dishing up the pie. The sound of his keys in the hallway sends such a flutter to her heart that she almost drops a plate and has to hide in the pantry for a moment to breathe. When she emerges, Gil is there, in his neat hair and his well-pressed suit and the shoes she'd identified this afternoon, a lifetime ago.

'Pie,' he says. 'Nice. Not too much for me, though, lunch went late. How're you?' He gives her a kiss on the lips and gets a beer from the fridge.

'Well, thanks,' says Frey. 'Did you reel them in?' She watches his expression closely.

'Reel them in?'

'The investors.'

'Oh, yeah. Maybe.'

'What niche assets are they interested in?'

Gil looks bemused, but Frey registers the expression as one of puzzlement over her uncharacteristic interest in his work.

'Well, they're carpark people, so no one's favourites, but they want to clean up their image, get into eco-tourism and arts and stuff.'

Frey is barely listening to his words. She instead watches his body language, his eyes, his hands. None of them behave suspiciously. *If he's lying*, she thinks, *he's good.*

'Hey, Tom?' Gil calls towards the couch. 'The bloody maritime board have changed their life-jacket laws again . . .'

Frey, excluded by default from the boating conversation, turns back to the pie and decides that one of two scenarios is possible: that the interaction between Gil and the woman in the blue coat was innocent, or that it was indeed a clandestine meeting, one of many that have turned Gil into a master of subterfuge. Either way, more conclusive intelligence is required.

She swallows down any further questions, pours herself a wine chaser and considers the possibility that the whole afternoon was a vivid, involuted dream.

𝄢

Only after consuming a second glass of wine, three old episodes of *The Bureau* and the serve of pie that Grace hasn't touched does Frey consider it safe to go to bed. She is not sufficiently prepared for any bedroom husband-and-wife interaction. Gil, with his early bike rides and his healthy habits, is most often asleep well before ten. It is past 10.30 when she creeps upstairs and along the corridor. She stops short before a line of light under Grace's bedroom door.

She knocks softly. There is no reply so she opens the door a crack and says, 'Grace?'

Grace is sitting up against the pillows, headphones on. Frey catches sight of her slipping something under the bedclothes.

'You should go to sleep, darling.'

Grace takes the headphones off and says, 'Shh.' She motions to the spare bed on the other side of the room, where Lily is a bundle of eiderdown and stuffed toys and sleep.

Frey frowns at Grace.

'It's okay, she can stay there,' Grace whispers. 'She was scared she might wake up all alone. She was, like, really worked up this afternoon when you didn't come home.'

Frey grimaces. 'I'm really sorry. I met some . . . some old friends and it was just, um, really nice to see them.'

Grace shrugs. 'It's okay.' She clearly wants Frey to leave.

'You should sleep, you must be exhausted.'

'I'm not, but okay.' Grace sets the headphones on her bedside table.

'Do you think you're overdoing it? With a Year Ten workload and dancing, it's a lot.'

'I'm all good, Mum.'

'Put your device away, please.'

'It is away.'

'Grace.'

'I haven't got it, Mum.' Grace's voice rises. Lily stirs.

Frey walks across the room and pulls back Grace's covers to reveal a notebook.

'See, no *device*. Jeez.' Grace snatches back the covers.

'Okay, good,' says Frey. 'Goodnight.'

Grace doesn't reply.

Frey leaves. In her own bedroom, she slips into bed, faces the wall and wonders how, after this extraordinary day, she will possibly sleep. It's the choir that gets her there, more quickly than she thought. The memory of their music starts to swirl her jarring thoughts, blurring them into a softer, circular motion that makes her limbs feel floaty and slipping. Rising harmonies, gentle hands and dark starlit eyes take her the rest of the way.

𝄡

Tuesday, 6 August 2019, 10.37 p.m.
Mum just came in and suggested I'm 'overdoing it'. Not a word about how hard I work to keep decent grades AND dance five days a week. Anyway . . .

Good things that happened today:

Harry.

Harry.

Harry.

(Three messages from him. All with kisses. One of them said, 'I think you're amazing, Grace.' Haha. Then xxxx. FOUR kisses.)

I nailed the grand jeté at Lyrical tonight. Do I dare include it in my end-of-year showcase routine? I want to dance for Harry. Eve says I'm dancing with more feeling and she can't see the tech anymore. 'Almost perfect,' she said. Look what love does. I could grand jeté all day if Harry tells me he loves me. I am NOT telling him first. That would be way too Year Ten of me.

Bad things that happened today:

Maths.

Mum went AWOL while I was at Lyrical and just didn't come back to pick me up. Then she didn't answer her phone or reply to any messages. Lily was shitting herself when I got home. Mum says she went for a walk and then met up with friends. WT actual F? What friends?

I had to get a lift home with Diana. Talk about awkward. She can't even look at me without crying about Tom. He says she was full-on bordering on psycho and is about cling-factor eleventeen, but I know he treated her wrong. Diana's mum has some sort of freaking eldritch crush on Mum. Or maybe she hates her. Sometimes it's hard to tell the difference. It's probably both. Why is everyone so weird?

𝄡

Stepping Stone Number 9, from *La Lista* by R.K.:
Look after one another. There is nothing so safe and knowing and comforting and annoying as family.

Chapter 6
La Lista Infinita

Rosanna Kalbfel can see a cluster of little blue men nibbling on her ribs. She zeros in until a gradual strobing appears above them, followed by a beam of light that strikes swiftly and cleanly, freezing them in a brief frame of terror before they flicker and disappear. Rosanna breathes out, gathers her fighting wit and scans around for more of the blue enemy foot-soldiers.

'Mum?'

'Aspetta, amore mia, sto combattendo.' Wait, my love, I am fighting.

Rosanna keeps her eyes closed, but the image she has conjured in her mind's eye is fading. She sighs, opens her eyes to find herself back in her sunlit bedroom with the mountain in its afternoon glow by the window and her daughter, Ilaria, standing doleful in the doorway.

'Stai bene, tesoro?'

'Non Italiano.'

'What's the matter, love?'

'Stephanie told me I can't play on the swings because I'm not in her friend group. She is so mean.'

Rosanna tries not to close her eyes again and flump back onto her pillows. 'And does she and her friend group own the swings?'

'No.'

'Well, she has no case, then. You can say to her in your sweetest voice, "*Stephanie, via a cacare figlio di puttana*", okay? But you must say it without anger so that no one ever, ever suspects that you have said "fuck off, motherfucker".' Rosanna hoots with glee. 'And if you like, we can do the meditation together and we can eliminate her with the white light.'

'Mu-um, this is why people think I'm weird.' Ilaria stamps her foot, stomps out of the room and shouts, 'Dad, Mum told me to say, "fuck off, motherfucker".'

Rosanna hears a door slam. A minute or two later, her husband, Jonathon, puts his best disapproving expression around the door.

'I told you I should not stay in bed,' says Rosanna.

Jonathon blinks. 'Have you slept?'

'No. But I think I killed some cancer. Probably gained another two hours of life in which I can think of other ways Ilaria can stand up for herself. Where's Matty?'

'He's on the couch messaging his mates about his little sister saying "motherfucker". Serra is laughing in the kitchen.'

'And Bella?'

'Having her nap.'

Rosanna glances at the clock on the bedside table. 'I'll wake her up. Or she'll have happy-happy playtime until midnight. Three o'clock is the very limit.'

'She didn't go down until two.'

'Does not matter. Oh, I should put that on the list. There was something else I thought of too,' Rosanna mumbles to herself as she rumples the bedclothes and opens a blue notebook. 'Come on, Rosanna's brain.' She takes a pen from the bedside table and speaks what she writes. 'Put Bella down at one, get her up by three at the latest. Keep daytime nap until she is four if you can, or she will send you crazy.' Rosanna twirls an index finger beside her ear and rolls her eyes. 'And now I forget what the other thing was.' She puts a hand over her eyes to think.

Jonathon brings his wiry frame into the room, leans over his wife and plants a kiss on her forehead. 'Don't stress,' he says. 'We have plenty of your wisdom to work with.'

Rosanna runs a hand through his hair and says, 'A mother's wisdom is given over many days. And I might not have many days.'

'But you have more wisdom than most,' says Jonathon, 'so it'll balance out.'

She rubs his hand, but is still thinking. 'It was probably to remind them that they don't have to marry. Look at the messes you are in. I am sorry to leave you with so many children, so many things to think of.'

Jonathon smiles and says, '*La lista infinita.*' He has been learning Italian, something he has been meaning to do since the birth of their eldest child, Serra. He has flung himself into it with gusto since the word 'terminal' entered his everyday thoughts.

'Yes,' says Rosanna. 'The endless list.'

'You don't have to do it for us,' says Jonathon. 'Only if it makes you feel better. And'—he sits on the bed and kisses her nose, her lips—'you know I wouldn't do anything differently. Except of course I should have married Sophia Grafton.'

Rosanna responds with a jarring punch to his upper arm. 'Sophia Grafton is nasty pieces of work.'

'I love seeing you light up with jealous rage,' says Jonathon.

'You'll be seeing my lights all the way from heaven if you match up with Sophia fuckhead Grafton.'

'Oi, easy on the swears. You won't be going to heaven if you keep that up. I promise not to marry Sophia Grafton, ever.' He kisses her again. 'Any pain?'

'Yes, I am hurting in the everywhere,' says Rosanna. She smiles. 'But not the sort of pain I need medicine for.'

Jonathon takes her hand and they close their eyes, dwelling on the pain for just a moment, letting it pinch, then pass. 'Are you still sure you want to continue with this trial?' he asks. 'It's giving you a hell of a time.'

'A failed trial is still a useful trial, but only if you complete it,' says Rosanna. 'And maybe the curing part is in the last few treatments.'

'Okay,' says Jonathon.

'And it is giving me time to write *La Lista*, which is a comfort, so I will keep adding to it until I know it is enough.'

'*Basta*,' Jonathon says, kissing her again. 'Enough. We probably won't even need a list anyway. You'll most likely outlive me.' But he swallows, takes a deep breath and tips his head back in a well-practised tactic to hamper tears. 'Well,' he says, 'if you keep on with *La Lista*, could you tell them more about you? The more you the better. They only need to be like you and they'll thrive in any scenario. This I know for sure.'

Rosanna is about to swipe him and his sentimental compliments away, but one of his tears escapes, leaving a silver thread on his cheek and it makes her heart clench.

'Okay,' she says. 'I'll write more things about me. With no swear-words.' She fixes her huge brown eyes onto his blue ones. 'And I will put that it will be okay for you to find another wife.'

Jonathon stands. 'Okay, that's really enough now.'

'But only if this new wife is kind. Kindness is everything. Always choose kind.'

He stands, brushes her words from the air with one hand and says, 'I'll wake Bella.'

Rosanna lies back into her pillows. 'I will sleep for just a minute. And then I will listen along to the Ilaria catalogue of complaints. She's just like me, you know, needs to put her feelings into the room.'

'Yes, I do know,' says Jonathon.

And they say, 'God help us,' together, only Jonathon's version is in Italian. *'Dio ci aiuti'.*

𝄡

Rosanna sleeps for much longer than a minute and wakes to darkness and the clatters of the evening meal. She feels a pang of missing out. Illness puts fuzzy, fast-forward patches into hours. She hates these missing bits, wonders what sunset colours have come and gone on the mountain, what birds have passed overhead as she slept. She feels the resentful throb of her heart just as the tail of a dream slithers off into the forgotten. *Something to do with home*, she thinks, and is shocked to find that 'home' means Italy. With a sense of urgency she picks up the blue notebook.

She writes in Italian, because her first language brings her hand gestures, her eyes and her facial expressions to words on a page, and it translates to this:

Thursday, 8 August 2019

Dear Serra, Matty, Ilaria and Bella,

Some people say that it's not helpful to see a diagnosis of cancer as a 'battle' or a 'fight', but I am not one of those people. I have a fighting instinct in me, because I have you to fight for. I want to stay here with you. I want you to keep your mother.

But if you are reading this letter then I have lost the battle. What do I say next?

I am sorry. So, so very sorry that you don't have me anymore but also sorry for me not to have you. Sorry that the gods of fate chose me, sorry that your grandfather smoked in the car with me in it. Don't ever smoke, please.

You must be feeling very sad. I should have probably been quieter around the house, smaller, so that the space I have left isn't so big. But we all have to take up as much space as we need, don't we?

I hope that none of you ever feels as though you have to make yourselves smaller for anyone, or change your shape. I want you to fill your rightful space. As well, don't let anyone feel they have to change their shape for you. But I will try not to lecture here.

I should probably be telling you that as I write this, I feel peaceful and ready. That I accept my no-future. But I can't say that. How can I ever feel peaceful about leaving you, my dearest children? I can say that I think the no-future has more in it than humans can know. I think there is more to this life than life. And I think it will be good because I have been as good as I can be. As you know, I have been writing you a list of things I would like to pass on to you. Things I have learnt and feel are valuable and would in better circumstances have given you over a lifetime. Of course, you can drink the soup or throw it out the window, but you should know that if you choose not to follow my instructions to the best of your abilities, then I will haunt you. Phantom Mamma will flick cold water when you are lazy and put broccoli in your *Bolognese* when you don't eat well. She will shout instructions in the night and leave long lists of things to do everywhere. She will leave the smell of baked tomatoes and garlic in strange corners of the house. Her love is terrifying. Be very afraid.

And now, here alongside your list, I give you a little story, for you to hold, and for it to hold you:

A young girl lived in a beautiful valley in a beautiful country full of lovers. Lovers of art, lovers of food, lovers of music, lovers of people, lovers of laughter, lovers of love. This girl was an especial lover of the mountains surrounding her city, and their snow. She thought snow was a miracle. She played in it, built things on it, skied on it and hid herself away in it when her mother called her in for chores.

She was the fourth child of six, one of two girls. Her mother and father ran a goat farm an eighth of the way up the Maiella, one of the tallest peaks in the Apennine Range. Their love was mostly reserved for their goats, their god, Jesus and the Holy Ghost. Their faith in the Roman Catholic Church was what guided their every decision, mandated their work, their rest, their laughs, their scolds, their ideas. It was the Church who warned the young girl's father that his daughter must not speak too loudly or laugh too often or see the wrong people or sing the wrong songs. It was the Church who said that courage is not becoming of women and education is the privilege of men. It was the Church who put the fear of God into her mother, shame into the ordinary and the looming threat of sin into every day.

So the girl watched her brothers grow and play and sing their songs and go to university. She kept quiet and good and waited for the blessings of God to bring her joy and peace. They did not come, the blessings. Nor did the joy or the peace. Instead she was disturbed at all times by frustration and rage that burst out of her at inappropriate moments and brought terrible disgrace to her family. One time during Saturday mass she stood up in the pew, shook her fist at the priest and shouted, 'Your god is not my god. You are an arsehole and fuck off to you and all your dead relatives.' Then she sang a bar or two of 'Take On Me' by A-ha before her mother slapped her hard across her face.

A terrible silence descended upon the congregation and put its claws into the girl's mother until she screamed. The father then dragged his daughter by the ear from the church, along the streets of their city, L'Aquila, to the Aterno River where he pushed her into the icy water. Much of the congregation had followed, and they stood on the riverbanks shouting ugly words about sin and retribution. Above them all, the icy peaks of the Apennine Mountains shimmered their own rebukes and some said they heard the distant rumbles of an avalanche, a sure sign that the wrath of God was stirred and very, very strong.

A place was found for the girl in a convent reformatory far away from L'Aquila and the Apennines and the Aterno, where the ways of a devout Roman Catholic God could be more intensively applied. While she waited for her punishment time to begin, her mother could not look at her and her father could not be in the same room as her, but one of her brothers, the youngest, Matteo, gave her a bag of money and the instruction: 'Run.'

So she ran.

She had learnt at some point during her limited schooling that her city of L'Aquila had a sister city called Hobart, which could only be found on the world globe after almost an hour of searching, on a tiny island that looked like it was slipping off the very bottom of the world. Her mind fixed quickly onto the idea that Sister Hobart, the farthest place she could go before she would freeze to death in Antarctica, was where she needed to be. She had read in a book that the city had a valley and a river and sat beneath a small but beautiful mountain. 'Mountains,' said the girl to the book, 'are what I know.' And because the island had its toes in the freezing Southern Ocean (which, by the way, said the book, is lit up at night by small fish with luminous scales and contained other fish that walked on tiny hands), the girl knew there would also be snow.

The journey was long, and when she reached its end, she saw that there was indeed a mountain, but that it was a bold dark blue with not a hint of white. The air, though fresh, was warm and filled with blossom and the river seemed more like an ocean, and the people, though they smiled and laughed, did not smile and laugh with her. She could understand only phrasebook things and nothing of what was funny. Almost as much as finding mountains did she want to find laughs. But in the warm blossom air she could only feel the cold of alone.

In search of some miracle snow, she took up her belongings and walked south, out of the sister city of Hobart, which didn't feel like a sister at all but a stranger. She thought she might find the Southern Ocean and if not snow, perhaps a lanternfish or a fish with tiny hands. She was still walking when the night began to fall and an unfamiliar moon rose smug above her. She took a path off the main road where she was safe from fast cars and the moon was hidden by trees. She paused in the dark and looked at the stars and asked them for a way out of this fool's errand.

Not a minute later, she heard from behind her a thunderous sound, which came so fast she had barely time to place it as the sound of a horse's hooves, and no time at all to move safely off the path and out of harm's way. Instead, she jumped. She dropped her belongings, bent her knees and sprang into blackness, her calf brushing the hot silken velvet of the horse's flank.

There was a grunt, a drama of hooves, a shout, and an immense searing pain all over the girl's body. *'Cazzo Madre di Dio,'* she screamed. *'Che due palle!'*

'Bloody hell,' said a man's voice from the darkness. 'What the . . .?'

'Help,' called the girl. 'Help us, please, thank you. *Sono in fiamme.' I am on fire.*

And so the voice came to ground level and moved nearer, then attached itself to an arm that reached out and gave enough help (please, thank you) to pull the girl out of her fire-trap.

'Bloody hell,' said the man again. 'You put yourself in a heap of nettles.' He helped her back onto the path.

The girl did not understand what the man was saying so she called him an ugly son-of-a-bitch bastard (*'Puttana bastardo'*) and began to sing a lullaby her mother had sung to keep the minds of her children from pain.

'Noo nonna nonna, a nenna mie, l'angele l'addorma . . .'
She closed her eyes tightly and imagined herself away.

The man continued to talk to her as she sang, and his voice was not an unpleasant accompaniment. She imagined Apennine snow being pressed onto her burning skin, and Aterno water washing away the nettle-pins, and mountain clouds taking her up. The girl wasn't sure how long it took to realise that she was upon the horse, and that the horse was loping gently towards a house with yellow light at the windows.

Under the yellow light, a woman's face came into view and the girl saw in that face the sort of kindness that can make you cry.

'Bonjour?' said the woman. *'Guten Tag?'*

'Italiano,' uttered the girl, with tears looming. *'Buongiorno.'*

'Right,' said the horse man, who was standing behind the kind woman, and who brought himself closer to reveal that he was in possession of the crying-kind face too. *'Buongiorno.'*

The girl sniffed. *'Buonasera.'*

'Right,' said the man again, and he offered up a glass of beer, which tasted of autumn and made the girl hiccup. The nettle-pin pain was subsiding, leaving behind an itch.

The kind woman touched her sternum and said, 'Kyrie.' She pointed to the kind-faced horse-beer-man and said, 'Jonathon.'

The girl touched her chest and said, 'Rosanna.'

And Jonathon said a phrase that Rosanna recognised. He said, 'Ma, Rosanna can sing.'

And that is all for now, my darlings. I know there are things I have missed. I will find a way to get them to you. I promise. If you lose this letter I have scanned it, saved it to the clouds and given Dad the link. I am not in the clouds, I am here with you. (Waving from the trees, winking *gibigianna* on the water, flying on the breeze, shimmering on the snow.)

Watch for nettles, sing your songs and keep riding your horses, but not in the dark. If you decide to love God, love the gentle version, the one who loves all the lambs, the white, the black, the fat, the weak, the girl, the boy, the ones who choose no gender, the sick, the lame.

And know that I love *you* and I love you and I love you, always and always.

Your Mamma. XXXOOO

𝄢

Stepping Stone Number 4, from *La Lista* by R.K.:
Always look for the laughs. And if there are none about, either make some of your own, or go and find them. Laughter is a universal language, like love and song. It is thought that laughter came to exist as a pre-linguistic signal of safety, belonging and social bonding. Real laughter requires a temporary shutdown of all emotions other than mirth, so it serves as an important detachment mechanism in times of stress. It should be taken deadly seriously. (This advice is derived from the work of Henri Bergson, 1900.)

Chapter 7
Hollow

In the days that follow, Frey allows herself to feel the aches in her shoulders, the catching pain in her elbow and the tender bruises on her thigh. But she puts herself at an emotional distance from the possibility of betrayal, from where she can watch Gil with concentrated calm.

His behaviour appears unchanged from the usual unshakeable self-assurance, but Frey can't be sure whether his 'usual' lifestyle includes a mistress whom he is accustomed to concealing. His sporting interests would certainly afford opportunity for illicit trysts, but his game reports (mostly directed at Tom) remain detailed and apparently genuine.

When Gil slings an arm over her and kisses her neck early on Friday morning, Frey's body wants to pull away. *This could be an important evidence-gathering exercise*, she tells herself, and turns to face him. And then he caresses her breasts and breathes in her ear and it is so much like it always has been that she forgets her aching limbs and her suspicious pride and gives her body a few moments of release.

She notices no contrite tenderness from Gil, no unusual movements or newly acquired lovemaking techniques. She just holds herself in the familiar terrain of his body and imagines away the woman in the blue coat.

𝄡

By Sunday, the bruises on her thigh are a furious purple. She welcomes the vivid proof that at least parts of last week were real. The photograph she took of Gil and the woman in the blue coat has turned fantastical with too much scrutiny. She has printed it, folded it, unfolded it and observed differences every time. The faces looking towards the sound of the smashing window appear innocently startled, then sheepishly shocked, then back to innocent. The woman looks frightened, then angry, then frightened again. Gil's hand on her arm seems protective, then casual. Frey puts the picture away from her, in a box labelled 'Fun With Maths!' at the very top of her wardrobe and hopes it might just disappear.

𝄡

On Tuesday, she wonders whether she should run back into the path of the yellow Fiat and slip again though the portal into Rosanna's eyes. Instead, she runs ten kilometres, fixes Lily's swings, prunes her apple tree then waits at dancing, joining a conversation about vacuum cleaners.

𝄡

On Wednesday, when she visits her father, Roger, at his flat in Battery Point, he says, 'Hello, The Girl. You're back again. I'll be sick of the sight of you soon.'

'Hi, Dad.' Frey sits herself opposite him at his pink laminate kitchen table, which is set up for the dismantling and re-building of an old transistor radio.

He twitches a brief smile at Acorn and says, 'Hello, dog.'

'You had tea?'

'Nope.'

He eyes her over his glasses and continues with his work. Frey watches as he removes the screws from the back of the radio and places them carefully on a large magnet.

'Have my big ugly brothers been in this week?' Frey asks.

'Nope,' says Roger. He prises the radio's knobs from their holes.

'Whose transistor?'

'Mrs Butler from number twenty.'

'What's wrong with it?'

'Probably sick of belonging to Mrs Butler from number twenty.'

Acorn rests his head on Roger's shoe.

'What's wrong with her?'

'She smells,' says Roger.

'What of?'

'Like a ruddy perfume shop.'

Frey snorts. 'She probably has a crush on you.'

Roger doesn't reply. He has removed the backing case and circuit board when Frey says, 'She paying you for this?' She picks up a tube and cleans it with a thick pipe cleaner.

'Nope.'

'Did you ever get sick of Mum?'

Roger inspects Frey over his glasses again. Frey wonders whether she should add, *'Because there's a chance Gil is so sick of me he's fallen in love with someone else. And I don't think I can fix a marriage the way we can fix a radio.'*

Roger turns his attention back to the circuit board and says, 'Nope.'

'Forty-one years together and you didn't once get sick of anything about her?'

A few minutes of cleaning tubes and tweaking wires pass before Roger says, 'I ate a few too many of her jam turnovers. Lynny's were excellent, but I can't abide a jam turnover these days.'

Frey sighs. She picks up the circuit board and says, 'This solder join is broken.'

Roger grunts.

Frey gets up and puts the kettle on, washes a few dishes, then says, 'I got hit by a car at low speed last week.'

'How'd you go with that?' Roger briefly scans his daughter for signs of injury.

'Not bad. I jumped. It was a Fiat 500.'

'Lucky.' He runs a pipe cleaner through a hole.

'Are bagless vacuum cleaners better?'

'Nope.'

'If I bring you my violin, can you fix its strings? You do it better than me.'

He looks at her again, this time holding her gaze when he says, 'Yes.'

𝄡

A week later, when Gil still seems completely normal and her life is bound back into its tight schedule, Frey has partially convinced herself that the afternoon of visions and grapefruits and Fiats and music was a result of perimenopausal hormones. *Well, if they can heat your body up in seconds and violently swing your moods, what else can they do?* Just to be sure, she drives to New Town and past the house where she'd seen Gil and the woman in the blue coat. Everything is as she remembers it. House, driveway, grapefruit tree. There is no one in the driveway, no car there either, and nothing parked out the front. Frey drives on for another block, parks and walks back. When she reaches the house, she lifts the lid of the letterbox, takes out an envelope, scans the print on its front, then replaces it and walks on. This is executed in one swift movement and in less than three seconds she has a name. *Skye Killinger.*

13

By the weekend, Frey has matched the name to the startled face in the driveway, and has compiled a Skye Killinger profile. It is not comprehensive, but detailed enough for her imagination to dervish about with inevitable self-comparisons. Skye is thirty-four, she is very pretty, *very* slim and an artist. *Of course she's something fascinating like an artist.* Her work as an illustrator and painter shows remarkable talent – particularly her portraiture, which most recently depicts beautiful people in water or gazing up to skies. They are clever and realistic, almost like photographs, but not to Frey's taste at all. Why would someone pay a fortune for a painting that looks like a giant photograph of a stranger? The idea seems creepy to Frey, but is evidently granting Skye Killinger some success. Her recent collection at Hobart's Handmark Gallery sold out in two days.

There are no obvious links from Skye to Gil, nor are there any to Barnes and Rutherford Property Development, cycling, golf, tennis or boating. There are, however, numerous pictures of Skye in a studio looking adorable in paint-stained overalls. Another of her in a gallery wearing the blue coat over jeans and a white shirt. Effortless elegance. Frey unclenches her jaw and thinks of her own over-tailored wardrobe. *My over-tailored life.*

At lunchtime, Frey comes downstairs to take Grace and Lily to their dancing school's annual fundraiser.

'Mum!' says Lily. 'You're wearing jeans! I didn't think you had any. Grace, look, Mum's wearing jeans.'

'Of course I have jeans,' says Frey, running a hand over her bottom and tweaking down her T-shirt.

'Skinny jeans?' says Grace, her disapproval upwardly inflected.

'Too tight?' asks Frey. 'I might have, you know, grown a bit since I last wore them.'

Grace just raises her eyebrows.

'They just *really, really* fit you, Mum,' says Lily. 'And no one wears skinny jeans anymore much.'

'Kate Moss does,' says Frey.

The girls ask simultaneously, 'Who?'

'Maybe just tuck your shirt in at least,' suggests Lily.

Frey nearly laughs. Lily's face is so serious. Fashion advice from an eleven-year-old in leggings and a cropped hoodie.

Frey tucks herself in, but her waistline isn't high enough to keep the T-shirt contained. She grabs a navy jacket and channels effortless elegance.

Grace laughs and hums 'Yesterday' by the Beatles.

When they arrive at the fundraiser venue – a rammed-earth-and-glass purpose-built structure with a view of a vineyard and a concrete minimalist interior – Frey finds herself feeling nostalgic for Laetare Gardens and its flounces.

'It finishes at three, Mum,' says Grace. 'See you then.'

'I'm staying too,' Frey says with a smile.

'Why?' asks Grace.

'You won't let us have pink lemonade,' whines Lily.

'Yes I will.' Frey massages her jaw.

'Oh, hello there,' says a woman in a floral dress after the girls have joined their friends. Frey recognises her as Teagan Wiley, the dance academy's costume manager and a woman well known for her gossip. 'You're Grace and Lily's mum, aren't you?'

'Freycinet,' says Frey. She clears her throat. 'Frey.'

'Yes, hello, Frey. Great that you've come along. Gawd, you must be proud of Grace. She's freakishly good, that one. We'll be sad to lose her when she goes.'

'She's not going anywhere,' Frey says with a laugh. 'Not for a few years yet.'

'No,' says Teagan, 'but she will in the end. At her standard, she could probably dance with the New York City Ballet and whatnot. We all wish we were her.'

Frey and Teagan look over at Grace, who is laughing with a group of her friends. All the girls have similar hairstyles, similar clothes, but Grace stands out. There are others in the room glancing in her direction, some openly staring. Frey switches to their lens and sees, after a brief moment of refocusing, a beautiful girl who is somehow not a girl. It isn't just beauty that marks her, nor her long slender limbs, but a sort of aloof knowing, and the slightly bored indifference of someone much older. It's like she's waiting for something and everyone wants to know what it is but no one is brave enough to ask.

'I can see where she gets her stunning looks,' Teagan says. 'You're such a beauty yourself, Frey. Do you dance?'

Frey feels her body wanting to get away. 'No. Not anymore. I used to a bit but I had lots of other interests. And I have three boofhead brothers, so, dancing wasn't really a thing in our family.'

'And what do you do now?'

'I work for our family business. My husband's property firm.' This is not untrue. She does spend three mornings a week typing up notes from recorded meetings. It is mind-numbing work. Balm to an over-thinking brain.

'Ooh, fancy,' says Teagan (by now, Frey is having trouble looking the woman in the eye). 'I'm a science teacher when I'm not organis-ing the bloody costumes for everyone. Got seventy-five lab reports to mark after this.' She blows air through her lips and smiles.

Frey hates herself for being surprised that gossipy Teagan has a scientific brain. 'Nothing more important than teachers,' she says.

A small girl in a tutu runs over then and says, 'Mum! Can I start Acro next term? There's a space in the Wednesday class.'

'Sure, sweetheart!' Teagan winks at Frey and adds, 'There's Wednesday afternoons gone.' They watch the tutu bounce away. 'They love it so much. Does my heart good to watch.'

Frey doesn't like to admit that she hasn't seen Grace dance at all this year. Grace hadn't wanted her to watch the mid-year Eisteddfods and Frey hadn't argued. Something about the manufactured smiles and the overdone faces makes her uneasy. 'I'm going to make sure my youngest isn't overdoing the desserts,' Frey tells Teagan. 'See you soon.'

'Nice to chat, Frey,' says Teagan. 'You'll be hearing from me about the end-of-year showcase costumes. Glad you came along at last. Ooh, there's Valentina, been wanting to catch her.'

Frey watches as Teagan scurries over to a petite woman with a sweet smile and a dark, glossy bob. Valentina Bellavance. Frey looks around for Paul and is surprised to find herself disappointed that he is not in the room. She would like to inspect him anew with her recently acquired context: Paul Bellavance, manipulative cad and pathetic penis exhibitionist.

Frey knows Valentina well enough to say hello to, but rarely does. They move in different circles. Or rather, Valentina moves in her circles while Frey skirts the edge of others. Valentina is known for her sweet nature, her charity work and her generous parties. Frey has seen the pictures; friends of friends on Facebook living it up at the Bellavance mansion or raising a glass on their boat. Frey wonders whether Skye Killinger has ever been in attendance, suspects so. *Hobart is a small place*, she thinks, *and all the beautiful people gravitate to one another*. She turns away from Teagan and Valentina and decides that it's time she made more of an effort to find some real friends. Sister friends. A choir of imaginary women from a different world doesn't count.

She attempts to join a conversation with a cluster of parents by the silent auction. They are talking about Netflix. Frey asks whether anyone has seen a documentary about the troubles in Haiti and feels suddenly and immensely lonely while waiting for a reply.

The party drones on, and when it is over, she leaves feeling annoyed with herself. *You think you're better than these people, you stuck-up bitch.* She feels hollow, even though she has eaten her own allocated chicken salad and most of Grace's.

₿

Even considering the rules of evidence in a civil proceeding (fact on the balance of probabilities), Frey is presented with another exhibit that does, on face value at least, actually prove the existence of the West Moonah Women's Choir. It comes on Monday afternoon when Frey's bruises have turned yellow and she is collecting Grace from dancing.

'Some girl gave me this the other day,' Grace says, tossing something onto Frey's lap. It's an envelope, creased from Grace's bag. Frey picks it up and sees her name written on the front in flourish-y, rounded cursive. *Freycinet Barnes via Grace Barnes.*

'What is it?' she asks, turning the envelope over. There is nothing written on the other side.

'How should I know?'

'Which girl gave it to you?'

'I don't know. Some little girl from dancing. She said it was in the office, and the office bitch asked her if she knew us.'

'Don't call her an office bitch.'

'It's a he, and he is. A bitch.' Grace picks up her phone, shutting down further questions.

Frey opens the envelope and pulls out a piece of card. The same extravagant hand has written a short note. An invitation.

Dear Freycinet,

Please join us at New Town Station Nursery for lunch on Wednesday (28 August). Half past twelve. We'll go along anyway so just show up if you'd like to come.

Warm wishes,

Bizzy, Kyrie and Rosanna, West Moonah Women's Choir (AWC).

'Oh, it's a lunch invitation,' Frey says, hearing her own delight. 'For Wednesday.' She smiles and imagines Rosanna's eyes. '*Grazie mille, mi piacerebbe venire.*'

'What?' asks Grace, her face disdainful.

'I said, "Thank you very much, I'd love to come." She's Italian, one of the women who invited me.'

'Since when did you speak Italian?'

'Since I learnt it. That and four other languages.'

'Right, Mum.' Grace goes back to her phone.

'And I have a brown belt in taekwondo, a Cert Three in electronic engineering, a diploma in special effects makeup and a motorbike licence. As well as my Arts-Law degree.'

Grace makes a *pfft* noise, which is a midpoint between scorn and disinterest.

'And I can dance, you know. I did ballet for a while. And gymnastics.'

'Right,' sighs Grace with a roll of her eyes. 'And you can ride a horse while standing on your head.'

'I haven't tried that yet.'

Grace rolls her eyes again.

Frey chuckles, then drives on with the card and its envelope clutched between her knees, its warm wishes thawing the air around her.

♭

Stepping Stone Number 3, from *La Lista* by R.K.:

Don't eat too much sugar. It feels like a treat until you feel ill. Always, whether you eat sugar or not, brush your teeth. Not brushing teeth is disgusting. They will turn yellow, then brown, then black and then they will fall out and no one will want to kiss you.

Chapter 8
Raspberries

Freycinet wonders why on earth she's never thought to have lunch at a café within a plant nursery in the second half of a Tasmanian winter. New Town Station Nursery is a study of hope and relief. Hoorays of winter blossom and fragrant Erlicheer wave her in. Kyrie and Bizzy are already seated and laughing along with the trumpeting daffodils at a table by a fountain. There is no sign of Rosanna.

'Freycinet,' says Bizzy, standing in welcome. 'I'm telling Kyrie off for making my pelvic floor sit next to a fountain. There must be no laughing over lunch or I'll be wetting my knickers for sure. And no jumping, dancing, running, skipping, galloping, prancing or . . . what have I missed?'

'Bouncing?' asks Freycinet. 'I don't last two seconds on a trampoline.'

'Yes, no bouncing. It'll have to be just plain old lunch.' Bizzy smiles. Her lipstick is bright blue, matched to her fingernails and her peacock-print dress. Kyrie is elegant in a black-and-white herringbone coat, her hair all long silver waves. Next to their statements, Frey feels like a whisper. She has ditched her Skye

Killinger–induced attempt at relaxed style and reverted to navy pants and a cream shirt.

'I'm so pleased you got our little missive,' says Bizzy, motioning for Freycinet to take the seat closest to the fountain. 'I knew the dance community would find you.'

'Thank you for the invitation,' says Frey. 'Can I ask . . . though I don't mind, um, I don't remember giving you my surname. Did I?'

'Ah, you didn't,' says Bizzy. 'I worked that out. There aren't so many beautiful women called Freycinet in the Hobart area.'

Freycinet blushes.

'She's incorrigible,' says Kyrie. 'A professional nosy parker.'

'Just imagine if everyone went about minding their own business,' Bizzy says. 'What a miserable old world it would be.' She absently touches a pendant around her neck – a brown circle, like a primitive coin, humble against the vivid peacock blues.

'Rosanna is so annoyed she's not here,' says Kyrie. 'She's not feeling up to much today but left strict instructions that we are not to frighten you away with our old-lady weirdness.' Kyrie sends Bizzy a stern look.

'Oh, I'm sorry,' says Frey. 'That's disappointing. She is so . . .' But she can't think of the right words to describe Rosanna.

'Yes,' agrees Kyrie, 'she is.'

And Bizzy adds, 'Very so.'

'I hope she feels better soon,' Frey says, and is pleased when the waiter arrives because her words seem so impotent.

They order toasted sandwiches and tap water, and Kyrie asks, 'How are your bones and muscles, Freycinet?'

Frey has to think about what she means.

'After the Fiat run-in.'

'Oh, fine, thank you. Fine. Is there any damage to the car?'

'Not a smudge.'

Frey knows instantly that this is a lie. 'There must be a dent?'

'No dent,' says Kyrie.

'We should be having a sneaky little glass of bubbles,' says Bizzy. 'To celebrate your survival.'

'Love to, but I can't,' says Kyrie. 'I have grandchildren to pick up.'

'Well, I will,' says Bizzy. 'I've just landed a nice Very Cross Stitches commission. Government House, no less.'

Kyrie places a hand on Frey's and says, 'Bizzy is a remarkable example of a woman who has successfully taken centuries of indoctrination and brain-washing and turned it into an artform that makes her a lot of money while blowing a big old feck-you raspberry to the patriarchy.' Kyrie demonstrates one of the raspberries, simultaneously shoving her middle finger in the air.

'Oh my goodness,' says Freycinet. 'Of course, Bizzy! You're the Very Cross Stitches woman. I saw your work in the *Guardian* recently. You stitched Julia Gillard's famous quote! "I will not be lectured about sexism and misogyny by this man."'

Kyrie claps her hands and says, '"Not now, not ever."'

'Yes, that article was a boon,' says Bizzy. 'I got another ten or so thousand followers on Instagram from it. Julia was very generous with her endorsement.'

'And I've seen your books, too. How silly of me!' Freycinet regards Bizzy afresh and sees new meaning in her poise.

'It's a bit of fun,' says Bizzy.

'Wow,' Frey says. 'Is there anything else I should know about the choir before I make an idiot of myself?'

'Bizzy is also the Liniment Girl,' says Kyrie proudly.

'The liniment girl?' echoes Frey.

'Ah, come on now, Kyrie,' says Bizzy.

But Kyrie ignores her. 'The song. You know it. From the eighties? Huge hit. Huge.'

'Oh *that* liniment girl,' says Frey, recalling the tune. 'Is that your song, Bizzy?'

'No, it's not my song, but it's about me. Allegedly.'

'Definitely,' says Kyrie. 'The band Barbara Takes a Trip was a proto-riot grrrl outfit. They were very inspired by Bizzy's feminist activism. It was an unexpected hit.'

'Very unexpected,' adds Bizzy. 'Given that the song is a load of steaming shite.'

'It's an iconic song,' says Freycinet. 'Very empowering for women. Deeds not words and all that.'

'Whatever it is,' says Bizzy, 'I'm terribly trapped in that song. Everyone always assumes I'm up to fight their cause.'

'You are,' says Kyrie.

'Hmm,' says Bizzy. 'I'd sometimes like to just sit upwind for a while, chat to the trees.'

'You?' replies Kyrie with a laugh. 'Chat to the trees?' She looks at Freycinet. 'This from the woman who wants to turn the fifth wave of feminism into a tsunami.'

'Anyway,' Bizzy says, clearing her throat, 'we're not here to talk about me. We wondered whether you'd like to join the choir, Freycinet? We've all decided that Kyrie was very clever hitting you with her car, because you'd be a good fit.'

Freycinet's heart flips. 'Join the choir? You don't even know whether I can sing!'

'Everyone can sing,' says Kyrie.

'And it doesn't matter if you sound a bit dog to start with,' says Bizzy, 'as most of our singers have excellent musicality. And we're more than just singing. At risk of sounding like complete twats, we're about energy, really. And yours is unusually . . .' Bizzy searches for the right word.

'Simmery,' concludes Kyrie.

'Yes,' says Bizzy. 'We could be wrong but we think you might be all a-smoulder inside those lovely fire-retardant fabrics. And we think you could add that smoulder to our fire and together we can all make sure we blow up in the right places at precisely the right times. Does that make sense?'

'Um,' says Frey.

'What Bizzy means, Freycinet,' says Kyrie, 'is that the choir needs a bit more . . .'

'Oomph,' says Bizzy.

'Well, I'm flattered,' says Frey. 'But surely you have masses of women clamouring to sing with you, some of them with far better energy than me.'

'Possibly,' Bizzy says. 'But we're very fussy.'

'She's lying,' Kyrie says. 'Very few people have the energy – good or bad – for things like women's choirs. Why do you think we're a choir of nine? We're barely an ensemble.'

'We *are* fussy though,' says Bizzy. 'The West Moonah Women's Choir won't take on just anyone.'

'Strictly speaking,' Kyrie adds, apparently not listening to Bizzy anymore, 'we need ten to meet the definition of a choir.'

'You'll bring just the right sort of classiness. And we just like you a lot.'

'Rosanna is adamant that you join,' says Kyrie.

'And you can't refuse a dying woman, can you?' adds Bizzy.

'Of course you can,' says Kyrie, frowning at Bizzy. 'It's entirely up to you, Freycinet.'

'I really don't think . . .' says Frey. 'Thank you but I don't—'

'Take all the time you need to decide,' says Bizzy. 'But you won't regret it. We're apparently a fascinating bunch, according to recent reviews. Would you like a potted history of our choristers?'

'Say yes,' advises Kyrie. 'She'll deliver it anyway. She's memorised them all.'

'Yes,' says Frey. 'Okay.'

'Now, all of this is confidential West Moonah Women's Choir business, of course,' says Bizzy. 'There is no formal code of conduct, but we will have your tongue removed if you speak of anyone's business with anyone outside the choir.'

'She's possibly not lying this time,' says Kyrie.

'All right, so, let's start with Sally,' Bizzy says. 'She's our retired doctor. She has a well-mannered but useless husband who doesn't have any hobbies other than venerating the Murdoch press with his poisonous mother, poo-pooing climate change and so on. Sally chose a career over children, thereby beautifully disrupting the grand Eyreton tradition of flattening women into cardboard cut-outs which look lovely next to the Cornish-blue crockery on the kitchen dresser.'

'Sally is always the first at rehearsal and the last to leave,' says Kyrie.

'Then there's Eleanor,' Bizzy continues. 'She's the tall one with the sausage doggie and the inconsistent fashion sense. Years ago, her husband erased her emotional motherboard with constant, protracted violence and other destabilising tactics before she knocked him on the head and buried him out near Leslie Vale somewhere. She's done twelve years in the prison hospital for the criminally insane but has since been declared stable and reformed by a team of doctors and a progressive parole board.'

'Oh, my God,' says Freycinet.

'She says the murder weapon was her cold, rock-hard heart,' says Kyrie, 'but it was a folded-up newspaper.'

'A Millwall brick,' says Frey.

'Bugger me,' says Bizzy. 'You know the Millwall brick?'

'Yes, a club made from a tightly folded newspaper, used as stealth weapons at English football matches.'

'That's the one,' says Bizzy with glee. 'I knew you were a keeper.'

'So,' says Frey, 'that's why Eleanor's dead on the inside?'

'Yes,' says Kyrie. 'We gave her Penelope the dachshund in the hopes that a dear little doggie might arouse some feeling in her. It's not working yet.'

'And then there's Irene Hawke,' says Bizzy. 'She's a founding member. She lost her husband Harvey years ago but keeps forgetting he's dead. She has a bit of a marble problem, in that she's losing them.'

'Poor Irene,' says Frey.

'Yes, poor love,' Bizzy agrees. 'She went home the other day and Harvey was sitting in the breakfast nook eating his eggs.'

'Oh,' says Frey.

'She was quite perky about it actually,' Bizzy says. 'Said he looked quite good for a dead man.'

'It's very sad,' says Kyrie. 'She has a dicky heart, too, which could stop if ever she gets startled or overexcited.'

'It won't happen,' says Bizzy. 'I've never met someone so expert at remaining underwhelmed as Irene Hawke. Now, as for Mary Dempsey-St Clair . . .' Bizzy pauses as the waiter delivers their sandwiches. 'Mary is an heiress to a fortune. Unfortunately her parents are fascists so she's pretty ashamed of her wealth. Her reaction is to make her own clothes, take up women's footy and do a post-grad in gender studies.'

'"Fascists" might be overstating it,' says Kyrie.

'If they're not fascists then they're alt-right reactionaries,' says Bizzy. 'At best. Dreadful people. Friends with Small Smellypants and those langers.'

Frey spends a moment thinking about Gil, and how he is likely to be one of 'those langers'. *And so am I, probably.*

'Are there really alt-right reactionaries living in Hobart?' she asks.

'Oh, the liniment girl,' sings Kyrie. *'Oh, she'll ruin your world.'*

Freycinct feels a shiver run up her spine. It is not unpleasant.

'Moving on,' says Bizzy. 'Our Rosanna is an associate professor of geology with lung cancer, secondaries in her bones. She is married to Kyrie's son Jonathon and they have four children.'

Frey looks at Kyrie. 'So Rosanna's your daughter-in-law! I wasn't sure what the connection was.'

Kyrie nods, smiles and puts a hand to her heart.

'She's on a chemotherapy trial that has prolonged her life somewhat,' says Bizzy. 'We're all hoping against hope that it'll create a miracle.'

Freycinet puts down her sandwich. Kyrie clasps her hand. 'The rest of the choir come to us with far less baggage, I promise.'

'And lots of happy stories,' says Bizzy. 'Avni is an Indian-Iranian refugee who's been offered a recording contract with Island Records for her glorious folk songs. She suffers badly from stage fright so we're all waiting to see how that goes. Quin is a reformed junkie who took herself to university and blew everyone's bobby-socks off with the calibre of her brain. She's almost an engineer now.'

'She's extremely badly behaved and a terrible influence on us all,' says Kyrie, with what sounds like pride.

'And you, Kyrie?'

'Ah, me,' says Kyrie. 'Boring boring. I've had four husbands, studied family law after my third and now I save women from being diddled out of their finances, and dote on my grandchildren.'

'What do you think, Freycinet?' asks Bizzy. 'Do we sound like a bunch you'd like to knock about with?'

Freycinet nibbles at the corner of her sandwich and says, 'So, we have a rebel princess, the actual Liniment Girl, a hero lawyer, a badly behaved genius, a doctor, a dementing woman, a rising star, a dying woman and a murderess.'

'That's about it,' says Bizzy.

'We're all that and more,' says Kyrie.

'We're just missing the member who's really got her shit together,' says Bizzy.

Frey laughs. 'You think that's me?'

Bizzy leans in and lowers her voice. 'The truth is,' she says, 'I'm sixty-five. Kyrie here is seventy-three, for feck's sake. Irene is losing a marble a day. Rosanna is ill. We need firey, respectable young women like yourself, Freycinet, to join our choir, sing our songs, carry our torches. We need fresh embers.'

But Freycinet has stopped listening. 'Fuck,' she says. She grasps both Bizzy's and Kyrie's hands simultaneously, then remains utterly still, staring down at her plate.

'What?' asks Bizzy. 'What's the matter?'

'That woman,' Frey hisses to her sandwich. 'The one who just walked in, with the hat. I think she's having an affair with my husband. I think it's her. She's over there in the lemon trees.'

𝄡

Stepping Stone Number 17, from *La Lista* by R.K.:
Know that it is scientifically proven that the energy of the dead still exists. It can no longer be organised into a body but it cannot be nowhere. It is everywhere. Sometimes you might be able to feel it. Things like music and singing and the wind in the trees might help it whirl about, so you can more easily tap into it and use it. Take mine, it is yours to keep.

Chapter 9

How to Clean
the Garlic Crusher

Freycinet, with her husband's alleged lover browsing the citrus section of New Town Station Nursery, has suddenly become very interested in her toasted sandwich. She sits back in her chair, smiles and says, 'I haven't had a buttery toastie like this since I was a little girl. I must remember to come back to this place; eating lunch surrounded by the scent of violets is very, very pleasant. Did you know that there are two plants in the world that have evolved to attract flies rather than competing for bee pollinators? They smell like rotting flesh.'

'Wow, really?' replies Bizzy. But she is more interested in Freycinet, who is suddenly and tangibly more relaxed. Sure of herself. Even more attractive, if Bizzy is to be frank. There is a languidness in the set of her shoulders that wasn't there before. If Bizzy didn't know differently, she would say that this woman, Freycinet, is an actress and someone has just called, 'Action!'

Kyrie, on the other hand, is rigid. 'What shall we do?' she asks from one side of her mouth. 'Do you want us to shuffle you out of here? Are you sure it's her?'

'No,' says Freycinet in a conversational tone. 'Yes. No.'

'Who is she?' Kyrie hisses.

'If it is her, her name is Skye Killinger,' replies Freycinet. 'She's an artist. She buys her clothes from Boden and her shoes from Country Road. She's recently had a toner put through her hair and she lives at 26 Tower Road, New Town.' She takes another casual bite of her sandwich.

'I knew there was something on the boil in you, Freycinet Barnes,' says Bizzy. She dabs her lips with her napkin. 'Excuse me a moment,' she says, standing from the table.

'Bizzy,' warns Kyrie.

'It's all right,' says Bizzy. 'I shall be a mere moment.' She walks towards the citrus display.

Kyrie raises a hand. 'I don't think . . .' But it's too late. She glances at Frey and says, 'Oh dear. I know that look, I think her pilot light is flaring.'

Freycinet sits up in her chair, her act-natural facade momentarily glitching.

'But don't worry,' Kyrie adds, 'she'll contain it. She's a seasoned professional. She'll be confirming identity and getting a bit of that woman's measure.'

'These dear little wrinkly limes,' says Bizzy to the slender blonde woman in a light-weight camel trench. 'They're so plain to look at but smell heavenly. I love them so.'

The blonde woman smiles. There is a sweet dimple on her right cheek. Bizzy looks at it with dismay and thinks, *Oh my dear*.

'It's a Kaffir Lime,' says the blonde woman. Her voice is as sweet as her dimple. 'They're deceptively aromatic but no good for putting in your gin. Best for Thai curries.'

'Thai?' repeats Bizzy, looking at the ugly little limes. 'Are you getting one?'

'No, I'm getting my mum a cumquat tree,' says the woman. 'She had two but one died, and now she's in a tizz about her feng shui.'

'Apparently,' says Bizzy, 'the juice of the cumquat is unbearably sour but the skin is very sweet.'

'Really?'

'Yes, so you just squeeze out the juice and eat the skin.'

'I'll have to tell Mum.' The woman suddenly seems to Bizzy more like a girl.

'I'm Bizzy,' says Bizzy, extending her hand.

The woman-girl frowns briefly before her courtesy catches it. She shakes Bizzy's hand. 'Skye,' she says.

'Are you Skye Waterstone, by any chance? Just that you look so like a friend of mine, Amanda Waterstone. I thought you just have to be her daughter.'

The dimple reappears. 'No, I'm sorry. Skye Killinger. I don't know any Waterstones.'

'Ah, right you are.' Bizzy notices that Skye Killinger's nails are neat and short, and rimmed with blue, as though she's had her hands in paint or dye. *Skye, the artist*, she thinks.

'Anyway, Skye,' says Bizzy, collecting up one of the smaller Kaffir Lime trees. 'I'll be taking one of these, thank you for the tip.'

'You're welcome, Bizzy. Enjoy the sunshine.'

You are actual sunshine, thinks Bizzy, turning back to see that Frey has abandoned her sandwich again. *Oh, my poor love.* She returns to the table, sets down her lime tree, takes a deep breath and squeezes Freycinet's arm.

'So?' asks Kyrie.

'It is Skye Killinger indeed.'

'What's she like?'

Frey doesn't want to hear the answer.

'Ah, as one would expect,' says Bizzy. 'There's very little to her. She's not even very pretty up close. So much makeup. She must smear it on to compensate for her lack of brain.' Bizzy avoids Kyrie's eyes.

'You're telling white lies,' says Frey. 'And she's not pretty, she's stunning.'

'Be off with you,' says Bizzy. 'You are much snazzier than that woman. Look how short she is, for a start.'

'Bizzy,' says Kyrie.

'Oh, I know,' says Bizzy through her mouthful. 'We mustn't find comfort in the flaws of other women. Internalised misogyny and all that. Don't forget, dearest Kyrie, that our care for all women mustn't ignore the fact that some of them are ridgy-didge arseholes. I bet even some dolphins are arseholes.'

'But we have to ask why they are arseholes, don't we,' says Kyrie, 'and how their souls got so wounded. Think of our Eleanor, stripped of any self-worth, then murderous and officially insane.' She looks at Freycinet. 'Did you know that loneliness causes inflammation in the body?'

But Frey is watching without actually looking as Skye Killinger moves to the cashier counter. Her face is obscured by the cumquat tree.

'Sometimes we don't have time to ask the dolphin how its soul got wounded,' continues Bizzy. 'And if we asked, for instance, Dagmar Overbye, whether we could inspect her soul, she would likely throw us in her masonry heater.'

Kyrie frowns. 'Dagmar Overbye?'

'Child killer from the nineteen-twenties,' explains Bizzy.

'Well, she was bound to have had an inflamed soul well before she took to murder.'

As Skye Killinger pays for her cumquat tree and departs the nursery, Kyrie says, 'You didn't just ask for her name outright did you, Bizzy?'

'No,' says Bizzy. 'I supplied a small amount of information, she supplied the rest.'

'Classic chicken feeding,' says Freycinet without thinking.

'Have you fixated on all the internet photographs of this woman until you're driven half mad?' Kyrie asks Frey. 'I've been there. Two of my husbands were philanderers.'

'Yes,' says Frey with an expression of grateful relief. 'Yes I have.'

Bizzy watches as the uncertainty returns to Frey. *I don't think this woman has any friends.* The thought occurs to Bizzy suddenly and with confident assertion.

'Are you all right, Freycinet?' she asks. 'Quite a shock for you.'

Frey sighs. 'I'm okay. My little adultery problem, if that's what it is – I mean, I only saw them standing together, I could have it all wrong – if it is adultery, it's a bit small bananas in the scheme of things. In the scheme of the choir.'

'It's very big bananas in the scheme of your life,' says Bizzy. She leans in, grasping Frey's hand. 'My love, even the nicest possible men are fucking us over even if they're not fucking us over by fucking someone else. Even the women with careers and support-ive husbands and shared domestic labour are being fucked over because they're the ones who know where the worm tablets are and how to read the mind of a teenager and whose birthday is coming up.'

'And how to clean the garlic crusher,' adds Kyrie.

'How to clean the garlic crusher,' agrees Bizzy.

Frey smiles. 'Gil puts the garlic crusher in the dishwasher without rinsing it and then everything comes out smelling of garlic.'

'Exactly,' says Bizzy. 'Here's how to clean the garlic crusher: don't. Buy pre-crushed garlic. It's feminism in a jar.'

'But not great for the environment,' says Frey. 'We can't win.'

'Re-use the jars for keeping your running-away cash in,' says Kyrie. 'Then hide them in mushroom bags in the fridge. I bet no one but you ever looks in the mushroom bags.'

Frey laughs. 'To be fair,' she says, 'I haven't changed a tyre since I was married.'

'Pfft,' says Bizzy, 'People call someone to change their tyres all the time.'

'You could call someone to clean the garlic crusher,' says Frey.

'But you don't,' says Kyrie.

𝄡

Forty minutes later, after Kyrie has hurried off to her grandchildren and Bizzy has insisted on another champagne, she leans in towards Frey and says, 'I am very pleased to have met you, Freycinet. You've left me feeling quite inspirited.'

Freycinet looks again at the presence of Bizzy, the blaze of her amber eyes and wonders how she could possibly be a source of inspiritment to her. She swallows a mouthful of champagne and says, 'Gosh, really? My children leave the room when I walk in. So thank you. It's nice to hear that from someone who is so motivated to change the world that she inspires hit songs.'

Bizzy tops up both champagne flutes and says. 'Well, I had a particularly motivated mother. She always had a cause, leapt gleefully from one to the next, waving flags and getting under the skin of the establishment and changing the world as best she could. I never knew any different, it's just what we did. Sometimes I wonder whether it might have been more useful for me to get some sort of qualification, but I never even went to school. My mother was my teacher, and occasionally I wish . . .' Bizzy trails off. 'Anyway, what are we going to do about your marital dilemma?'

Frey feels a pang of gratitude to hear the word, 'we'. She sighs and says, 'I really don't know.'

'Well,' says Bizzy in a comfortingly decisive tone, 'I think first you have to find out for sure whether this carry-on with Skye Killinger is indeed an affair. You could be imagining all sorts of things when all you saw was a business chat. And if it is an affair, then you get to choose your own adventure.' Bizzy speaks as though she might be issuing instructions on how to tune a television. 'You either confront him or move on. If you confront him, you can forgive, get couples therapy, leave him, kick him out. Or you keep mum and issue small acts of revenge in satisfying little increments. That could be fun.'

'I did think about replacing his hair-loss tablets with contraceptive pills,' Frey says.

'That'd be a start,' says Bizzy. 'Grow him some lovely bosoms.'

Frey snorts. 'And shrink his balls.'

'Or,' says Bizzy, her eyes flashing, 'I could pop an anonymous note in that woman's letterbox. Some sort of crusade libretto that expunges all romance from an extra-marital affair by illuminating its contribution to an unbalanced society. *Dear Skye Killinger, Your lover's wife is at home caring for their children, cleaning the rubbish bins and wondering how she can make herself more attractive to her husband. She is lonely. She washes his underwear. Do you tell him he is wonderful? Do you love the scent of him? That's the smell of the fabric softener she buys because he likes his towels fluffy. You are working for the patriarchy.'*

Frey laughs. It's a satisfying relief of a laugh. 'That's deeply heartbreaking,' says Frey, 'and so true. I don't know why I'm laughing. It's brilliant.'

'Evidently I still have some feck-em in me,' says Bizzy.

And then without thinking, Frey says, 'I'd love to join the choir.'

Bizzy's eyes widen. She beams. 'You will?' She claps her hands. 'Well, that's just wonderful, Freycinet. Very good news.'

Frey has shocked herself but is moved by Bizzy's genuine pleasure. 'It has to be on a trial basis,' she says. 'You try me out and if I lower the musical tone too much, kick me out.'

'Done. Excellent.' Bizzy holds her champagne glass in the air and says, 'Welcome aboard the West Moonah Women's Choir train,

expect turbulence and fun. This is the first leg of the feck-em tour.'
She downs the rest of her champagne.

Frey glances at her watch, does a rapid schedule recalibration and
says, 'I think we should have dessert.'

They spend the next thirty minutes coming up with creative acts
of revenge.

'What are his favourite things?' asks Bizzy.

'Sport,' says Freycinet. 'Golf mainly, cycling. And boating. He's
nuts about his boat. And his work. Actually he doesn't love the
work as such, just the status it brings. I'm making him sound like a
complete twat.' She pauses, puts down her dessert spoon. 'God, he's
a complete twat, isn't he?'

Bizzy deftly avoids the question. 'So,' she says, 'I wonder if we
could arrange for a flock of birds to take to his boat. Nothing more
undignified than a snazzy boat covered in cack.'

Frey laughs. 'Terns are apparently the worst. Their poo is like
cement.'

'Or you could get a size smaller in his cycling gear. That'll mess
with his ego.'

'Great idea,' says Frey. 'Because another of his favourite things is
his looks. He's very good looking. Good physique.'

'Spends far more hours worrying about his physique than his
children I'm guessing.'

'Yeah,' Freycinet says. 'Possibly.' She sighs. 'It's a shame he can't be
subjected to the same amount of expectation that women are when
it comes to ageing.'

'Well, you could buy him an appointment at one of those god-
awful places that position themselves in the dubious field of "cosmetic
science". They'll put him in a machine that takes photos of his skin,
projects his future wrinkles, gives a ghoulish printout and prescribes
a range of expensive services that'll leave him looking like a shiny
blowfish. I know how they work those places; I went undercover

and had my "skin assessment" done, then staged a protest outside. It did nothing other than attract the disdain of the Y–Z generations bobbing in to have their lips puffed and their "prophylactic Botox". Very disheartening.'

'Gosh, you could be onto something. He could actually fall for that.'

'It would give the patriarchy a right look at itself.'

Frey is pondering this as an option when she notices an elderly woman making her way slowly towards the end of an aisle of hedge plants. At right angles to her, hurtling at five times the speed is a small child. By Frey's rapid calculation, the two are on course for maximum impact collision. She is out of her chair and has reached the hedge plants before she's had time to think. Positioning herself in front of the child – a little boy in a yellow hat – Frey collects him up in her arms, swinging him nimbly up and over a tray of daisies, then puts him back on his feet before he has even registered the situation. Bewildered, he puts a finger in his mouth and stares up at Frey, then skips back to his mother, who is oblivious in the succulents. The elderly woman ambles on.

'Freycinet Barnes,' says Bizzy in amazement when Frey returns to their table, 'you just saved a sister from certain death.'

Frey smiles. 'She would have just got a knock. I don't think—'

'A broken hip is what she would have got. Our bones are leached and chalky after eighty. And we all know it's downwards to the grave from a hip fracture. You saved her life.'

Frey brushes her away and says, 'I should get going. It's been such a lovely lunch, thank you, Bizzy. Eventful and lovely.'

They split their share of the bill and head for the carpark. Again, Frey is reluctant to leave. It feels a little too much like stepping out of the magic, in a backwards direction.

'Do you have a career, Freycinet?' Bizzy asks as they walk towards their cars.

'I used to.'

'Well, you still do. Even a stalled career is a career. Marriage and children can't take that away.'

Freycinet gives a burst of laughter. 'Oh my goodness, it can. My career is so far behind me, it literally belongs to a different life, a different person. And anyway, I studied for longer than I worked, and now I've lost touch. It's not stalled, my career, it just doesn't exist.'

'Still a career.'

There is more silence. Freycinet is aware that she is meant to fill it with the name of her profession. There is a rush of pride that deepens her breaths, a fleeting image of that different Freycinet, in that different life, with colleagues and challenges and people saying, 'You've done well' and 'Congratulations'.

'I was in foreign affairs,' she says, 'based in Canberra, then China, then the US.'

'Are you a spy?'

'Ha,' says Freycinet, 'I knew some people in intelligence, but I was in the diplomatic corps.'

'Right, but you wouldn't say if you are a spy, so there we are.'

'I'm definitely not a spy,' says Freycinet.

'But perhaps you *were* one,' says Bizzy firmly.

'Ha,' says Freycinet again. 'Nice try.'

'That arrogant bastard took you away from your beloved, interesting, important spy work.'

'I left *the diplomatic corps* because I got pregnant, and I fell in love.'

'Right. And how's that going for you?'

Freycinet feels a prickle of heat in her cheeks and decides she's quite ready for the next leg of the West Moonah Women's Choir feck-em tour.

𝄢

Stepping Stone Number 166, from *La Lista* by R.K.:

You can wash many things other than dishes, pots and cutlery in the dishwasher. Hairbrushes, combs, dish brushes, canvas shoes, rubber shoes, shower heads, sponges, toys, makeup brushes and potatoes. You can also use the dishwasher to cook salmon (dress with lemon and dill, seal in foil, sit on top racks and put through a normal 65 degree Celsius cycle).

Chapter 10
All the Little Daisies

Bizzy drives home aggressively, weaving in and out of Hobart's peak-hour traffic without indicating, mounts the edge of a roundabout into the leafy suburb of Dynnyrne and then, in a final display of furious renegadery, pulls sharply into her driveway and causes a small gravel spray. This rewards her a certain satisfaction until she observes that the house itself, partially obscured behind its unpruned hawthorn tree, seems wearily embarrassed, like a fifteen-year-old boy who doesn't find his mum's jokes funny anymore.

Bizzy sighs. The fizz of adrenaline from her lunch with Frey and associated renewed vigour is already beginning to fade. She wonders whether it's possible to develop a resistance to adrenaline.

'Okay,' she says to the house, 'I'll come in and be normal. I'll have a cup of tea and a sit, and fall asleep in front of *Gardening Australia*. That make you happy?' The house continues to hide behind the hawthorn tree. Next door, the tousled head of a small child trampolines at intervals above the fence. Bizzy gets out of the car and calls, 'Hello there, Ferris!'

The head turns and Bizzy glimpses a rosy-cheeked smile twice more before it disappears, then appears again after some clambering up onto the fence.

'Bizzy!' shouts Ferris. 'You should see my mum's tummy now, it's even fatter than Mrs Milkbar's, and Mrs Milkbar eats a block of jelly bean choccy a day.'

'Jelly bean choccy?' replies Bizzy.

'It's chocolate with jelly beans in,' says Ferris helpfully. 'I'm not allowed it.'

'It sounds awful,' says Bizzy, wrinkling her nose.

'No!' Ferris disappears momentarily on account of falling off the fence. There is some scrabbling before he bobs up again. 'It sounds yum! Mum says I can have some after the baby's come out.'

'Excellent,' says Bizzy.

'What treat would you ask for, Bizzy?'

'Hmm, I think that I would probably ask for more time with my mam, if I could have anything.'

It's Ferris's turn to wrinkle his nose. He rolls his eyes and sighs in the dramatic way of a six-year-old boy who hasn't met his inhibitions. 'Nooo,' he says, 'a *treat* is something you eat or something you play with. Don't be boring, Bizzy.'

'My mam played the best adventures with me.'

Ferris looks puzzled. 'Mums aren't for adventures,' he says. 'They're for baths and stuff.' He appears momentarily worried that he may have caused offence. 'You're not boring, though, Bizzy, are you? 'Cause you're not a mum.'

Bizzy smiles. 'Perhaps I'd ask for a cola spider too.'

'What?' Ferris is incredulous now. 'A spider?'

'It's a fizzy cola drink, like Coke, with ice cream in it. It's good with Guinness too, funnily enough.'

Bizzy watches Ferris think, his eyes slowly widen. 'Coke and ice cream together?'

'Yes.'

'Wow, that could even be better than jelly bean choccy.' He falls off the fence again. 'I'm telling Mum about spiders.' These last words are uttered out of Bizzy's sight, and on the run.

'Bye Ferris,' calls Bizzy, but he is already gone. She turns to her house, which seems now to be peeking out with a suspicious expression. 'It's all right,' she tells it firmly. 'I'll come in and be sensible.'

She unlocks the front door and wanders in, thinking, *What I would give for a cola spider and another adventure with my mam. That'd properly bring my oomph back.*

𝄢

Bizzy Nancarrow considers her very first adventure with her mother, Winifred Nancarrow, to be the one in which Winifred was raped at knifepoint in a horse stable in 1953. It happened on the Nancarrow family farm in Galway. The stable was one of many on a property made rich by the luck of the Irish and the uncommon horse knowledge of its patriarch and flat-racing trainer, Cillian Nancarrow.

The perpetrator was a recently acquired stable foreman by the name of Sean Byrne. Fifteen-year-old Winifred had seen him only once or twice before school when she and her sisters helped muck out stables for pocket money. He had a well-to-do accent and an overly chirpy 'hello sunshine' manner that set her teeth on edge. It was just on dawn, Sunday the twenty-second of March, while Winifred was challenging herself to pile the manure barrow higher than ever before, that Sean Byrne pushed her against the stable wall, held a knife to her neck, ordered her not to look at him and fumbled the buttons of her jodhpurs undone.

'Scream and I'll cut your throat,' he whispered, wrenching the jodhpurs and her knickers to her knees. 'Tell a soul and I'll do the same to your sisters.'

But Winifred's hands were already clenched, her mucking-out arm muscles taut. A wellspring of fury she didn't know was there shot up from her boots at around the same time Sean Byrne shot his semen into her. She felt his grip weaken in his climax and without a conscious thought, she followed some animal instinct that had her twisting to face him, thrusting her knee into his groin with fierce, trauma-sprung force. He grunted, he doubled over, he swayed. She kicked him again, this time in the face, with her heavy-booted foot. He fell, grasping at his nose. She trod heavily on his forearm, took the knife from his hand and said, 'No, you will not, be doing anything like this to anyone else.' And with that, she took the tip of his exposed, still partially erect penis in one hand and, with the other, cut it off at its base.

'You will harm no one, not ever again,' she said into his bleeding face.

His bowels evacuated as she threw the severed penis on the wheelbarrow with the heaped horse shit, pulled up her jodhpurs and wheeled the barrow out to tip on the compost heap. *And now I'll have to shovel up his shit too*, she thought, from a stunned, dissociated distance, where she floated in shock. She also thought, from way over there, that cutting through a penis felt very like cutting through a finely minced, thickly cased pork sausage.

The plaintive rises and falls of Sean Byrne's wails, Winifred occasionally claimed, were the foundation of a melody she hummed to a well-known Russian composer named Igor Stravinsky, who later used it as a motif in his biblical drama 'The Flood'.

The veracity of this last statement is questionable, but the rest of the story is true. Bizzy knows this because she has lived the consequences, perhaps more so than even Winifred did. And because, once that single microscopic sperm made its way to that viable, sizeable (22 mm) follicle, in those minutes following this indecent act, she – Bizzy – was there.

Winifred's father, becoming aware of the 'incident' in the stable, had Sean Byrne swiftly dealt with. Cillian was a powerful man in the racing world; he knew people and authorities in the business of eradicating pests and disturbances. Most of Sean Byrne disappeared without a trace (while a small piece of him vitalised the compost and later fed the turnips). But Cillian had difficulty looking his eldest daughter in the eye. He didn't need to ask, 'What did you do to attract such attention?' or 'Was there really cause to take the man's willy?' Winifred could see the questions written on his face.

He said only one thing about what Winifred came to refer to as The Great Cherry Heist of '53, and that was: 'Byrne had a sharp mind, and ran a tight shed row. Shame the war taught him bad lessons.' After that, the offender's name was not mentioned again, and Cillian avoided Winifred as though she had a newly acquired menace.

As it turned out, she had acquired Bizzy, whose presence, according to Roman Catholic decree, was indeed a menace to society. A fallen woman is a fallen woman, regardless of how she fell. The only thing to do with an unmarried girl and her swelling belly was to send her quick-smart to a place where she could receive maternity care and a firm Godly hand to steer her from recidivism. The Bon Secours Mother and Baby Home in nearby Tuam was selected by Cillian and presented to Winifred's mother as 'the only responsible course of action'.

'Please,' said his distraught wife. 'Do not ask me to make decisions at this time. I cannot see the future for the hoary shadows of disgrace that have beset our family.' (Brigid Nancarrow had a touch of the theatrics about her.)

'The Bon Secours sisters are trained in these things,' Cillian assured her. 'And they have a laundry set up where Winifred can properly join the working class. She'll come back to her glossy ponies good as new. It's an opportunity, Brigid, to better all our girls.'

Brigid agreed, sighing profusely and adding, 'Perhaps she'll come back more accepting of the world. I'm exhausted by her questioning. She'd ask a cloud to explain its rain, that girl would.'

Neither of them referred to the growing 'disgrace' as a tiny human being. And so, Winifred and Bizzy were shipped off to Tuam for their second adventure.

B

It was immediately clear to Winifred that the Bon Secours Mother and Baby Home (or just 'The Home' as it had become known locally) was very badly haunted. Winifred had previously experienced some garden-variety hauntings – a chill in a cemetery, a fleeting glimpse of the old man on the Maam Cross road, a shudder on the Long Walk in Galway City – but none like what gripped her in the hallways of The Home.

A crucifix, erected by the sisters in the grounds of the building, memorialised six IRA volunteers who had been executed onsite in 1923, but that only went a small way to explain the heavy, melancholic air and the constant thrum of something so utterly Other it had clearly sent the nuns mad.

'You will be with us for approximately four months,' said the first unhinged nun Winifred encountered. Her name was Mother Hortense. 'This includes up to two weeks postpartum during which time the infant, if not half-blooded, will be put up for adoption. You will then be returned to your family and allowed to resume your childhood with the grace of God.' Mother Hortense finished her statement with a brisk double swipe of her hands, reminding Winifred of that smug Mary Poppins. *Jiggety jog, pish posh.*

Winifred's frank amazement must have translated as pitiful, because Mother Hortense leaned in and, in a lowered voice, added, 'No one, my dear, would expect you to raise the product of an indecent and violent act.' She produced a facial expression that was apparently meant to portray sympathy. Winifred regarded it with horrified fascination.

'All for the best,' said Mother Hortense gently.

Winifred decided she preferred Sean Byrne, his willy and their traditional version of violence. One can only take a knife to certain kinds of assault.

'If this is all for the best,' she whispered to the bulge in her belly later. 'The best is not for us.' She startled herself with the word 'us', then let it fill her with a warmth that might have been – under a thin blanket on a hard mattress in a haunted dormitory – something like belonging.

Other signs of hellish influence and possible demonic possession came thick and fast. The Bon Secours sisters worked the pregnant women from dawn to dusk, and longer if they happened to be carrying a half-caste baby. 'For the good of their soul' they were told to work until they hurt. Mops were not allowed because 'down on hands and knees before our gracious Father' was ruled as essential. Some of the women and girls (especially the girls) worked themselves to agony or illness, and thanked God for their suffering.

The 'residents' nearing their time were not allowed bed rest, but were worked harder. If their waters broke, they were sent to pace the gardens and ordered not to scream, to pay for Eve's original sin and learn the consequences of their own. Winifred understood then that these nuns were no longer human, but dangerous beings, smote by desperate spirits. She emptied her mind of bitterness, forced her good humour into form, dished it out as balm and on days besieged by fear or sorrow, still managed tiny pipettes of antidote cheer. Not once, not ever, did she allow herself to feel ashamed.

'What a glorious morning it is!' she would announce to the pallid girls waiting for breakfast, followed by, 'I can smell spring in the air,' which made some smile because spring was months away and actually the smell was burnt porridge.

'Right-ho,' she might shout to the line of girls waiting for the latrine. 'Who wants a smutty song?' (Winifred had a whole collection gathered from the racetracks.) Someone might say yes, but Winifred would sing on even when they didn't.

Four and twenty virgins came down from Inverness,
And when the ball was over, there was four and twenty less!
Oh, the village postman he was there, but he had the pox.
He couldna' do the ladies so he did the letterbox!

When she ran out of collected songs rude enough to cause diversion, Winifred made up her own. One in particular became a favourite among the women and the children:

Whorey whorey Hortense,
Built a great big tall fence,
Locked up all the mammies,
In their prison cells.
Holy Mother Hortense,
Full of self-importance,
Pilfered all the bebbies,
And fell down into hell.

Only the bravest or most bitter of the girls giggled at this one. It was sin enough to say 'hell', let alone send one of Christ's chief brides down into it.

Sometimes Winifred knew to be more sober.

'You have done nothing wrong,' she whispered one day to a girl of fourteen named Aisling who had never been fully informed about human reproduction and was still confused and dreadfully ashamed. 'This is not your fault. You must know this because it is the shame that will get you.'

'I hope when the waters break, I and my bebby will be taken,' said Aisling. 'It is the just and rightful ending.'

'Ah, be off with you,' said Winifred. 'A birth is not an ending. Do I need to be teaching you your opposites as well as the birds and the bees?'

But Aisling's wish came true. The following week, she went into labour and before two days had passed, both she and her baby girl were 'gone to their Heavenly Father'. Winifred, with her growing disdain for the Heavenly Father and a billowing blossom of love for the mound under her dress, kept a picture of Aisling's destroyed expression in her mind's eye, to fend off any shame.

There were other things she held close to the surface, as though she might need them one day, like the lewd songs. The sight of a nun dragging a dark-skinned infant across the floor by his arm; the image of older children having their heads shaved to discourage lice; the heavy, blistering boots they were made to wear; the fall of a little boy whose spindle legs could no longer hold him up; a screaming mother, emptied of everything, standing on the steps as her baby is driven away. All the little daisies on the front lawn of The Home, there to reassure passers-by that things were felicitous within.

When Winifred's labour began in the middle of the night and progressed with agonising speed, she screamed blue murder and continued to do so despite the hushings and shushings and threats from the sisters.

'This is God's will,' said one of them between contractions. 'The original sin, along with your own misfortune, decrees that we must suffer. And you must do so in silence, as our Lord Jesus did.'

Winifred screamed louder until someone pushed a wad of cotton into her mouth. Her eyes darted wildly across the faces of the nuns. By now they seemed to Winifred the demonic faces of pure evil.

Through her pain and outrage, and in the face of such blatant insanity, Winifred felt the solid ground of maternal love, and it gave her purchase. *That's it, little one*, she willed, *let's not dilly-dally.*

Baby Bizzy did not dilly-dally. She was born just two hours after Winifred went into labour. 'Do not look, do not look,' said the nuns in their horrifically gentle voices. 'No touching for now, it's for the best.' So Winifred caught only a brief glimpse of the tiny red face of her daughter as she was whisked away to be assessed and wrapped. And with that glimpse came a surge of want and need and love so explosive, she was sure she could hear it. It coursed through her, pulsing as she pushed a nun aside, pulled the cotton from her mouth and screamed again, louder than ever before.

'She is mine! She does not belong to you or your church or your God!'

The words were almost indecipherable but the sisters knew blasphemy when they saw it.

Hands went on her, ten or more, pushing her to the bed. There was a bright sting of something on her thigh and then a slowing down of things. The screams softened to a wail.

'Luke 18:17,' said someone. 'Whosoever shall not receive the kingdom of God as a little child shall in no wise enter therein.'

Another said, 'Don't smite that infant with your shame.'

Winifred thrashed about and through the blur she fixed the preaching nun with her wild gaze and said, 'I am not ashamed. I am not ashamed. I will not reward your maniacal convictions by saying so. I have not sinned, you have. I have seen the babies disappear. And they will come back to you in the night. They will nibble at you until you feel all the pain you have caused, every last agony. And all your wrongs will come back to bite you.'

And with that, she picked up one of the hands and bit it as hard as she could before she fell into enforced sleep.

𝄡

Bizzy ties a purple, green and white striped scarf around her hair, then watches as ice cream settles layer by layer into stout. She pokes at it with a spoon until it bobs and fizzes, then lifts the glass to her lips and takes a long drink.

'Ah,' she says when she's done, 'that's the way to drink Guinness, Mammy. And wouldn't those swaying, ruddy old men lose their rag over me saying that.' She stares into the creamy blackness. 'If I look hard enough I might see Mary Magdalene, d'ye think? Ha, or your sweet face.'

She sighs and touches a hand to the silk of the scarf. 'Mam, it's been such a long time without you. I'm a bit tired. I'm still trying, but can you send me some of your wildfire, please?'

𝄐

Stepping Stone Number 19, from *La Lista* by R.K.:

If you want to touch someone's sexual parts, or if someone wants to touch yours, permission MUST be sought. And permission is only granted by an audible and voluntary 'YES'. However (and this is very important) 'yes' is not 'yes' unless 1) it is an enthusiastic YES, 2) it is a YES from someone who is close to you in age and over fifteen, 3) it is a YES that is not under the influence of alcohol or drugs, 4) it is an informed YES (if the yes is for touching a bottom, you need to ask again before you touch anything else), and 5) it is an ongoing YES, because people are allowed to change their mind.

Being unsure of any of this or having a worried 'eeek' feeling in your tummy cancels out the YES. 'Eeek' means NO.

Chapter 11
A Wilderness of Mirrors

Gil holds Skye's hips and thrusts into her from behind, his breaths voiced in time with his movements. Skye is standing on her tip-toes, her smooth calves tense, her head thrown back against Gil's shoulder.

'Slower, Gil,' she gasps. 'Slow down.'

Gil does as he is told, but only for a short time before his movements speed up again. 'I can't,' he says in a voice distorted by desire.

They are both completely naked. Skye's magazine body seems photoshopped. Their clothes are dripped across the room from the doorway to the bed

'Skye,' breathes Gil. 'Oh, Skye.'

A loud, high-pitched groan shudders out of Skye and shimmers from the bedroom into the hallway, where a woman stands watching every move.

This woman's hair is a shocking red, styled in a long, thick bob and parted in the middle. She has a beauty mark just above her lip and large, vividly white teeth. Her eyes are concealed behind mirrored sunglasses and her lips are painted the same colour as her hair. She is wearing a long red vinyl coat, black leather gloves, a Pepsi T-shirt and black leggings. Slung across her back is a yellow satchel. She is chewing gum and holding a small Nokia flip phone.

Skye and Gil, both preoccupied with their approaching orgasms, have not noticed the woman in the hallway. She has only been there a moment or two, and she takes another to silently take five photographs using the phone. She could turn on her sneakered heel now, leave undetected, but she doesn't. She moves right to the bedroom doorway and lingers there, watching the fevered lovers a little longer.

'Skye,' breathes Gil. The word ripples out of him.

The woman in the hallway turns to the paintings on the wall, studies them as though she is there for an exhibition. There are three large canvases depicting women in various poses beside the same house. All three have expressions of joy, bliss, pleasure. The detail is astonishingly realistic.

'Oh my God,' says the naked woman. 'Oh my God.'

Oh my God, repeats the red-haired woman in her head. She reaches down to pick Gil's suit trousers up from the floor and catches his eye.

'Jesus Christ!' he shouts, and the red-haired woman turns and slips away.

'Hey!' calls Gil. 'What the fuck?'

The woman doesn't run, just walks swiftly, moving with confidence, all swaying hips and shoulders, jaw working her gum.

There's another 'Hey!' from Gil, followed by some indeterminate exclamations from Skye.

The woman is down the stairs in a few seconds and out the front door before Gil has left the bedroom.

'What are you doing in my house?' yells Skye.

The woman closes the front door gently, walks along the garden path and exits the front gate. Without slowing, she kicks over a wheelie bin, crosses the road, turns into a side street and slips between trees within a tall stand of yews. There, she takes off the satchel, the vinyl coat and the T-shirt, revealing a black lycra running shirt that matches her leggings. She opens the satchel and takes out a black bum bag, a pair of silver headphones and a denim baseball cap. She clips on the bum bag, removes the red bobbed wig and replaces it with the cap. She stuffs the wig and the phone into the bum bag, the clothes and sunglasses into the satchel and Gil's trousers into a yew tree.

She puts the headphones on and jogs out to the end of the side street and onto a busier road, where she passes several people, shops and cafés and reaches a St Vincent de Paul charity bin, into which she deposits the yellow satchel and the gloves. That done, she circles back the way she came. As she jogs, she scrapes the beauty mark from her lip. She leaves the side street and turns away from Skye's house, but not before she glimpses Skye standing on the pavement looking in astonishment at the contents of her wheelie bin spilled out over the footpath. Gil is nowhere in sight.

'What are you doing with my husband?' asks Freycinet quietly as she jogs. In another minute or two, she is on the bike path with the other lunchtime joggers, many of whom are women dressed in black lycra with bum bags and baseball caps.

13

An hour and a half later, showered, changed and heart rate decreased, Freycinet is able to sit down with a cup of tea and review the operation, her performance and the outcome.

Her first thought surprises her. *That was boringly easy.*

It's true, gaining resolute confirmation and material proof of Gil's affair was a relatively straightforward blackball job without too many challenges. The greatest impediments had been her own mistakes, such as adding too many elements to what was classified as a 'light disguise'. Too much pocket litter, not enough pockets. As a working intelligence officer, she would never have needed to slip into shrubbery to perform a quick change; she would have managed well in under thirty-seven seconds while still on the move. The teeth facade was, however, necessary, given her proximity to the targets. That was her other mistake, getting too close.

Two factors appear to be at play in the decision to stand in plain sight, and then to move closer even after the photo-intelligence take. The first is that she simply couldn't help herself; she was evidently drawn to every brutal detail – things to process later, emotional involvement signifiers, self-flagellating weaponry. And she hadn't been able to resist taking Gil's trousers.

The second is that it was possible she compromised what was meant to be a clandestine operation by switching from covert operative to provocateur because she was too eager to prove (to herself, apparently) that she could be audacious again. That she hadn't forgotten her tradecraft. Had she reassembled the 'Roxy' disguise (as she had nicknamed it years before) for its bold legend and its total departure from the tastefully courteous, careful woman she has become? Had she wanted to be seen or pursued, or to be identified? Or all of the above?

There were other factors to consider. Skye's incredible artwork on the walls – definitely too spiritual and soppy for Frey's tastes, but incredibly skilful. Hyperreal, joyful expressions that were hard to look away from. And of course, how firm Gil's bottom appeared from that angle, in that action. Skye's outrageously perfect proportions.

What is doggie style called when it's standing up? Freycinet thinks, and then, *Oh, I think it's just 'from behind'.* This analytical question, she realises with a thrill of pride, proves that she can still manage an element of professional distance. Except that she'd kicked over the rubbish bin. Hardly professional.

'Oh, Skye,' Gil had gasped. A flash of pain grabs Frey in the throat. She closes her eyes.

This element of her long-ago ASIS field training (Applied Psychology: Limbic Control, Class of '95) has never gone unused.

Since leaving the service, Frey has necessarily practised ICBM (instant calm breath methods) on a regular basis and talked frequently to her amygdala (the almond-shaped cluster of cells in the brain that controls fear). She uses it now as she ponders that Gil has never, in their eighteen-year marriage, gasped out 'Freycinet!' while they made love. Not even in its diminished 'Frey' form.

The pain dissolves, and she switches back to her performance evaluation. The photographs had been her planned take, so why did she need to swipe Gil's trousers? An operative's remit should never involve mischief. Or malevolence (flashback to the wheelie bin). But she had successfully located her targets, achieved surreptitious entry (she'd always been great with locks), got her PHOTINT (had the HUMINT indelibly printed on her memory), performed a successful E&E (evade and escape), secured a jogging backstop (alibi) and safely returned home. Whether her Roxy cover held, she can't be sure.

She returns the wig and teeth facade to the Fun With Maths! box at the top of her wardrobe, then realises that Roxy's lipstick is still in the pocket of the red vinyl coat, left for a St Vincent de Paul volunteer to find. This doesn't concern her; she had probably destroyed any DNA evidence when she used the scarlet lipstick to write a small, neat letter 'A' on Skye's fence post on her way into the house. More unnecessary malevolence. In her seven years as an Intelligence Officer, she always prided herself on her moral integrity and focus. But then she thinks of Bizzy and her sweet little increments of revenge, her beatnik version of morals and allows herself a smile. Then she phones a local medi-spa and books Gil in for a massage and comprehensive skin assessment for his upcoming birthday.

The final remaining task is to return Grace's silver headphones to their precise spot in her bedroom. It is neat, the bedroom. Grace's bed is tightly made with a carefully arranged collection of pillows and cushions. The bookcase is meticulously organised from tallest book to smallest, trilogies and series kept on a separate shelf in their correct order, school texts gathered into subjects. On their own shelf, only slightly less tidy, are Grace's collection of dancing books. Biographies, photographic compilations, instructional books, many of them given to Grace by Frey. She smiles, remembering her own bedroom at age sixteen – just as orderly, just as methodical, but displaying a wider range of fixations.

Don't forget to live, my darling, Frey thinks.

The photo collage on the pinboard is also neat, but neglected. Grace put it together so carefully one winter holiday, and now there are curling corners and vacant spaces. Some pictures have been cut. One has been torn in half and another has a thumbtack pressed over a face. Freycinet leans in to inspect this one closer. *An old crush?* she wonders, but then recognises the sleeve of the windcheater and realises that the redacted face is Grace's own.

There is a smattering of family pictures, all of them at least five years old. Other photos of beaming, pre-teen girls, groups of summer friends jumping from jetties, giving peace signs or pretending not to sunbake. Familiar faces, though Freycinet realises she hasn't seen many of them, perhaps any of them, for a while. Grace's current friends – four or five leggy, frighteningly gorgeous girls with concave midriffs – are mainly from dance class, not school. These girls perform stretches at odd times, such as when dinner is served. They wear their hair in high buns, fry their vowels and display veneer manners with 'please' and 'thank you' in shiny voices that drop to a whisper if Freycinet stays near. They are, Freycinet reflects, pretty awful. And Grace is one of them.

On the desk, perched against the wall is Grace's childhood teddy. He is dusty, gazing blankly in the direction of Grace's bed as though he's given up longing.

'Sleeper agent deceased,' Frey says with a sad smile. 'You could have been a very valuable asset. I'm sorry you were considered a throwaway too.' She scans the room's details and whispers to it, 'What else can you tell me?'

The top of the bookcase catches Frey's eye because it is empty. A substantial parade of dance trophies used to march along it, glinting with gold plastic glory. Frey can't be sure how long they have been missing. She frowns, opens a wardrobe door.

The wardrobe offers something of a relief. It is messy, normal teenage messy. An illustrated testament to adolescent preoccupation. Animated, actually, because as the door slides open, a sleeping bag slips off the shelf into which it has been stuffed and takes with it a tangle of belts and handbags, revealing a large cardboard box with a tiny gold hand reaching upwards. Pulling the box towards her, Frey finds a calamity of trophies dumped together, entwined with medals. She frowns, then after a moment returns the wardrobe contents to their previous positions (disarray is far trickier to replicate than order) closes the door and turns back to the bed.

Taking her phone from her pocket, she photographs the position of the cushions, then systematically removes them, pressing and kneading them one by one until she reaches a large, square cushion printed with an image of Frida Kahlo's defiant face against a backdrop of flowers. Frey locates a hard object inside the cushion and unzips it, digs among the batting and pulls out what she has been looking for – the notebook Grace hid beneath her covers that night last week. A lifetime ago.

Frey stares at the cover, plain yellow with 'Journal' written in white.

'Shall I read you?' she asks.

'You shouldn't,' replies the diary. 'But you will.'

And so Freycinet opens the diary, at a middling page, and the words she reads are these:

I will dance with lonely today.
We will sway in the hall of disappointments
And turn all the people away.

These words are followed by a series of question marks and the word *ballad*.

Freycinet shuts the diary. The words are so un-Grace-like that she wonders whether she has come across someone else's diary. Yet they are written in her daughter's immaculate hand. She opens the diary to another page.

Lunch: says the diary. *Fifty sit-ups, thirty push-ups, sixty squats and a bottle of water.*

On another page it shouts, *WHERE ARE ALL THE GOOD ROLE MODELS?*

'Jesus Christ,' Freycinet says to the diary. She flips to a page from the month before.

Monday, 22 July 2019, 9.55 p.m.

It is my birthday today. SIXTEEN. Harry gave me a necklace and a kiss. I love his lips. When he kisses me I feel like I'm living the film version of my life. I'm glad I'm not sweet sixteen and never been kissed. Mum and Dad gave me a voucher for Sportsgirl and a fancy restaurant dinner because They Don't Know Me At All.

In my seventeenth year I will: get fitter, get more flexible and strong (gym in mornings), train harder and CRUSH the grand jeté (until it's automatic), GET INTO ADI, not talk to Tom AT ALL because he is fucking negative energy, walk away when someone tells me I am just like Mum.

I asked Grandpa Rog whether he thinks I am like Mum and he said, 'Yes and no.' I'm running with the no. She irons pyjamas FFS. It shits me how she stares at me like she's trying to get at my soul.

I can't stop thinking about Harry. I really think I want it to be him. We're meeting on Friday night so it could be THE TIME!!!! SO excited!!!! I haven't told him so it'll be a surprise. I know he wants to. He would never pressure me because he is SO NICE but I know in the way he kisses me. And we've done pretty much everything else.

With a racing heart, Frey flicks a few pages forward, to Saturday, 27 July.

IT HAPPENED!!! We did it and he was amazing and he told me he loves me!!!! I'm happy that he has done it before, because it would be SO AWKWARD otherwise. It feels so STUPID not to be with him ALL THE TIME. The rest of my life is just a stupid boring drone, even Derwent Academy fucksake. I can't wait to dance out of there. But none of it matters because Harry loves me and I love him.

The perfect handwriting has started to swim. A searing pain in Frey's throat spreads to her chest. She closes the diary and looks at it.

'I told you not to,' it says.

She zips it back into its cushion, then restores the bed precisely to its previous perfection and swiftly leaves the room, a barrage of questions chatting along with her. *Who the hell is Harry? How can my daughter be having sex, she's just a baby? And ADI! The Australian Dance Institute. Surely Grace wouldn't want to leave home so soon, oh my God . . . Why shouldn't I iron the fucking pyjamas?*

She shuts herself in the bathroom, sits on the floor and surrenders to the pain.

𝄐

Later, when the family arrive home in their dribs and drabs, Frey has washed her face, forcibly pulled herself together and is displaying calm, neutral normality.

Lily galumphs in to say that chocolate eclairs are *godly* and that she has to make them for French class. Frey smiles and gets out the recipe books.

Tom arrives home with a friend. They eat all the Weet-Bix, guffaw at something on their phones and track mud through the house. Frey asks them about footy and cleans up.

Grace mumbles a greeting, changes for dance and leaves again, insisting she will jog to class. Frey does not look too closely at her in case she sees something irreversibly different. Also so Grace does not suspect attempted soul-theft.

When Gil arrives home just on dinnertime, Frey's heart misses a beat or two but she successfully throws a nonchalant, 'Hi, darling,' in among helping Lily with English homework. She clocks immediately that Gil is wearing navy trousers with factory creases and no matching blazer.

'Abstract nouns,' she says to Lily, 'are things that you can't touch or see or smell or hear or hold in your hands. They are ideas or feelings, like . . .' Freycinet sifts through some words to find one that isn't too loaded '. . . humour or kindness.'

'Or love?' asks Lily.

'Yes,' says Freycinet, aware that Gil is pouring himself a drink. 'Or adventure.'

'Patience?' suggests Lily.

'Yep, you've got it.'

'Anger? Hate? Pain? Hurt? Disgusting?'

'Disgusting is an adjective. Disgust is an abstract noun.' Freycinet manages not to look at Gil. 'Can you set the table please, Lil?'

'I did it last night. Is worry another one?'

'Yep.' Freycinet opens the cutlery drawer and thinks, *So is suspicion, jealousy, lust, betrayal.* She imagines what betrayal might look like if she could hold it in her hands. Dark red, almost black. Cold. She glances at Gil. 'How was your day?'

'Pretty good,' he replies. 'Yours?'

Freycinet decides that he is looking at her more intently than usual. He was the first in the family to look through her. Also, he doesn't normally ask about her day. *Does he?*

Freycinet crafts some convincingly mundane, good-humoured anecdotes about hair clogged in a plughole, Acorn, school. She asks him several vague questions relating to the transcriptions she's been working on. After a few minutes she notices that he has stopped listening, and has almost finished his drink.

Bit stressed, are we? she thinks, then rattles off an observation about the new school art building. She wonders about throwing in, *'And I tracked your phone, picked you up at your lover's house and watched you shag her from behind.'*

'What did your day bring?' she asks, then has to hide her shaking hands while he lies.

Domestic life, she concludes, is a wilderness of mirrors.

13

Stepping Stone Number 6, from *La Lista* by R.K.:
Be honest. Please. Always. Even when it feels too hard. Especially when it feels too hard. (But don't tell your grandmother her feet are ugly, she's worried about them her whole life.)

Chapter 12

Endless Upside

'I'm fucken pregnant.'

Quin's words bounce around the Laetare Gardens hall, shimmer off the light fittings and settle into the silence that has befallen the choristers.

Freycinet, having arrived at choir rehearsal feeling uncertain then positively vertiginous about attending, immediately wishes she'd stayed home. She doesn't feel eligible to hear such personal information outright. The imposter at the party. But the cannonade of emotion that comes next switches her discomfort to a feeling of pleasure, perhaps honour. It surprises her, puts a lump in her throat.

Rosanna is the first to react. 'Holy shit and dear God. What in the heck?' she shouts, clapping her hands together. 'This is some fantastic news.'

The fact that she has mustered the strength for such a lusty, Rosanna-like exclamation is stirring in itself. She appears childlike in stature and is as pale as a ghost.

'Oh my goodness, a baby!' says Avni. 'This is wonderful, Quin.'

'It wasn't perimenopause after all,' Sally says. 'Or lactose intolerance. How far along are you?'

'Sixteen weeks.'

There is a burst of exclamation.

'Fecking heck,' says Bizzy. 'How did you not know?'

'Show us your tummy!' says Mary.

Quin lifts her Metallica T-shirt to display a perfect round stomach. 'My bloat is a baby,' she declares.

'Quinella Doyle,' says Bizzy, clasping the circular pendant at her neck. 'How can this be?'

'Well,' says Quin. 'The penis enters the vagina, and then the—'

'She means,' says Mary, 'when did you have sex with someone and who was it and how can your poor gorgeous abused body actually make a baby?' Mary bursts into tears. 'You're going to be a wonderful mother, Quin.'

'Steady on,' says Quin. 'I'll be shithouse and it'll potentially ruin a career that hasn't even got fucken started yet, so I'll be resentful as fuck, probably.'

'You know abortion is a safe and valid option,' says Sally.

'Yeah, nah,' says Quin. 'I thought about that but Mary's right. I've abused the shit out of this body and now it's somehow going to give me a baby, so I reckon it's about time I gave it some respect.' She scans the faces around the room and smiles. 'So I'm going to have a baby.'

Frey realises she hasn't seen Quin's smile before. Some of her teeth are grey and others are missing but the smile puts dimples in her cheeks and light in her eyes.

'You're going to have a baby!' says Avni, rushing to pull Quin into her arms.

'And youse are all the godmothers,' Quin says over Avni's shoulder. 'Because I can't do this on my own.'

'Where's the father?' asks Sally.

'Is he the nice one with the good penis?' asks Mary.

'That's him,' says Quin. 'He's a fucken dream come true. Bit of a geek, likes music, drinks craft beer, says "interface" a lot. He's beside himself with excitement to be having a baby with me.'

Frey observes that the smile has faded.

'You haven't told him,' says Mary.

'Yeah, I have,' Quin says. She looks briefly at the floor.

'What did he say?' asks Bizzy.

Quin laughs. Her shoulders are rigid. 'He didn't say anything. He just ran.'

'He *what*?' asks Sally.

'He fucken, like, actually ran. I said, "So anyway, Roland—"'

'His name's Roland?' Mary laughs.

'Yeah, after the keyboards. His dad's an old rocker. I said, "So, Roland, we've kinda like, you know, got ourselves up the duff and that. I mean, I'm having a baby and it's yours, I think. I mean, I know. It's your baby." And he looks up at me – he's really short – he looks up at me and kinda like sways, and then he just runs off, out of the cafeteria.'

Avni gasps. 'No!'

'Yep.'

'Gee,' says Sally. 'Nothing like living up to the legends.'

'Well, it was more of a trot, really. Like this . . .' Quin demonstrates a fast walk interspersed with bursts of running. 'I mean, he was carrying a heavy backpack and he had to dodge the tables, so . . .'

'The little arsewipe,' says Sally.

'Holy crap,' says Avni. 'You have to find him.'

'Nah,' Quin says. 'He has a fucken great relationship with Alexa and Siri, but not with me. I'll pass.'

'Arsehole,' says Eleanor.

'I wish I could tell him what I'd like to shove up his arsehole,' says Mary.

Bizzy just takes Quin's rigid body into her arms.

Lyrics from 'The Liniment Girl' float into Frey's mind.

She'll raise you from the steps and rub the liniment
Into your weary knees . . .

She's had the song on high rotation since the lunch at New Town Station Nursery. She'd also found an article describing how the members of the band Barbara Takes a Trip recall being 'rescued and awoken' by a mysterious woman who opened their eyes to the gross oppressions and mind-washing of the patriarchy.

She'll take your chalky hands and strike up the band,
Put whiskey in your tea.

The meaning of the lyrics is still not entirely clear to Frey, but the words and their melody bring a powerful confluence of nostalgia, excitement and fear that has been especially uplifting while washing the lunchboxes or wondering whether one's husband is somewhere having sex.

She watches now as Bizzy says into Quin's hair, 'We are here, we can do this,' and then quietly arranges some sheet music in preparation for the singing.

𝄡

They sing a song about falling. And boats. Frey struggles along for a while and then stops to listen as the harmonies swell and Rosanna's alto rises and runs to pitch some sort of pronged implement straight into her solar plexus. She places a hand on her middle and expects to feel heat. *At least I know I'm not dead inside.* She casts a glance at Eleanor, who is singing without expression in the contralto section, the voices around her building and twinkling off her monotone. Quin's rich, low voice sits alongside Eleanor's while Kyrie, with her eyes closed, sends her glorious soprano straight to the ceiling where it wafts around the pink chiffon star.

The choir launches immediately into another song, this one about being found. It has a musical theatre cheesiness about it but it makes Frey feel ever so slightly found, and that's fine with her.

When the singing is done, Frey watches how easily the women move in and out of one another's spaces. Someone asks about a plumbing problem, another about a fallen tree. Hands are placed on Quin, an arm is thrown around a shoulder, everyone gives the room a laugh. Freycinet feels an unexpected and intense sensation of care as she turns with a start to see that Rosanna has taken her hand. It is a small, unaffected gesture but it brings tears to Frey's eyes.

'You are enjoying the music magic,' Rosanna says.

'Yes,' says Frey, though it didn't sound like a question. She looks up at the shimmering ceiling and says, *'Mi sta facendo qualcosa.'* It is doing something to me.

Rosanna's eyes widen, her smile is huge. *'E incredibile quelle che puio sentire con le tue orecchie.'* It is amazing what you can feel with your ears. She laughs. 'Your accent is *perfetta.'*

'Thank you,' says Frey. 'It's definitely better than my singing. I'm a bit shit. But I can read music, I played the violin for years. And my anger has definitely billowed.'

Rosanna gasps. 'Freycinet can play the violin!' she says. 'And quick, everyone sit, I think she has a Fury to give.'

'Um,' says Frey.

Bizzy regards Frey's uncertainty and says, 'A reminder, Freycinet, that none of this goes beyond Laetare Gardens. And no Fury is too big, or small.'

'Give us your embers, Freycinet,' Kyrie says. 'There's an unlimited word count for your first one.'

'Well,' begins Frey. 'My husband is having an affair.'

No one seems very surprised.

'With a much younger woman.' Frey twiddles her wedding rings. 'And I've been feeling really sort of numb about it, which I think is like, a sort of white rage. I mean, I've never loved anyone else, and I can't believe he'd just go and do that, like that . . .' Frey tries to find her thoughts and match them to words. 'And, you know, for all these years I've been faithfully toeing the line. I changed my name, then I named our children after members of his family – Tom, Grace and Lily – which sounds like some expensive boutique selling children's gumboots. I'm like a poster-girl for a settled life, and that hasn't come naturally to me, I worked really hard at that. I was never, ever a settled person. I pack the same sanitised, wrapper-free lunchboxes at the same time every weekday. And everyone tells me that my kids are so amazing and full of energy and focus but no one acknowledges that they've got that much energy and focus because they probably sucked it all out of me. I'm just a sort of ghost. Not even a scary one. I feel proud by how well I iron Gil's work shirts. And now—'

Frey finds a sob in her words. She pauses to let it subside.

'And now I think my newly sixteen-year-old, dance-obsessed daughter is switching her obsession to the school football captain *and* lost her virginity to him. He's two years older, if I've got the right boy and I know I have. He comes from a long line of football "legends" with gambling tendencies. And the last thing I want to do is talk about it to my husband when the *first* thing I should be doing is talking to my husband. My son is in love with himself, closely followed by a mixing desk, and my other daughter is eleven but sometimes twenty and very often six. I'm just lugging all this baggage around, wondering where to put it. So, yes, I'm angry that what I get in return for the baggage is a delightful whack of infidelity.' Frey stops for breath. 'There's my anger, can you take it, please? I'm, like, murderous, I think.' She sneaks a look at the group and is relieved to see that they haven't run away.

'Well,' says Eleanor after a minute, 'you're welcome to talk to me about feeling murderous. Anytime.'

'Thanks, Eleanor,' says Freycinet. She is feeling giddy again.

'And thank *you*, Freycinet,' says Bizzy, 'for feeding directly into our rage repertoire, which needs work.'

'Has he denied it?' asks Quin.

'Quin,' says Bizzy. 'No questions.'

'Has he, though?' asks Mary. 'These are important fire-starters, Bizzy.'

Bizzy offers a concessional silence.

'I haven't confronted him,' says Frey.

'Have you confirmed that there is actually an affair?' asks Kyrie.

'Yes,' says Frey. 'I have photo evidence.'

'Ha,' says Sally. 'You can take him for everything. Can't she, Kyrie?'

'She may not want to,' says Kyrie.

'Oh my Gods,' says Rosanna. 'I would not be able to keep that knowledge under my hat. The whole neighbourhood would know if Jonathon had done adultery behind my back. How can you be in the same house with him and not scream?'

'Everyone is different,' says Bizzy.

Rosanna continues. 'And if my daughter is losing the virginity I will have to make properly sure she loves this boy.'

'She says she does,' says Frey, unable to add how she knows. Reading a private journal is not likely to be viewed favourably on the high ground of these morally venerable women.

'The football captain and the gambling could be a black flag,' says Rosanna.

'A red flag,' corrects Kyrie.

'But love is a beautiful thing, is it not?' says Rosanna. 'Remember the first bit of love? I was only just eighteen when I fell in love with Jonathon. And if she is a dancer, she can put the love into her body and make it do incredible things. Dancing is what you do when you don't have the words or the music. It tells all the stories, and love is the best story of all.'

'Ah, Rosanna,' says Bizzy, 'you can take the runaway out of Italy but the romancing will come along with her.'

'Are you going to break his balls?' asks Quin. 'Cut up his suits? I'd cut up his suits.'

'I don't know what to do,' says Frey. 'I'm just numb. I won't let him get away with it, but I need to be careful. I have three children to consider.'

'He hasn't considered them, though, has he,' Mary points out.

'I like it,' says Sally. 'You have proof, and a serious upper hand. You could do anything.'

'Do you love him, though?' asks Avni.

'Yes,' says Frey, forgetting that she is in a circle with nine virtual strangers. 'Yes, I do. I feel in actual pain, like I've had a layer of skin removed.' A sob sits in her throat, threatens to escape.

Avni gives a sad little squeak and takes a notebook from her bag.

'Look out,' says Quin. 'Avni's after song lyrics.'

'She has a songs book filled with ideas,' says Rosanna.

'I think you're displaying good sense,' Kyrie tells Frey. 'Be measured about this. And I am more than happy to give legal advice, no charge. I did, after all, hit you with my car.'

Frey smiles at her. 'Thank you.'

'While we're talking,' says Bizzy. 'And before we move on to the rest of the Furies, I want you all to know that I have made our rally official. I have contacted City Council and the police and put in the permit applications. The date is set: Saturday the twenty-ninth of February, 2020. We need to start drumming up participants.'

'Oh Lordy,' says Irene. 'She has that soap-box look about her. Buckle up, lassies.'

'In the lead-up,' Bizzy continues, 'I will be campaigning to raise awareness of the rally, to identify and demonstrate creative ways to open people's eyes to everyday acts of oppression and then help them build activism and feminism into their busy schedules.'

'Hear, hear,' says Mary.

'Are you really oppressed though, Bizzy?' asks Sally. 'You're white, you're rich, you're free. Isn't being all "Girls Just Wanna Have Fun" about feminism itself a form of oppression, because it's shifting focus from say, stopping First Nations people from dying in custody?'

'You're right, Sally,' Bizzy says. 'Of course there are bigger issues at hand. The focus of our rally is to make accessible ways of thinking and behaving that can ultimately have far-reaching effects for all.'

'And you're kind of proving the point, Sally,' says Mary. 'We don't even feel the subjugations anymore, they're that ingrained.'

Bizzy nods. 'Take Freycinet, for instance. She's experiencing, before our very eyes, the same emptiness and dismay experienced by women the world over, brought about by a devaluing of the work that goes into caregiving. She carries the emotional, physical, social and logistical burden of everyone in her house including her eejit husband. For very little in return. That's exploitation.'

Bizzy pauses. Goosebumps sweep up Frey's arms.

'And when her dismay shifts,' Bizzy continues, 'it's only to let in the shame she's made to feel because she has wealth and a home and freedom and safety and can't seem to find her gratitude. But how free is she really when she's so burdened down? How safe is she when she feels like a ghost?'

Frey feels the prickle of tears.

'Okay,' Bizzy continues, 'so in Frey's situation this is mostly a cisgendered, heterosexual issue for those lucky enough to have a family, but if we can shift to a world where caregiving and empathy is seen and valued in the same way as, say, technology or finance, then everyone will benefit. First Nations people, refugees, Mother Earth, even the fecking patriarchy. All those fellas worrying about the size of their houses and their willies, they can hurry up and help undermine the socialisation patterns that emotionally cripple them. Devaluation strips people of their agency and lets systems of oppression thrive. So, I'm just saying, maybe we start there, with the reimagining. Carry on the struggle of generations, honour the suffragettes and invite one and all to join our chorus in any way they can.'

Mary and Rosanna burst into applause.

'Join the chorus,' says Irene.

'That's a catchy hashtag,' says Avni.

'We could get women to stop work,' Mary suggests. 'Ditch the chores, go on strike.'

'We don't want to put any children at risk,' says Sally.

'This,' says Kyrie, 'could be a lot of effort for a small gathering of disgruntled women and a lot of institutional scorn.'

Bizzy looks at Kyrie. 'As my mother's ghost keeps telling me, if I want to rest on my laurels, then I need to have some fecking laurels. And what do we have to lose? We can't seem to attract anyone to the West Moonah Women's Choir unless we run them down with our cars. But perhaps we can get them to join this chorus.'

'Join the chorus!' shouts Rosanna.

'Well, surely we don't front up to this rally as the West Moonah Women's Choir,' says Mary. 'We have to be the Angry Women's Choir.'

'I still think it all needs a clearer focus,' says Kyrie.

The door swings open then and a tall, handsome man with salt-and-pepper hair strides in saying, 'Knock-knock, ladies.'

'Fucken here we go,' says Quin.

Frey recognises him instantly as Paul Bellavance, Liberal Member for Lyons, wealthy property tycoon and West Moonah Women's Choir nemesis. Also Gil's friend and Derwent Dance Academy parent. She tries to shrink into herself.

'Saying "knock-knock" is not actually knocking,' says Bizzy.

'Apologies, Ms Nancarrow. Rude of me, you'll have to put me in one of your little embroideries.'

'You're in many of them already,' replies Bizzy. The frost in her voice makes Freycinet shiver.

Bellavance's eyes narrow briefly. Penelope growls. He looks down at the dog and frowns.

'No dogs allowed, I've told you that before, Eleanor. But I'll let it slide because you're my cleaner. And he's a cutie.'

'God, you love saying that, don't you, Paul,' says Mary. '"You're my cleaner".'

'And Penelope's female,' Sally says.

'Of course she is,' Bellavance says.

'To what do we owe the pleasure?' asks Irene.

'If it's about the rent increase,' says Bizzy, 'you'll have to wait until your insanely inequitable demands have been assessed by the tenants' union. It's in their hands for the moment.'

He smiles his devastatingly handsome smile, but it too sends a shiver up Frey's spine. 'Those are some impressively big words, Byzantine Nancarrow of County Galway, Ireland. Look I won't keep you from your singing, or your chit-chat or whatever it was you were doing, but—'

'Paul,' says Bizzy, 'perhaps we can try to be civil. I have a feeling you've been treated badly at some point in your life. May we offer you some kindness?'

'Gee,' he says, 'imagine if blokes interrupted women halfway through a sentence. We'd be hung, drawn and quartered.'

'Ah, well,' says Mary. 'You've had a good run at it.'

'Look,' Bellavance says, 'I'm here to say that I will no longer be raising the rent.'

'Right,' says Bizzy. 'Go on.'

'And to offer you the courtesy of telling you that the reason I will not be raising the rent is because I've sold the building. To developers. They'll issue notice to tenants but I suggest you start looking at alternative venues for your little shindigs.'

'You keep talking down your nose at us like that and I'll give you a fucken shin-dig,' says Quin.

'Quinella,' warns Bizzy.

'Quinella,' repeats Bellavance. 'Don't get your knickers in a twist again.'

'Ugh,' says Quin, 'don't you even think about my knickers, you sleazebag.'

'Who says the new owners won't just keep running Laetare Gardens, and keep us on?' asks Mary.

'The building still has four regular tenants,' says Kyrie. 'Plenty of event bookings. It's an asset.'

'It's an eyesore,' Bellavance says.

'It's an important part of Hobart's cultural history,' says Kyrie.

Bellavance snorts. 'What, did you lose your virginity here at a school dance in 1973? Look, ladies, I've been in property a long time and this place is good for nothing but the wrecking balls, quite frankly.'

Irene emits a squeak.

Frey finds herself sitting up. 'Oh,' she says, 'I just worked out who you are. You're Paul Bellavance, aren't you? Sorry, I didn't recognise you at first.' She feels his eyes on her, sees his surprise. Her voice is higher pitched and accented with a blend of British and Toorak.

'Frey Barnes?'

'Freycinet,' says Rosanna.

'Yes,' says Frey. 'My daughter dances with yours at Derwent Academy. And my husband is—'

'Gil Barnes, yes.' Bellavance appears off-kilter for a moment. 'He worked for me on a shopping centre. Barnes and Rutherford did the waterfront development, near the art school.'

'Oh, welcome to Mansplainia,' says Mary. 'Here we all are.'

Bellavance ignores her. 'What are you doing here?'

Frey smiles. 'I'm a member of the choir. I've wanted to join for so long; they're amazing. Now that the children are old enough, here I am.' She giggles. 'I just love to sing. Gosh, to think I used to see you at school events. I think we were in the same year. Everyone had a mad crush on you.' She giggles again.

Paul Bellavance smiles, clears his throat and adjusts his tie in a show of modesty.

Bizzy shifts uncomfortably in her seat.

Frey hurries on. 'I just love the northern suburbs, don't you? Such working-class character. There's a definite on-the-brink-of-gentrification feel in this area, isn't there, which would be why you've had success on the sale. Congratulations, you must be thrilled. Actually, it's so funny because we've been considering this property since you put it on the market . . . when was that? Would have been . . .' She taps a finger to her lips.

'Three months ago,' says Bellavance.

'Yes, of course, back in May when it was first listed, we discussed it.'

'I didn't list it,' he says.

'Not formally, no,' continues Freycinet. 'But Tasmanian property development is a very small world, I'm sure you'll appreciate, news gets about. So you went with, let me guess, Evermor Holdings? BMDG?'

Bellavance shakes his head. 'No, but I really can't disclose, as I'm sure *you'd* appreciate.'

'Oh,' says Frey. 'Must be Firebrand, then.'

'I can't say—'

'Unusual move for them, they normally aim for high-end water-side assets. But that's great. I have good contacts there and they'll definitely be expecting a local re-sell offer. Probably why they bought it. We'd usually offer another ten per cent on what they paid, but they're bound to push us to thirty.' Freycinet rolls her eyes and lets out a peal of laughter. 'But that's okay, you had an extraordinarily low price on it anyway, for a trophy asset with endless upside. Our fault for umming and aahing too long. But Gil will no doubt be overzealed by the foreign-ownership factor. He's so fiercely Tasmanian, he'll probably accept a fifty per cent mark-up on the re-sell.'

Bellavance attempts a laugh. 'Wait, but I didn't . . . you can't—'

'Oh, sorry,' says Frey. 'I talk fast when I'm keyed up. Property is my passion, can you tell? Did you stipulate against pre-settlement re-sell in the contract before Firebrand made an offer?'

He scratches his head, jiggles his tie again. Frey watches his body language with glee.

'Ha,' says Quin. 'Take that, Small Smellypants.'

Bellavance turns on Quin, leans towards her and says, 'I've spoken to you about that before, Quinella, Trifecta, whatever-your-name-is Doyle.'

'Jesus Christ,' says Quin. 'Your breath could kill Tutankhamun.'

Bellavance doesn't move. 'I know where you've been,' he hisses.

'And you have no idea how far she'll go,' says Avni, surprising herself.

'Frey,' Bellavance says. 'Great to see you. I think you should visit the TSO chorale if you want to sing. Don't join these women. Trust me, I've put up with their nutty squirrel shit for years and you don't want to be getting mixed up in it.'

Frey smiles sweetly. 'Thanks for the concern, Paul, so much. Lovely to see you again. And thank you for all you've done over the years for the choir. You'll leave a void in the lives of these women, for sure.'

Paul Bellavance struggles with the door on his way out. The choristers wait ten full seconds before they erupt in a chorus of joyful astonishment.

'Oh my Lord,' says Sally, wiping laughter tears from her eyes. 'Freycinet, look at you go.'

'You should be on the stage,' says Rosanna. 'That was a five stars performance.'

Frey beams. 'Thank you. I have to do something to make up for my sketchy voice.'

'I can teach you some singing exercises that helped me,' says Rosanna with a smile.

'Thank you,' says Frey. 'But I'll never sing like you, Rosanna.'

'Did you see his stupid face?' Mary asks.

Bizzy is very still. 'It's been sold,' she says. 'Our Laetare Gardens has been sold.'

'Yes, but Bizzy,' says Irene, 'Freycinet and her business are going to buy it back, aren't you, Freycinet? It's a high-end trophy asset.'

Frey's smile fades.

'I think that might have been just a ruse, Irene,' says Bizzy.

'What?' replies Irene.

'I'm sorry,' says Frey. 'I was just trying to bring him down a peg or two. I had no idea he was such a shit.'

'He has the worst case of palsied imagination I think I've ever seen,' says Bizzy. She looks at Frey. 'Empathy requires imagination and his is so impaired it should be in rehab.'

'So all his support for victims of sexual assault really was pretence, wasn't it,' says Frey.

'Yep,' says Mary. 'Posturing. Opportunism. It won him a seat and probably a lifetime supply of extra-marital blowies. He's done diddly-squat for women since he got in.'

'Except for when he voted against paid paternity leave,' says Kyrie. 'That was most definitely directed at women.'

'Oh, the music in these walls,' says Bizzy. 'The laughs and the rejoicement and the glorious rage.' She looks at Frey. '"Laetare" means "rejoice", you know, in Latin.'

'We can rejoice in being the West Moonah Women's Choir anywhere, Bizzy,' says Mary. 'It will be okay.'

'And the new owners might just keep it how it is,' says Avni. 'It's kind of retro kitsch.'

They look around at the shamelessly hideous surroundings.

'You couldn't call that carpet retro, could you?' asks Sally.

'I don't want us to be anywhere else,' says Bizzy. 'This is not just a rehearsal space, it's our family home.'

'Can we buy it?' asks Eleanor.

'I could make enquiries,' says Frey, but she knows already that Firebrand will have tagged the site for units or industrial infrastructure, possibly storage facilities. Years of transcribing acquisition documents have taught her more than she'd prefer to know about property markets.

'I can't afford to buy a building,' says Quin. 'Not even to chip in.'

'Nor me,' says Eleanor.

'Goddamn that man,' says Bizzy, 'and the men who destroyed his vision and the horses they rode in on.'

Mary shakes her head and looks pointedly at Bizzy. 'If I can't convince you that a rally led by the Angry Women's Choir isn't appropriate, then let that arsewipe do it.'

'All right, dog jammit,' says Bizzy. 'You're right, Mary. Let's get the Angry Women's Choir out from behind closed doors. For Quin's baby, for us, for Freycinet's avenging, for September. It's finally spring and I have a properly loaded spring in my step. Let's raise our flags and rally the troops and get an army to join the chorus. Fight the fuckheads and bring this interminable struggle home.'

'Bloody hell, Bizzy,' says Kyrie. 'I've never been able to resist your orations. Let's do it, God help us.'

'He won't,' says Rosanna.

'Sally?' asks Mary.

'Well, I have to go along now, don't I?' replies Sally. 'To keep you lot out of trouble.'

'I'm totally in,' says Quin.

'Me too,' says Avni.

'I'll help,' says Freycinet. 'Where I can.'

'What are we agreeing to again?' asks Irene.

'Yes, good point, Irene,' says Mary. 'Let's work out a mission statement.'

'Wait,' says Eleanor, 'can we sing first? "Amazing Grace", maybe? I think I'm having an emotion.'

The Angry Women's Choir takes its place on the stage and with some particularly fervent conducting from Bizzy, sings a seething version of the famous hymn. It is generously dedicated to Paul

Bellavance, Gil Barnes and Quin's runaway Roland. Frey, though she stands with the choir, does not sing. She is too stunned by all the seeing of things she hadn't before, the most immediate of which is the revelation that such a sweet redemption song could actually be interpreted as an anthem of outraged vindication.

𝄐

Stepping Stone Number 68, from *La Lista* by R.K.:
Don't be rude to Siri, Alexa or any other artificial friends you might encounter. They are probably the way of the future and if you are mean to them, a superiority complex can develop and destroy every-thing. I keep going on about kindness but please and I mean it, be the kindest person you know.

Chapter 13
Ellipsis

Just as Frey falls silent among the harmonies, Grace Barnes is waiting in the low-lit foyer of Derwent Dance Academy, grasping fiercely to her own melodic, lovestruck take on the world.

She is watching three pulsing dots on the screen of her phone. A much anticipated reply from Harry after a gradual crescendo of messages to him about when she might see him again. The dots blink on. She forces her eyes to the framed photographs of outstanding academy alumni, perfect ballerinas mid-pirouette, musical theatre stars, and one young woman who was a featured extra in a Mariah Carey film clip. Grace used to dream of being in one of those frames on that gold wall. Now she dreams of bigger things. Getting off the island, big cities, elite schools, changing her name.

What shall I call myself? she wonders. *Grace works, Barnes is too blah. Grace Fenton?* She looks back at her phone. The dots are still there, still winking. Three little dots of promise. *It's a long message, Harry Fenton. What do you have to say?* She smiles. *My heart actually just skipped a beat.*

She puts her phone down and reminds herself to focus. *Elite dancers don't make it by dreaming about boys.*

Except that Harry Fenton isn't 'boys'. Harry Fenton is The Boy. He is the one she's reserved all her crushes for (her friends have had a giggling multitude). He is hot enough to make her strong dancer knees go weak, cool enough to have hordes of friends, respected enough to be a prefect, clever enough to have a place at Sydney University Law School for next year. And now, unbelievably, he has told Grace he loves her and she has had quiet, precious sex with him. Twice. This has become a secret so sparkling and weighty she wonders whether people can see it.

'You're beautiful,' Harry had said when they'd skipped a party to stay in his car and kiss. 'Like, really beautiful. Everyone says so.' And he'd bounced the heel of his hand on her hip bone in a shy sort of way, then leaned in to kiss her again before reaching under her shirt for a bra strap. Not long after, they were lying together naked and he was asking, 'Are you okay? I hope that was okay?'

He was gentle too, and thoughtful. *And he loves me.* She is proud that he has ignored the attentions of the girls in his year, and some older, to be with a Year Ten girl. She thinks that it shows how little he cares what other people think. That he is his own person. And she loves that he has promised not to tell anyone about their new relationship, that it's too special for other people to know. Too early to share. 'It's our secret,' he'd said. And later he'd picked her up into his footballer's arms and whizzed her around and it had felt a little bit cheesy but mostly amazing.

Grace shifts her thoughts back to the routine she is about to perfect in her solo class. But they sneak off again to imagine Harry watching the class. She knows her arabesque is exquisite. Her ballet teacher Eve told her so. She allows a brief foray into a scene where Harry is in the front row of a theatre while she performs something extraordinary. Something *prima*, with a standing ovation. Look at the way he smiles and does a little disbelieving shake of his head. Look how much he adores her.

'Hi, Bumhole.' The voice intrudes on her glorious anticipation, filling her with intense and instant aggravation. She looks up to see her little sister, Lily, standing before her, beneath the weight of her schoolbag and a hefty French horn case.

Grace tucks her phone away and wrinkles her nose. 'Ew, the stinkiest bumhole in the place. Why are you here?' The French horn and the way one of Lily's pigtails has gone wonky annoys Grace even more, though she wouldn't be able to say why.

'Mum said she'd pick us both up after your class and that I have to wait here.'

'Why?'

'I don't know.' Lily drops her bags and looks around her. 'It smells in here.'

'That's because you just walked in.'

'Which one's your favourite?' Lily nods at the pictures on the wall. 'I like her.' She points at a ballerina in a tutu filigreed with gold, a beatific expression on her pale face. 'She's so pretty. I like those fluffs on her arms.'

'They're not fluffs, they're feathers. She's Odette.'

'She's who?'

'Odette. From *Swan Lake*. One of the most famous parts for a ballerina.'

'Odette,' repeats Lily, gazing back up at the picture.

'So where's Mum?' asks Grace.

'You'll be Odette one day, Spacie Gracie.'

Grace snorts. 'Yeah, right.'

But Lily looks at Grace with a serious expression and says, 'You will. You'll be one of the people who have left here and everyone talks about, like, "Oh, she's on the stage in Boardway now, she was like, our best ever student and now she's worldwide famous."'

'Broadway,' says Grace.

'What?'

'It's *Broad*way.'

'I wish it was me going to *Broad*way. I wish I was like you, the world-famous Grace Barnes.' Lily puts her face very close to Grace's, and then rests it on her shoulder.

Grace pushes her away and laughs. 'No you don't, Silly Lily. You want to be like you.'

It's Lily's turn to wrinkle her nose. 'No I don't. I should be more like you. Pretty and dancery and beautiful.'

'Practise more, then. And you are beautiful. Mum tells you all the time.'

'She has to.'

They are silent for a moment. And then Lily says, 'You should eat your lunch, though, Gracie.'

'Don't start, Lily.'

'You tip your lunchbox into the rubbish bin at the bus stop before we get home. You won't be beautiful if you get bony. Harriet's sister is all bones now and she looks like a camel. All humped over, with hollows in her face. She has "disordered eating", that's what Harriet said. And it's frigged up her brain so now she can't eat anything without shouting at everybody.'

'I don't want to hear any more about Harriet's sister,' says Grace. 'That's not going to happen to me. I just choose to eat from the canteen because I'm sick of Mum's lunches. They're always the same. And I have to eat certain things for my dancing and she just doesn't get that. Okay? I'm not going to turn into a camel and I have to go to class.'

Grace gathers up her things, glances at her phone. The ellipsis continues to pulse.

'Mum's being weird,' says Lily.

'What sort of weird?'

'I don't know, just weird. She forgot to sign the thing so I can watch a film in class. I had to go to the library. And she bought condoms at the supermarket. She was all sneaky with them but I saw. She's probably having an affair with them.'

'No, Silly Lily,' Grace says, looking at Lily's worried face. 'She bought them for me. Gave them to me yesterday. She was like, "Now that you're sixteen, you should probably have some of these handy and if you want to talk about anything" and blah, blah. She got some for Tom as well. It's awks but not that weird, it's what mums do. They think we're stupid.'

Grace's phone dings, her heart leaps. But it's Freycinet.

Hi darling. Lily is being dropped off to Derwent after her music lesson. I'll pick you both up together. She has maths homework to do. Can you text me and let me know she's safe please? Mum xx

Grace rolls her eyes and says, 'See, she's worried that you can't possibly survive without her.'

'Did she say why she didn't pick me up from music?'

'Nope. I have to go in.'

'Okay.'

Grace looks at Lily. She suddenly seems very small, sitting on the couch on her own with that wonky pigtail. Grace gives a put-upon sigh, because to be an empathetic big sister would be properly weird, and will turn lip trembles to tears. 'Come in with me and watch if you like. You'll see why you don't want to be me.'

But later, when Grace has executed a perfect routine to Christina Perri's 'A Thousand Years' and Lily is gazing at her as though she's never seen her before, Grace remembers Harry saying, 'I love you, Grace' and realises that for the first time in ages, maybe in forever, she is actually happy to be Grace Barnes. The feeling is only marginally diminished when she checks her phone again to see that there is still no message from Harry and the ellipsis has disappeared.

𝄡

Wednesday, 18 September 2019, 8.30 a.m.

Harry still hasn't answered my messages or my calls. He's been
on Snap Maps heaps so I know he's not dead. He can't even
be bothered to block me. Can boys for real be this insensitive?
I am SO DUMB to think he would love me. Why would
he? At first I thought he might be kind of reeling with the
overload of emotion he has for me. Or feeling bad because
I'm younger than him. But I'm an idiot because he's obvs just
a prick who USED ME FOR ONE THING. I've stopped
messaging him. Can't believe all those texts I sent him.
So stupid.

The Derwent Academy showcase is a little over two months
away. Apparently there's going to be an Aus Dance Institute
person there checking us out, and a casting rep from the
mainland. It's probably just rumours but I need to be 150 per
cent prepared. I'm still going to do the Thousand Years routine
but NO MORE THINKING ABOUT HARRY, I HATE HIM
HE IS DEAD TO ME.

I have to go because I have exercises – DOUBLE REPS –
before I have to leave my room and be normal for Dad and
Grandpa's birthday lunch. (I don't want any stupid lunch.)

Mum does Grandpa's birthday every year for her own guilt,
not for Grandpa. I know he'd rather be at home tinkering.

I hate Harry Fenton. I love Harry Fenton. I hate Harry
Fenton with all my heart. There are stupid tears coming out of
my stupid face.

𝄡

For Roger and Gil's party, Lily has dressed herself in sparkly tights,
Tom's Fleet Foxes T-shirt cinched in with a sequinned belt and a blue
faux-fur jacket.

'Happy Birthday, Grandpa!' she shouts when Frey opens the door to Roger.

'Happy birthday, Grandpa,' Grace says, hoping her face isn't showing signs of the stupid tears.

'I'm here for the cake,' says Roger, winking at Lily and giving Acorn a pat.

'Good,' says Lily. 'Because we made you a ginormous chocolate one.'

'That's the way,' says Roger.

Frey leads him to the kitchen. 'Happy birthday, Dad,' she says.

'Thank you, The Girl,' Roger says, following along.

'Gil's at golf, but he'll finish in time for lunch.'

'He needn't,' says Roger.

Grace realises that she's never seen her grandpa and mother embrace. Not even a quick hug.

'Happy birthday, Grandpa,' Tom says from the stairs.

'Thank you,' says Roger. 'How's the loop station, Tommy?'

'It's awesome. I got a MIDI grid controller.'

'A what?' asks Roger.

'Musical Instrument Digital Interface grid controller,' says Tom. 'I'll show you if you want.'

'You could give Grandpa a demo for his birthday,' says Frey. 'He spends *hours* with that thing, Dad. Saved all his work money for the whole set-up. It's like a professional studio in there these days.'

Grace feels a twinge of irritation at the sound of Frey saying 'demo'. And another at the way she makes everything sound so wholesome around Grandpa, when really she's mostly yelling at Tom to go outside and get some fresh air.

'He just makes creepy Oingo Boingo mixes, Grandpa,' Grace says. 'So if you want one of those for your birthday . . .'

'I made a birthday mix for him actually, *Grace*,' says Tom. 'And one for Dad.'

'Did you, darling?' Frey seems surprised.

'Oingo Boingo is just fine,' says Roger, heading upstairs towards Tom. Frey and Lily follow.

Grace rolls her eyes and heads to the kitchen to scrutinise the lunch offerings. In the pantry, she leans in close to the cake and inhales the sweet smell of chocolate and icing and childhood, then feeds a pork pie to Acorn.

They don't come back downstairs for half an hour, by which time Grace has made her own lunch. Salad, no avocado.

'Grandpa knows how to loop his own vocal tracks now,' says Lily. 'He just said "la la" into the microphone and now he's the baseline beat in a Tom Barnes DJ mix.'

'It's the most words I've heard Dad say in years,' says Frey. 'The birthday songs are amazing, Grace. You need to hear them. He's mixed about ten different birthday songs together.'

'Amazing Grace,' says Roger with a chuckle.

'There are fourteen songs total, actually,' says Tom.

'Cool,' says Grace, but she's thinking about Harry again, and it comes with a stab of pain.

'I'm sure I had six pork pies,' Frey says, frowning. She opens the fridge and checks the lower shelves. 'Did you eat one, Tom?'

'No.'

'I don't mind missing out,' says Grace.

'You can have half of mine, Gracie,' says Lily.

'No thanks.' Grace avoids Lily's eyes. 'More room for cake.' Grace checks her phone and realises it's become a reflex. *He's not going to miraculously message you now, idiot*, she tells herself, flicking the phone onto its front.

Gil doesn't get home in time for his birthday lunch, which no one is particularly surprised about. When he does arrive it's just as Lily is about to wheel out the cake.

'Rog,' he says, shaking his father-in-law's hand with vigour. 'Sorry I'm late, mate. Happy birthday. What are we today? A hundred and thirty?'

'Happy birthday,' says Roger. 'Mate.'

It strikes Grace that her grandfather doesn't like her dad very much. She's not sure why she hasn't noticed it before.

'We gave Grandpa some new trousers with thick knees and a new set of sprockets,' says Lily.

'Dad got a facial,' says Tom with a snort. Roger frowns.

Freycinet smiles. 'It's a massage and a skin consultation,' she explains. 'He's at the right age to start a proper skincare regime. He got a golf ball cleaner too.'

'Sit down, Dad,' Lily says. 'I've been waiting, like, forever for the cake!'

'Ooh,' says Gil. 'I've been told, Rog.' He sits down beside Frey, who sends a smile in his general direction but doesn't actually look at him.

Why is everyone being so weird? Grace wonders, but she doesn't have the right sort of energy to be bothered thinking too hard about it. She looks at Roger, who would rather not be made a fuss of, and the way his smile crinkles his eyes so much they almost disappear, and how his hands are so worn in and seventy-two. She remembers this smile at Granny Lynn's funeral and how it wobbled on his pale face, how he didn't cry but made a tiny noise in his throat when their wedding photo appeared on the screen.

The cake, after a few misfires with the candles, finally appears. Grace sings 'Happy birthday' as loudly as she can, and puts her hand on Grandpa Roger's. He smiles and says, 'Strewth, this girl can sing.'

𝄡

Stepping Stone Number 28, from *La Lista* by R.K.:
Before you give your heart away to anyone, make sure they are kind to animals and think farts are funny.

Chapter 14

A Day Out

Stuck in morning traffic on Davey Street in central Hobart on a Thursday in October, Brent Fenton is lecturing his son Harry about the importance of stoicism on the football field.

'Pain is just weakness leaving the body,' he says, 'and you can work through it just like anything else your brain has to process. If the opposition see you on the ground just a moment longer than you need to be, they've gotcha. They see you hesitate, they've gotcha. Now all I saw last season, Harry, was a big boy behaving like a little girl.'

'Dad, I cracked a rib.'

'And what did I crack the year we beat Clarence for the premiership? What did I crack?'

'Your knee.'

'My fucken patella, right in two. And what did I do?'

'Kicked another goal.'

Brent Fenton gives the steering wheel a whack and rests his elbow out the open window. 'Kicked another goal. Fentons are built tough, Harry, all of us. Now this Saturday, I don't want to see a little girl on the field with number four on her back. I don't want to see a big boy with number four on his back. I want to see a man.'

Harry is silent. He stares down at his phone.

'And if you're going to stare at that bloody thing, watch the game again, see what you coulda done better.'

'I watched it twice.'

'Watch it again.'

The traffic begins to move. On the approach to the corner of Sandy Bay Road at the entrance to St David's Park, Brent Fenton sees three women in Victorian-era full skirts, high-necked shirts and wide-brimmed hats with puffed hair and placards painted with @ANGRYWOMENSCHOIR, #ANGRYWOMENSCHOIR and #JOINTHECHORUS.

'What the hell?' he exclaims. 'What are these old boilers up to?'

He presses a terse foot to the accelerator and careers straight into the back of the car in front. The sound of metal on metal reverberates through both driver and passenger. They jolt forward with a simultaneous shout. Harry's phone flies out of his hands, hits the dash, ricochets at an angle out the driver's side window and smashes on the bitumen below.

𝄡

'Fucken hell,' says Quin, looking out from under her hat brim towards the sound of the crash.

'Oh dear,' says Bizzy. 'I hope we didn't distract a driver. We must look a bit—'

'Like knobs,' says Quin.

'Oof,' says Mary, craning to see through the traffic. 'I think it's a Range Rover.'

'Fuck,' says Quin. 'Looks new too.'

'Quin,' says Bizzy, 'I never usually mind your potty mouth but given we are Victorian ladies today, do you think you could rein it in? We're not going to resonate with any CWA types with that language.'

Quin sniffs. 'I bet them suffragettes weren't all jolly hockey sticks with their language. Tough birds, they were.' She straightens up her purple, green and white sash and scratches under her hat. 'If this gets us any followers I'll eat these stupid boots, Bizzy.'

'Actually,' says Mary, 'the suffragettes are one of the most identifiable symbols of the women's movement. They really tap into people's emotions. No one wants the bravery and struggle of those women to be for nothing.'

A passing driver toots her horn and waves.

Mary waves back. 'See?'

'You just get your rocks off on these fucken underskirts,' says Quin.

A pedestrian shoots Quin a shocked look.

'Please, Quin,' says Bizzy. 'Swearing is not a sensible awareness-raising tactic.'

'How about flashing my arse crack?' asks Quin.

Bizzy experiences a rush of irritation. 'Then you'll be arrested for indecency.'

Quin snorts. 'Well, it would be worth it so I can say, "Actually, Your Honour, let me tell you what's truly indecent: rape statistics, that's what. You know what else? That."' She points to a homeless woman dozing on a bench, a clutch of overstuffed shopping bags by her side. '"And while I'm here, I could also tell you about honour, Your Honour. Not very many of you rich white fuckwits have any."' Quin laughs. 'Get me in that dock, I tell you.'

'So,' says Bizzy, evidently giving up on keeping Quin's decorum in check, 'I've brought a map of our proposed movements.' She takes the map from her basket and unfolds it. 'We'll stay here for morning peak hour with our pickets, then we'll circle the CBD via Salamanca and the waterfront with the pamphlets, up Campbell past the theatre and around, closing in until we end up in the centre at lunchtime. We'll picket at Centrepoint, have a break and then back here for the afternoon peak hour.'

'Perfick,' says Quin, 'and that way we can leave some of our shit with Petal.'

'Petal?' asks Bizzy.

'Petal.' Quin thrusts a thumb in the direction of the woman asleep on the bench. 'She'll do anything for anyone, Petal will. I'd sleep rough with her any day. Have done a few times. She'll be here all day, this is her beat.'

'Great,' says Mary. 'Sounds like a plan.' She holds her placard aloft and shouts, 'We're women and we're angry. Support the choir and you support women's rights!'

From the scene of the crash, someone else is shouting.

𝄢

By 10 a.m. when peak hour has passed and the three suffragettes are canvassing the waterfront, Bizzy is beginning to sweat. Getting the AWC campaign ball rolling with a fun bit of costume drama was her idea, but she is fast losing control of her recruits. Already they have gone off-piste and stuck missives written on sanitary pads to telegraph poles, noticeboards, bus shelters and rubbish bins. The messages are written in red pen and say things like, 'If you don't care about feminism you don't care about care' and 'Homemakers have been hoodwinked for the sake of GDP & civil order'. They are lucid, punchy notes that Bizzy might have written herself, but the chosen medium turns her stomach slightly. She has also missed the one that Quin stuck on the Constitution Dock sign which said, 'Your mum is on antidepressants because she is trying to exist in a world that exploits her. Stop fucking her over, motherfucker.'

When they circle back from the docks to Parliament Square, Bizzy watches as Mary thrusts her sign towards a woman carrying groceries and says, 'Coloniser capitalist men keep you busy with all the domestic duties and emotional labour so you don't have time to think about how the current treatment of homemakers is EXPLOITATION!'

The woman alters her direction to give Mary a wide berth.

'Unpaid care work contributes up to fifty per cent of GDP!'

Quin eyes a passing man who is eating a sandwich. 'Your wife make you that, did she, mate?' she yells.

The man shies to the left and drops his sandwich. It falls apart on impact and he scrabbles to pick it up and hurry away. The tomato gets left behind.

'Okay, that might be enough,' suggests Bizzy. 'That *is* enough.' She looks at the tomato on the ground, her skirts feeling suddenly heavy.

Quin's attention is diverted by the appearance of a small camera crew on the steps of Parliament House. 'Oi!' she screeches. 'Come and get a load of us! The Angry Women's Choir!'

'Right,' says Bizzy. 'I think we can get ourselves some morning tea before we move on. I'd kill for a coffee.'

But Quin is galloping towards the camera crew.

'Oh Lordy,' says Bizzy.

'Look at her,' says Mary. 'All belly and mouth. I don't know where she gets her energy.'

They watch as Quin talks animatedly to the journalist, then to the camera. She waves her placard.

'Quin!' shouts Bizzy. 'Come here to me, woman! Ah, Mary, can you fetch her back? I need a little sit-down.' She sinks onto a nearby bench, but is on her feet again within seconds because Quin appears to be gathering her skirts right up above her hips.

'No, oh dear, no,' says Bizzy.

Quin exposes her bare, untamed pubic region and shouts, 'And no I won't shave my beaver for nobody!'

Mary claps a hand over her mouth and gasps out some astonished laughter.

Bizzy puts her hands on her hat.

Quin completes her performance by bending over and wiggling her bottom at Parliament House, a dignified old building with perfect symmetry and elegant curves. A security guard appears through the front doors and calls out, 'Hey there, stop that!'

'You stop!' Quin shouts back. 'Stop your privileged-white-manning!' She drops her skirts, picks up her sign and runs, laughing, back to Mary and Bizzy. The camera follows her as she rejoins her fellow suffragettes, one of whom looks like she might give Quin's bare bottom a good hiding.

13

Bizzy's day does not improve. Nor does her mood. In the Cat and Fiddle Arcade, where they'd been granted permission to sing a few rousing trios, Mary and Quin vanish briefly, then reappear in the display window of R.M. Williams. They stand alongside the neat-shirted mannequins, their signs aloft, perfectly still but for the occasional almost-giggle. A number of shoppers photograph the pair on their mobile phones as they pass. A group of older women clap and cheer. Spurred on by this, Quin once again bares her nether regions. Cameras snap. The R.M. Williams staff evict the pair and Bizzy marches them out of the arcade and onto Liverpool Street, where Quin flips the bird at a man in a Porsche and yells, 'Oi, mate, got any tips on tax havens? I'm over paying tax for bullshit like health and education!'

Over toasted sandwiches and soup at Cultura Café, Bizzy does her best to rein them in. But Quin is on fire, and Mary's uncontrollable laughter is pure ethanol to the flame.

'I'm sorry, Bizzy,' Mary says, 'but it is a bit funny. You would have loved all this not so long ago, wouldn't you? Didn't you say we should be putting the fun back into feminism?'

'Yeah,' says Quin, 'some of them women in the Cat and Fiddle looked dead jealous they weren't with us. They'll be on board quick as a flash, I bet.'

Mary snorts and says, '"Flash" being the operative word.'

'But that's the thing, Quinella,' says Bizzy. 'You're not actually giving anyone a call to action. You're just making a spectacle of yourself. We can raise eyebrows by all means but we also need to be raising consciousness. And not our skirts.'

'Yeah, but I'm the spectacle, the attraction, then you step in to follow up with your calls to action and your hashtags, don't you? I reckon it's working great. Everyone's loving seeing a preggo suffragette with a hairy fan and something to say.'

Mary spurts soup through her nose.

'It's a fine line between fun and disrespect, though, Quin. You're putting people off. And breaking the law.'

Quin blows a raspberry. 'Public nuisance is activism, Bizzy, you taught me that. And law schmaw. I'm not hurting nobody. The criminal stuff is happening within the fuckwit patriarchy. Don't fucken tell me I'm taking things too far. Not that stale old chestnut.'

'You were nasty to that man in the park. And his sandwich. We're about care and kindness, remember? Not bullying.'

'Ha!' says Quin, startling several people in the café. 'I was a bully to a poor man and his sandwich, was I? Come on, Bizzy, I did him a favour. Gave him something to think about that will most likely change his life for the better. He'll never take his fucken sanger for granted again, will he? And it's not like I rubbed my hairy growler on him, did I?'

People are staring now.

'That's it,' says Bizzy, brushing breadcrumbs from her mouth. 'I need to get home. I think we've done quite enough for one day.' She rummages in her basket and fishes out some cash. 'I'll see you on Tuesday.'

'Aw, come on, Bizzy, we're going so well. Think of all the times men get their stupid wangs out *and* rub them on people without asking.'

But Bizzy has already gone. Quin looks at the staring people and adds, 'Well, it's a valid point.'

𝄡

Bizzy is having trouble thinking straight as she makes her way across Murray Street towards the Centrepoint carpark. Standing at the lights, waiting to cross, she can't work out whether she's furious with herself or with Quin and Mary. An inner voice keeps saying, *Simply not decent,* and it sounds just like Sally's dreadful mother-in-law. She can't stop thinking about the startled man with his sandwich, the forgotten tomato. Something about her had wanted to protect him. The same instinct that wants to keep Ferris safe from harm. A tiny part of her wants to make a sandwich for someone.

'Pull your sorry bones together,' she mutters to herself. 'What's the matter with you?' She wonders whether she might be losing her marbles, like Irene. An elderly man tips his hat at her and she wonders whether he might be a ghost. Her fingers worry the brown circular pendant at her throat.

When she reaches the carpark stairwell, the heavy door shuts behind her and she pauses in the cool, concrete-scented enclosure for a moment before going up to the green-doored level where she is almost sure her car is waiting. At the first door, which is yellow, she second guesses herself and pauses to think. While she is doing that, the yellow door opens and through it come Freycinet and a gazelle.

Bizzy blinks and wonders whether Irene's dementia began with seeing strange and mystical creatures in unlikely places. She blinks again and the gazelle turns into a girl, a slender, leggy girl with silky skin and the most devastating pout Bizzy has ever seen.

'Bizzy?'

'Freycinet. Well hello there. Goodness, look at me, I've been raising awareness with Mary and Quin, God help me.' Bizzy sees that the girl is a lanky, longer-haired, fuller mouthed version of Freycinet. 'Support the Angry Women's Choir and you support women's rights,' she chants, winking at the girl.

Freycinet seems flustered. Bizzy hasn't seen a flustered Freycinet before. 'Grace,' she says, 'this is my friend, Bizzy.'

'Hello, Grace,' says Bizzy.

'Hi.'

Bizzy notices how the pillowy mouth doesn't bother leaving its pout. And how her eyes flick towards her mother.

'We're off to buy ballet shoes,' says Frey, evidently composing herself. 'Grace has worn hers out again. Plus she's grown about a mile.'

'You're a dancer, Grace,' says Bizzy. 'Do you sing too?'

'Not really,' says Grace.

'She does, actually,' Frey says. 'Well, she used to. She has a lovely voice.'

Grace looks at the floor. Something unspoken wrinkles the cold air of the stairwell. The yellow door makes its final delayed bang as it closes. The sound echoes unreasonably around them.

'A stairwell is a wonderful place to sing, you know,' says Bizzy, 'if you feel like having a sing now. It would vastly improve my day and flip knows it needs a boost.'

'How did you go with your awareness raising?' Frey asks. It is a question designed to hurry things up.

'Ah, it's a long and sordid tale,' says Bizzy. 'Suffice to say we've had a day out, but we haven't toppled the establishment and its innovations.' She laughs and shoulders her bag in a gesture of departure. 'So you won't sing for a barking old woman in a stairwell, Grace?'

'No, thanks,' says Grace, not unkindly. She sends Bizzy a brief but beautiful smile.

'Ah, I wouldn't either.' Bizzy laughs and is rewarded with another hint of smile. 'I'll let you get on. Enjoy your afternoon.'

'Bye, Bizzy,' says Freycinet. She smiles but she doesn't look back as the stairwell swallows them up and sends back their retreating footsteps and Grace saying, 'I know where we can have lunch.'

I'm forgotten already, thinks Bizzy, and she stands listening for a moment, imagining what it might be like to take a daughter to buy ballet shoes, to discuss where to go to lunch.

13

Bizzy enters the front door of her house and surveys its interior with weary, fresh, Freycinet-and-Grace eyes.

'Who is this doolally Byzantine Nancarrow, then?' she asks the walls. 'Show her to me.'

She traces a hand on the turquoise-and-gold wallpaper, inspects the assemblage of Very Cross Stitches in mismatched frames, most of them gold or silver, all of them ostentatious. She rolls her eyes at the bookcase (overflowing with books she hasn't had time to read), then inspects the sitting room, which has an electric blue ceiling with gold stars, a pink couch, a large aquamarine chandelier, an orange fringed floor lamp, hectic pink carpet and not an inch of wall-space free of some picture or quote that has tickled Bizzy's fancy over the forty-two years she's lived here.

'Ha,' Bizzy says. 'Not an ounce of understatement do you have, Bizzy, m'girl. So why was today too much for you?'

She looks at a framed quote on the wall which says, 'Make it your job to remind people just how wonderfully, ludicrously fantastical it is to be alive.'

'Ludicrous,' she says, pouring herself a whiskey.

With drink in hand she hovers over another image, this one on the sideboard beside the drinks stand. An old photograph, framed in walnut and bleached by years, cracked in parts. A young man stands at its centre in dark water up to his knees. He smiles up at Bizzy, smiles and smiles until she slaps the frame face-down onto the sideboard. 'And where did you feck off to? You and your smile? I could have made you a sandwich, sat under the trees with you.'

There is a sudden knock at the window. Bizzy jumps, spills her drink. 'Feck and jingoes,' she exclaims.

A little face is pressed against the window, trying to see in. 'Bizzy?'

Bizzy yanks the sash upwards. 'Ferris? You scared the full clappers out of me.'

'We saw you on the news, Bizzy Nancarrow!' Ferris shouts. 'Put the telly on!'

𝄡

Stepping Stone Number 199, from *La Lista* by R.K.:
Don't be a bozo on the roads. Be patient, tolerant and safe or you will injure yourself or someone else. And don't tailgate. Tailgaters are, without exception, complete fuckwits.

Chapter 15

Sing the Mountain

Frey is sorting through mail in the office when Gil emerges from around the corner and says, 'I'm home!'

Frey almost drops the letters in fright. 'Bloody hell, Gil.'

'Jumpy,' says Gil. After a beat he takes her in his arms, says, 'Hello,' then kisses her.

Frey can't help wondering where his mouth has been. It has, in the last few weeks, become clear even without active surveillance, that Gil's infidelity is an actual affair, not a mere dalliance. He has taken to saying things like, 'My bad, I went to the pub for one after work and ended up having too many beers' or 'Don't tell anyone but I took the afternoon off and played golf, then stayed back at the club rooms. I'm a menace.' Frey knew this tactic well. The cover within a cover: admitting to doing something less serious so as to divert attention from the true behaviour.

She has documented his movements in a notebook and hidden them with Roxy's phone and its photos. *Artillery stores for when I strike*, Frey thinks, but cannot yet see what form her strike might take. Or whether it will happen at all. During her research, she has read that strong women throughout the eras clocked their husbands' affairs and refused to let them ruin things. In some cases, an affair has even enhanced the marriage. The institution of matrimony was, after all, manufactured when humans weren't expected to live much past fifty and monogamy didn't ask for sixty years of unswerving faith.

Frey wills her body to relax beneath Gil's kiss. But the familiar aftershave smell of him sends a draught of emotion through her. She clears her throat, clears her senses and says, 'You're home early.'

Gil sifts through the mail. 'Actually I'm home on time, I just never get out of the office when I'm meant to.'

'Why today?' Frey asks.

'Well, I finished a job, it was too late to start another one, and, you know, it's a nice day.'

'Yes, spring's finally here.' Frey motions towards the window and thinks, *And now we're talking about the weather.* 'You heading out on your bike?'

'Nope, might just hang with my family.'

'Well, Tom's in his sound cave, Grace is out running and Lily's in a mood.'

'Excellent, it's just you and me then.' He nuzzles her neck.

She breathes him in.

'Is there something you want to tell me?' He looks at her and smiles.

Frey almost drops the letters again. *He knows I know.* 'Hmm?' *Relax, you idiot.* She smiles back. 'Like what?' Images of the Roxy disguise flash through her mind. *Of course he knows it was me in that disguise; he knows me so well.*

'Like, I don't know, you've joined a choir?'

'A choir?' Frey breathes again. *Maybe he doesn't know me that well.* 'A choir. Yes, yes, I suppose I have, sort of.'

'Sort of? Paul Bellavance said he met you at your choir practice.'

'Yes,' Frey says. 'Gosh, that was a blast from the past. I haven't seen him since school. I didn't know you'd worked together.'

'I didn't know you'd joined a choir.'

'Well, I'm sort of trialling it. I mean, I can't sing very well, so.'

'What made you go there? Moonah, is it?'

'West Moonah.'

'Why there? I mean, I think it's great you're doing something for yourself. I kind of thought yoga or tennis.'

'I don't really like yoga. And I've played heaps of tennis. I wanted to do something that challenges me.' Frey is improvising, but the words are true. 'And the West Moonah Women's Choir is really good. They're properly talented.'

'Right, okay. Choir's cool with me.'

'Does it need to be cool with you?' Frey feels the prickle of hot irritation.

Gil's eyebrows go up. He raises his hands. 'Hey, not at all.' He laughs. 'You don't have to tell me what you're doing. I'm just your husband.'

The outrageous paradox of this statement – and the sarcastic tone with which it is delivered – takes Frey's breath away. She rips open the water bill and shoves it in a tray marked *To Pay*.

'Just that Paul told me they're a pack of mad bitches,' Gil continues. 'One of them went to jail for murdering her husband.'

'I know. He destroyed her first.'

'Right. Just be careful, okay? Paul said it's like some sort of cult.'

Frey laughs. 'They sing eighties songs and laugh a lot. If that's a cult it's a pretty benign one.'

'Righto. Okay.'

'Rehearsals are Tuesdays,' says Frey. 'Five thirty until seven.'

'Ah, so that explains the takeaway dinners.'

'Yep. Sorry I didn't tell you. I just wasn't even sure I wanted to stay on.' Frey can't believe she's apologising. 'But I do, I think,' she says. 'Want to stay on.'

'Well, I guess your violin playing could make up for your mediocre singing.'

'Yes, maybe,' she says. 'I'm not brilliant on the violin either these days.' She considers what an ugly word 'mediocre' is. And then she realises that Gil's suggestion has merit. *I must take my violin to Dad for new strings.*

'Think I might go for a ride after all,' says Gil. He kisses the top of Frey's head as he leaves the study.

'Okay, be careful.' Frey imagines adding, '*It would be terrible if you fell off and landed on top of a woman in Tower Road, New Town and accidentally pierced her with your penis.*'

She sighs instead, puts her face in her hands for a long moment, then turns back to the bills.

𝄡

An hour later, Frey is washing potatoes when Grace puffs into the kitchen.

'Wow, that was some run,' says Frey.

'Mmm,' says Grace, helping herself to Frey's glass of water.

'Where did you go? Kingston?'

'Nope. Fern Tree.'

'As in, halfway up the mountain?'

'Maybe. I don't know.'

'I'm going to Fern Tree tomorrow.'

'Cool.' Grace puts her earphones in and flops onto the couch with her phone.

Frey watches her and mutters, 'Because one of the women in the car that hit me a few weeks ago, just before I saw your dad with another woman, is going to teach me how to sing. She's dying of cancer, which is a travesty because she's the most alive person I think I've ever met.' She tosses the potatoes into a pot.

Tom walks through the kitchen to the fridge. Frey is relieved to see he also has earphones in. *I could say anything in this house, tell them everything, and no one would hear.* She starts to sing a choir song. The one about sinking ships.

𝄡

'Mum, can I have pointes too?' Lily asks later when she's half-heartedly setting the dinner table.

'When your foot bones are stronger,' says Frey. 'Couple of years.'

'Couple of years?' Lily repeats. 'That's forever. And they are strong.' She looks down at her feet, points her toes.

'They're spongy,' says Grace. 'You have spongy foot bones.'

'Shut up,' says Lily. 'You have a spongy face.'

'Nice,' says Grace.

'Come on, girls,' says Frey. 'Grace, can you please make the salad? I'll crumb the fish.'

'Get Tom to do the salad,' says Grace. 'He's sitting on his arse in his stinky room.' She looks at Frey. 'I don't want my fish crumbed, thanks.'

'Tom!' yells Lily at the top of her voice. 'He can set the table as well. The women shouldn't be in the kitchen while the bumhole men—'

'Sit on their bumholes,' says Frey.

'He'll never hear you,' says Grace. 'He'll have music in his ears, mixing the next alt-rock medley for his ten YouTube followers.'

'At least he's being creative,' says Frey.

'I'm creative *and* I get off my arse,' says Grace.

'I wasn't saying you're not creative,' says Frey. 'Using your body to tell stories is about the most creative thing there is.'

Grace, if not surprised, seems unable to think of a smart response.

A few minutes later, Tom does come in. He switches the television on.

'Don't watch telly,' says Lily. 'You have to make the salad.'

'I have to watch the news for school.'

'You do not.'

Gil appears then, freshly showered from his ride. He drinks the rest of Frey's water. 'Hello, family,' he says. 'Fish for dinner again?'

'And today in Hobart,' says the newsreader from the television, 'a women's choir strikes a shocking blow for feminism.'

Frey jerks her gaze to the television and a still image of Quinella Doyle exposing her pixelated nether regions to Parliament House. She freezes, her mouth open in astonishment.

'Look at this crazy bitch,' Gil says with a laugh. He reaches for the remote control, turns up the volume and raises his eyebrows at Frey.

With a half-smile on his face, the news presenter continues. 'Three women dressed in the dignified floor-length skirts of Victorian suffragettes have been hard to miss in Hobart's CBD today. However, the skirts did not stay on the floor, and some say their antics have been far from dignified. Adam Riley reports . . .'

'Would anyone like an olive?' asks Freycinet brightly, popping one in her mouth. 'I'm a little behind with dinner.'

'Shhh,' says Gil, holding up his hand.

Adam Riley's voice takes over. 'Three modern-day suffragettes have taken to the streets today in a bid to put women's rights in the spotlight, and to raise awareness of their new women's choral group, the Angry Women's Choir. Their promotional day out – supposedly designed to inspire others to join their all-inclusive chorus – included committing indecent exposure outside Parliament House.' Here the footage of Quin has been inserted, complete with her screeching, 'I won't shave my beaver for nobody!'

Grace snorts.

'Ew,' says Tom.

'Oh, come on,' says Gil. 'When are women's rights *not* in the spotlight these days?'

Adam Riley continues, his voiceover matched to various wobbly videos evidently taken by civilians on their smartphones. 'Sanitary pads bearing messages of women's oppression and exploitation were stuck to landmarks around the city, peak-hour commuters were picketed, and shop windows invaded. Images of the trio have been shared multiple times on social media platforms, with commenters either slamming the behaviour or applauding it. The women have been identified as possible members of the West Moonah Women's Choir, apparently re-branded as the Angry Women's Choir. No arrests have been made today, but police have issued a warning.'

'What did I tell you?' Gil exclaims, looking at Frey with an expression of triumph and disgust. 'They're a pack of mad bitches.'

'Mum, that's the woman we saw in town,' Grace says. 'The one with the—' She stops talking when she sees Frey's face and the barely perceptible shake of her head.

'Yeah, Mum's a member of that choir,' says Gil. He makes an ugly scoffing noise.

'She is not,' says Lily. 'Choir is so boring.'

'Are you, Mum?' asks Grace.

'Yes,' says Frey. 'I am.'

Tom laughs. 'But you can't sing.'

'Well, I have a voice.'

'Shhh,' says Gil again.

The story cuts to a police officer, who says, 'We are taking this matter very seriously. Lewd acts and civil disobedience will not be tolerated in Hobart and we will certainly be making further enquiries. We wouldn't like to see any copycat behaviour occurring in our city.'

The story ends on a shot of Quin, Mary and Bizzy singing in Hobart's Cat and Fiddle Arcade.

'Bloody hell,' says Gil in disgust. 'Some people just have too much time on their hands.'

Freycinet feels a red-hot smack of anger hit her with force. She wrestles with it, searching for the right words to say.

Grace finds them in the end. 'Oh well,' she says, 'if they want to kick off the revolution, good on them. No one else is.' But then she adds, 'Except everything has already turned to shit, so Mum, you and your choir are better off planning what to sing when the world burns down.'

𝄢

Rosanna's house is tucked into the foothills of what most Hobartians have nicknamed 'the mountain'. It also goes by its traditional name, kunanyi, and the name given to it more recently: Mount Wellington. Her suburb, Fern Tree, is officially part of Hobart, but is more like a mountain village. To Freycinet, as she drives up the winding road, passing Greens Party signs and a banner shouting *NO CABLE CAR*, it feels as though the ten-minute drive has taken her light-years away. Nothing in her life, not her career or Gil's work, her children, her children's friends, their interests or their inclinations, ever requires her to go to Fern Tree. *This is where all the good people live*, she thinks with a tremor of guilt. *The ones we're all depending on to save humanity.*

Rosanna's yard doesn't contain Frey's idea of a garden. Rather a large, upward sloping piece of Tasmanian scrub, a bit of scruffy grass and an embankment of rock. The house sits modestly in one corner, like an afterthought. Its back rests against the rock while the sun dapples the front deck. A sudden, close whinny from a horse startles Freycinet. By reflex, she almost jumps back into her car but is halted by the sight of a beautiful golden pony with a white mane. He stands in his muscled beauty and regards Freycinet suspiciously, his nostrils huffing.

Freycinet watches him for a long, silent moment, as if waiting for a signal.

'He's enough to make you want to take up horses, isn't he?'

Freycinet turns to see Rosanna walking across the lawn towards her from the back of the house.

'I've never seen such a beautiful horse. I could look at him all day.'

'Don't let him hear you,' says Rosanna 'He is so arrogant already.'

'Is he yours?'

'No, he is Jonathon's latest commission. Okay to ride but no manners on the ground.'

'Jonathon breaks horses?'

'Yes. But not this one. Jonathon's horses are sold far and wide for their perfect skills. He doesn't really break them, he just understands them. This one has been sent to him for correction. He's a fixer-upperer. Like me. Poor Jonathon, all the things to try and fix. And now he is rolling his eyes around about Quin and her misbehaviours.'

'Oh my goodness, did you see the news?'

Rosanna nods. 'I talked to Bizzy this morning. She is nearly laughing about it, but not quite. It is helping that the Angry Women's Choir social media page has got so many more followers now.'

'It has?'

'Yes.' Rosanna claps her hands. 'Thousands of people talking. And all because of Quin and her woman parts.'

'The hairy beaver!' Frey laughs.

Rosanna's laugh echoes the richness of her singing voice. 'Come in, we have the house to ourselves. My baby is asleep.'

The interior of the house almost has Frey laughing with glee. It's busy, eccentric, there's a harp in the corner of the sitting room and a bowl of coloured stones on the table. A wall of books spills out into piles, some of them acting as coffee tables and pot stands. On the opposite wall hangs an array of colourful plates, framed butterflies and a large, elaborate cross-stitch in a bright green frame that says *Home is where the fart is*.

'Is that Bizzy's work?' asks Frey with a laugh.

Rosanna laughs too. 'Of course. She does not like it because it is not chipping away at the patriarchy, but it makes everyone laugh and that is always a good thing.'

'Well, it pokes fun at convention, and that's a start, I think,' says Frey.

'I agree,' says Rosanna. 'When you are laughing, you are hard to oppress.'

'This is such a gorgeous house,' says Frey. 'I love it.'

'It is a clutter,' says Rosanna. 'I see things and I feel sorry for them and I have to bring them home. It has always been a problem for Jonathon and me. But I love it. Bizzy thinks that I am trying to out-clutter her. We are both proud maximalists.'

Frey looks at three mismatched pendant lights and the yellow paisley wallpaper on the ceiling and says, 'It really works.'

'They will have a hell of a time sorting through it all when I'm gone.' Rosanna laughs again.

Frey stays silent.

'Now, we will sit and talk about the singing but would you like a juice first? Water? Champagne? I won't offer milk because it is not good for singers.'

'Juice would be lovely, thank you.'

When Rosanna returns with the juice she also brings a small oxygen tank on wheels and a coil of green tubing. 'I am having a low oxygen day, so I'm sorry but I need to look exactly like a terminally ill person for a short while.'

'Don't apologise! I don't mind. We don't even have to sing if you're not feeling well.'

'I am always well enough for singing, Freycinet.' Rosanna inserts the tubing into her nostrils and loops it around her ears. 'Now, the first thing that I learnt from my horrible Sunday School teacher in Italy was that I needed to have good posture. She was right, damn her. Good posture is very important.'

Frey watches Rosanna's tiny frame demonstrate correct singing posture, then explain the different kinds of resonance. 'If you want to shout at the children,' she says, by way of example, 'always use your deep chest resonance with your diaphragm engaged or you will injure your vocal folds. But if you want to sing to the mountain, send the notes right up through the top of your head. They will be thin, but they will be beautiful. Like your daughter, Grace.'

Frey frowns, puzzled.

Rosanna smiles. 'My daughter, Serra, is a little younger but she does some dancing at the Derwent Academy.'

'Oh, does she?' Frey's heart sinks a little.

'They are not in the same classes but Serra says Grace is slim and beautiful and very wonderful at the dancing.'

'Thank you. She's certainly very dedicated.'

'Dancing is something I wish I can do,' says Rosanna.

Frey sees again how fragile Rosanna is but also how strongly her hands speak while her eyes listen. Frey wants to howl with rage against the injustice of the world.

They sing, and Frey is carried effortlessly along through a slowed down version of 'Somewhere Over the Rainbow'. She surprises herself by not ruining it.

'You have very well matched vowels,' Rosanna tells her. 'And a pure, breathy sound. I wish I had all that breath. Your vocal colour is a beautiful pale blue. Grow it stronger and Bizzy will have you doing the solos.'

Frey knows she is just being kind. It brings tears to her eyes, the kindness. She can't remember the last time she has been nurtured like this. Without thinking she says, 'I'll need about one hundred lessons from you to go from pastel to bright,' she says.

'I do not even have one hundred days in me, Freycinet,' Rosanna replies, and Frey wishes she'd thought before she spoke.

Rosanna picks up a brass horse figurine, puts it back, taps a finger on its head. 'They are saying I don't even have fifty. This medical trial is finished, so . . .'

'Oh, Rosanna. I'm so sorry.'

'No sorries,' says Rosanna. 'This is how it is. Sometimes I have such terrible rage that I wish I had God so I could send it all to him. But I just have to shout at the mountain and then sing it all to the clouds and put it to use. That is that. I am not scared.'

'You're amazing,' says Frey. 'I don't know what else to say.'

'Thank you, Freycinet. I *am* amazing.' Rosanna laughs. 'You are amazing. We are all amazing.' She sings a few bars of 'Amazing Grace'.

Frey swallows a large lump in her throat.

'Please, Freycinet. You cannot tell this to anyone. Kyrie knows, of course, but I am still trying to work out how to tell the choir. None of them ever want to believe that I am actually dying.'

'It is very hard to believe,' says Frey. But she looks at the marked rise and fall of Rosanna's chest, her tiny wrists, and knows that it's true. 'And of course I won't breathe a word, but I think you should tell them sooner rather than later. If you don't mind me saying.'

'Yes, I know you are right. I have to tell my parents first, though. They are in Italy, so this is difficult too.'

'I can't imagine.'

'Ah, they have God very, very close so they will be okay. And they have been praying for my soul for almost twenty years.'

'Will they fly over?'

'I think that they will stay near their god. My funeral will not have the right one. But my brother will perhaps come.'

Frey leaves some silence in case Rosanna wants to keep talking.

'And I have Bizzy to give a eulogy, she is good at those. And she shares the same no-god as I do. She gave her mother's eulogy and she said it was helpful to her healing. I will have to tell her very soon, give her the time to prepare. Telling you has got the right balls rolling, so thank you for that. I can work on a plan. Well, I can work on working on the plan. Does this make sense?'

'Yes,' says Frey. 'Yes, it does.'

Rosanna smiles. 'Like you with your marriage, yes? Working on working on a plan.'

'Yes.' Frey is having trouble speaking.

'You are very hurt, Freycinet. I knew even before we hit you with the Fiat. You had aching written into your face, there on the footpath. Are you all right?'

Frey can't believe she is being asked about her wellbeing by a woman with less than fifty days to live.

'Yes,' she says. 'I'm okay.' She points to the bowl of stones on the table and says, 'I have all those sitting here, in my stomach. They are hot sometimes, and heavy. And I'm empty at the same time. But I think that emptiness has been there a long time. I'm used to it. And I will be okay.'

'You will.' Rosanna presses her hands onto Frey's cheeks. 'You will know the right thing to do. It will be nice to look at and easy to recognise. And now, it is almost three and I have to wake my baby and you have to go to your afternoon. I will see you on Tuesday at choir.'

She plants a kiss on each of Frey's cheeks and sends her on her way.

Back outside, with the day so full of mountain and golden horse and fading music, Frey stands with a singer's posture and lets herself feel the hurt that Rosanna has seen in her face. It washes over her and heats her skin. She looks back over the years and sees how her colours have faded. How she has matched her finishes to please no one. How her shoulders have begun to round. She squeezes her eyes shut in pain, opens them again and sways a little in the mountain air. It seems so honest, this air, no secrets, no fraught interactions.

The scraggle of bush around her is unaffected and undemanding. Rosanna's world. A place where it's nice to match your vowels but everything else is welcome to be what it is: paisley and lace and butterflies, greenstone dolerite and the sun over the horse shed, a baby waking to her mother's face. Frey looks at it, this world, and glimpses a flash of future so bright it makes her squint. The right things. *Nice to look at and easy to recognise.* Somewhere beyond the pain and the empty what-ifs, Frey senses euphoria. A hint of it squeezes her heart.

It is with reluctance but improved clarity that Frey turns away from Rosanna's place and takes the first step into her afternoon. The gravelly crunch underfoot reminds her of broken promises.

𝄡

Stepping Stone Number 108, from *La Lista* by R.K.:
To get a baby to sleep, try passing an open tissue down her face from forehead to chin, so that it very delicately strokes her. Nine times out of ten her eyes will close. Keep it up until the little one can't keep her eyes open anymore.

Chapter 16

Bang!

Eulogy for Winifred Brigid Nancarrow

<u>8 March 1983, Royal Botanical Gardens, Hobart, Tasmania</u>

How best to send off my mother, Winifred (Winnie) Nancarrow? It's not something you discuss with your mother when she's just forty-five. Dying so young was not on our cards, not on our palms, not in our tea leaves. I know because she liked all those sorts of things. She was always on the look-out for something beyond religion. Apologies to those believers present, but she had a hard time believing in a god when she bore such witness to terrible cruelty.

It's a sure thing that she would have liked a fuss. Just what sort of fuss was the question. I know that she wasn't one for expense, or the fluffy sort of fuss. Nothing too stylish, nothing too exclusive or elegant or intimidating. She loved trees, especially the mountain ash, or what we call the rowan tree. And of course she adored her adopted homeplace of Tasmania. The island that's not feckin' Ireland, she called it. So, here we are, then, at Hobart's Royal Botanical Gardens, under the rowan tree.

Thank you, one and all, for coming along. I never would have thought I'd see such a number. And some of you from Ireland and all.

There are many faces that I don't recognise but I know she must have held in her thrall in some way. It was quite a thrall. You'll all have your stories about the redoubtable, incorrigible, rude, headstrong, glorious Winnie Nancarrow, and I ask that you tell them, keep them fresh. She would like that. Exaggerate them, by all means – she'd like that too.

I have just two stories that I'd like to share. The first is the story of the second greatest adventure my mother and I ever had, and it's the reason I have wheeled in a cannon for this occasion. My mother liked to do things with a bang, as you will shortly hear, and to go out with a bang would have given her great pleasure.

Many of you will know that our adventures together were plentiful, so you know this will be a good one. It takes place in the Royal Albert Hall, London, in November 1970. I was sixteen, pretending to be eighteen. My mother was thirty-two. We had been living – or hiding, I suppose – in various parts of London for most of my life. It was an exhilarating existence – a life in communes and squats, which I know sounds at odds with a secure childhood but was, in fact, the best possible childhood I could have hoped for. We were protected by a burgeoning underground scene whose alternative, human-rights-driven politics included taking care of their own. It also meant having fun, knocking about, laughing a lot. We were part-libertarian adventurists, part idiots. And as you must all know, with Winnie alongside, no one could ever harm me.

This group of 'dropouts with brains', as the press later described them, went on to protest against all sorts of right-wing regimes. Each time, they pushed the envelope a little further in the hope that they might attract media attention. But media policy was to ignore this kind of nuisance, so the group began to get slightly more explosive, so to speak. They sent out cheeky calling cards, tried to make national security look like eejits, that sort of thing. They called themselves the Angry Brigade, but much of the time I think Winnie was one of only a few who were truly angry. When the tenets of conservatism dealt blows, she was a direct hit. The pain of her injuries burned bright and long and furious. She wore her anger like armour, slept with it under her pillow, armed me with it too.

The night in question, just a few days shy of my seventeenth birthday, was the very first time my mother allowed me to accompany the group on one of their missions. We were protesting against the Miss World pageant and the media's role in perpetuating unrealistic ideas of womanhood. At two in the morning, my mother and I and two others placed a small amount of TNT wrapped in the *Times* newspaper under an American broadcast vehicle and blew the floor out of it. We knew we wouldn't be hurting anyone. We knew no one was around, but given that the attack targeted the media itself, we thought our protest would at least make the news. It didn't. Regardless, I saw my mother light up like a beacon that night. Without her action she would rumble about and pace and worry. She needed deeds not words.

A month or so later we caused a couple of explosions at the home of the Minister for Employment, and it was, as they say, on! After a total of twenty-five what they called 'bomb attacks', we had evidently caused quite enough niggle to the government, and they had had enough. Eight members of the group were put to trial. To this day I have no idea how my mother got us out of it. Pleaded for her daughter, perhaps. Handed over most of our savings, probably, because by the time she paid for two plane tickets to Australia, we had next to nothing.

We landed in Melbourne in late February 1971, to a thirty-six degree day. Winnie said, as only Winnie can, 'Smeg and feck, Byzantine, we'll have to go further south before this place burns our feckin' eyes out.' She needed her eyes to look over her shoulder every few seconds. Two of the Angry Brigade were sentenced to ten years in prison, so I suppose she had good reason. And so, after a few months of selling hairbrushes at a market stall, we flew as south as we could go, to Hobart. She was satisfied to see that it was raining when we landed.

But as I said, that was our second-best adventure. Now to the greatest adventure of all. This goes back in time a little more, to the fifties, in fact, when I was just a tiny baby. Many of you will know that my mother was just fifteen when she fell pregnant with me. As a result of rape. She will not mind me saying so, as she was never ashamed of her condition, never ashamed of me, despite *every single person* in Ireland telling her that shame, repentance and punishment were her only salvation. She wasn't having that.

On top of hard physical labour in the Home's affiliated laundries (which, by the by, laundered the stinking linens of the Department of Defence, the Bank of Ireland and several golf clubs), my mother was expected to tend to the children and babies of other women, pray to the Holy Father every morning and night, accept cruel treatment inflicted by many of the Bon Secours sisters. Regardless of how she was treated, and here's the clincher, she was expected to give her baby up so she could return home herself again, all disgrace erased.

Most of those young unmarried mothers did give up their babies. They handed them over or left them behind. And when they fought, they were separated from their infants by brute force. Their signatures were forged on adoption papers, sometimes birth certificates were falsified. All told, of the thousands and thousands of mothers and babies that crossed the hallways of these institutions, every single one of them was done a terrible injury. And from that injury, some of them never recovered.

My mother, our Winnie, was one of the ones who just knew from the start that of course she had a choice. And this is where the adventure part takes place (I'm sorry to bog you down in the suffering bit just there).

After my birth, when my mother woke from her drugged sleep to find herself alone, her baby gone, her milk coming in and her hands tied to the bed, she knew that she must do as she was told. Obedience, she understood from her upbringing around horses, gains reward. So, in her words, with every particle of her screaming for me, she tamped down her hatred and acted the part of a good little schoolgirl. She ate what little they brought her without complaint, she thanked them for their care. She drank chasteberry tea under supervision without objection, and when she was told later that it was prescribed to dry up breast milk, she did not react. She let them bind her breasts. And when she identified a kindly sister, Winnie told her funny rhymes and talked lovingly about God and asked her very politely whether she might take her to her baby, to give a proper Godspeed.

The kindly sister agreed and led my mother to an internal window, through which she could properly look at me for the first time. Apparently she sang me a little tune, some old nursery rhyme about Jesus that would please the sister. But she told me years later that the rhyme was a cover for the explosions that were happening inside her. She said that people in there had accused her of insanity, and that this moment at the nursery window was the only time in her life she felt actually insane.

'Bizzy, you caused an electricity inside of me,' she later told me, 'that could light up the whole world. I imagined for a moment that it might charge out of me and smash that glass between us, and even as I was being led away from you, I could still hear the last of the shattering, and was honestly unsure whether the glass was intact or not.'

A week or so later, as was this particular home's custom, my mother was pressed into the clothes she had arrived in, those months and a lifetime ago. A yellow frock, a cream cardigan, black Mary Jane shoes. Her hair was fixed and her makeup applied, along with a borrowed corset to hold in the empty flesh of her belly. She was brought to the front steps of the Bon Secours Mother and Baby Home, where the gardens were admirably groomed and the attendant nuns in their starched white were half-smiling in their forbearing way. She was told to clasp her hands and keep her chin down, and she duly obliged. Another nun, Mother Hortense, the one in charge, arrived and stood a step or two below my mother. In Mother Hortense's arms was me: two weeks old, dressed in frilly pink and screaming my head off.

Winifred must have lost some of her strict composure at that point, because Hortense hissed at her over my din, 'This is your final lesson, your moment of redemption. Your immense gratitude should be immediately evident.'

My mother set her face into a grateful smile as a smart station wagon turned into the driveway. It was driven very carefully, as though there was a baby already inside, and as my mother watched it approach she said she just sizzled with dread and irritation. I continued to scream.

Winnie said she can't remember much about the appearance of the couple that exited the station wagon. She just remembered that they were 'a queasy beige', and that the woman's hands, when she reached them out to take me from Mother Hortense, were as white and flawless as porcelain.

She stayed stock-still, my mother. She knew from the whispered accounts of others that a nod from one of the sisters would summon a burly man or two from some watching place. She hid her disgust as Mother Hortense switched on a sweet Godly voice to exclaim at the health of my lungs, as the beige woman jiggled me and laughed and avoided my mother's eyes. And then Winifred said in a loud, robotic voice, 'Thank you for your kind and generous act. I am most grateful to you both.' She unclasped her hands and crossed her fingers behind her back.

And then she watched while I was put inside the car and driven painstakingly away. She stayed still on the steps until the sisters' faces returned to their tight efficiency and began to move inside. Only when Mother Hortense called back to her, 'For God so loved the world that he gave his only son,' did my mother move.

She took a few short moments to lunge at Sister Hortense, grip her about the jaw with one strong hand and reply, 'Woe to those who call evil good and good evil!' then she booted Hortense in the shinbone and leapt down the steps three at a time, shouting over her shoulder, 'Book of Isaiah.'

She must have timed herself perfectly because no burly men appeared, and the only witness to her flight was an elderly gardener with a wooden leg, who wheezed after her, 'Run, duckie, run,' and waved his trowel.

The gates were still open and the station wagon was still doing its slow, self-important glide along the Dublin Road. But it was a long way ahead, and though she was fast and fit, my mother's confinement had willowed her quite a bit and she was no match for a motor car. She ran as fast as she could, but the vehicle moved further away. She told me that watching it get smaller as the distance between us grew was like having her heartstrings drawn out of her ribcage and pulled tighter and tighter until she was sure that even had she stopped running, she would have been dragged along by them, those invisible ligatures, and that maybe the pain of having her skin grazed against the road might at least put her heart-pain into some sort of relief.

And then, just before the car veered right and disappeared, she saw it pull over to the verge and stop. She thinks that by then she mightn't have been running at all, that the elastic stretch on our threads was pulling her along and that perhaps her feet weren't even touching the ground, and that there was a chance the ghosts of all the little vanished babies from the home were carrying her along too. She caught up with the car, and by this time the beige woman was out of it, jiggling me on the roadside. Her back was turned but her fluster was evident. There was something, Winifred said, about the way the woman's legs were slightly bent at the knees, how the toes of her shoes were just slightly turned in, and how her beige hat sat so prettily atop of her curls, that spoke of rampant uncertainty. And it made Winifred feel a wave of pity. She approached quietly. I screamed on.

'Put your finger in her mouth,' said my mother, and the woman wheeled around.

'What?' said she, wavering between astonishment and fear. Her eyes were saying, *How do I make it stop?*

'Like this.' My mother put out her hand and placed the knuckle of her index finger into my mouth. It was the first time she ever touched me. I stopped crying.

Mam asked her then, very nicely, whether she might hold me for just a second. 'They wouldn't let me have a true *slán leat*. And you know what they say about a baby who doesn't receive the goodbye blessing from her blood mother?' Winifred put on a very grave face and whispered, 'She will grow horns.' The beige woman's hands trembled and her knees bent a little more. My mother reached out and put her hands around me and the woman released her hold.

There's every chance, of course, that Mam's memory of this has changed with time, every chance that actually she snatched me back and gave this woman one to the shinbone too. She could be stretchy with the truth. But I like to believe this version. She said that in that moment, as she took me into her arms for the very first time, she felt a transfer of womanly understanding. It was interrupted, as these things are, by a shout from a man. The woman's husband.

'Sweet Jesus and Janey Mack,' he yelled. 'What the blazes is going on here?'

And with that, Mam was off and running again, this time with me in her arms. She began turning blindly back the way she came, but was cut off by a Bon Secours lorry filled with the burly men, who were properly burly but not very fast. They clambered out onto the road and ran after her but by then she'd already shimmied down off the verge into the ditch and back up the other side. And then she rolled me under the gap in a tall iron fence, squeezed herself after me and landed us in the midst of the Tuam Christmas races. The Parkmore Racecourse, you see, was just a stone's throw from the home.

Some of you will know that my mother grew up on racetracks, that her heart was always there, no matter how many other places it was putting itself. She knew these places like the back of her hand. She slowed to a respectable walk and carried me down to the rails, where she could weave us both into the thickest part of the crowd, then across to the grandstand and behind it to the backside, which is what they call the private stables where the horses are kept. We hid beneath the guinea stand, and this is where, she told me, she crouched and gave some long hungry moments to looking at me, to finding herself in the shape of my eyes and holding my wee hand. I cried again, though – hungry, I suppose – and a female hotwalker, an older woman, looked in on us.

'Ah,' said she. 'Ye must be why there's a ruckus out there. Ye be from the receiving home.'

Mam didn't offer a reply. The woman had a cigarette in her hand, and she took a few moments with that, then said. 'C'mere to me, then. Hurry up about it.' And she walked off towards the stables.

Mam and me followed.

'Do you know horses at all, at all?'

'I do,' said my mother.

'Know them well?'

'I do.'

'In here with you, so. Round the corners on the hay. You'll know what next.'

She swung open the door of a stable in which a wild-eyed chestnut thoroughbred stamped. 'He has the devil in him, but you look to me like you can manage even that.' And she pushed us inside and shut the gate behind us. We crouched down in the corner but were close enough to feel the heat off of the horse. Mam said she sent him up some clicks of her tongue and no scent of fear, and knew we were safe.

'Ah, be dog-wide of this one,' she heard the old woman shout before long, 'Only myself, his trainer and some sort of eejit would go near this horse. He'll kick your teeth in and your lights out quick as sin.'

Mam couldn't hear what the burly men said by way of reply, and she held me to her breast to keep me from crying. But the milk wouldn't let, and cry I did. The old woman gave a whistle and the horse neighed his almighty neigh, which might nearly have covered us, only didn't quite. The thoroughbred's gate was once more swung back and we were discovered.

(Now, I am thinking that many of you are sick of the sound of me by now, but I'm nearly there. And I promise that we'll keep the pies hot for you and the ale cold, don't worry.)

Anyhow, so our old woman bellowed, 'You've gone done it now, feck ye. You've upset His Highness, I'll have you ruled off quick as look at ye.' And then she gave another of her magical whistles and the great horse reared up over two of the men, then threw its hind hooves out at the other. No hoof connected with any of their lug heads, but the men were sent reeling long enough for Winifred and me to skedaddle from the stable and into the hotwalking yard, where a nervy-looking filly was frisking about on the end of a shank, awaiting her jockey.

The three men ignored the old woman and were on Winnie's heels as she shoved aside the filly's young hotwalker, grabbed the shank and hoisted us both up onto the filly's back. There was a bridle, but the incoming jockey had the saddle, so for the sake of an accurate picture, you have a stablehand on the ground, three big men running and a wild girl with a baby in her arms in a yellow frock astride a frisky bareback filly.

I see some disbelieving faces, or perhaps astonished ones. I also see some knowing nods. I don't think any of you are surprised to know that I can swear to you that all of it is true.

You might not be so surprised to know that we – being Winifred, the filly (whose name was Llanheld, by the way, it was etched into her bit) and myself – didn't get all that far. We did, however, get not very far extremely quickly. The filly was terrified, which is excellent for speed but not so good for safety. Winifred, who had exercised race horses since she was ten, had control of the horse physically but had not the experience to control her nerves. So we managed about six furlongs, which was all it took to deliver us to the Tuam train station in under a minute. There, we dismounted, and Winifred waved a five-pound ploughman at a boy.

'This is yours,' she said, 'if you return this filly to the racetrack. But you have to say you found her alone up by the saw mill. Say you promise.'

'I do,' said the wide-eyed boy. 'I promise.'

'And you know what happens to brown-haired boys who break their promises, don't you? Your father will have an accident on the twenty-fifth of May. This is truth, heed it well.'

The brown-haired boy nodded, took the money and the shank and led the twitching filly away. Winifred held me close and hid her ring finger and cried to the porter about losing her ticket, who took pity on her and let her on the train to Dublin without one.

'Where are your belongings, Madam?' he called out after her.

She did not reply until we were safely on the train, when she whispered into my little ear, 'You are my belongings.'

I am so terribly sad that she is leaving me, and all of us, so early. I might cry about now, yes, there we go. She wouldn't mind me crying. She had a hide like old boots but knew the value in a well-shed tear and a bit of wallow time. She would also ask me to laugh, because, let's face it, to think that Winifred's heart stopped while she was asleep is laughable and ludicrous. Died in her sleep when just the day before she was on the top of a bus flying an enormous *NO DAMS* helium balloon wearing just her knickers. She'd abseiled off buildings, set wild horses free, camped up trees and she died in her fecking sleep. Just goes to show that we shouldn't rest too long. And frankly, it's not funny to me. I'm just angry about the unfairness of it. She's been taken from me far too soon and that's not a bit funny. Her passing is a terrible thing. The pain of it is sure to burn bright and long and furious. I'll wear it for the rest of my days.

If I were to say something directly to her, it would be this:

Mam, you were my belongings. All I needed. I caught you looking from your hands to me many a time and I knew what you were thinking. You were thinking of the beige woman with the porcelain hands on the steps at Bon Secours. But Mam, I am far, far better off being raised by your colourful ways and your callused, resourceful worker's hands. Your hands lit other people's torches, they changed things for good, they taught, they *did*. I promise to you that I will carry on lighting the torches as best I can. Bright and long and furious. I will not rest too long.

Thank you all for listening. She loved every one of you, I know she would want me to tell you that. You can have a pie in a minute but first, off she goes with a bang.

(Cue cannon: BANG!)

𝄡

Stepping Stone Number 148 from *La Lista* by R.K.:
To pick up tiny shards of broken glass, press them with a thick slice of soft bread.

Chapter 17

How High We Can Climb

'While we haven't really gone anywhere near breaking the internet,' says Bizzy at choir rehearsal the following Tuesday, 'we have managed to go sort of low-grade viral.' She pauses, scanning the eyes in the room.

Some of the eyes are amused, others lowered in what could be shame. Quin's eyes are defiant, and Mary's eyes are not yet there because she is coming from footy training and is running late.

'We are receiving a great number of messages of support – and quite a few distinctly unsupportive ones – from all over Australia. We reached the national news.'

'Go me,' says Quin.

'This was not entirely part of the plan,' Bizzy continues. 'The suffragettes were meant to be a gentle starting point. Some singing and a wee bit of picketing. Instead, we displayed some *very juvenile* behaviour.'

'Oh, come on, Byzantine Nancarrow,' says Quin. 'You had the most fun since you helped decriminalise homosexuality in the nineties. We razzed that fire of yours right up.'

'And,' says Bizzy, ignoring Quin but unable to contain her smile any longer, 'though I don't like to admit it, the Join the Chorus campaign has kicked off with far more success than I could have hoped for. And we still have more than five months before the actual rally day.'

'Ha,' says Quin.

Bizzy continues. 'We've caught the attention of the masses, which is what a consciousness-building initiative is meant to do. We've had a zillion suggestions from people wishing to further the feminist cause, from caregiver groups to the LGBTQI+ community, arts organisations, Soroptimists, the women's football league . . .'

'The Safe at Home initiative wants us to help raise funds for their helpline,' says Kyrie. 'A vital resource for victims of domestic violence.'

'And, to bring it back to my original muse,' Bizzy says, winking at Freycinet, 'there's a group working to revive the wages for housework project of the 1970s.'

Frey smiles, but feels mildly uncomfortable. 'That's great news about Safe at Home.'

'There are a great many angry women out there,' says Rosanna.

'Yes,' Bizzy says. 'At last look we have 58,000 social media followers.'

'Heck!' says Irene. 'We'll have to section everyone into brigades.'

'It's war!' shouts Quin.

'Oh God, is it that bad?' Mary has come in, flushed with rush and panting. 'Are we under arrest?'

'I don't think so,' says Bizzy. 'Though it wouldn't be such a terrible thing. You could do a hunger-strike protest and we could bail you out after we make a stinging statement about use of police resources, civil disobedience harm versus domestic violence and so on.'

Mary sits on Bizzy's knee. 'Do you still love me, Bizzy? I am sorry. I was under the intoxicating influence of Quinella Doyle. And it was fun, wasn't it. Wasn't it?'

'Don't blame me, Mary Dempsey St-Clair,' says Quin. 'You're the one working on the reinvention of the feminist manifesto.'

'I never said anything about flashing your growler.'

'Well, I'm not one to beat about the bush,' says Quin with a guffaw.

'Get off me, you great sweaty heffalump,' says Bizzy, giving Mary a shove.

'Everyone at footy has seen us on the interwebs,' Mary says as she finds herself a chair.

'I think Quin's done us all a service,' says Sally. 'Nature gave us pubic hair to reduce friction during intercourse. It's ridiculous to have to wax it all off for the sake of misshapen ideals.'

'I'll bet there's been some backlash, though,' says Irene, 'regarding the growler.'

'Yeah, heaps of people have been sledging us,' says Eleanor.

'But the point is,' says Bizzy, 'with every rebuke from some sexist or pre-enlightened member of the public, there is a response from someone who is standing up for us, someone who agrees. We've started the conversation again, and now we're going to have to keep it going. We owe it to our forebears.'

'So what is it we're doing, precisely?' asks Irene.

'Irena,' says Rosanna, 'we are giving the world a reimagining. Building a beautiful road to the mountaintop.'

Avni gasps, takes up a notebook and pen.

'More songs coming?' asks Eleanor.

'I think so,' says Avni. 'You wondrous women fill me with songs. Soon I'll have one for each of you.'

'And a campaign song?' Rosanna suggests.

'Well,' says Avni, 'I can try.'

'If we have a song,' says Irene, 'we'll need a salute.'

'A salute?' asks Mary. 'Of course, a salute! Every effective movement has one.'

'You mean like the Nazis?' asks Eleanor.

'Not like the Nazis,' says Irene. 'You know, like a raised fist or something.'

'Probably not a raised fist,' says Bizzy, 'since it's already aligned with communism.'

'I'll ask Harvey,' says Irene. 'He loves the military.'

'How about a raised hand?' suggests Kyrie. 'The left hand, with a straight arm, like you're in a classroom asking to be heard.'

'And if we raise the index finger, pointing to the sky, to show how high we can climb,' says Rosanna. She raises her hand and demonstrates, her arm poker-straight and close to her ear.

Frey looks at how big Rosanna's hands seem on the end of her spindle-like arms and wonders whether today she will share the news of her failed cancer trial.

'I like it,' says Bizzy, trying the salute herself. 'See me, listen to me, I am not invisible.'

All the choristers raise their left arms and point straight up.

'The AWC salute,' says Mary.

'Can we promise not to get all Shulamith Firestone and suggest that women can't be free until all babies are made in laboratories?' asks Sally.

'Shulie Firestone's ideas were quite prescient, though,' says Bizzy. 'I wouldn't be surprised if they don't seem so extreme in the near future. And I think she was right when she said that liberating women means liberating children. Helicopter parenting is a very real threat to human development.'

'And I'm all for baby-making in labs,' says Quin. 'Now that I'm carrying one and *my* lab is as bloated as fuck.'

'You are very big for your first,' says Eleanor.

'Can always rely on Eleanor to call a spade a fucken spade,' says Quin.

Bizzy gives Quin a hard look. 'Quinella, thank you for kickstarting things but consider yourself on warning. You are not to embark on any activity without clearing it with one of us first. And clearance may not come from Mary. You two are dangerous together, and we must keep one another safe.'

'We could throw confetti around, or uncooked rice,' suggests Eleanor. 'It makes an unholy mess. I know because I've started cleaning St Matthew's Church in Glenorchy.'

'Can we try,' says Bizzy, 'to remember my point about this being a consciousness-raising exercise? A gentle one. If we get all disruptive and shove all of society's inauthenticities and compromises in everyone's faces all at once, we risk pissing people off, or sending everyone barking mad.'

'Or pushing their default detachment settings into overdrive so they just switch off,' says Sally. 'We've all seen that happen.'

'I sometimes miss my switched-off days,' says Kyrie. 'It was quite relaxing being shut off to the injustices of the patriarchy. I've broken two teeth with my jaw-clenching since I met you, Bizzy.'

'Oh my God,' says Frey. 'I'm always clenching my jaw.'

'You'll break a tooth soon too, no doubt,' Kyrie says. 'I have to wear a nightguard now. Cost a bomb.'

Rosanna laughs and sings a few bars of 'The Liniment Girl'. *She'll show you all the lies, baked into apple pies and served up with cream . . .*'

Bizzy hesitates. Rosanna's voice seems huskier than ever. She glances at Kyrie, who is also looking at Rosanna with a worried expression.

'I think my broken teeth improved my resonance,' says Irene.

'My mother-in-law completely denies the existence of the patriarchy,' says Sally, 'and she has dentures. So I'm thinking we'd carry even more tension in our jaws if we hadn't been enlightened.'

'Has Frey met your mother-in-law yet, Sally?' asks Kyrie.

'No,' says Frey.

They watch as Sally alters her posture to a poker-straight back, then peers at the choristers with a supercilious expression.

'Oh, hello, Mrs Eyreton,' says Rosanna. 'We haven't seen you in a while.'

'Well, hello, Freycinet,' Sally says in an upper-class accent. 'How nice to meet you. I see you're hobnobbing with this lot. I do hope they haven't corrupted you into thinking women are oppressed or anything like that. It's all in their mainds, you know, all in their hypersensitive mainds. And I hear you've had a spot of trouble with your man. You know this infidelity is not his fault, don't you? You mustn't have been giving him enough attention. A ram won't jump the fence if the clover is at his feet, will he? Have you tried a scented douche? A ribbon in your hair? The poor man, having to do all that clever deception and go to all that inconvenience for his wellbeing.'

Frey laughs. Sally stands and performs a little clap, a couple of steps of dance and a dramatically embellished pose right in front of Frey.

'Sally was wasted in the health science,' says Rosanna.

'Why thank you, Mrs Eyreton,' Frey says, 'I will take your advice on board and—'

'Shove it up your clacker,' shouts Quin, raising her left arm in the AWC salute.

'Avni,' says Frey, still laughing, 'maybe you should write a song called "Broken Teeth".'

'Or a satire song in the voice of Mrs Eyreton,' says Mary.

'Speaking of songs,' says Bizzy. 'Let's sing. We're a choir, after all.'

𝄐

The choir only just manage to get to their second song ('The Flower Duet', which has startling menace when arranged for an angry women's choir and translated into English – 'rowdy birds' and so on) when Bizzy's hands suddenly cup a downward 'stop' motion. Frey, floundering in the altos, misses the gesture entirely and her breathy high-C is left hanging alone for an undignified second in the air before she stops, mortified, and sees that Paul Bellavance has strode into the room.

'Don't stop on my account, please sing on,' he says. 'Sounding excellent, ladies.'

'We only sing for an invited audience,' says Bizzy.

'Well, in that case, I won't keep you. I just wanted to pass on some news. The new owners of the building were in two minds as to whether they wanted to demolish and start from scratch. They had put it on the backburner and were happy to maintain their existing tenant agreements.'

'And?' prompts Bizzy, impatient with the obvious relish Bellavance is taking in the delivery of his news.

'And, in light of your recent, er, exposure'—he looks at Quin— 'and the elevation of your profile, they've decided instead to proceed with demolition.'

'You're full of shit,' says Quin. 'I bet they're not.'

'They are a Chinese firm, you see. A family firm, with very traditional beliefs, one of them being that modesty is essential. They are justifiably horrified to be in any way associated with groups considered lacking in common decency.' He seems unable to control the disgust on his face, his top lip curling upwards and his nose twitching. Bizzy wonders how he could ever have been considered handsome.

He directs his sour look at Freycinet. 'And Frey, I had a chat to your other half.'

Bizzy watches as Frey makes a valiant attempt to hold herself still.

'He thought your idea of Barnes and Rutherford buying this place was hilarious. He's not the slightest bit interested in this old shitter.'

'Yes, I imagine he did say that, Paul,' Frey says. 'He's Hobart's most successful property developer, unlikely to give away anything to a rival. He was cross with me for talking about it. So I'll stop right now.' She places a cheeky hand over her mouth and giggles.

Paul Bellavance and his swagger both waver a fraction.

Heavens, thinks Bizzy. *She's good.*

'The other thing you might like to know,' he continues, recovering, 'is that I am shortly, owing to a cabinet reshuffle, taking on the role of Minister for Arts *and* . . .' He dishes up his most charming smile. 'Minister for Women.'

'Piss off,' says Quin.

'Now you really must be joking,' says Mary.

'I think,' says Bellavance, 'that owing to my past history of service to women, I am a superb choice.' He smiles his Guy Smiley smile.

'And giving us this news is a threat, yes?' says Rosanna. 'You will shimmy things around in the Arts portfolio to ensure we have no voice?'

'It's too late for that,' says Quin. 'We already have a voice. And a platform.'

'Hey, hey,' Bellavance says, 'keep your pants on, Quinella.' He laughs at his own joke. 'You all know how much I value the contribution of women *and* the arts. My wife and I are ballroom dancers, we like to go to the theatre. I was quite the thespian at school but I had to choose leadership over drama as I was footy captain and head prefect, so . . . Anyway, I'm very much looking forward to my new gig. But I won't stand by and watch the highly regarded Tasmanian arts scene denigrated by one very outspoken group, whose views are not shared by the masses and who *must not* speak for everyone.'

Quin sneers at him and says, 'Off you fuck, then, if you don't want to watch.'

𝄡

The angry repertoire feels a little saggy to Bizzy after Paul Bellavance's interruption and haughty departure. Instead of lifting their determination and engaging their diaphragms, he has evidently depleted the choristers. Bizzy glances up into the spangle of Laetare's unsuspecting walls and dusty, oblivious flowers and finds her own voice wavering. There is a drift of spray-on snow in the corner of a window from some long-ago Christmas. It makes her heart ache.

'Shall we sing a sad song, to match our mood?' she asks as they draw Aretha Franklin's 'Chain of Fools' to a close. 'Just wade on in and wallow?'

'Yes, that is a good idea,' says Rosanna. 'There is some wallowing to do, before we organise all our strength together for rally. We should sing "Meet Me in the Middle of the Air" by Paul Kelly.'

'Oh, gawd, no,' Mary says with a grimace. 'Not that miserable dirge again.'

'Please?' says Rosanna. 'For me.'

'Oh, Rosanna,' Kyrie whispers, trying not to cry.

Bizzy's heart aches a little more as she lifts her hands to conduct the choir into Paul Kelly's interpretation of Psalm 23. A little way in, Bizzy feels Rosanna's eyes on hers. She looks into them, two dark windows filled with telling and sorrow, with a beautiful, husky voice to match. It snakes out and takes Bizzy's sunken heart and gives it a squeeze. By the final few lines, Bizzy's hands are motionless in the air and she can't see the choir for her tears. She wants the song to go on and on so she doesn't have to hear the words that are in those eyes.

But it does end, and Rosanna does speak. 'Thank you,' she says. 'You have confirmed for me that you will sing this song at my funeral, please. In about four weeks.'

'What?' exclaims Mary.

'My chemotherapies trial has ended,' says Rosanna. 'We are laying down our weapons so I can enjoy the last part in peace.'

There is a hubbub of emotion. Bizzy finds herself unable to move. She feels Kyrie's hands lead her to a chair.

'Bloody stupid fucken cancer,' says Quin. 'I'd like to rip it a new arsehole.'

'It should be me dying,' says Eleanor, who has turned white.

'No, no,' says Rosanna. 'Not when you are just finding your feelings again.'

'What can we do?' asks Irene.

'Just as I have said,' Rosanna replies, 'please sing at my funeral. Also, raise your voices, get others to join your chorus. Take my ashes with you to the rally so I can join the chorus.'

Mary whimpers.

'And one more thing: when I am on my death bed, I want you all to, one by one, bring me a secret.'

'A secret?' says Sally.

Rosanna nods. 'A secret. Because I love a good secret, and there is no better person to take your secret than a dying woman. I will have them to keep me company in the hereafters.' She looks around the room. 'Bring those tears too, if you need to. Tears are good. And if you want to bring a goodbye then that is okay too. But I will not have goodbyes to give. No goodbyes from me.' She puts a hand on Bizzy's shoulder. 'Too many demolitions today, Bizzy, I am sorry to add more. This news of Laetare is unexpected and too much. Was this the wrong way to tell you now?'

'No,' says Bizzy through her tears. 'You told me with music, and there can't be any better way.'

𝄡

Stepping Stone Number 52, from *La Lista* by R.K.:
Don't peak in high school.

Chapter 18
Tell the Bees

Each member of the choir departs rehearsal carrying the news of Rosanna's dwindling days in their differing ways. But all of them, without exception, re-enter their individual lives and find them cast in a new and gloomy light.

𝄡

Sally takes the news out into her garden, where the fading yellow of her wattle tree tries to shout it down. She sits among vanilla lilies, the acaena buzzies and the pigface flowers and the kind, soothing whispers of the sagg grass. She takes off her shoes and socks and scratches her toes into the earth, tugs out a young ribbon of sagg and chews its white end. And she waits for the sadness to seep into the earth, to rest with taken songs and lost words and other sorrowful things Country can hold.

𝄡

In Avni, the sad news is music – brooding melodies and dark lyrics and heavy beats. They flush her cheeks and threaten to burst her capillaries. She scribbles them into what Rosanna called her songs book, thrums them into her guitar and sings them in a new tone that halts her boyfriend as he walks past the doorway. 'That,' he says to her when she sees him, 'is a sound that could break the hearts of journeymen and riddle believers with doubt.' He kisses her burning forehead and pours her a cup of settle-down cardamom tea.

𝄡

Irene unpacks the news with the groceries she'd picked up before choir. She sits, looking at it sadly, until Harvey shuffles in at long last and says, 'Are you all right, Myrene?'

And Irene says no she's not all right, that her friend Rosanna from choir is dying and will be gone very soon. 'And she wants us all to visit her and tell her a secret. I can't think of a secret good enough. I keep my marmalade recipe a secret but that's not something she'll want to be taking to her grave. Is it?'

'I can give you the best secret of all,' says Harvey, sliding into the breakfast nook beside Irene.

'Go on, then,' says Irene, shuffling over.

'I am on the Other Side.' He pauses for dramatic effect. 'And it is very nice, thank you very much. No luggy things like dying eco-systems and war. Everything has to float, you see. We can have wings if we like. Tell her that one.'

Irene smiles. 'Thank you, Harv.' And she rests her head on his shoulder and he puts his warm arm around her, the way he always did. 'Don't forget to tell the bees,' he says. 'Else they'll feel left out, get in a huff and stop their work.'

'Can't have that at the height of spring,' says Irene. 'I'll tell them now.' She ambles outside with her sadness in one hand and Harvey's secret in the other.

𝄡

Eleanor has no idea at all what to do with the news. She carries it clumsily around with her until the following week when she goes to clean St Matthew's and thinks to place it neatly at the feet of the priest, Father Mac. He accepts it with such practised humanity and careful wisdom, that Eleanor feels a twinge in her chest she has never felt before. It alarms her, the twinge, and she fumbles a hymnbook and rips a page, which brings a tear to her eye. A tear! She mends the hymnbook with sticky tape and extra care, re-polishes the candlesticks and hurries home to Penelope, hoping the Rosanna sadness will stay with Father Mac for long enough to let her sleep.

'Sleep,' she whispers to Penelope later that night, 'is very disturbed by feeling. No one sleeps like the dead. Or someone that's dead inside.'

She stares into the darkness of her small bedroom and discovers that she is slightly wistful for her previous, very recent life without emotions. She wonders whether she can give them all to Father Mac.

𝄡

Mary takes Rosanna's news, scrunches it into a ball of focused determination and uses it to finish the first draft of her thesis, which does indeed take on the tone of a manifesto for revolution. Thoughts of her dear Rosanna's brutal kindness powers her work, swirls it into pages and pages of wild, woolly and imaginative disruption.

𝄡

Quin takes the Rosanna news to a bench in St David's Park, where her friend Petal is dozing among all her worldly possessions. These include a Queen Elizabeth jubilee mug, a ginger cat called Mango and a spinal fusion that makes sleeping rough even rougher. Quin knows she won't have to speak, that Petal will be able to hear her even without words. Petal has heard it all.

13

After a night of tossing and turning with Rosanna's news, Bizzy gets up at dawn and stands in her garden, lights up a cigarette, draws on it luxuriously and blows a perfect smoke ring into the air.

A screen door bangs, and a minute later, a small rumpled head pokes up above the fence line.

'Hello, Ferris.'

Ferris's face appears. It is squashy with sleep. 'Hi Bizzy,' he says. 'How are you?'

'Not good,' says Bizzy. 'My dear friend is going to die soon.'

Ferris blinks, and Bizzy feels a wobble in her stomach, realising how much she loves this boy. The way his thinking shows in his face and in the dear little movements of his hands. His flexible acceptance of things. 'What's their name?' he asks. 'Your friend?'

'Rosanna.'

'Rosanna,' he repeats. 'Why will she be dead?'

'Because she has a terrible disease and she can't recover from it.'

'My Opa has a terrible disease. The top of his head went all spotty and so did his ears. They had to cut off a lot of his ears but they left a bit at the top for him to rest his glasses on. He has some dints on his boiled head.'

To Bizzy's dismay, she loses her grip on a short burst of laughter.

Ferris smiles, then shouts some laughter too, then a bit more. The two of them laugh together until finally Ferris recovers some solemnity and says, 'Shall we do some crying for your Rosanna?'

'Yes, that would be grand, Ferris, thank you.'

So Ferris produces some tears so perfect that Bizzy has to put her hand on his hair over the fence. The rounded warmth of his head is so comforting she feels that it must be actually absorbing some of her sadness.

'Thank you, Ferris,' she says, feeling a Ferris-sized bit lighter, 'for letting me share my sad news.'

'That's all right. Bye, Bizzy.'

'Bye bye, Ferris.'

𝄡

Kyrie, lighter now that she's given Rosanna's news to the choristers, drives away from Laetare Gardens and reflects on what Rosanna has brought to her life: both a lively effervescence and a profound settling, with the additional carbonating effect of four grandchildren.

'Thank you, universe,' she says to the sky, 'for the gift of Rosanna. And curse you for taking her away again.'

She shakes an angry fist, then stops and buys a bottle of prosecco, because, despite her recent unburdening, everything in the atmosphere feels entirely flat.

𝄡

Rosanna sends the news in emails to Italy.

Wednesday, 16 October 2019

Dear Matteo,

I am sorry to say that I am going to die soon. The medical trial kept me going for much longer than we thought, so I do not feel too sad. If you dearly wish to come to Tasmania for my funeral, then my family would very much like to see you. We can pay for your trip because I never paid you back the

money you gave me to run away. I know I have said this to you
before but here it is in writing: You gave me everything that
day, Matteo. You have seen my Jonathon and our beautiful
children so you know what I mean.

If you cannot come, then please know that this is fine, and
I will be floating over to you anyway. You will see me in the
mountains, and in the Apennine when the snow melts into it.

In case I do not write again, thank you for your letters and
FaceTimes over the years. They have brought me home. And it
has been a great joy to see you healthy and happy. I cannot do
FaceTimes now because you would not like to see a skeleton on
the screen! I look very scary with death, especially because you
haven't seen me for a while. No more round face!

Cry for me, laugh like you always do, then get on with being
the kind person you are.

With greatest love,

your sister, Rosanna.

P.S. I will send a letter to our mother and father now too.
They could need you to tell them (if you can get them out of
the kneeling position in the Santa Maria del Suffragio) because
last time I sent them a letter was in 2009 just before the
earthquake, and they might burn it before opening this time
around.

𝄢

Thursday, 17 October 2019

Dear Mother and Father,

I wish to tell you that I will be dying soon. I am telling you in
my English words because I think they will translate softly for

you. And because now I dream in English and it feels better.
I hope it is better for you.

We tried with the medicines but they have not worked. I do
not want you to attend to me in Tasmania because I know the
flight to here will be difficult. Do not feel badly that you will not
be here for my funeral. You will be there in other ways, I know.

I do not have any bad feelings for you. I know that everything
you have done is with your best intentions. One day I hope that
you might meet my children in L'Aquila, if they choose to travel
there. If they do, they will take me home with them when they go.
It is still home, just as much as Tasmania is home. You will always
be my mother and my father. I will always be your daughter.

I thank you for the prayers you have sent out for me. I wish
health and love to you both and to my siblings.

Rosanna

𝄡

Frey uses the news of Rosanna's imminent passing to sharpen the blades
on the lawnmower, mend a faulty catch on the washing machine and
sand back the peeling windowsills at the back of the house. When
that is done, she is dismayed to see that it is not yet noon. The hot
stones in her stomach have turned cold and are beginning to make
her feel queasy. Mending a piece of loose guttering on the roof eases
the nausea only slightly, so she searches for something else to fix. Her
pacing of the house eventually takes her to the wardrobe, where she
dresses in a grey pants suit, red heels and Tom's Metallica T-shirt.
In the bathroom she applies lipstick to match her shoes and messes
her hair into ragged waves. Then she leaves the house with her heart
turned expertly to stone, and demolition on her mind.

At the entrance to the trendy warehouse offices of Barnes and
Rutherford on Hobart's Mac Point, a receptionist tops up a large vase

filled with cream-coloured tulips. Above his head is a row of identical glass balls containing retro light bulbs. On the wall is an oil painting featuring various shades of white and a slash of cream. Frey chose it to match the leather couches, the tufted rug on the floor. Today it also matches the tulips, and the receptionist's tie.

Frey walks in through the glass doors, smiles at the receptionist and says, 'Hello, Alistair, I have an appointment to see Gil.'

'You do?' says Alistair, looking puzzled.

'Under the name of Vida Goldstein.' Frey laughs. 'It's a private joke.'

'Right,' says Alistair. 'Well, you look snazzy. Vida.' He regards Frey's appearance approvingly. 'I love your hair like that. He's just on the phone I'll let you know when he's done.'

'Thanks.'

'How're the kids?'

'Very well, thank you.' Frey wonders whether he'd asked Gil the same question this morning. She presumes not. 'How're your dogs?'

'They're great,' Alistair says. 'I'm getting a third because I've been diagnosed with high blood pressure, and patting dogs can lower it again, apparently. Oh, he's off the phone. Go ahead, Frey. He's free until two.'

'Thanks, Alistair.' She walks towards the lift, turns back and adds, 'We should inject some colour in here. Maybe some scatter cushions? Purple and green.'

'Okay?' replies Alistair, looking sceptical.

'We could get you a purple, green and white striped tie to match.' Frey leaves him looking even more puzzled and enters the lift. Once the door closes, Frey whispers to herself, 'Deeds, not words.'

In his glass-walled office with a view of the docks, Gil sits at his immense, Huon-pine-topped desk. He glances up as Frey enters. 'Hey,' he says.

'Hi, sweetheart,' she says with a smile.

'You look nice, what are you . . .? I have a one o'clock appointment, Alistair—'

'*I'm* your one o'clock,' says Frey, taking a seat and stroking some dust from the rubber plant on Gil's desk.

Gil laughs. 'You're Vida Goldstein?'

'Yes, and we need to talk business.' She shifts forward in her chair. 'I have sent you an email. You won't have read it because you never read my emails, but I sent it at twelve forty today. It might even be in your junk folder. Could you have a look, please? Subject line, "Hello, Darling".'

'Right, well, this sounds exciting.' He doesn't seem excited, though, Frey notes. His face is expressionless.

I don't excite him at all, Frey thinks. She waits as Gil scans his inbox.

'Got it.'

'Okay, open it.'

Gil clicks on the email. Frey watches as his eyes register the contents. 'Oh, God,' he says. 'Oh my God, Frey . . .' His expression is blankly shocked.

Frey stands and walks briskly to his side of the desk. 'Ooh, I especially like this one,' she says, pointing at a photo of Gil's naked body as he thrusts into Skye Killinger. 'Look at the definition in your arms.'

'Don't, Frey,' Gil says, clicking out of the email.

Frey fixes her gaze to his darting eyes and says, 'You're saying "don't" to me?'

He stands, paces the room, closes his eyes, rubs his hair.

Frey watches.

'So,' he says eventually, 'I don't get it. You sent that woman? Was she a private detective or something?'

'Yep,' says Frey. 'She's something. Her name's Roxy and you seriously don't want to mess with her. Now, I'd like you—'

'Look, Frey, this isn't—'

Frey raises her hand and says, 'Shhh,' then returns to her seat and gestures to Gil to do the same. 'I need you to answer some questions, and I will know if you are lying. First, are you in love with Skye Killinger?'

'No.'

'That's a lie.'

'I don't know.'

'That's a lie too.'

'Not the way I love you.'

'How do you love me?'

Gil looks confused. 'You're my wife.'

'Does she love you?'

'She says so, yes.'

'Are you planning to leave me for her?'

'No.'

'So were you planning to continue the affair behind my back? Behind your children's backs?'

'No.'

'Lie.'

'I hadn't really thought about it. I wasn't thinking.'

'How long has it been going on?' Frey watches resignation droop his shoulders.

'Not long.'

'Liar.'

'Three and a half years. On and off.'

Frey only just manages to stop her mouth from opening in shock. *Three and a half years?* She clears her throat. 'On and off?'

He looks at his hands. 'I tried to call it off.'

'Another lie.' Frey brings her fist down onto the desk.

Gil jumps. 'She called it off twice.'

'Why?'

'Because we felt . . . she felt bad.'

'Where did you meet?'

'At the Blundstone Arena development. She provided some artwork.'

'Did you instigate the affair?'

'I suppose I did. I called her first. Frey, I—'

'Do you love me?'

'Yes.' Gil's eyes stay on hers as she silently counts to ten.

'As much as you love her?' She counts again, holding his gaze.

'More,' he says, but at four seconds he looks downwards and to the right. 'I love you more,' he says to the carpet.

'No further questions,' Frey says. 'I've booked you into an Airbnb for seven nights. During that time you need to find somewhere else to live. I will pack up the things you need myself, and have them delivered when you have a fixed address. Any further correspondence can be done through my family lawyer, Kyrie Kalbfel, who will be in touch regarding my custody of the children, and a division-of-wealth plan. And, just so you know, I'm not even sure what might happen with these photos because my anger could well take control of that.' She stands. 'I mean, your mum's always asking for family shots.'

Gil stares at her, the odd blankness strange against the anger in his eyes. His face is pale, sheened with sweat. 'Frey, come on. We can work through this. People do all the time, and come out stronger. I fucked up, I wasn't feeling connected. I fell for someone because she seemed so completely into me. It fed my ego, I don't know. Please, I don't want to lose my family.' He begins to cry. 'I'll do anything.'

Frey watches him for a long moment, then sits back down. 'You will end this affair with Skye Killinger?'

'Yes.'

'You will work harder at our marriage? For our family?'

'Yes, yes of course.'

'You will accept that I may not make you feel "connected" for a period of time? Because I'll be grappling with quite a lot of hurt and anger that I will have to "work through" in my way. I'm not sure how that's going to manifest.'

'What does that mean?'

Frey opens her bag and takes out a small aerosol can. Without leaving her chair, she leans down and sprays a large, bright-red capital A on the cream carpet.

Gil leaps out of his chair. 'What the fuck, Frey!'

Frey sprays a circle around the A. 'Oops,' she says, 'the old scarlet-letter trick. That's the kind of thing I mean. Small acts of revenge. Feels a tiny bit better already.'

'Jesus H. Christ.'

'He won't help you.'

Gil is wary. 'Look, Frey, I know you have a bit of bad-arse about you, I've witnessed it before – especially on the tennis court, even though you try to hide it. And now you're mixed up with that Angry Women's Choir, I can see where this could be headed. But can we just, like, go to therapy?'

'Yes, we need couples therapy, too.'

'You won't send those photos to Mum?'

'No, if you end the affair, I'll get rid of the pictures so at least I can't stoop that low.' She imagines crossing her fingers. More lies.

'Okay.' He stands, leans over Frey and tucks a wave of hair behind her ear. 'I'm an arsehole, I've done the wrong thing, and I will make it better, I promise.' He kisses her.

She wonders who has taken the word 'sorry' from his vocabulary and how deeply they buried it. But her heart is softening; there are tears threatening. She puts her lips to his ear and says, 'I don't want to lose our family either. Don't ever do this to us again.' Noting the catch in her voice, her bravado wilting, she pushes him away and stands up. 'There is another thing you can do, Gil. Something that means a lot to me.'

'Yes?' Gil's eyes display what looks like genuine eagerness to please.

'I sent a second email, subject line "Laetare Gardens". You just need to follow the instructions.'

𝄡

Stepping Stone Number 58, from *La Lista* by R.K.:
Take photos. Not hundreds for each occasion, just one or two. Scenery photos are better with people in them, unless you are a very good photographer. At the end of the year, have them printed and put them in an album with captions and give them to someone in your family (or yourself) for Christmas.

Chapter 19

Raar

Grace arrives at Derwent Dance Academy's Sunday morning class shortly after it has started. She'd risen early but decided just a little too late to run the nine kilometres from Lower Sandy Bay to the Lenah Valley dance studio. The other dancers have almost finished their warm-up when Grace slips into Studio Two.

She is instantly aware of the change she brings to the room, recognises the temperature drop. She steels herself against it, smiles at the teacher and says, 'Sorry I'm late. I hope you don't mind me joining this class.'

'Not at all, Grace,' says the young instructor. 'We're more than happy to have you.' But the teacher seems wary too, her face flushes and she blinks a lot, like shy people do.

They all hate me, thinks Grace. But she pushes the thought aside and takes herself to a far corner of the room.

Grace had been about twelve when she discovered the power of pairing beauty with aloofness. And by the time she grew tired of that game, the facade had taken hold – at least in the minds of her peers – and become hard to shake. Her awareness of her beauty had come well before that, reflected back by people all around her, all the time.

She sees it now in Studio Two: the darting eyes, the heightened gestures, the feigned disregard.

She knows most of the other dancers; many of them around her age, few of them at a standard to match hers. One male dancer, Lyric Chen, has recently moved to Hobart from Burnie and been in the paper as Tasmania's next big thing. Grace is interested to see his form. His dance partner, Harper Goodwin, performed with the National Ballet when she was thirteen. Both of them are there, pretending not to have seen her.

Grace also identifies Hannah Farrell and Serra Kalbfel (both good but not very focused), Chelsea Edwards (too tall), Tara Dabrowski (weird feet), Claudia Le Strange (too cute), and Esperance Bellavance (too bouncy).

At the barre, Grace notices that Lyric Chen's *fondu* is shallow and in *relevé* it shudders. In the centre, Harper Goodwin's *grand battement* is imprecise and at the end, her *reverence* looks hammy, like something from a Shakespeare comedy. These small imperfections keep Grace buoyed, because she senses deficits in her own performance too. She is tired, wishes she hadn't run to class. But she glimpses Harper's thighs through the sheer material of her training skirt as they head for the change room, and she is pleased she ran. *No one wants a chunky ballerina*, thinks Grace. Her mind strays to Harry. *Piss off*, she thinks.

'So you're doing Sundays as well, are you, Grace?' Harper asks as Grace is changing her shoes. Her voice is a semitone away from baby.

'Yep.' Grace keeps her back turned.

Harper presses on regardless. 'What are you doing for Showcase?'

'I don't know yet,' says Grace. This is true. Her 'Thousand Years' routine has begun to feel a bit forced. Dancing to a love song when love has made a dick of you will do that.

'Oh gosh, really? We've known for ages what we're doing. Took us a while to decide which routine, though. Lucky we get pairs and solo.'

Grace closes her mouth against the question Harper is fishing for, but thinks it instead. *Why do you get pairs and solo?*

Harper can't help herself. 'We reckon we're getting both because Lyric's the only dude in Seniors. Also he's Asian so, you know, diversity!' She laughs again. 'And my background with the National attracts new enrolments.'

Grace can't help herself either. 'Oh my gosh, you're sooo amazing, Harps,' she overenthuses. 'I'm sooo jealous.'

Harper's cute facade falls away. 'Are you taking the piss?'

'Yes.' Grace holds Harper's gaze until Harper looks away.

The other girls, who have been chatting, fall silent.

'You think you're so great, Grace Barnes.' Harper yanks her track-suit pants on under her training skirt.

'Harper,' says Serra Kalbfel.

'No, Serra, she's been strutting around acting superior for long enough.'

'I couldn't give a shit who's in the room, Harper,' says Grace. 'I'm just here to dance.'

Harper laughs. 'Yeah, horizontal folkdance with Harry Fenton.'

'Harper, shut up,' says Serra.

'Yeah, shut up, Harper,' says Tara Dabrowski.

But Harper's words have slapped Grace. She hasn't told a soul about Harry. She catches a kind smile from Serra but doesn't return it. *I want no part of this fucked-up Gen Z confederacy*, she thinks as she turns to face the wall, shoving her AirPods in her ears. But she doesn't switch on any music. She listens instead to the furious pounding of her heart and the ragged breaths she is struggling to control. *That fuckhead Harry*, she thinks. *How could he be such an arsehole?* But a heartbeat later, *How could I be such a moron?*

She sits on the bench to tie her shoes, dizzy from the weeks since Harry reduced himself to a ghost. The nights of tears, the reliving of every second of their every interaction, from the moment he first indicated interest (a smile at Tom's footy game) to those last three message dots inside their vanishing bubble. Not a word from him except this, now, his silence broken via fuck knows how many gossiping people. This new pain, betrayal pain, swells up alongside the ache of rejection. It seems to take up just as much space in her chest as the fluttering joy of first love. But instead of languishing in her limbs and softening her focus, the pain sharpens her, flexes her resolve, makes it clear that no one can ever really understand anyone and that everything is about your own survival. *I don't think it's even pain,* Grace thinks. *I think I'm just angry.*

'Grace?'

Grace opens her eyes. Most of the girls, including Harper Goodwin, have left the change room. Serra Kalbfel is standing before her, bag on her shoulder, looking torn between running away and giving Grace a hug.

'Are you okay?' Serra asks.

Grace takes a deep breath and picks up her backpack. *Please, no hugs.* 'Yep,' she says. 'All good.'

'You know that Harper's just really jealous. She gets kind of sick with competitiveness. It's not good.'

'It's okay, I get it.' Grace walks to the door, throwing 'Thanks' over her shoulder.

Serra follows. 'I hear my mum gave your mum a singing lesson.'

Grace wishes Serra would leave her alone. 'Did she?'

'They're in the same choir. West Moonah. My mum and my gran have been in it for, like, ever.'

'Cool,' says Grace. 'She's not really a singer, my mum. But that choir's really making some noise.'

'Yeah, they've kicked up a storm lately. Sixty thousand followers on Facebook or something.' She gives Grace a sideways smile. 'Doing their bit.'

Grace looks away. 'Ha,' she says. 'Good on them.' They leave the academy building. Grace contemplates the long walk ahead of her, feels the weight of things and heads towards the nearest bus stop.

'See you,' she says to Serra.

'Hey, we can give you a lift home if you like.' Serra points at a nearby car. 'Dad won't mind. It's Sunday, so no rush.'

'No, I'm good, thanks. I'm all the way in Lower Sandy Bay.'

'Okay,' Serra smiles awkwardly, waves. Her wave is small and kind and makes Grace want to cry.

'Actually,' says Grace, 'a lift would be awesome. The buses on Sunday are, like, never.'

Serra's smile widens. 'Sure.'

Grace settles into the back of the car, next to a baby seat and a pile of books.

'Sorry it's messy,' says Serra. 'It's always trashed. Dad, this is Grace.'

The man in the driver's seat turns. 'Hi Grace, I'm Jonathon.' He reminds Grace of Keanu Reeves. Dark and hairy and nice.

'Hi, thanks for the lift.'

'She lives in Lower Sandy Bay.'

'You can just take me wherever. I can walk from the city if that's easiest.'

'Lower Sandy Bay it is,' says Jonathon. 'How was your class?'

'Good,' says Serra.

Grace doesn't reply. They drive on in silence for a while before Serra adds, 'Harper was being all, *raar*.' She mimes a cat, complete with claws.

'Right,' says Jonathon. 'Harper seems to have a lot of hackles.'

'And she has really weird hackles,' says Serra. 'Grace is like'—she glances back at Grace—'I hope you don't mind me saying, like, the most incredible dancer. She's probably better than our teacher, and it's magic to watch. I mean, I just follow what you're doing and *my* technique improves. Anyway, Harper can't handle it.'

Grace is unsure what to say, eventually mutters to the car window, 'Thanks, Serra. I'm not incredible, though.'

'You are.'

'You're a great dancer too.'

'Thanks.' Serra's smile is a beam so bright that Grace has to look away.

They drive another kilometre or so in silence before Jonathon says, '"Harper Can't Handle It" is a good name for a band.'

'Or "Harper's Hackles",' says Serra.

'Or just "Raar",' say Grace.

'Ah, that's the best one,' says Jonathon. 'Raar, live onstage tonight with their new album, *Incredible Dancer*.'

A small laugh finds its way through Grace's pain.

𝄐

Frey and Gil are reading newspapers at the outside table on the terrace when Grace arrives home via the garden gate. She stops short of the terrace steps and says, 'What's going on?'

Frey lowers her newspaper. 'We're having an al fresco breakfast.'

Grace frowns. 'It's ten thirty.'

'Brunch then,' says Frey.

'Aren't you missing golf, Dad?'

'Yes, very much,' says Gil, then clears his throat. 'I'm having some time off golf. I'm not playing so well.'

'Where have you been, darling?' Frey asks Grace. 'I thought you must have been out running but you've been gone for hours. I've been calling your phone.'

'I had a dance class.'

'Another dance class? Grace, is that overdoing it? You'll risk an injury. Rest is an important part of athletic performance.'

But Grace has stopped listening. She is looking at the wheelie bin beside the house. It has three golf clubs sticking out of it. One of them is bent at an almost ninety-degree angle.

Frey follows her gaze, coughs, and says, 'I, um, accidentally ran over Dad's golf clubs.'

Gil shuffles his newspaper and adds, 'My fault. I left them in the way.'

Grace looks at her parents, narrows her eyes and goes inside.

'She's never very chatty, is she,' says Gil.

Frey gives him a long look, then says, 'Spending more time with us is going to be a blast.'

𝄢

Grace heads straight upstairs towards the shower. Tom is evidently in his room because walking along the corridor is like entering a David Guetta music video. The beats build as she walks, both in volume and speed. She fits her step to the tempo. As she reaches the bathroom, she hears the unmistakable lyrics of Robin Thicke and Pharrell Williams's 'Blurred Lines'. Her feet keep time with the beat, all the way to Tom's door, which she throws open.

'Argh!' Tom shouts over the music. 'Grace, you scared the shit out of me, what the hell?'

Grace finds the powerboard and flicks off its main switch. The music stops. 'Do you even know what that song's about?' she asks.

'You can't just switch it off like that!' Tom shouts back. 'It damages the motherboard. I have to shut it down properly. Get out of my room.'

'I'll damage *your* motherboard if you keep mixing up *rape songs*, you dickhead.'

'It's a cool song.'

Grace takes the collar of Tom's shirt in one hand and twists it, pulling him towards her. 'It. Is. Not. Cool.'

'I don't even—'

'Listen to it. Just listen.' She lets go of his collar, shoving him back in his seat. 'For fuck's sake.'

'Jeez, why are you so pressed?'

'I hate that song.' Grace picks up Tom's drink bottle, which is next to him on the floor. 'And another thing. You know how you ghosted Diana Millane?'

'What?'

Grace holds the drink bottle above Tom's mixing desk and says, 'Don't pretend you don't know.'

'Fuck, Grace, stop!'

'You know how you ghosted Diana Millane?'

'I talked to her.'

Grace tips the bottle.

'Stop! Okay, yes, I know. What about it?'

'And the way you treated Abi Neilson?'

Tom makes a lunge for the drink bottle, but Grace is quick to jerk it out of his reach. Water flings through the air.

'Grace!' They watch as drops fall onto the desk. 'Stop! This stuff is worth a lot of money and you'll be paying for it.'

'You keep on treating girls like they're nothing, and playing rapey music, and I will come in here and wreck all your shit. Because it means a lot to you and guess what? Being treated like a human means a lot to Diana and Abi too. And all the poor women you lure into your future. At some point we have to stop tolerating shit treatment of women, or it will be normal forever and ever, the end.'

Tom holds his hands up. 'Okay, okay, Jesus. Just give me the water.'

'You'll stop being an arsehole?'

'Yes.'

'And you'll delete that song from our house?'

'Yes.'

'Good.' Grace puts the bottle back on the floor, and Tom immediately snatches it up.

'You're a salty freak.'

'And you're a fuckwit. Turn it around, Teddy.'

Confusion breaks through Tom's rage. 'What?'

'I think I just made that up, but I like it.' Grace thinks for a moment, then asks, 'Can you help me make some music?'

'What kind of music?'

'I need a song to dance to. I'm sick of all the usual tracks.'

'No.'

'Okay, arsehole.'

'I'll think about it if you get the hell out of my room.'

'I'm out.' Grace slams the door behind her.

𝄡

Sunday, 27 October 2019, 10.15 p.m.

I have had an idea. It's crazy but I wonder whether I can make my own accompaniment for the showcase. I don't think it's something people do, which is surely why it's a good idea? Maybe I can even do the vocals? I've never written music but Tom can help with production and beats and stuff. Mum's getting singing lessons so maybe she can be my backup singer HAHA.

Actually, maybe it doesn't even need a beat. Maybe I can dance to something a cappella? Is that a thing? Surely if there's no audible beat, then giving them a beat they can SEE could be something, couldn't it? At the moment I feel like I have a beat inside me that everyone can see just when I'm walking around. Sometimes it hurts but mostly it's just pumping pure anger into me. This is good. Strong emotion enhances performance, everyone always says. And it burns energy. I have burned A LOT of energy today. Maybe I should be thanking Harry.

Grande battement translates to BIG BEAT. My grand battement felt crappy today. Not even 100 degrees. Développé better but not ideal. Teacher said it's probably a strength thing but I don't want any more bulk in my thighs. I'll get up early and stretch some flex into my hips.

Song lyrics brainstorm: (What do I want to say?)

I think I want to say sorry to myself for giving myself away like that, to an arsehole. For putting myself in a trash film version of my life. For trusting.

. . .

I've been living lies and breathing smoke
I gave all your time and love to ghosts

. . .

Or a message to All Men? Turn it around, Teddy.

. . .

I don't want to write a song about FUCKHEAD HARRY.

In schools our children should be taught that men have a natural tendency to be arrogant knobs. Boys should sit exams about how not to be and girls should be taught how to be. To protect themselves, how not to trust, how to be a role model for their daughters. Put that in a song and dance the bejesus out of it.

Raar.

𝄐

Stepping Stone Number 201, from *La Lista* by R.K.:
Google Keanu Reeves. He is a lesson in humility and kindness. I am proud to say I had a crush on him when everyone else was coveting Brad Pitt.

Chapter 20
Next Level

'Mum?' says Lily. 'You know how you're in the Angry Women's Choir?'

Frey is reluctant to answer. She has been stuck in a traffic jam on the same strip along Hobart's CBD for fifteen minutes, about to be late for dance class and she is not in the mood for a Lily conversation.

'Mum?'

'Yes?'

'Are all the women in the choir really angry? You don't seem that angry. Only sometimes.'

'Um, well, yes. They are angry. Some of them more angry than others, for various reasons.'

'What reasons?'

Frey watches as a woman on the footpath wrestles shopping bags, a pram, a dog and a screaming baby.

'Well, the specific reasons are private, but . . .' The traffic still isn't moving; Frey decides to be a mother. 'Well, you see, Lily, thanks to popular opinion and some very stubborn myths, throughout the ages women who are partnered with men have just been expected to give away their time, their energy, their care, their priorities, for free.

It's kind of built into the idea of heterosexual relationships. But the stuff they usually do – the care-taking, the putting food on the table, the wiping bums, the sitting in traffic – is badly devalued because it actually lays a solid foundation for our economy. Only that's never reflected in what we get paid. We just do hours and hours of work for free, while men work for actual money.'

'Is that the gender pay gap?' asks Lily.

Frey thinks for a minute. 'Yes. Well, no, but maybe it should be. The gender pay gap is about women and men in the workforce. But I would argue that caregiving should be considered an integral part of the workforce, because how can the business people go about their business without someone looking after children they might have at home?'

Lily is silent for a long moment. *I've made it too complicated*, Frey thinks, *she's stopped listening*. But then Lily asks, 'Can't the women just go and get a job that pays them money?'

'Yes, and lots of women have to, but someone still has to wipe the bums and watch the children. And statistics show that even if women already have a job, they're still doing a lot of the bum-wiping. So they actually have two jobs, or more, for one salary.'

'They could pay someone else to wipe the bums.'

'And then they don't see their children enough.'

Lily thinks. 'Can't the dads share their money with the mums?'

'Yes. But then they have control over it. Which means they control the women.'

Lily thinks for a minute, then says, 'If I get married, my husband will wipe as many bums as I do.'

'Well, that's what we all hope for. But there's another gap people get cross about: the gap between how we imagine our lives to be and how they actually end up.' Frey speeds up for an orange light.

'But not everyone's angry, are they?'

'No,' says Frey. 'Some are just bone-weary with disappointment.'

'Right.' Lily looks out the window at an elderly woman holding a cabbage at a bus stop, staring into space. 'So that's why lots of people want to join the choir,' she continues, 'because they've all got rage about the gaps?'

'Do lots of people want to join?' Frey asks.

'Some of my friends do. Even some of the boys. And my teacher. Hashtag AWC is trending.'

'Wow. That's good.'

'They probably all want to help warn people about the gaps.' Lily sighs. 'We're going to be late for class.'

'We might not,' says Frey. The traffic moves encouragingly, but then slows again at another intersection.

Lily looks in the window of a nail bar. Lines of women staring at their phones having their feet buffed and polished and tended. Frey follows her gaze.

'Those women aren't doing caregiving,' Lily says.

Freycinet sighs. 'No, they've been tricked into thinking they need perfect nails.'

'You do your nails.'

'I know. I've let myself be tricked too.'

'My friend Paige's mum gets her lips puffed up and her head wrinkles are all smoothed and ironed out with Botox until she can't move her face. Paige says it's scary because she never looks angry so there's no warning for when she's about to yell and throw stuff.'

Freycinet presses the brakes a little too hard in the realisation that Gil's slightly unsettling neutral acceptance of her small acts of revenge isn't neutral acceptance at all. It's Botox. She laughs, loudly, then thinks, *Holy shit, his skin 'diagnosis' must have warranted intervention by injection.*

Lily takes her laughter as a response to her story and adds, 'She threw her favourite mug once and then cried over it and Paige said her face didn't even change. It's all shiny and stuck.'

Frey stops laughing. 'Poor Paige's mum,' she says. 'Shiny and stuck. Look what they make us do.'

'Do you ever smash things at rehearsal?' Lily asks. 'Throw plates and stuff?'

Frey laughs. 'No, darling. Anger doesn't always have to be aggressive, it can be contained and poised and healthy. Like, I don't know, activated almonds.'

'Right.' Lily frowns. 'So you put the anger in your singing?'

'Yes, of course, that's why we're a choir. Anger can be really beautiful. You can actually turn it into music, I've heard it. Or you can turn it into compassion or progress or determination.'

'Or muesli.'

'What?'

'Activated almonds are for muesli.'

'Okay, forget that analogy. Sorry.' They pull into the street that leads to Derwent Dance Academy. 'Anger can be courage too,' Frey says. 'The word "courage", translated literally from its origin, means "heart rage".'

'Cool,' says Lily. 'We're only a tiny bit late.'

'I'll wait for you today, darling,' Frey says. 'I have some paperwork to do and I want to chat to Teagan about costumes.'

''Kay,' Lily says. 'Can you tell her I *hate* my tutu? She said it's dusty pink but it's actually brown.'

'Maybe.' They pull into the carpark. Lily jumps from the car and runs to the building's entrance.

Frey watches her go. 'Mind the gaps,' she says to the already closing door.

$$\mathbf{B}$$

Frey locates Teagan among a swarm of parents and children in the academy common room.

'Teagan, hi,' she says. 'Thanks so much for your work on the costumes so far. Lily is in heaven with her tutu. I have to hide it so she doesn't ruin it before the showcase even starts.'

'Oh, you're welcome. I love doing it. Has Grace got hers sorted? She said she doesn't need my help with a showcase costume this year. I'm dying to know what she's wearing. I hope it's not going to be something better than my costumes!' Teagan hoots with laughter. 'Kidding, she'd look perfect in a hessian sack, it's no wonder she doesn't need me.'

'Right,' says Frey. 'I don't know. I just assumed she was still waiting for hers. Maybe she wants to spare us the cost. Lily's was quite expensive.'

Teagan's smile drops. 'We don't like to get the cheap stuff. They don't last. And they're made in sweatshops.'

'Of course.'

'Dancing is actually a really reasonably priced activity,' Teagan continues. 'It really gets up my nose when people complain. I mean, horse riding or rowing are so much dearer.'

Frey looks at Teagan and decides that the last place she wants to be is up her nose. 'Yes, that must be very annoying. Especially when you give so much of your time for free.'

Teagan's smile reappears. 'I do, but as I say, I love it.'

Frey sees the in, and heads directly for it. 'Teagan, I wonder whether you might help me with something *I'm* passionate about. Have you heard of the Angry Women's Choir?'

'God, yes, who hasn't? Mad lot, but good on them, I say. Eccentrics have their place, and who doesn't relate to an angry woman?'

'Exactly. Well, I'm . . . I'm just helping with this one thing.' Frey takes a breath and wonders why she feels the need to exempt herself from the choir for this woman. 'I've been giving them a hand to raise funds for the Safe at Home scheme in Tasmania, in particular for more counsellors on the Family Violence Response team.'

'And you'd like the academy to sell some chocolates or something? Petra Gibb is the one to talk to about that. She's in charge of fund-raising and I dare not tread on her toes.' Teagan gestures towards a tall woman searching through the lost property, and leans closer to Frey. 'She's a proper fiery redhead when she wants to be. Don't mess with Petra.'

Frey smiles and moves slightly away. 'Actually, I just want your opinion. You see, we need a high-profile spokesperson to do a snappy little call to action for us to share on social media. You know, the importance of expert counselling, donate now and so on. It's a partially government-funded organisation so I'm going to approach Paul Bellavance, given his ongoing advocacy for victims of sexual violence and his new role as Minister for Women.'

'Oh, good idea. Paul's a total sweetheart.' Teagan giggles. 'I mean, swoon!'

'I'm glad you said that. Without meaning to be weird, I need to make sure he's exactly the right person to ask, that he doesn't have any, you know, skeletons in the cupboard so to speak. I don't want to bugger up the appeal before it even starts. Like, he hasn't been violent towards women or anything?'

Teagan gasps. Frey decides that if Teagan were wearing pearls, she'd be clutching them.

'I mean,' Frey says, 'has he always treated women with complete respect? In case you've heard of any stories from the past that could mar our campaign. You know how . . . *litigious* things can be these days. If he's representing Safe at Home, then he has to be squeaky clean.'

Teagan's eyes flutter. 'Gawd, well, there's the usual stuff you hear from back in the day. Probably girls who had their hearts broken by him.'

'What do you mean by "the usual stuff"?'

'Oh, you know: "he stuffed me around", "he was an arrogant prick" and the rest of it. He was always a heartbreaker and people love bringing down a tall poppy like Paul, being the sports star he is. But really he just *loves* women. Adores Valentina – they are the most loved-up couple I know. Yep, I wholeheartedly endorse him. He's your man. Great cause.'

'Excellent,' says Frey. 'That's good to hear. Thanks, Teagan.'

Teagan leans in close and lowers her voice again. 'I'm glad you didn't ask Petra. She *despises* him. I think she's probably secretly a bit in love with him. I know I am.' She expels another whoop of laughter.

Frey glances back to the lost property bin, but Petra is gone. 'Okay, thanks again, Teagan. I'm going to wait in the car for the girls. I have some calls to make.'

'Good luck with the fundraiser,' says Teagan. 'Let me know if you need any help.'

𝄢

Frey hurries to the carpark and spots Petra backing her station wagon out of a spot in the far corner. Frey jogs over and knocks on the driver's side window.

Petra looks startled, opens the window. 'Hi?'

Her greeting is a puzzled question. Frey realises at once that it's a response to her being so persistently distant over the years. Petra's son has danced with Lily for three years, but Frey has never spoken to either of them.

Frey thinks fast. 'Hi, Petra, I noticed you were checking lost property. Were you looking for a Derwent T-shirt by chance? Lily brought an extra one home, unnamed.'

Petra smiles. 'No. Liam's lost a tap shoe. How he can lose one shoe is a mystery.'

'Oh, that's a pain. I'll ask Lily to keep an eye out.'

'Thanks.' Petra eases her car forward slightly.

'I'm Freycinet,' says Freycinet.

'I know. Hi, Freycinet.'

'Hi. Sorry, I know you probably need to go, but do you mind if I ask your advice about something?'

Petra looks wary. 'Sure.'

Frey gives Petra the same Angry Women's Choir/Safe at Home fundraiser spiel she gave Teagan, then adds, 'I'm interested to know whether people think Paul Bellavance would be a good spokesperson for this kind of fundraiser? I don't know him at all, only what I see in the media, so if you've had anything to do with him, do you think he really is as . . . lovely as he seems?'

Petra blows out a sigh, as if she doesn't know where to start. 'Wow, okay, Paul Bellavance and the Angry Women's Choir.' She laughs suddenly, then looks down at her hands. Frey suspects that whatever has made her laugh isn't very funny. 'You know, I have to do some grocery shopping before Liam's class ends, so . . .' She sighs. 'I think I'm just going to say, "no comment", if that's okay.'

'Of course,' says Frey, seeing instantly that Petra must not be pressed. 'No problem. I'm happy to give Liam a lift home, I'm waiting here anyway—'

'That's okay, I'll come back. Thanks, Freycinet. See you.' Petra drives away.

'Okay,' says Frey. 'Bye then.'

𝄢

The following weekend, Frey opens the door to Roger and his toolkit.

'Dad,' she says. 'This is a nice surprise. Come in.'

'The Girl,' says Roger, walking into the hall. 'Tom didn't mention me coming over?'

'I'm lucky if Tom mentions his presence in the house.'

'Hmm,' says Roger. 'He wants another sample.'

'A what?' Frey feels alarmed.

'A vocal sample.'

'Oh.'

'You thought faecal sample.'

'Ew, Dad. No, I didn't.' She goes to the staircase. 'I thought wee. Tom!' She calls up the staircase. 'He won't hear me. Just go on up. Mature-age-man vocal samples must be all the rage.'

'Hmm,' says Roger, heading up the stairs.

'Why have you got your tools?'

'For your violin.'

'Oh.'

'You keep saying you'll fetch it over, then you don't.'

'Okay, thanks. I'll bring it up to Tom's room while you're leaving your sample.'

But Roger has been swallowed up into the sick beats of the hallway leading to Tom's bedroom.

Frey thinks for a moment, then heads upstairs too, takes the opposite corridor down to her bedroom and its walk-in wardrobe. She drags a chair across the space and stands on it, opening the highest cupboard. She reaches past the Fun With Maths! box to a large suitcase, which she drags out then puts on the floor and unzips. She pauses a moment before opening the suitcase. 'This is a can,' she says, 'and inside are worms.'

She lifts the lid and looks in. Inside is a box and a violin case. She puts her hand on the violin case, then lifts it out and sets it down beside the suitcase. She is about to close the suitcase again when she hesitates, then opens the box. A brown cardigan is folded neatly on top. Frey lifts it up to reveal a large bra, a pink blouse, beige slacks and a pair of green rubber clogs.

Frey smiles and says, 'Hello, Freida.'

She has just returned the suitcase to its shelf, replaced the chair and is about to leave the wardrobe with the violin when she hears Gil's voice as he enters the bedroom.

'I don't know,' he is saying. 'I think maybe Thursday. Soon, anyway.'

Frey stops dead. There is a warmth in Gil's voice that catches her attention.

'No, her dad's here, they're in Tom's room, otherwise known as the DJ den. You wouldn't hear an earthquake in there.'

Frey holds her breath.

'I don't know, Skye. I'm sorry, it's so messed up. I panicked and I can't just . . . yeah, okay . . .'

Frey feels her knees buckle. She gives in to them, lowering herself into the chair, the violin case held to her chest. She rests her forehead on it.

'Of course I've considered that. I'm not a monster, babe.'

Babe. Frey stands up and moves quietly into the bedroom. Gil has his back to her, shuffling things absently on his dressing table as he says, 'I know and that's fantastic, I'm so proud of you.' He turns, sees Frey and says, 'Whoa,' before he regains control of himself and switches to, 'Yeah, yep, got that. Yeah, no worries. We can talk more about it in the office. Okay now, see you, bye.' He swipes clumsily at his phone and says, 'Hi, Frey. Jesus, you're starting to . . . hey, your violin.' He attempts a smile, but looks at her face and says, 'Oh, shit.'

'Hi, *babe*,' says Frey.

'I was just . . . oh, Jesus. It was three years, Frey. She's hurting, I'm just trying to, you know . . .'

Frey closes her eyes and says, '*She's* hurting?'

'Shit,' says Gil. 'You don't need to hear that, do you.'

Frey shakes her head.

'Right.'

Frey opens her eyes and fixes them on a striped tie hanging on the mirror above Gil's dressing table. She nods in its direction. 'That's your old footy club president tie, yeah?'

'What?'

She whips the tie off the mirror and carries it into the en suite.

'What are you doing? Frey?'

Frey throws the tie into the toilet and flushes it down, then returns to the bedroom, where Gil is pressing his hands to his shiny head. 'Jesus Christ, can we just—'

'How's it going with Laetare Gardens?' Frey smiles.

'Good,' says Gil. 'Good. It's happening.'

'Great. I'm so proud of you.' She leaves the room, carrying her violin.

𝄢

Frey takes a moment in the music outside Tom's room and uses it to find her breath and quell the threatening firestorm in her chest. She wishes she could feel nothing, like Eleanor, or master her heart, like Irene. A startling assortment of audio samples shouts at her through the door – 'here we go again', 'kick it', 'ladies and gentlemen' and 'pump up the volume' are all interspersed with scratches, dum-di-dums, screeches, horn blasts and sirens. The effect is almost psychedelic. The walls seem to oscillate. She holds herself upright, clutching her violin case until finally she hears a familiar 'Hmm'. And another. 'Hmm.' It's Roger, on loop. 'Hmm, hmm, hmm.'

She opens Tom's door. Roger is sitting at a microphone, while Tom flicks switches and turns dials.

'It's a rum thing,' Roger says, looking up at Frey.

'Oh, Pa, there's another one,' says Tom. 'You're full of them. Say that again and I'll record it.'

'It's a rum thing,' says Roger on cue. He looks at Frey's face, then down at her violin case.

'Good-o,' he says, taking the case from her and opening it without a thought.

Frey looks at the polished maple instrument, then leaves the DJ and his artist to it.

'Good-o,' she hears as she walks down the stairs. 'Good-o, good-o, good-o.'

𝄢

Roger brings the violin downstairs an hour or so later, when he and Tom come seeking refreshments and find a plate of blueberry muffins on the bench. Frey is just outside the window weeding the herb garden at a furious pace. Lily is with her, squirting Acorn with the hose. Roger nods at her and lifts the violin case. Frey smiles at him and thinks, *Ah, Dad. Here we go.*

'It's fit as a fiddle,' Roger says when she comes inside.

'Thanks, Dad.'

'Give us a jig, then.'

'I knew you were going to say that. Can you let me have a go on my own? I'll be so out of form.'

'Can I've a go?' asks Lily.

'Come on, Mum,' says Tom. 'If you're an Angry Women's Choir member you're going to need to exercise your music muscles to keep up with those ladies. Some of them are, like, actual singers. Avni Sasani is getting a real glow up.'

'Which is my point,' says Frey. 'Glowing singers don't need a rusty fiddler.'

'You should never lose your tradecraft,' says Roger.

Frey frowns at him.

Grace walks into the room and gets a glass of water. 'That your violin, Mum?' she asks.

'Yeah, and she won't play for us,' says Tom.

'I will,' Lily says. 'Please?'

'She's scared,' says Roger.

'I'm not scared, Dad.' Frey gives him a hard look.

'Remember when you played at the school trivia night and got twenty house points for Collins?' Grace says.

'Did I?' asks Frey. But she does remember. Gil had laughed off all the compliments and called her a show-off. The violin went in the wardrobe after that.

'Come on, Mum,' says Tom.

'Don't make her, Tom,' says Grace. Frey detects an unusual amount of vitriol in her voice. 'Maybe she just wants to weed the herb garden.'

A line from Grace's diary flashes across Frey's vision, lit up by a flare of shame. *WHERE ARE ALL THE GOOD ROLE MODELS?*

'No, it's okay,' she says. 'I'll give it a go.' She picks up the violin. 'Don't expect anything amazing.'

The gentle press of the instrument against her neck feels like a homecoming. *Aren't I already home?* she thinks. She feels Swansea at her feet, the fitful seascapes, the ocean on the air. *This is the trouble with having a wonderful, exciting childhood*, she thinks. *Once you leave it you're never quite home again.*

The first note is enough to engage all the memories in her left hand. The second shuts out the room and the third drowns out the world. She doesn't register any passing of the next eighty seconds, until she trips on a bowing and stumbles to a stop.

'Oh dear,' she says, 'I told you I couldn't do it.'

But the look on Roger's face says she can. He doesn't even need to use one of his few words. He uses them anyway. 'There she is,' he says. 'My girl.'

Gil walks in clapping his hands. 'You've still got it, Frey,' he says, and his eyes are trying their best to say more, maybe even 'I'm proud of you', only Frey finds she's not all that interested in what Gil or his eyes have to say. What his unsettlingly smooth face can't say. Her thoughts give a sigh, her heart is a stone again and her left hand squeezes its nimble fingers into a fist.

'How do you wobble your hand like that?' asks Lily. 'It's kind of weird and amazing.'

'It's called vibrato,' says Tom.

'People do it with their voices too,' says Grace. 'That was next level, Mum.'

Frey's stone heart softens. 'Thanks, Grace. Not really. I forgot the last bit.'

'Just practise it,' says Grace. 'It's obviously there somewhere.'

Frey smiles at her. 'I will.'

Roger helps himself to a muffin. 'Mmm,' he says. 'Good.' He pushes the plate towards Grace and says, 'Put one of those in your cakehole, Bones.'

'No thanks,' says Grace. 'I had a sandwich before.'

The doorbell rings.

'I'll get it!' says Lily.

'I'm gone,' says Roger. 'Better get back.'

'Thanks, Dad,' says Frey.

Roger lifts his eyebrows at her, smiles and says, 'Hmm.'

There's some gathering of toolkits and packaging of muffins before Frey sees Roger out. She has forgotten that someone rang the doorbell, until she sees Petra Gibb standing at the top of the front steps, looking striking in green and a little bit terrified.

𝄢

Stepping Stone Number 301, from *La Lista* by R.K.:
If you are making berry muffins, roll your blueberries or raspberries in flour before you mix them in. It stops them from sinking to the bottom of the muffin.

Chapter 21
Buzzies

'Mum,' says Lily, 'this is Liam's mum. She's here to see you.'

'Liam's mum,' says Roger, with a little tip of an imaginary hat as he passes.

Petra nods at him and smiles.

'Hi,' says Frey. 'Petra.'

'Hi,' says Petra.

'Bye, Dad,' Frey calls, but Roger is already at the gate. He waves without looking back.

'Come in,' says Lily. 'Mum has been playing us her violin.'

Frey smiles. 'I promise I've put it away. Come in.'

Petra's smile fades. 'Oh, no, I won't come in, thanks. I can't stay long . .' She looks at Frey.

'Darling,' says Frey to Lily. 'I promised Petra I'd show her how to fix a chainsaw. Want to come too?'

Lily wrinkles her nose. 'No thanks,' she says, and heads for the trampoline.

'Some things are a sure Lily-repellent,' Frey says as she leads the way to the garden shed. 'Firewood is one of them.'

Petra smiles. 'Lovely garden,' she says.

'Thank you. I'm no expert but it's a nice place to get lost in. Come in.' Frey opens the door to the shed. It's small, but immaculately kept, everything in its place. The walls are lined with similarly organised, oiled tools.

'Wow,' says Petra, 'this is impressive. Can you really fix a chainsaw?'

Frey laughs. 'Not really.' She watches Petra's hands as they tweak at her clothes. 'You don't have to tell me anything, Petra. I can tell you're not comfortable. I shouldn't ask these things—'

'It's okay,' says Petra. 'I realised I might have been waiting for someone to ask, actually.'

'Okay.' Frey waits.

Petra takes a long breath. 'Paul Bellavance is not someone to have on your side. He was my sister's boyfriend. Years ago – 1995 to 1997. They were together for eighteen months.'

Frey stays silent.

'He was completely charming. Intelligent, handsome, perfect manners – a dream, really. My sister was just nuts about him. We all were. And then'—Petra looks upwards, as though searching for the right words—'she started to act differently. She didn't want to see her friends, withdrew from her family, changed her appearance. When we realised that something was really wrong, it was just too late.'

The silver sound of a blackbird reaches them from a nearby maple tree.

'Anyway, she tells it better than me.' Petra pulls a folded piece of paper from her back pocket. 'Please don't use her name, or mine, but you need to know why he should never represent anything to do with Safe at Home. And if it helps the Angry Women's Choir . . .'

She holds the paper out to Frey, who looks at it and asks, 'Are you sure?'

'He's been appointed the Minister for Women, for fuck's sake. It makes me sick.'

Frey takes the piece of paper, unfolds it. It's a photocopy of a neatly written letter. Frey glances back at Petra, then reads.

2 February 1998

Dear P.,

I'm sorry I haven't seen you but I promise you don't want to see me. I'm not winning at the moment. My hair is falling out, people on the bus are scared of me. And that was when I could catch the bus.

I got scheduled but I can't go back to hospital, I JUST CAN'T. When they feed me through a tube it's like being tortured. So I ran away. The eating disorder therapist tells me my brain won't function properly until I gain weight, that my thought processes can be rewired, but when they torture me the wiring goes all wrong again.

I'm still trying, on my own. I promise I'm trying. I'm doing my best to stick to the plan. I try to sleep instead of exercise and I am eating things that are not my safe foods. But it's still a bit like torture because even while I'm exercising I'm planning the next kilojoule burn. I've banned celery. I really like hummus. I know I'm too light, I just can't see it, can't actually feel it.

I feel a little bit like giving up. I'll be sorry if I die but not sorry because you will definitely all have an easier time without me.

The eating disorder group has been trying to talk more about how we ended up so sick. It's important that you know (you and Mum and Dad) that nothing you did caused this. It's my fault for letting it get so bad. And I'm not trying to make excuses but I think Paul is responsible too. I know you think it's my fault we broke up but for YEARS he made me believe I'm not good enough.

He used to call me his 'chubby cupcake'. I told myself it was cute. Once he tripped me over in front of his friends and laughed about how clumsy I was. Other times he told them how I failed Level Two Maths, and that I am really highly strung. Things I thought were important he would smirk at, and then someone else would tell him about it and he'd take it seriously. He never wanted to hang out with you or my friends, and a lot of the time he didn't want me to, either. Once he told me that all his friends thought it was weird we were together. Sometimes he just wouldn't call me for weeks or not touch me for days and then say I was too needy. He always made me feel that I was wrong to be upset. It really annoyed him if I cried, and if I complained, he'd say, 'You always take stuff the wrong way' or 'Don't overthink everything' and stuff like that.

I could go on and on, but I don't know whether any of it is even worth mentioning. It's all so small, I wonder whether I'm too sensitive. But all the little things add up, you know. They make one big thing that seems like it can break me.

I wasn't highly strung until I fell in love with Paul Bellavance.

I truly believed I didn't deserve him unless I changed. So I wore the clothes he wanted me to wear and I didn't go to the parties where I thought I'd embarrass him and I stopped myself saying things and doing things and I waited and waited for him to love me. And in the end I was too sick and gone in the head for anyone to love me.

I especially can't love myself. Maybe not ever again. I know because I've tried. I've tried everything.

I love you, I'm sorry I always said, 'I'm fine.' I'll keep trying to be well, I promise. But it's really, really hard. And I'm not fine. I'm just so tired.

B. XOX

'Oh, Petra,' Frey says when she's finished reading. 'That's heartbreaking. Did she get through it?' But Frey already knows the answer.

'No,' says Petra. 'No, she didn't.'

'I'm so sorry.'

Petra takes a deep breath. 'I've been following the AWC's social media stuff and I'm about a hundred per cent sure that if my sister was here now, she'd want this to be in the hands of other angry women. Ones with energy.'

Frey nods. 'Okay. Thank you.'

'At the very least it'll answer your question about the fundraising spokesperson.'

'I appreciate that, Petra.'

'And just so you know, I'm semi-friends with his wife, Valentina, and I'm pretty sure she's copping his shit too.'

'Semi-friends?'

'She's hard to get to know.'

Frey feels an instant and strong affinity with Valentina.

They hear Lily call then. 'Mu-um?' She's close.

Frey reaches immediately for the chainsaw. 'And once you've made sure it's sharp and fuelled up, you should be able to . . .' She pulls the saw's ripcord and it fires into a roar. Lily appears with her hands over her ears. Frey kills the chainsaw. 'And that's it. You can just borrow mine if you like.'

'Thanks,' says Petra. Her expression is one of puzzled amusement. 'You really can fix a chainsaw, can't you. I'll let you know if I can't get ours going.' She walks back out onto the path and says, 'See you at the dance showcase, Lily.'

'Yep,' says Lily. 'Bye.'

Petra nods a smile at Frey and walks away.

𝄢

Freycinet arrives early at Tuesday's choir rehearsal, inflamed by Gil's continued dishonesty, emboldened by Petra's letter and armed with her violin.

'Glory be,' says Bizzy when she sees her. 'Someone's been filling up your beans, by the look. Is that a fiddle?'

Frey feels suddenly self-conscious. 'Yes. Just in case it's useful. I used to play a bit.'

'Useful!' says Mary, rising from the piano stool where she's been practising. 'It'll be brilliant. Finally, something to cover my terrible piano playing. I keep asking Avni to bring her guitar but she's so eternally stagestruck.'

'Rubbish, Mary,' says Irene. 'You're a fine pianist.'

'You really are, Mary,' says Freycinet. 'And I'm very out of practice.'

'Play us a tune, Freycinet,' says Sally. 'We'll soon tell you if you're shit.'

So, while some choristers are still arriving, Frey plays a quick Irish jig, dedicated to Bizzy.

'Oh, my heart,' says Bizzy when it's over. 'I think you've raised my mother from the dead. She's sitting in the garden by the wishing well, dreaming of O'Connell's Bar.'

'We should post a video of you playing that,' says Mary. 'It's so shareable.'

'Haven't we been shared enough, for the moment?' asks Bizzy. 'I'm quite enjoying the sunlit plateau we're on. Sixty-five thousand followers is plenty for now. We've barely done any active campaigning yet and still Kyrie and I can't keep up with the emails.'

'That's how fast things move now, though, Bizzy,' says Mary. 'Social media is so immediate. And we've struck something.'

'We're offering people an outlet for their anger,' Sally adds.

'But people keep sending me audition tapes of them singing Disney songs and asking to join the West Moonah Women's Choir,' says Bizzy. 'Which is great but, I mean, I'm focused on the Angry Women's Choir for the time being. We don't need princesses.'

'Ooh, keep them on file, though,' says Irene. 'When this "join the chorus" madness is over we'll all want a little snuggle down in the West Moonah repertoire.'

'Bizzy!' says Sally. 'We're only just gathering steam. You talked me into this and now you're flagging?'

'Not flagging,' says Bizzy. 'Just mindful of our battery life.'

'Pfft,' says Sally, 'we'll rest after the rally. The AMA is on board and so is the nurse's union. Both using the AWC as a springboard to lobby for improved pay conditions for carers and healthcare workers. There's a real groundswell, can't you feel the earth rumbling?'

'No,' says Irene.

'We're preaching to the choir, though,' argues Bizzy. 'Literally. How do we convince the ones who don't want to hear us? How do we have them join the chorus?'

'Some of the men in the footy league have accepted a challenge to stitch some of Bizzy's designs,' says Mary. 'Can you imagine? Boofhead footy blokes, sewing your Very Cross Stitches, Bizzy, taking up the cause. That's evolution right there. I phoned Rosanna to tell her and she said it helped her get out of bed for the afternoon.'

Frey is surprised to observe that Bizzy's eyes don't light up with her rather forced smile. *She's exhausted*, thinks Frey. *Or burning out?*

'And Bizzy,' says Mary, 'even the choir needs preaching to. Sometimes they forget to listen. Or feel overwhelmed. We're here to help them find simple, accessible ways to make a difference. After they've washed the baked bean tin, they can call out misogyny.'

'In the garden this morning I was thinking,' says Sally, 'we need to be like buzzies.'

'Buzzies?' echoes Mary.

'You know, piri-piris, bidibids, bidgeewidgees – those little ground-cover plants with the sticky prickles?'

'Pesky little buggers,' says Irene.

'Exactly,' Sally says. 'Pesky, determined, virulent and extremely ground-stabilising. And you can make tea with them.'

'I love this,' says Mary. 'Bizzy's buzzies.'

Avni, who has just arrived, immediately takes out her songs book and furiously takes notes.

'Also,' continues Sally, 'I think we need a second rehearsal each week. And maybe even a separate meeting for admin. It's almost November, it'll be 2020 in a minute.'

'We don't even have a secure rehearsal space,' says Bizzy. 'I can't bear to find one, frankly.' She puts a hand on Laetare's wall.

'Don't worry about that for now,' Frey says. 'Something will come up.'

'And there have been Small Smellypants ructions already,' says Bizzy. 'He's been digging up stories about me and the Angry Brigade, says I'm a trained assassin and I should be deported.'

'He can't prove anything,' says Mary, but she doesn't look sure.

'I have a feeling that man has plenty of buried stories of his own,' Freycinet says, 'and is about due for his comeuppance.'

'Ha, look at us rubbing off on you,' says Bizzy. 'Glad we've pulled the wool off your eyes, Freycinet.'

Kyrie arrives then and says, 'Oh, a violin! Wonderful.' But her smile doesn't reach her eyes.

'Rosanna's not coming?' Bizzy asks.

'No,' says Kyrie. 'She's just not well enough.' She attempts another smile. 'Still as bossy as ever, though. She's made a schedule for you all to visit her with your secrets. Wednesday in a fortnight, the thirteenth, if you can. You just need to put your name in the spot that suits you best.'

'Okay,' says Irene, who has mastered her heart. Everyone else stays quiet.

'I have some good news,' Kyrie says to the quiet. 'One of the partners at work has a share in a printing company. She's offered to donate ten thousand dollars worth of printing services.'

'We can get merch!' says Mary.

'Yes,' Kyrie says. 'They do brochures, cards, mugs, pens, T-shirts, bags, aprons – whatever we want.'

'Not aprons,' says Bizzy. 'And nothing plastic.'

Quin (and her belly) arrive. 'Did I hear merch?' she asks. 'I think we should do a range of dildos.'

'T-shirts for sure,' says Avni.

'Maybe they could do decks of cards that have rousing quotes on them,' Sally suggests. 'Or sweets wrapped with little stories about ordinary women. Veterans of the Homefront.'

'They could be called "Fannytales",' says Quin.

'Or,' says Mary, 'the cards could have civil disobedience ideas on them.' She looks at Bizzy. 'Nothing illegal. Just small acts of rebellion.'

Eleanor's miniature dachshund suddenly trots into the room.

'Penelope,' says Bizzy. 'Where's Eleanor?'

Penelope sits herself down beside Eleanor's spot on the contralto side of the stage.

'She can't be far away,' says Kyrie.

Avni raises her hand as if she's in a classroom. 'While we're talking about publicity things,' she says. 'I've written eight songs so far, and have more half-done. I think there's going to be one for each of you.'

'Avni,' says Bizzy, 'that's so clever of you.'

Avni blushes with pleasure. 'They're probably not great. They've come in a rush. But if at any stage, you want to collaborate with me, or use the songs for the competition in some way, they are yours, for your voices. I will copyright them to the AWC. I have two for Rosanna.' She looks at the floor. 'So far.'

Eleanor comes in through the main entrance, puffing, sweating and wearing what looks like a large, tie-dyed pillowcase. She spots Penelope and says, 'Goddamnit, dog, have you lost your skinny mind? I thought you were sausage meat. She jumped out of the car and ran off before I could get her lead on. I was sure she'd get skittled.

We were out on the main road.' Eleanor sits heavily on the stage next to the tiny dachshund and looks awkwardly at the bit of floor next to her tail. Penelope looks at the ceiling.

'You were worried, Eleanor,' says Bizzy.

Eleanor is silent for a moment, gauging her emotional state. 'I don't know if I was. Was I?'

'I think you were.'

'You might give her a pat,' says Kyrie. 'She was obviously just keen to get to choir.'

Eleanor reaches down and taps Penelope gently on the head. 'Stupid pooch.' She stares a moment into space, eyebrows raised, then collects up the dog and looks into her little black eye-pools. 'Well I'll be jiggered,' Eleanor tells her. 'I think I might have been worried. Yep, I was anxious and worried. And now I'm relieved.'

'That's wonderful,' says Frey.

'Yeah,' says Eleanor. She looks around the room, slightly dazed, then asks, 'Where's Rosanna?'

'She's not well enough today,' says Mary.

Eleanor, with Penelope still against her chest, bursts suddenly into tears.

There is momentary, disbelieving silence before Bizzy says, 'Eleanor, dear heart, come here to me,' and Irene says, 'That's the way, my love,' and Sally says, 'Let it out.'

They gather around Eleanor in a big, murmuring hug. A choir of a hug. Freycinet stands back awkwardly before a flapping hand from Bizzy catches her by the shirt sleeve and pulls her in. She smells the powdery scent of Bizzy's hair and the fabric softener smell of Sally and something else which she can't place but makes her think of teapots. And there's a warmth that spreads from the choir into her chest, as though she'd had a gulp of tea from that teapot, with something potent laced into it, perhaps buzzies, or Irish whiskey, which would match nicely with the violin.

'Not so tight, Kyrie,' says Quin from within the hug, 'I got a full goon bag up this jumper and you're about to pop it.'

𝄡

The music that follows – two ballads, one hymn, a folk song and a furious rap – seems, to the more experienced choristers, enriched by Eleanor's newfound feeling, Avni's spirit of giving and Freycinet's improving pitch.

Surrounded by it, Freycinet allows her mind to turn to Gil, and the pang that follows sends tension to her diaphragm, straightens her spine and adds volume to her voice. The tone that comes from her vocal cords to her middle ear sounds as though it could be quite sweet.

𝄡

Stepping Stone Number 62, from *La Lista* by R.K.:
If a prospective partner/lover says any of the following, run for the hills. Run for your life, actually.

'I want you in my plans.' 'Boys will be boys.' 'I've never really enjoyed the company of women until now.' 'I miss more than just your body.' 'Are you wearing that?' 'Calm the fuck down.' 'She knew what she was getting into.' 'You're my whole world.' 'You're being dramatic.' 'Wow, you're so brainy.' 'I won't ever change.' 'I love Jane Austen.' (He's probably lying, double check by getting him to name his favourite and quote it.), 'I'm a meat and three veg man.' 'I shot a tiger once, but it was really old.' 'Why are there no potatoes?'

Chapter 22
Thick Gloves

Paul and Valentina Bellavance's house, located at the city end of Hampden Road in Hobart, was originally built as Queen Alexandra Hospital for Women. Errol Flynn was born there in 1909. The Port Arthur gunman was also born there, in 1967. After it closed in 1980, the hospital was converted into welfare flats, then holiday apartments for a brief time before it was boarded up. Paul Bellavance, unable to resist the Errol Flynn connection, bought it in 2005 and had the building gutted and reinvented into 'Queen Alex'.

'She's a true queen,' a magazine once said of the dramatic conversion. 'Golden-age Hollywood meets humble Hobart, complete with indoor fountain, pool room, sunken conversation pit and a feature wall of convict-bricks.'

A stout elderly woman in possession of a cleaning caddy, a tapestry handbag and two rather voluminous chins peers at the vivid white building through high-security gates. She wrinkles her nose at the palm trees in the garden, then looks at the large 'Queen Alex' sign on the gate post and says in a thick German accent, 'Hello, your majesty.' She presses the buzzer on the gate, smooths her short grey hair and waits.

A minute or so later, a pleasant voice crackles out. 'Hello?'

'Hello,' says the stout woman. 'I am Freida. I am here to clean.'

'Sorry, what was that?'

'Hello,' says Freida again. 'I am Freida, I am here to clean.'

'Oh, clean,' says the voice. 'Yes, come up.'

There is a buzz and a click, and the gates open. Freida takes her time walking to the front door. The garden is not really a garden, she notes, more a display of landscaping skills. By the time she reaches the panelled front door, the friendly voice is there, along with a dimpled smile, a perfect black bob and their owner, Valentina Bellavance.

'Oh, you're Freida.' Valentina does her very best to hide her distaste, but her eyes settle too long on Freida's chins, the chunky crucifix around her neck, and finally on her green clogs.

'I can take the shoes off, if you prefer,' says Freida.

'No, no, it's fine. Come in. Thank you so much for filling in for Eleanor. I hope she's not too unwell.'

There is no upward inflection on the end of the statement, which conveys a clear lack of interest as to Eleanor's wellbeing. As a result, Freida does not respond.

'You needn't do the full clean, like Eleanor does. I'll just show you the essentials. It's the bathrooms, mainly.' Valentina leads the way through the entrance hall, past an under-lit marble fountain and up the matching staircase.

'Your windows are not good,' says Freida. 'I will clean windows.'

'Oh, gosh, don't do that, there are acres of them. And I have a professional window cleaner.'

'There will be scum around that fountain.'

Valentina gives a weak laugh. 'Just the bathrooms and kitchen is fine. And some vacuuming in the lounge.'

So Freida cleans the bathrooms. There are six of them. It appears that Paul, Valentina and their daughter, Esperance, all have their own, then there are two guest bathrooms and one out in the pool pavilion. It takes Freida two hours. In the black-tiled bathroom belonging to Paul, she checks inside the mirrored cabinet for good measure and finds a packet of Viagra and a canister of Wart-Off. She dips his toothbrush in the mop bucket and puts toilet water in his mouthwash.

When she is done, she heads back downstairs and takes her anti-bacterial wipes to the wrought-iron banisters.

Valentina finds her halfway down the staircase. 'Oh, Freida,' she calls, 'no need for that. Thank you, though. I'll show you the vacuum cleaner.'

'On banisters there is urine, faeces, blood and mucus,' says Freida. 'And probably some semens.'

Valentina's dimples disappear.

'I clean,' says Freida. 'I have thick gloves.'

'Okay,' says Valentina. 'Thank you.'

Freida is almost at the end of all the curlicued iron rosettes when Paul Bellavance appears in the hall from a side doorway. 'What's all this?' he asks.

Freida sends him a brief glance and says, 'I clean.'

'Where's Eleanor?'

Freida feels his disdain, it echoes off the marble. 'She is sick.'

'She comes on Thursdays. Today is my work from home day, she knows I do that every Monday. I would prefer you to come on Thursday, thank you.'

Freida contemplates the phrase 'thank you' and how the slightest shift of tone can rob it of its courtesy. She stands and looks at him, watches his expression flinch at the sight of her. 'Eleanor told me that. But I am busy on Thursdays. I am free only Mondays.'

Bellavance sniffs and walks on. Freida quickly finishes the banister and ambles in the same direction. Both Valentina and Paul are in the cavernous kitchen, eating lunch. Freida switches on the vacuum cleaner and attaches the crevice nozzle, which sucks air through its narrow opening with an ear-piercing squeal. She dabs it on every foot of all twelve dining chairs before she looks up to find Paul staring at her, his eyes thunderous. She switches off the vacuum cleaner. 'This is too loud for lunch?' she asks.

'Yes,' says Paul. 'Way too loud. I'm trying to have a break from work. What are you even doing with the chair legs?'

'All the human skin sheddings gather on the feet of the chairs. I am vacuuming them away.'

Valentina wrinkles her nose. 'Oh, well perhaps just finish them off and move into the lounge or the pantry, if that's okay, Freida.'

'I said I didn't want the help here on a Monday,' Paul says to Valentina with a hard stare. 'Jesus, it's not much to ask.'

Valentina looks stricken.

Freida turns to them, clasps the cross at her neck and says, '*Es tut mir leid, aber ihr seid schreckliche Leute.*' I am sorry, but you are terrible people.

'What?' asks Paul.

'I said that I am sorry to disturb. I will move to the lounge now.' She picks up the vacuum cleaner.

In the lounge, Freida vacuums cat hair from the carpets and a tax invoice from the coffee table. In the butler's pantry, she scrubs the sink, wipes the cupboard doors and tips half a bottle of Henschke Hill of Grace down the sink. In the study, she cleans two computer keyboards, switches the A and the R and dusts a set of BMW keys into the bin. When she is done, she gathers her things and presents herself back in the kitchen, where Paul is drinking coffee and Valentina is switching on the dishwasher.

'I can do your filthy dishes,' says Freida.

'No, all done,' Valentina replies. 'Thank you, Freida, that's all we need today. I'll arrange your fee through Eleanor, if that's okay.'

Freida nods, then pulls a football from her handbag and shows it to Paul. 'I have grandson who is big football fan of yours. Will you sign his football, please?'

She watches as Paul tries to pretend this is a tired old request. He clears his throat. 'Sure,' he says. 'I can do that.'

'Well, that's adorable,' says Valentina. 'How old's your grandson?'

'Forty-one,' says Freida.

'Oh,' says Valentina. 'Lovely.'

'Also,' says Freida, once she has taken back the autographed football and put it in her bag, 'Eleanor asks me to say to you that she is very, very grateful for your donation to the Angry Women and their choir. She said they are very happy to receive your twenty thousand dollars.'

'What?' says Paul.

'What?' says Valentina.

'Eleanor asks me to say that she is very—'

'Yes, we heard what you said,' says Valentina. 'But I think you must be mistaken . . .' She looks at Paul, whose face is now thunder and lightning. 'I don't know what she's talking about,' Valentina says, her voice pitching upwards.

'Oh,' says Freida. 'I might have you mixed up with some other rich people with enormous ugly mansion. I am sorry. Goodbye.'

She presses a hand to her crucifix, then leaves the kitchen and moves through the house to the front door with uncharacteristic speed. The voices behind her are rising and heated.

Once outside, Freida runs around the side of the house, sets down her bag and caddy and makes her way swiftly to the back garden. There, she ducks down and creeps under the windows. The furious voice of Paul Bellavance escapes through the static vent above Freida's head. She reaches up and presses a smartphone to it.

'Don't start that again. Jesus, Valentina just answer the question. I shouldn't have to put up with this shit all the time. You need to clear this stuff with me first.'

'But I promise, I have no idea what she—'

'I promise,' Paul says in an ugly imitation of his wife. 'I don't know anything.' His voice drops to a menacing tone. 'I don't know either, Valentina. I just don't know.'

Valentina's fearful whimper hits Freida's ears and straightens her legs. Through the window, she sees Paul towering over his wife, his left index finger less than an inch from her face, which is crumpled with fear. Freida holds up her crucifix for a brief moment, then shouts, 'I am very sorry!'

Valentina jerks her frantic gaze to the window. Paul is a beat behind her.

Freida holds her crucifix higher, presses a tiny button on its base and captures the moment and its threatening tensions. 'Forgive me, oh Gott, I remember now!' she shouts. 'This is my mistake. The Angry Women money was coming from the other famous Tassie football man. The young one. Peter someone? Not Paul. He is giving the twenty thousand dollars. *Entschuldigung und auf Wiedersehen.*' She runs, gathering up her belongings from the side of the house.

On the driveway she realises that the security gates are closed, and switches direction towards a willow tree by the fence. She throws both her caddy and bag over the fence, grabs the weeping branches of the willow and hoists herself up into the tree. She climbs a further three branches.

'Hey!' Paul roars from somewhere near the front of the house. 'If you're hiding in my garden, you creepy nut job, I'm opening the gates. Get out and don't come back.'

'Okay,' mutters Freida. 'Did not need tree stunt.' She shimmies along the fourth branch until it clears her of the fence to the other side. From there she swings downwards and drops neatly onto the paving below. 'Oof,' she says, then takes a moment to recover before gathering up her scattered cleaning equipment and her bag. She sprints to her car, which is pointing in a getaway direction around the corner in Davey Street.

As she drives, she breathes heavily and mutters, 'Creepy nut job.' She eyes herself in the rear vision mirror and drops the German accent. 'You're an idiot.' She whoops, then laughs. 'Nice one, Freida.' She whoops again and takes off her gloves and her grey wig. 'Oh my God, that felt good. Oh my God.' She stretches off her latex face prosthetics, her smile fades. 'I'm sorry, Valentina. *Verzeihung.* Let's get you out of there.' She pulls off Davey Street into a side street, changes out of Freida's clothes and into Freycinet's, then drives home.

𝄡

Stepping Stone Number 23, from *La Lista* by R.K.:
Don't just be yourself, be someone kinder, braver and more generous than yourself.

Stepping Stone Number 222, from *La Lista* by R.K.:
If someone suggests that you carry your keys in your hand to protect yourself against predatory men, you could suggest that keys are better used by men to lock themselves in their houses whenever they are feeling predatory.

Chapter 23

The Day of Secrets

Rosanna knows how close she is to death. She knows this because *La Lista* has been lying untouched for five days. The blue book has only four pages left blank. Her commitment to the list of 'stepping stones' has at times bordered on obsession. She has carried them with her everywhere in case something came to mind and slipped out again before she could write it down. Since being told that she would most likely die, every tiny household detail, obscure quirk or possible amenity that might contribute to smoother runnings has seemed utterly vital. But in the last few days, she has struggled to think of anything to add, and the sense of urgency has receded. She picks up the blue book and flicks to the last two entries:

Stepping Stone Number 305:
Ironing is a terrible waste of time. And time is everything. Cherish time, decorate it with music, don't wish it away and don't use it to iron clothes. Unless there's a job interview or a funeral. Only very occasionally can you disregard time, in moments when you are very excited for something. In Italy, in these moments, we say, '*Non veto l'ora!*' which translates to 'I don't see the hour'. Otherwise, treat

time like you would your best friend or it will slip away and never speak to you again.

Then she has added:

Stepping Stone Number 306:
And while you have this extraordinarily long list about how to live well and how to run the household, have a look back at Stepping Stone Number One, because really the only important thing is filling yourselves and the household with love and kindness and keeping it there. Love and kindness make all the other things fall into step.

Rosanna can see that these words have the shape of an ending. A sign that her beloved time is running out.

Physically, too, she is very obviously dying. Her once rounded frame has not just sharpened, it's begun to concave. She needs help to adjust position in the bed, which Jonathon wheels to various parts of the house and garden depending on where the family is. Or the sunshine. She has no pain but the syringe driver by her bed keeps her drowsy.

Her voice is husky and not as voluminous as it once was. She can sing, but her tone is thready at times. She can still laugh, though. Really laugh. Ilaria spends a lot of the time sitting beside Rosanna with her eyes closed so she can hear her mother's wonderful laugh and not see the strange disaster zone of her body.

Rosanna, with Jonathon and Kyrie's help, has now scheduled The Day of Secrets (as all the Kalbfels have come to call it). The visiting choir members have been entered, appointment-style, into a printed spreadsheet. Kyrie is frowning at it.

'I don't know about this, Rosanna,' she says. 'You're all booked up from nine until five. You'll be exhausted.'

'Not exhausted,' says Rosanna. 'Cross-country skiing for a day, marathon running – that would be exhausting. Today is going to *give* me energy.'

'But all the emotion,' Kyrie argued. 'It should be done over two days, or three.'

'I do not have enough days,' Rosanna says. And Kyrie looks at Rosanna's shoulder bones and stays quiet. There is a certain brightness in her dulling eyes, though. *Perhaps*, thinks Kyrie, who has read the extraordinary blue book, *those eyes need to stop seeing the hours.*

𝄢

Irene, who always books early and sometimes books twice, is the first to arrive at 9 o'clock sharp. 'I wrote the time and day in my diary,' she says when Jonathon welcomes her inside, 'on my calendar and on my car windscreen, just to be sure I wouldn't forget. My colander brain forgets all kinds of important things. None are as important as this, though.' She reaches up to hold Jonathon's shoulders and says, 'Here's a tip: Harv went twenty years ago but on occasions I still wear mourning clothes. That way my friends know that I have woken with gloomy old grief sitting on my bed with his horrible long arms. Sometimes I have to drag him around with me for the day, give him some attention or he will eat me up. Oh, he can get real mean if I push him away too often. And if I do shove him off he's likely to take all the precious memories.'

Jonathon smiles and says, 'Thank you, Irene. That's an excellent tip.'

When she enters Rosanna's sunshine-filled room, Irene says, 'Oh Lordy, you poor love, nothing but a wafer. Where are those beautiful bosoms?'

Rosanna sends her a blissfully narcotic smile and says, 'They are spread into my armpits and down to my belly button.' She laughs her Rosanna laugh.

Irene sits on a chair next to the bed and leans in close. 'I hear you don't want goodbyes. This is a very good thing, as I wasn't going to give you one. Because my secret is this: you will not be gone.' She leans back in her chair and nods knowingly.

'I thought this,' says Rosanna, 'but I wasn't sure.'

'You probably won't be seen for a while,' continues Irene, in a whisper now. 'Not until people are in the right sort of brain – somewhere between the griefly sad brain and the smartly working brain. I haven't always been able to see Harvey, but I have started to lately. And I know that he's been there all along. Anyway, the other bit of the secret is from Harvey. He says that it's lovely on the other side of here. All warm and cradle. You'll have your bosoms back. Harvey has his strong jaw, which disappeared into jowls when he was sick.'

'Thank you, Irena,' says Rosanna. 'God bless you.'

'And you.'

'See you soon.'

'Indeed.'

𝄡

Quin is next. She stands in the doorway as if afraid.

'Quinella, come closer,' says Rosanna. 'Cancer is not catching and I want to see your beautiful bump.'

Quin takes a few steps forward. 'Rosie, look at what that bastard cancer's done to you. Fucken criminal.'

'Fucking criminal, I know. I look like an alien, Matty told me. All eyes and hands.' Rosanna laughs. 'But it is nearly worth it for all the secrets I am going to hoard under my pillow. My coffin will be humming with them!' She claps her hands. 'Give me yours.'

'So I'm having a baby, that's no secret.' Quin sniffs.

'Excellent news.'

'And I swore I was having a girl.'

'You are not having a girl?' Rosanna wrinkles her nose. 'This is disappointing, but you have a village to help with emotional intelligence, sense of humours and musicality. And you have very strong, effective flag bearers.' She narrows her eyes at Quin and adds, 'You look scared. You are never scared.'

'I'm not having a boy either,' Quin says.

Rosanna frowns. 'What?'

'I'm having *three* of them. Three fucken boys. I'm fucken fucked. At least one of them will definitely be the mayor of Dicktown.'

'My God,' Rosanna puts a hand to her mouth. 'Tell Bizzy immediately. The village must prepare.' Despite her industrial-strength aversion to religion, she crosses herself.

𝄢

Eleanor comes into the room with a candle and this: 'I have been cleaning at St Matthew's Anglican Church in Glenorchy for a while now.'

'Yes,' says Rosanna.

'And Father MacKenzie has always been kind to me, even though I cleaned around him and hid behind the hymnbooks so's I didn't have to talk to him.'

Rosanna nods.

'He said that he looks forward to Wednesdays because he wants to see what "tremendous outfit" I am wearing. And then he gave me some leftover communion wine even though I am the worst of all the sinners. And he complimented my brass cleaning and gave me a candle because I prised all the old chewing gum off the bottom of the pews. Some of it looked like it had been there since the seventies.' Eleanor fiddles with the fringing of her skirt, which is actually a chenille bedspread.

Rosanna waits.

'And I wanted to ask you, Rosanna, whether, if you dust dry skin bits and tissue lint from the shoulders of a man and you feel a bubble swell and go pop in behind your ribs and you want to touch his hair and darn his jumper, could that be love?'

Rosanna's response is this: 'Yes.'

13

Bizzy is holding a Russian *Matryoshka* doll in her hands when she walks quietly into Rosanna's room. 'Oh, my love,' she says.

Rosanna raises a hand and says, 'I know, it's amazing to me that I haven't been asked to be in a fashion magazine with these xylophone ribs.'

'You're far too fat,' says Bizzy. She sits not on the visitor's chair but on Rosanna's bed, where she places a hand on the childlike shape of Rosanna's leg and says again, 'Oh, my love.'

'Have you come to tell me you are not an Irish dissident but a Russian princess?' Rosanna is looking at the doll.

'Yes. I am Anastasia Romanov.'

'*Mio Dio*, Anastasia, you are looking so good for your age.'

'Thank you.'

They smile at one another and the thought passes between them that these effortless little banters will soon have to end.

'Winifred gave me this doll when I was very small.' She hands the Russian doll to Rosanna. 'She said it had different meanings to her over the years.'

'Tell me,' says Rosanna, touching the doll's painted face.

'Well, it meant, at first, what these dolls are meant to mean: maternity. The passing down of life and lessons from mother to child. I think the literal translation of *Matryoshka* is "little matron".'

Rosanna opens the first doll to reveal another painted face inside. A winking boy. 'What a cheeky little boy,' she says.

'Yes,' says Bizzy with a smile.

After the boy is a little girl holding a red rooster. And then another girl with a sheep. 'These are so beautiful.'

'All hand-painted.'

'So very clever.'

'I used to imagine that they were all my siblings, all the fun we would have. But I was an only child, of course. And I have no babies, so they must represent my family: my choir.'

'Which one is me?'

'You're in the eyes of the matriarch, with Winifred. And in her smile.'

Rosanna smiles. 'And we will watch you forever.'

'Well, that's creepy,' says Bizzy, and they laugh. 'Winnie also said that perhaps the dolls are all part of the one woman. Because every woman is necessarily many different people.'

'That is very true,' says Rosanna. 'I am a carer, a cleaner, a cook, a singer, a driver, an entertainer, *mediatrice* – those people who stop the arguments.'

'Mediators.'

'Yes. And a historian.'

'A sexy person.'

'Magician.'

'Curator.'

'Keeper of secrets.'

'Guardian of hearts.'

'We are people inside people.'

Rosanna is quiet for a moment before she says, 'Kyrie has been all these people for me lately. No one could make a Russian doll big enough to contain all the people she has been for us.' Rosanna looks at the fragments of *Matryoshka* doll on her bed, sighs and asks, 'And so, your secret, Bizzy Nancarrow – is it here somewhere, among all the people of you?'

'Yes,' says Bizzy. 'It's here. It's a silly, flutter-hearted thing but it's here and I can't seem to be rid of it. Can I give it to you?' She holds the winking boy in one hand and with the other she touches the dull brown pendant that hangs around her neck.

𝄢

Stepping Stone Number 253, from *La Lista* by R.K.:
If you leave a tissue in the wash and end up with tissue fluff everywhere, put your clothes in a bucket of hot water and three to four soluble aspirin tablets. The aspirin dissolves the flecks of tissue.

Chapter 24
The Impossible Beach

When Byzantine Nancarrow tells of her arrival in Tasmania in May 1971, she likes to adage that her mother, Winifred, marched her from Hobart Airport to the top of the Post Office Tower in Elizabeth Street and shouted, 'Hello, Tasmania, we're here! Where do you need us?'

It wasn't quite like that. But the move from airport to hostel accommodation to the Tasmanian offices of the National Council of Women was swift and categorical.

'Top of the morning to you,' Winifred said to the woman at the desk in her most charming Irish accent (she never usually said, 'top of the morning'). 'We would like to join up, if you please. We're fresh in from the mother country and would like to help get this antipodean outpost gumptioned on matters of women's liberty and common goods. We are experienced, smart, brave, and ready to serve Daughter Australia.' She performed a perfect military salute, followed by a nimble click of her heels and a little trumpet noise.

This cheerily eccentric approach did not seem at all peculiar to Bizzy. She was well versed in the idea that effective activism often involved making a complete fool of yourself. And also that getting other women onside is a very good start.

'The first thing a Japanese geisha learns in her training is how to charm another woman,' Winifred taught her at an early age. 'My charm is the singular reason you didn't grow up with Mr and Mrs Beige, useless dainty shoes and a hollowed-out soul.'

It worked on the Council of Women too. Lurlene Wallace, the woman at the desk, lifted her weary face and said, 'Well, thank the baby Jesus for that. I was having a bugger of a time finding volunteers for the Crafts for Cash initiative. Can you start now?'

So, Winifred and Bizzy began selling craft items door-to-door around the suburbs and businesses of Hobart. The crafts – knitted and stitched bits and bobs, decorated ribbons, birthday cards, miniature paintings, beaded collars, poems, recipes – were the product of 'unskilled' women struggling to make ends meet. 'The cohort of invisible indispensables,' Lurlene called them. 'Might get them a bit of pin money, if nothing else.'

Bizzy rather enjoyed the work. She was very taken by the creative skills of these unskilled women. She loved the poems and the paintings and especially the colourful costume jewellery. And she was genuinely thrilled when a sale led to an order for more products from a certain craftswoman. One housewife's knitted creations led to her opening a shopfront in Salamanca Place. Winifred, however, was restless. 'I'm not put on this earth to be a costermonger. Nothing wrong with costermongering, of course, but I can't like these trinkets, and I can't abide much more of this door-knockery. It's not coal-face enough for me.'

The door-knockery ended soon after when Winifred's charms worked their magic on an alderman, convincing him to back the Council for Women to form a market on Salamanca Place.

And so, the first Salamanca Market, replete with six stalls, was held on Saturday the second of November, 1971. Winifred and Bizzy were put in charge of the Council for Women stall, where they spruiked the rights of women, recruited new members and sold purple-and-green striped headscarves, pocket squares and neckties for sympathetic passers-by. (One of the neckties was repurposed as a headband by Mick Jagger when the Rolling Stones played Randwick Racecourse in 1973. Helen Reddy wore a pocket square tied around her wrist later that same year when she performed one of the first ever rock concerts at the Sydney Opera House.)

Another of the stalls featured paintings by an artist named Patricia. Bizzy was particularly taken by her work, especially her gentle, muted watercolours, which seemed to Bizzy to portray far, far away landscapes of calm. The kind she had never known.

'I can hear this painting,' she said to Patricia, pointing to a small picture of tea-coloured water, soft sky and a beach of pale pink.

Patricia chuckled. 'What does it sound like?'

'Bewitching silence.'

'Well, you're quite right,' said Patricia. 'It's a place that seems silent when you get there, but after a while you can hear that it's not silence at all, but a great chorus of delicate sounds. Lappings, birdsong, rustlings, distant, water-carried things . . . it *is* bewitching. Magical.'

'I want to go there,' says Bizzy.

'You'll need to hurry up then,' says Patricia. 'Very soon it will likely be gone.'

'Gone?'

'It's Lake Pedder. A lake in what they call "the wilderness". The government plans to drown it in order to form a hydropower catchment.'

'Drown it?'

'They'll dam the nearby rivers so that it floods an area big enough to power everyone's houses. That lake will become a big water impoundment.'

'Electricity?'

'Hydroelectricity.'

'But that's a tragedy! A travesty. They can't do that. Can they?'

'What travesty?' asked Winifred, interrupting the conversation with glee. 'And who can't do what?'

13

That's how Bizzy found herself walking at Winnie's strapping pace with a crew of artists and protesters across a mountain range in Tasmania's south-west. Under a sky of scudding clouds and changing colours, they arrived at the lake, with its miraculous, twinkling, pink inland beach.

They stayed for nine days. There was a filmmaker, two pilots, a Lithuanian photographer, a member of the newly formed United Tasmania Group, three painters, a poet, two professional hikers and two loony Irishwomen. They set up camp on the edge of the wide beach and went about their work.

Winifred threw herself in with the politician and the protesters while the artists set about doing what they could with pigment and canvas, written word and cameras, to stop the disappearance of a lake. That or a pre-emotive memorialising of a vanishing place. None of them felt the need to talk.

Bizzy wandered, mesmerised by the feeling of being held by dark mountains in a bright valley, listening to a tearing wind in the trees above but feeling nothing on her skin. Utterly protected. She walked the half mile across the beach and put her feet in the tannin lake, waited for the silence to bring out its chorus. And it did. She sang along.

She was at the northern shore of the beach, smiling at the squiggly trees with their feet in quartz when one of the pilots, the one called Charlie, emerged from the rocks.

'Oops,' he said. 'Sorry, didn't mean to intrude.'

'Oh, no intrusion. It's fine.' She'd spoken a little to Charlie on the walk in, liked his thoughtful presence.

They looked at the water and after a bit, he said, 'Everything feels a bit intrusive here, doesn't it.'

'Yes,' said Bizzy. 'Like we should be walking on tippy-toes. But that's not going to help this lake, is it? I feel so stupid that I can't do anything to stop them taking it away.'

There was another silence. Bizzy wondered whether Charlie might be painfully shy, and whether she should leave him to it, ease his pain. She started to walk away.

But he spoke. 'I'm going to fly a plane above Parliament House in Canberra and write *Save Lake Pedder* in the sky.'

'Wow,' said Bizzy. 'I wish I could do that.'

'You could come.' He looked away. She could feel his blush.

'I think,' said Bizzy, cushioning his embarrassment, 'if we just take in as much as we can, then we're doing something. We can tell people about it forever. Be the eyes that saw Lake Pedder before it was lost.'

'What will you say when you tell them?' he asked. 'It seems hard to put into words. For an apricot farmer with a thing for planes. I'd need to be a painter or a poet.' He pointed at the tiny dotted people on the far shore.

'Well,' says Bizzy, 'what if we try using all our senses, not just our eyes? Like you have to with apricots. And flying. Name five things we can see.'

'Brown water,' Charlie said.

'I see little wizened trees that look like old ladies trying to run away.'

'Ha, they do,' said Charlie. 'I have to do better than "brown water", don't I?'

'I like people who get to the point.'

He smiled at her then, a lopsided smile that made Bizzy look at his upper arms, then his longish dark hair, then his mouth.

'I see . . .' He pauses to think. 'Mountains like giants having a meeting.'

'They do look like giants having a meeting! Or are they an audience? They seem so interested.' Bizzy laughed. 'I see an impossible beach that shines pink even underwater.'

'And I see forty winds.'

Bizzy looked up and saw that the roaring forties winds were making shapes with the clouds. 'Four things we can hear.'

'Those winds again.'

'I hear a frog singing a middle C.'

'You know what the note is?'

'No, I was trying to impress you.' She couldn't look at him but could tell the blush had returned.

'I think I can hear the ghost of a Tasmanian Tiger,' Charlie said.

'I can hear that too!' They laughed again. 'What can you smell? Three things.'

'Trees,' says Charlie. 'I think the main smell is trees.'

'I smell water.'

'Does it count if the air is so pure it doesn't have a smell? So it smells like nothing?'

'I think so.' Bizzy nodded. 'Two things we can taste.'

He cupped his hands into the lake and lifted water to his lips. 'I taste, um, lake.'

She drank the lake too. 'Yep,' she says. 'Ancient glacier flavour. Very popular in Canada and places like that. And I taste salt, from where I clambered over those rocks and got sweaty and bothered.'

Charlie looked away and Bizzy thought, *Damn, I hit his shy nerve again.* But when she hurried on to, 'Name one thing you can feel; the last of the senses,' she found that Charlie wasn't shy at all, or if he was, there was some greater force, some ancient-lake spellwork that had him forgetting himself.

'Ah, well, I feel a lot more things than I can see or hear,' he said. 'I feel this water, cold enough to make me *not* feel my feet. And I feel the sun, and an itch on my neck where my shirt tag rubs.

And I feel pleased to be in this place, sad that it's in trouble, worried that I can't do enough. I feel my heart beating fast, and, to be completely honest, I feel like I might be falling in love.'

She stared at him. He was looking down, smiling at ripples.

Bizzy followed his gaze in confusion. 'With the lake? Falling in love with the lake?' She realised that her words were flush with hope.

'Nah, I already fell in love with that years ago, when I was a nipper.' He looked at her then, and she saw that his eyes were precisely the same tawny brown of the water that surrounded them.

$$\mathbb{B}$$

Twenty-one year old Charlie Herondale is the 'silly, flutter-hearted' secret that Bizzy gives Rosanna on her death bed. She gives it all – Charlie and the mass of baffling, rueful trailing threads – so Rosanna might take it all finally away.

She gives her the lake, where two young people with possibility all over their faces and a spring in their step found themselves in an extraordinary, vanishing place where anything could happen. Where people could write on the sky and pink beaches appeared far from the coast and painters made a masterpiece out of time.

'He gave you the ferromanganese quartzite,' says Rosanna, pointing at the disc around Bizzy's neck. 'A Pedder penny.'

'Yes,' says Bizzy. 'I didn't know you knew what it was.'

'I understood not to say,' Rosanna explains. 'I know a precious secret when I see one.'

'Ridiculous, but precious,' Bizzy says, 'I mean, I threw caution to the roaring of the forty winds and fell headlong into love with a tannin-tinted splash. Charlie and I lost ourselves in the Frankland Range, kissed under a full moon, swam naked in the far reaches of the lake, made love at the foot of a two-thousand-year-old tree and laughed until we thought we would die from lack of air. I mean, Rosanna, it would make you sick with sweet romance.'

'It does not make me sick,' Rosanna says. 'I am already sick. This makes me better. So much better. I love this secret story.'

So Bizzy tells her more. She gives Rosanna all the sights, the sounds, the smells, the tastes and the feels. She hands over her wishes to fly with Charlie the pilot forever.

'But the nine days were soon over and Charlie had to fly the politician out, while Winnie and I walked with the artists and the hikers. He held my head and kissed my face and he found the Pedder penny at the bottom of the lake.' Bizzy touches the small brown disc. 'He gave it to me and told me he would find me at the boarding house in Hobart, and then he flew away.

'And all the walk home over the Sentinels I trudged like a broken-winged thing, wishing I could fly too. And there was Winnie, tut-tutting and saying things like, "Love will do you in, my darling" and "Let's get you home", as though I was poorly with something, and as though I had a home when I'd never before felt such an absence of one.'

Rosanna, with her hand pressed to her mouth, says, 'And what happened next?'

'Well, soon after that it was reported that a pilot and a protester were flying to Canberra to write their lament in the sky but the plane vanished. Crashed, perhaps sabotaged.'

Rosanna gasps.

'And Winnie took me and my distress from the guest house to Launceston and buried us deep in the battles for a women's hospital.'

'Oh, Bizzy. This is so sad.'

'But it wasn't him flying the plane.'

Rosanna gasps again, smiles, claps her hands.

'We found out months later that it had been another pilot, one I didn't know. Even though Charlie said he would be going, it wasn't him. I cried with relief but then I couldn't find him and I started to think he really wasn't real. That I had dreamed him.

'And next the dams were opened and the water flowed and all through that winter of '72, the great valley was flooded. Some of the artists went back in a boat and saw the waters swirling around the tops of the little old lady trees, and they saw the last of the pink beach before it was altogether swallowed up. The skeletons of trees still stand all over that valley today, nearly fifty years later. Dead and colourless as anything you ever saw. And if you went there, you'd not even know where that little glacial outwash had ever been.'

Rosanna gives a tear in return for the secrets.

'The Lithuanian photographer died not long after. Drowned in a river. One of the hikers was killed in a fall. One activist was on the vanished plane. But the artists continue to paint Lake Pedder and the lost pink beach as though they've been haunted by it ever since.'

'And Charlie? Did you find him?'

Bizzy takes a deep breath. 'Winnie and I were caught up in the Gordon-below-Franklin resistance after that, and soon after that she died and I had grief to contend with. And as I said, it's like I dreamed him up. If it weren't for the penny I'd reckon he'd have been a trick of light on that blinding beach.' Her eyes fill with tears. She removes the Pedder penny on its chain from around her neck and hands it to Rosanna. 'Could you take him now, Rosanna? Take him with you? Because he's been beating on the door of my dreams of late and I can feel regret dampening me down and like Winnie said, love will do me in.'

'But I think you should find him, Bizzy,' Rosanna says. 'Find him. He will probably be a leery old man expecting you to darn his horrible old socks and your regret will turn to triumph.'

'But that would be worse,' says Bizzy wearily. 'Another sure sign that the dark of the world can leach even into the very light.' She pressed the stone into Rosanna's hand. 'So take him?'

'Okay,' says Rosanna, clasping the warm brown circle. 'I will take these precious things with thanks. But will you promise me you will run free with the Angry Women's Choir? That you will throw your passions into our rally and try to project your voices further than ever before? I am worried for your fire, Bizzy. It is low, yes?'

'Very low,' says Bizzy. 'And I don't know if I can do it without you.'

'You will never be without me.'

𝄡

Stepping Stone Number 142, from *La Lista* by R.K.:
Swim in the nude, whenever the opportunity arises. There are few things so wonderful.

Chapter 25

Sisters

Mary arrives at the Kalbfel household early, while Bizzy is still in telling her secret. She helps Kyrie and Serra in the kitchen, plays cards with Matty and Ilaria and is still chatting to Jonathon long after her appointment time has passed.

'Bizzy must have a ginormous secret,' Matty says when he's beaten Mary at a second round of memory cards. 'It's going for ages.'

'Yep, sorry, Mary,' says Jonathon. 'I could hurry them along. Avni and Sally are still to go in, too.'

'No, don't do that,' Mary says. 'It's okay. I don't have a secret anyway. I've told everyone everything, even about ticking yes on my parents' gay marriage votes while telling them the postie hadn't delivered them.'

'Vigilante,' says Jonathon.

'No secret romance?' suggests Kyrie.

'Nope.'

'Are you a little bit gay?' asks Matty.

'No,' says Mary wistfully.

'Do you have a crush?' asks Serra.

'Well, I've had a crush on you for years, Jonathon, but that's no secret.'

'Have you ever done shoplifting?' asks Ilaria. 'Or killed someone?'

'No,' says Mary, then bursts into tears.

Kyrie takes her in her arms and coos, 'Oh, Mary.'

Mary sobs. Rosanna's family watch. Jonathon pats her hand.

'Look at you all,' Mary cries. 'Oh my God, sitting here in this tragic ending with your incredible bravery and those gorgeous cooking smells. I'm so sorry to bring my blubbering in. Just that it feels like I'm losing my sister.'

'We don't mind, Mary,' Ilaria says.

'Maybe you should just stay with us,' suggests Serra. 'Instead of a secret, just be here.'

This makes Mary cry harder and apologise again.

'Imagine if no one sobbed at the kitchen table,' says Jonathon. 'That would be worse.'

Mary blows her nose into a tissue and says, 'Oh gawd, you're such a lovely man. We could get married if you like, once you've done your mourning. That's really inappropriate, isn't it.'

'Well,' says Jonathon with a smile, 'I probably shouldn't marry my wife's sister.'

𝄐

Avni loiters at Rosanna's door so quietly that Rosanna senses her before she sees her.

'Avni Sasani,' she says quietly, 'you needn't come in if you don't want to. I have the look of death.'

Avni walks into the room and says, 'I was worried about waking you but I am not afraid of death. My mother brought me here from Iran after my father was killed and she taught me the Baha'i law that dying is not an ending, but the beginning of the most important part – when the soul is free and able to reach its full potential without the restrictions of a body. We also believe that the freed soul will continue to influence our world and loved ones. My father's Persian culture appears in my music, I don't force it, it just does, Rosanna, like a miracle. My mother says I have an open, sing-song mind that lets things through.'

'I believe that,' says Rosanna. 'I hear it in your heavenly voice.'

'And your soul, Rosanna, I think it will be the strongest, most beautifully influential, musical soul there can be. It is already strong, think what it'll be able to do.'

'Ah, I knew something was growing inside of me,' Rosanna says. 'Even as I am fading I can feel it steeling itself. This explains why.'

Avni nods, then sits on the visitor's chair and lets her next words come out in a rush. 'And my secret is that I haven't signed the recording contract with Island Records. I've changed my mind.'

Rosanna gasps.

'I'm not made for stages and all the things they promise me. My music comes from a place that is bigger than me, and so how can I take reward? It comes to me so I can use it for my community, for my world.'

Rosanna's words of protest stay on her tongue.

'The record company asked me to change my pronunciations of things,' Avni continues, 'alter my tone so that I sound kind of like a drunk baby. They don't like the songs that carry influence from my cultures. They say I will have money and travel and fame and luxury, but if I take those things then I think the music will stop and the songs won't come anymore. And so I said no. And I am so, so relieved.'

Rosanna nods and says, 'You are keeping your soul safe.'

'Yes. I want it to still be singing when it leaves this world.'

And then she sings a Persian ballad so luminous and beautiful that Rosanna can feel her soul swelling with every note.

𝄡

'I'm not highly regarded for my bedside manner,' Sally says from the visitor's chair, 'so I won't subject you to it for long, but I thought I'd tell you that I got breast augmentation in 1999 and while I know it reinforces damaging patriarchal beauty expectations and taints my feminist stance it has definitely made that stance stronger, taller and more confident. People thought I went through menopause and got bolshie. They were wrong – I got a cleavage and a lot more front. My husband loves them so much that I was able to withhold sex until he stopped insisting the neighbours cut down their black peppermint gum. The tree is now thriving and the neighbours have become our friends. I haven't regretted my boobs for a moment.' She coughs, holds Rosanna's astonished gaze and says, 'You can respond now. I'm ready.'

So Rosanna takes her hand and says, 'Look at you go, Sally – turning the enemies' weapons back on themselves, saving the trees and avoiding the wars. Boobs are life-giving in so many ways, yes? Maybe after this rally of Bizzy's, the choir can lead a global sex strike. You could probably achieve climate change reversal and nuclear disarmament.'

Sally presses Rosanna's hand and says, 'I'm sorry I couldn't whip up a cancer cure in time for all that excitement, my friend.'

'I am sorry too but thank you to your colleagues for trying.'

𝄢

Freycinet arrives at Rosanna's house just as Bizzy and Sally are being seen out by Kyrie. For a fleeting moment, Frey doesn't recognise Bizzy. Her posture is different – not stooped, exactly, but almost. Her cheekbones are not highlighted with rouge and her clothes are a muted green. Her bright hair is hidden under a plain blue scarf.

'Hello there, Freycinet,' she says.

'Hello, Bizzy.'

Sally sighs deeply and says, 'It's really happening.'

Frey gives a slight nod. 'I'm very, very sorry.' The phrase hangs, useless, between them, so Frey adds, 'It's so unfair.'

Bizzy takes a minute to look at the sky. 'Yes,' she says, 'life is a brute. An ugly, evil brute.'

'It is a brute,' agrees Kyrie. 'But not always.'

'A lot of the time, though,' says Bizzy. 'Most of the time, frankly.' She is so heavy with sadness that she has to sit on the edge of the verandah. Kyrie and Sally sit beside her and the three lean into one another, murmuring and gazing into one another's faces with the easy proximity of sisters.

Freycinet looks away, wishes herself away. *I'm an imposter here*, she tells herself. It's a thought she's had many times before.

'I'll just . . .' she says, but Kyrie and Bizzy are still murmuring. She looks at the rise of rock behind the house and tells it, 'I'll go in.'

Inside the house there is laughter and the smell of something baking.

'Hi, Freycinet!' Mary stands from the couch. 'This is Freycinet, everyone. Freycinet, meet Ilaria, Matty, and this gorgeous thing is Bella.' Mary holds up a chubby baby with the biggest, blackest eyes Freycinet has ever seen. 'Ilaria had to make me cakes so I don't actually eat this baby up, she is so delicious.' Mary blows a raspberry on Bella's round belly. The baby erupts into laughter.

Freycinet is momentarily stunned by the warmth in the room, the open, not-sullen confidence of these children and the lack of regard given to death, whose presence is undetectable, except perhaps in a trace of redness about Mary's eyes, some scrunched tissues.

'You're her last secret,' says Ilaria. 'And then we're going to bring her back in here. She's got a wheelie hospital bed.'

'It has electric sit-up and a speaker for music,' says Matty. He climbs onto the couch, balances on one foot and pulls a silly face at Bella. The baby laughs uproariously again.

'Oh, Bella,' says Mary, laughing along. 'My heart.'

Serra pokes her head into the room, sees Freycinet and says, 'Wow, you and Grace are really alike.'

'This is Serra,' says Mary.

Freycinet is surprised. 'Hi Serra,' she says. 'You're at the same dance school as my Grace.' She feels a ripple of worry.

'Yes. We're in the Sunday class. She's like the best dancer in the state, pretty much.'

'Oh, I don't know about that.'

A grown-up version of Matty arrives, bringing a shadow of concern into the warm room. He is handsome, with long-ish dark hair and fear written into his brow. 'Hello,' he says. 'You must be Freycinet. I'm Jonathon.'

Frey shakes his hand and says, 'Thank you for having me. I hope this isn't all too much.'

'No, no, thank you for coming. Rosanna is so grateful. She's having the best day.' But everything about his face says that it is most definitely all too much. 'She's looking forward to seeing you.' He motions towards the door.

Rosanna's room is sunny and filled with flowers. The hospital-style bed is draped with a cheery quilt of patchworked vintage squares and beneath it is Rosanna. She is tiny and oddly coloured, her hands so thin and limp, seem too long to be human. There is a hint of something unsettling in the air, beneath the scent of the flowers. Frey averts her gaze to a beautiful oil painting of cottages against a snowy mountain. Thick, layered strokes, muted colours and an ornate gilt frame give it an old, precious appearance.

'It's by Ulrich Gleiter,' says Rosanna, and Freycinet is startled by the strength of her voice. 'The choir gave it to me for my fortieth birthday. My mountains. My brother is due to arrive from Italy tomorrow. I'm pulling all my mountains to me.' She chuckles and gestures to the visitor's chair.

Freycinet sits. 'You even have a piece of our mountain in your backyard!'

'Yes.' Rosanna's smile is almost bigger than her face. 'We knew this was the place because it sits at an actual toe of kunanyi.' She waves to the window, where Freycinet can see the rise of mossy rock. 'Sometimes I think I see it move, that mountain toe.'

'How are you feeling?' asks Freycinet. 'Is that a terrible question?'

'I am pleased that you asked. Nobody does anymore. I feel . . .' Rosanna shifts in her bed. A square of quilt turns towards Freycinet. It has the exact orange and brown flowers of her childhood sheets. 'I feel dying.'

'Oh.' Freycinet stares at a cartoon-like orange flower. 'And does that feel awful?'

'Not so awful. Now that I have stopped the fighting. But, yes, I will die within the week. I'm aiming for Tuesday, to give you all something to sing about at choir meeting. Not Sunday. It is not a good thing to die on a Sunday, too many gods hovering around.'

Freycinet doesn't have time to think of a response because Rosanna moves swiftly on.

'Now, enough about me, everybody dies, yawn, yawn. You.' She turns her body towards the visitor's chair and the orange flowers ripple. 'Everybody is fascinated with you. You don't have to tell me a secret, you don't know me so well enough, perhaps. But tell me just about you. None of us can see you properly, behind your beautiful mask. Telling about you is secret enough.'

Freycinet looks into the huge windows in Rosanna's face and sees herself reflected back. She takes a breath. 'Me? I am a lot of things. But mostly I *am* a secret. *Sono un segreto.*'

𝄡

Stepping Stone Number 57, from *La Lista* by R.K.:

Do things that exercise different parts of your brain and keep it healthy. Learn a language, read music, dance, build a labyrinth from stones, make cheese, read poetry, sit and look at the stars, do nothing.

Chapter 26
Take That, Nancy Drew

Freycinet Blewes was born on a Thursday, the only daughter of Lynn and Roger Blewes of Swansea, Tasmania. While the Blewes family – six in total – were all dark haired with curls, Freycinet grew to have straight, fine, fair hair. Her parents were told regularly, 'She'll go a long way with those looks' or, conversely, 'She'll be trouble.' Lynn wasn't one for favouritism but Frey's beauty gave her a different sort of hope than anything she'd ever held for herself. She had always wanted to be a little bit fancy, but could never pull it off. So she made Frey's dresses from the prettiest fabrics, instructed her to stay clean and enrolled her in violin, equestrian and ballet lessons.

Frey's response was to scrunch-dry her hair every morning in the hopes it might curl and dig in the garden to dirty her fingernails. She would jump her horse out of the equestrian arena and gallop away. Unable to escape quickly with a violin or in ballet shoes, she simply worked swiftly and smartly, sailing through exams and recitals on her own terms and with flair, so that no one could pester her into extra hours of practice. She worked hard at school as well, achieving good results, but argued teachers down until they lost their tempers. She had regular bouts of indignation and was disciplined for them by her mother, made to scrub potatoes or fold sheets or help with whatever chore Lynn was encumbered with.

'You have so much potential,' Lynn would tell her. 'Don't throw it away just to prove that you have a mind of your own. Listen to the advice of others, keep your head down and you could do anything, my girl, be anyone. Now, this is how you fold a fitted sheet.'

Freycinet watched the pride with which Lynn smoothed the orange-and-brown flowered sheet into a neat square and swore to herself never to be proud until there was something worth being proud of. 'I can be anyone,' she'd tell herself. 'Maybe everyone. Anything but this.'

Roger, an electrical engineer and diesel mechanic, watched his daughter with fascination, and wondered vaguely whether she could really have sprung from his loins. Or Lynn's, for that matter. 'I swear I heard St David's Cathedral ring the bells backwards the day that girl was born,' he'd say whenever Freycinet raised another commotion. Meanwhile, Lynn bought her a box of Nancy Drew mysteries and hoped she might be satisfied with vicarious daring and adventure.

Most of Freycinet's contemporaries had a phase of being obsessed with Nancy Drew. They all wanted to be her. Accomplished, capable, confident, attractive and brave. Freycinet's obsession was slightly different. She decided, after scornfully making her way through the box of books, that she would be better than Nancy Drew. That Nancy Drew would one day want to be Freycinet Blewes.

So, at the age of fourteen, she studied psychology books until she was attuned to the powers of suggestion and association, well versed in behavioural and cognitive psychology and schooled to university level in the science of human nature. She took up French, German and Japanese at school, Italian and Spanish in her spare time. (Nancy Drew could only speak French and English.) Frey's grandmother taught her to cook, her grandfather taught her golf. She played tennis to state level, and was taught poker, driving, diving and how to mix a cocktail by her brothers.

By the time she had entered university to study Arts-Law, she had obtained a boat licence, a driver's licence, a motorcycle licence, a gun licence, a first-aid certificate and a brown belt in taekwondo. She joined the university drama club, specialising in roles that required accents and mimicry, and declined an offer from a talent scout to audition for *Neighbours*. Freycinet left the University of Tasmania with first-class honours in Law, a masters in European Studies and a diploma in violin performance. Her final year was spent in Berlin and when it was over, she had saved up enough money from violin gigs to travel home via the rest of the world.

There was no time for friends but she wished very much that she could meet Nancy Drew so she could show her a thing or two.

In Vienna she busked on the streets to gathering crowds and learnt how to trounce a pickpocket. In London she learnt how to tell a decent joke, appreciate Morrissey and laugh at herself. In Seychelles she learnt how to climb trees and how to move her hips. In Brazil she mastered the art of flirting. In Zanzibar she learnt how to make love. In Budapest she learnt how to drink. In Milan she learnt how to wear a suit. In Hollywood she learnt how to paint her face and how to be someone else. In Idaho she learnt how to ski cross-country and how to access her spiritual side. In Fiji she learnt how to talk to children. In Japan she learnt patience. In Suriname she learnt how to be alone and in New Guinea she learnt how not to show fear.

When she finally faced recruitment officers at the Australian Secret Intelligence Service in Canberra, her curriculum vitae was waved in the air and scoffed at.

'So,' said an innocuous-looking man in a yellow jumper, 'you have made it to round three of the selection process for an Intelligence Officer position, which means that your credentials check out, but they still seem somewhat preposterous for a twenty-four-year-old woman.'

'Would they seem somewhat preposterous for a twenty-four-year-old *man*?' asked Freycinet.

The only other woman in the room smiled.

'*Siapa kamu sebenarnya?*' fired Yellow Jumper Man at Freycinet. *Who are you, really?*

'*Saya adalah semua orang dan bukan siapa-siapa,*' replied Freycinet.

Yellow Jumper Man frowned and looked at his colleagues. 'She says that she is everyone and no one.'

Some of the officers nodded and raised their eyebrows, which looked like approval.

'You are a musician?' asked the woman.

'Yes.'

'And a horsewoman.'

'Yes.'

'And an electronics expert.'

'Yes.'

'You have a law degree but you do not want to enter the law?'

'No. I want to enter the foreign service.'

'Have you told your family and friends about your ambitions?'

'No. They think I want to play the violin and get married.'

'And you don't want to marry?'

'No.'

'Why not?' This from Yellow Jumper Man, whom Freycinet had identified as a bit of a twat.

'Because I have worked hard for my independence. I don't want to be tied down. I have a sense of vocation that is not compatible with family life.'

'Do you have friends?'

'Yes, a few close friends.' Freycinet glided through the lie.

'Do you enjoy recognition for your many achievements?'

'Not particularly. I play music to save money for travel and I generally don't talk about myself unless I have to.'

'You have lived an exciting life. Are you looking for more excitement?'

'Yes, of course. But I am aware that much of the work is not about excitement in the classic sense of the word. I am excited by being in the field just as I am excited, for instance, by the prospect of helping our politicians to develop appropriate foreign policy.'

'Do you consider yourself unusual?'

'No. I have a brain that I would like to put to good use. I have an appetite for learning and for how we fit into the world. I am fascinated by human relations and psychology and I love my country. I don't think any of that is unusual.'

'Well, I think you're *very* unusual,' said Yellow Jumper Man, as he slid Freycinet's application to his right.

He turned out to be ASIS Director-General, and a slide to his right side meant the candidate was approved for the assessment stage.

Within six months Freycinet was accepted into the ASIS Intelligence Officer training program and six months after that, she received her first overseas posting, for which she was flown to Mali to assist with the recovery of a kidnapped Australian fisherman who had been lured to Africa by a fake mail-order bride. The recovery took only a few days but Freycinet played a key part in the fisherman's rescue by locating the hotel he'd been lured to and his trajectory from there. She was quickly posted again, this time on a longer-term assignment in which she was to gather intelligence in the Middle East that would inform anti-terrorism policy. Her life, loosely based in Canberra, was dictated by the unexpected. She loved every minute of it.

13

Seven years into her work, after being promoted to Senior Intelligence Officer, Freycinet was living briefly in Oxford, England when she met Gilbert Barnes. The assessment agency had given a clear directive for her to gather human or financial intelligence on a wealthy British businessman and his side hustle of human trafficking between the Philippines, the UK and Singapore. She successfully liaised with foreign partners and useful agents, one of whom had helped get her a violin gig at the event and another who was present, handing around hors d'oeuvres.

It was one of the rare times that Freycinet could get into an outfit worthy of everyone's expectation of the glamorous spy. It wasn't a job that called for high-octane action (so few of them were), but she did take a moment to appreciate her years of violin practice and to think, *Take that, Nancy Drew, you and your sports gear. I have a regulation-issued designer outfit and a security clearance, how're you going with that old clock?*

Her job occasionally called upon her to operate under 'deep cover', which gave her false names, nationalities and appearances. (Roxy had turned up at an art gallery covering a drug operation; Freida was a violin tutor to the teenage son of a big-time tax cheat.) She relished those jobs especially, but on this occasion, she was to perform as herself, Freycinet Blewes, at a benefit reception at the Divinity School next to Oxford's Bodleian Library. Her target, Robert Hannaford, was the reception's guest of honour, having donated a sizeable sum to the cause of children's literacy. She quickly chose a flute of champagne over a brandy and dry, not because she particularly wanted it (no drinking on the job) but because indecision is anathema to effective espionage. She took a tiny sip of champagne and scanned the crowd under the guise of admiring the space, but barely saw the astonishing beauty and storied intricacy of the tracery windows and the fan-vaulted ceiling.

Gilbert was the fourth person she clocked as familiar. The other three, one of which was Robert Hannaford, were all strangers but turned up a name, an occupation and a relationship to the target. Gilbert's handsome, tanned face didn't come with particulars, just an odd feeling that she was looking at someone she knew. He was dressed in a check shirt, a wonky tie and shiny R.M. Williams boots and looked just like upper-class Northern Tasmania at the autumn races. When she moved past him through the crowd to her violin and heard his Tasmanian boarding school accent (possibly undetectable to anyone but a Tasmanian spy) she was momentarily floored. It was like being caught out after curfew by your dad. She reminded herself that she was not undercover, merely being Freycinet. So she worked a little harder at that. It didn't come as easily as being in disguise and speaking a second language.

After her performance, it was possible that Gilbert caught a glimpse of home too, because he approached her and said, 'That was really nice. You're really good at that, aren't you? I mean, really good.'

His words were so simple and not wanky that Freycinet was ever so slightly disarmed.

'Thanks.'

'Pretty bloody impressive venue too, isn't it?'

'Yes, amazing.'

'Man, it would have seen some brain activity, this place. Think of all the thoughts that have been thought in here. A school of divinity. I don't know what that is but it sounds pretty up there.'

Freycinet smiled. 'It's just a fancy name for theology. Religion.'

'Jesus,' said Gilbert with a twinkle in his eye.

They laughed.

'You're Aussie,' he said.

'Yes,' replied Freycinet, thinking quickly. 'But I live here in Oxford for the moment. And my brother's dyslexic so I'm a big fan of this literacy initiative.'

'Oh, is that what this is? I met Robert at a work thing years ago and I'm just back visiting so he asked me along. I'm not really involved in this stuff, but we're having dinner afterwards. Where in Oz are you from?'

'Tasmania.'

'You're kidding. Me too. Launceston.'

'Swansea.'

'Ah, I knew you weren't classy enough for Launnie. I'm Gilbert. Gil.'

'Freycinet.'

'As in . . .'

'The peninsula, yes.'

'My family has a shack there. Coles Bay.'

Of course they do, thinks Freycinet.

'Beautiful place,' Gil says with a smile.

The smile Freycinet returned was genuine. She was pleased to be talking to a friend of Robert's, but even more pleased to be talking to Gil from Tasmania. She had an invitation to that dinner in her sights mostly for intelligence reasons, and a little not. He was so familiar and comfortable with being out of context. Freycinet was trained to find context and place herself into it. She was suddenly tired, and thinking of her mother's faded apron and the bit of worn carpet by her father's chair. Homesickness wafted through her, and Gil began to seem like the only person in the room. Like they weren't standing near a chair carved from timbers taken from the first ship ever to circumnavigate the world. He told her about his urge to travel clashing painfully with a job offer from a top property valuation firm.

'I just sort of want to go for beers and surf and explore coastlines,' he said. 'Growing up seems like a lot of boring, hard work.'

From her complicated, high-alert place in the world, Freycinet was beguiled. But she was also beginning to doubt the dinner invitation tactic. Gil was downing drinks rather quickly and could end up playing confusion agent, talking over valuable assets or changing subjects. Also she could tell he was attracted to her, and honeytrapping wasn't part of her tradecraft. She put eyes on Robert, who had nodded in Gil's direction and was slowly making his way across the room.

'Gil Barnes, you old sod,' he said when he finally reached them. 'How the bloody hell?'

Freycinet took in his small frame, his cowlick and the weakness of his chin and thought, *Right, well, you don't frequent the part of the arrogance spectrum I thought you might.*

'Bobsy, look at you, mate. So spiffy.' Gil tweaked the lapel of Robert's suit.

Exquisite cut – tailor-made, for sure, thought Freycinet. She guessed Savile Row, probably Anderson & Sheppard, by the flare of the drape. Patek Philippe watch. *This man has serious money. But where is his hubris?* She was fascinated.

'Thank you for the music,' he said not quite to Freycinet but very nearly. 'I'm Robert.'

'This is Freycinet,' Gil said, 'She's from Tasmania too. What are the chances, here in the hall of divinity or whatever it is?'

Robert raised a questioning hand. 'Tchaikovsky?'

Freycinet was surprised. 'Yes. The violin concerto, second movement.'

'A very sad piece. I should like to hear you play something more uplifting one day, perhaps.'

He looked at the floor just as Freycinet's heart sank. *This man is not going to brag about his schemes.* 'Oh, but there is so much beauty in the sad,' she said. 'And far more resonance.'

Robert looked her in the eye for a brief moment and said, 'I have a bit more ingratiating to do, and then I think the three of us should go for dinner. You Tasmanians will have much to, er . . .' He didn't finish his sentence, but just sidled off.

'He's a funny old thing, Robert,' said Gil, once they'd watched him go. 'Do anything for you, though. So, will you come for dinner? We're bound to have mutual friends to gossip about.'

'Thank you,' said Freycinet. Later, as she left with Gil, Robert and several others, she paused to take an hors d'oeuvre from the Filipino NICA agent standing by the door.

𝄢

Rosanna has more eye than face. '*Madonna fucking mia*,' she says. 'You are a spy?'

'I *was* a spy,' says Freycinet.

'This is unbelievable. And fantastic. You win, Freycinet Barnes. Freycinet Blewes. You win the secret of the day. Did you really use your future husband to spy on a criminal?'

'Yes.'

'Does he know?'

'No.'

'That you are a spy or that you were using him?'

'Neither.'

'Oh my gosh, I have so many questions.' Rosanna rearranges her body against the pillows. The brown-and-orange flowers bulge out towards Freycinet. 'Who else knows this?'

'My father.'

'That is all?'

Frey thinks. 'Well, Bizzy hit on it with a wild guess but I denied it.'

'Oh my Goddy God.' Rosanna's huge eyes widen even further. 'But finish the story, please. Did you get the human trafficker man? With the weak chin?'

'Yes. I learnt that he was brought up in an upper-class household that lamented the loss of what they called "service", which to us is "domestic servitude" or "slavery". So he drummed up quite a racket amongst a ring of like-minded twats, and made a lot of money supplying them with nannies, housekeepers, drivers, gardeners and whatever they needed to augment their lifestyle. We sent home forty-nine Filipino nationals, all of whom had worked almost twenty-four seven for a pittance. Some of them slept in cupboards.'

'Holy hecks. And your Gilbert, he does not know you brought down his friend?'

'No.'

'So you dedicate your life to espionage and then you don't tell your husband, the man you marry, what you do?'

'No.'

'He does not wonder why you speak so many languages and can kick a man in the nuts so lightning quickly that no one will see?'

'Occasionally he is surprised by some of my D.I.Y. skills, but I have a very practical father who is obsessed with fixing things, so . . .'

'And you have three brothers who taught you how to kick arse.'

'Yes.'

'I have five brothers.'

'You do?' Freycinet experiences an odd feeling of kinship.

'Yes. They taught me how to run away. I became a doctor of rocks, not anything so extraordinary as a spy.'

'Much more sensible,' says Frey.

'You don't want to show off? My God, I would want to show everything off. Look at me! I am a ballerina, I can ride horses and fly over a tall building in a single bound. What do you tell him instead?'

'That I was a musician. Which I was.'

'So you did not have to tell a lie. Brilliant!'

'Oh, I told a lie. I told many lies. Our wedding was a cover for an operation to bring down a paedophile ring.'

'Your wedding?'

Freycinet glances at the wedding photograph on the bedside table. Jonathon and Rosanna on the mountain, surrounded by family. Real and true. 'Yes. He had no idea.'

'You never told him, ever?'

'No.'

'How did he not know?'

'Gil just sees the things he wants to see. The power of suggestion.'

'Why did you marry him?'

'I loved him. It was wonderful, passionate. He had a gloriously simple view of the world. A haiku view.'

'Haiku?'

'A really simple little poem that reduces everything to the essentials. No overthinking.'

'Give me his haiku. You have thought about it, yes?'

Freycinet pushes her hair back self-consciously and quotes,

'He said, "This is nice."

And for his light, simple view,

I gave him my heart.'

'Ah,' says Rosanna. 'Does he still have it? Your heart?'

Freycinet feels an ache in her stomach. 'Yes.'

Rosanna leaves some silence.

'I think,' says Freycinet after a long pause, 'in hindsight, that for all my measured risk-taking and high-flying and danger zones, Gilbert actually posed the single most life-threatening thing I have ever encountered. I mean, above Somalian pirates and raging oligarchs.'

'Oh,' Rosanna whispers.

'Yes.'

'And how long did you do this, travelling with your violin, being the mysterious musician lady spook?'

'For two years after I moved back to Tasmania. For one of those I had a baby.'

'You used your baby as a cover?'

'No! Never.' Freycinet bit her lip. 'Only once.'

'Fucking the hell, Freycinet Blewes.'

'I know. So, you see, I really have no legs to stand on when it comes to deceit and risking the family unit. My anger has no legs.

And I've dished out some bits of revenge. I flushed his favourite tie down the loo, wrecked his golf clubs. And I sent him to a cosmetic clinic for his birthday and now he can't move his face.'

Rosanna's whoop of laughter is incongruous with her tiny frame. 'Ha! You got him right in the egos.'

Frey laughs too. 'So,' she says, 'maybe Gil's infidelity is a fair balancing of things.'

'Or maybe you just can't see the injustice of it because your self-worth is a little worn away.'

'I wore it away, though. I did that.'

'No one tells you you're useful, do they?'

'No.'

'Do they have a cupboard for you to sleep in?'

Freycinet shifts uncomfortably. 'Rosanna, I've been out of the Service now for sixteen years but still, I have never told anyone that I used my husband, and my baby, as unsuspecting acorns.'

'What is acorns?'

'Intelligence agents.'

'I think that if Gil were using you as his acorns, and never telling you, then no one would think twice. Least of all him. I think you could be indignant about that.'

'I even named our dog Acorn, because to this day I use him as a cover.'

'Hmm, acorns and sexpionage. You are a very, very excellent spy.'

'I am a very excellent fraud. In a glass house. With stones in her belly.'

'And no legs.' Rosanna smiles.

'I told you that I am a secret. A master of disguise.'

'Maybe you don't know what else to be.'

'Well, exactly.'

They sit in some silence before Rosanna and her flabbergast speak again. 'I think,' she says, 'that you need to take those stones you carry in your stomach and start throwing some of them. I think they might pave all sorts of new ways.'

Frey lets the ache rise into a burn. 'Yes,' she says. 'You're probably right. More stepping stones.'

'Yes,' says Rosanna. 'Stepping stones.'

There is another silence before Rosanna snorts and says, 'Imagine if your name is Winifred, like Bizzy's mother. You would have been called Winnie Blewes. Ha!' Rosanna mimes smoking a cigarette and laughs, then coughs.

Freycinet waits for the coughs to subside before she says, 'I am glad I've made you laugh. *Sono contento di averti fatto ridere.*'

Rosanna stops laughing and says, 'Say that in Spanish.'

'*Estoy contenta de haberte hecho reír.*'

'Say it in German.'

'*Es tut mir so leid, dass du weg sein wirst.*'

Rosanna beams, but the German words mean 'I am so sorry that you will be gone'. Freycinet tries to match Rosanna's beam, hoping that it will hide her tears.

𝄢

Freycinet drives a circuitous route home, around the mountainside to Neika, down to Longley and back towards Hobart on Sandfly Road. At the town of Margate, she pulls off the road beside a postbox and pulls out two identical envelopes, one bearing an address in Hobart, marked to The Leader of the Opposition, Labor Member for Clark, and the other addressed to AAR Media in Sydney, addressed to The Editor, *Woman* magazine.

Freycinet carries the envelopes to the postbox, whispers, 'Deeds not words,' and slips both envelopes through the slot.

𝄢

Stepping Stone Number 211, from *La Lista*, by R.K.:
How to fold a fitted sheet: roll it in a ball, toss it in the linen cupboard then go and laugh with a friend, for goodness sake.

Chapter 27

Mountaineer

The ending does come on Tuesday. At eleven twenty-two on a bright November morning, it creeps in and gently takes the mountain woman from her mountainside. Her voice remains audible right up to the hour. And with her family, two of her brothers, her bosom friends and the toe of the mountain gathered at her bedside, she says this:

'I am not angry and I am not afraid, because I have very great hope for what lies ahead for me. It is not a fashionable thing to believe in afterlife, and science is dismissive, but there are a great many things science has not discovered. It has not, for instance, been able to see the soul. And therefore it seems to think our souls do not exist. But how arrogant of us to assume that, to expect to know all the mysteries. Why did not my siblings get this cancer like me, when they were sitting in the same car with the same cigarillo smoke? Why can the horse hear the tree screaming well before it falls? How do we know to turn and find the person looking at us? How do we explain a mother's knowing? What about all the things that do not fit the pictures of evolution? How do we know my energies won't reappear by all of your sides all over the world and in other universes? The stardust makes the beautiful women on the catwalks just as it made the coconut crab. So in my imaginations I have a picture of going everywhere and nowhere, of staying and leaving and being home, all of them, all at once. For this you must not pity me.

'But you must allow some sadness, for your health, and you all must remain both afraid and angry. Fear will keep away the apathy. And anger will drive you forward. Forward, forward, forward, my loves. And do not forget to rest sometimes, because there is a very long way to go.'

She leaves a moment's silence, at which her family and bosom friends widen their eyes. They lean closer. To those eyes and that leaning, the mountain woman smiles her indelible smile, lifts an acrobatic hand and says, 'I thought up a haiku. Do you know what that is?'

The mountain woman's eldest daughter, relieved to hear her mother's voice remove the cusp of silence, whispers, 'A tiny Japanese poem with seventeen syllables.'

The mountain woman nods, takes a long, reedy breath and on a fading voice says,

'All the women sing,
their chorus so thunderous,
the world must tune in.'

She closes her eyes wearily, holds up a finger and adds in a whisper, '*Il frigorifero é puzzolente. Prova l'essenza di vaniglia.*' The finger and its hand float gently to the part of her below her ribs where scientists might have looked for a soul. '*Andiamo,*' she breathes.

Only one person speaks, the soulmate friend named Mary who grips the bed clothing with white knuckles in a last-order hope to hold time still. 'A scientist at the turn of the century,' she says, 'found that souls do exist, and that they weigh three quarters of an ounce.'

But the mountain woman, though she smiles very faintly, does not open her eyes again, she speaks no more, and a few brittle minutes later, when the leaning is so acute it could become falling, she releases her very last breath. With it comes a barely traceable sound from the very back of her vocal folds. Those listening closely and of musical mind might recognise it as a note in the whistle-tone register, perhaps a coveted E7? Or three-quarters-of-an-ounce worth of wonder departing the scene? It is beautiful and pure and it puts an unmendable crack in the hearts of everyone in the room.

Outside the house, the great number of birds who frequent the electric wires overhead and in the blue gum trees take sudden, unanimous flight. The horses in the paddock by the mountain rock feel a shudder through their hooves and set off along the fence line with their heads tossing towards the sky, where the clouds gather, freeze the rain to sleet and leave an unseasonal small white flag of snow on the mountain's summit.

𝄡

Bizzy, having stopped the clocks at eleven thirty-one (the minute Mary phoned to report Rosanna's departure) and letting time pass on a slant, arrives for that evening's choir rehearsal forty minutes early. She is surprised to find the door open and Irene sitting neatly in the foyer. Eleanor, with Penelope in tow, is in the hall sweeping the stage.

'Shit the bed, Cheryl,' says Irene, staring at Bizzy in astonishment. 'Your hair.'

Bizzy touches her hair, which has been freshly dyed jet-black. 'Yes,' is all she says.

'Black,' says Eleanor.

'Yes.'

They silently acknowledge the dramatic change for a moment before Eleanor carries on with her sweeping and Irene says, 'We've been here since three. It seems the only thing for today. Eleanor has cleaned everything, I've been telling the flowers and comforting the walls.'

'Is she here?' Bizzy asks.

'No,' says Irene. 'Not yet. Give her a while.'

Most of the other choristers also arrive early, all of them bringing their sorrow and their comforting hands and their reactions to Bizzy's hair. Freycinet catches hers in time to change it from 'Oh no!' to 'How appropriate, Bizzy, and elegant.'

Mary bursts in just after five-thirty and runs straight into Bizzy's arms.

'Ah, Mary,' says Bizzy, reaching up to press Mary's hair and swaying her gently.

Kyrie comes in behind and Avni takes her hand.

Freycinet swallows down tears and feels once again that she is intruding on something.

After a long moment, Mary leaves Bizzy's arms and moves around the room, embracing each woman. 'Rosanna asked me to do that,' she says.

'Are you all right, Mary?' Sally asks.

'Not even close,' says Mary. 'But I will be. Thank you for asking.'

'Was it awful?' asks Avni. 'The end bit?'

Mary looks at Kyrie and says, 'No, it wasn't, was it, Kyrie.'

'No,' says Kyrie. 'Just how she'd like it to be. She just sort of went to sleep, snored a bit, which would have made her laugh. And then . . .' The words trail off into the various imaginings of death.

'Can we sing?' asks Mary.

Bizzy smiles sadly. 'Of course.'

To keep demands on everyone's wits to a minimum, Bizzy has selected songs from the choir's 'old-favourites' repertoire. 'Over the Rainbow', 'Six Ribbons', a traditional Tamil song, 'Odi Odi' and then Gurrumul's 'Bayini'. They come easily, but are steeped in the absence of Rosanna's voice, which was always, but for those moments when Bizzy unleashed her compressed belt, the loudest in the room.

As the final notes of 'Bayini' settle around the women, Bizzy keeps her silence gesture in the air for longer than usual, her eyes pressed closed.

The choristers feel the quiet swim around them, filled with Rosanna. It occurs to Freycinet what a gift it is to be able to curate silence like that. So precisely that it hums. She imagines it closing wounds.

When Bizzy opens her eyes and lowers her hands, she smiles and says, 'I know some of you would like to sing an elegy of sorts, and I have the sheet music for one here if that's how we proceed. But I wonder whether it might in fact be more fitting to launch into . . .'

'"Bloody Mother Fucking Asshole" by Martha Wainright?' Quin offers. '"Break Stuff" by Limp Bizkit? Or "Fuck You" by Damageplan?'

'Or "Touch my Tooter" by Ween?' suggests Mary.

Bizzy snorts. The room echoes with memories of Rosanna's raucous laugh.

'Well *I'd* like to sing an elegy,' says Sally with a sniff and a frown. 'There was a very nice tone in the room before you said that, Quinella.'

'Nice tone, but it was just so full of empty,' says Mary.

'What about "Everybody Hurts"?' Sally suggests.

'Oh, give me strength,' says Quin. 'We've already had "Over the Fucking Rainbow". Rosanna would be turning in her grave.'

'She's not in her grave yet,' says Eleanor with a sob. Penelope snuffles and dabs her perfect black nose onto Eleanor's leg.

'Are you bawling again, Eleanor?' asks Quin. 'Fuck me, now *that* Rosanna would be proud of.'

There is a small beat of agreement. Bizzy pats Eleanor's arm.

'Can I sing you all a song?' asks Avni nervously. 'One that I wrote for Rosanna?'

For a brief moment, Bizzy forgets her grief and says, 'Avni, yes please. Of course! I thought you'd never ask.'

'Are you sure?' says Mary, observing Avni's shaking hands.

'Yes. I would like to give it to her children. Tell me if you think I should.' She shuffles about with her guitar, sits on a chair, tries another chair, then says, 'Do you think you could all not look at me?'

'Christ on a cracker,' says Quin. 'How will you ever front the stadiums of your future?'

'I won't be in stadiums,' Avni says, then plays her song's introduction so skilfully that it halts any further questions.

You know you have her eyes,
You know you have her ways,
You know you'll take her smile
As you travel through your days . . .

The song is called 'Mountaineer' and it leaves not a dry eye in the room. At its end, there is applause and tears and admiration and a lot of flustered delight from Avni.

'Oh,' sobs Kyrie. 'She would be so proud, our mountaineer.'

'Ah now,' says Bizzy as she wipes her eyes, 'That's what art can do, look what it can dream up.'

Quin clears her throat. 'In other news, just to balance the circle of life up for yas all, I'm having three babies. All fucken boys.'

There is a brief, floored silence followed by a burst of astonishment. A few of the women need to sit down. Bizzy is one of them. 'Jesus, Mary and Joseph's balls,' she says. 'There is much work to be done. The world will need to be vastly different if we don't want those boys shackled to misogyny.'

'Yeah,' agrees Quin, 'and churned out of the fuckwit factory.'

'Did Rosanna know this, Quin?' asks Kyrie.

'Yep. It was the secret I took to her. She said I have to gather the village, so . . . here we all are.'

'Jeez, Quinella,' says Mary. 'Isn't it lucky that Roland didn't stick around. The last thing you need is another man.'

'You'll have to tell him, though,' says Kyrie. 'He needs to provide financial support.'

'He's a student,' says Quin. 'He doesn't have finances. And I don't want him moping around after I ruin his life. I don't need him.'

'You'll need us, though,' says Irene. 'And we'll be right here.'

'Yes, we *will* be right here,' says Freycinet, seizing the moment. 'Because Barnes and Rutherford have successfully bought Laetare Gardens, and plan to keep running it as is. No rent increases, no reinventions, no demolition.' She watches as the expressions in the room transform back into amazement, and then something resembling joy.

Bizzy bursts into tears again. 'Oh thank heavens,' she sobs, 'with Rosanna in them.'

'Freycinet,' says Mary, 'you brilliant woman, how did you do it?'

'She shoved that upper hand of hers fair up her husband's rectum,' says Quin triumphantly. 'What else did he agree to? Is he going to ditch his shagpile?'

Frey nods. 'He says so.'

'Do you believe him?' asks Irene.

'Okay, no more questions for Freycinet,' says Bizzy, standing and taking Freycinet's hand. 'I just want to say thank you, from the bottom of my heart. Thank you.'

'You're so welcome,' says Freycinet. 'It's the least I can do.'

'Was that the secret you gave Rosanna?' asks Mary.

'Sadly no,' says Freycinet. 'I didn't hear until yesterday. I wish I could have told her.'

'She knows,' says Irene looking up to the shimmering ceiling.

'What were her final words?' asks Sally after a moment.

Mary looks at Kyrie, who says, 'It was "*Il frigorifero é puzzolente. Prova l'essenza di vaniglia*" which means, "the fridge is smelly, try vanilla essence". And then she said, "let's go".'

'*Andiamo,*' whispers Freycinet.

'The fridge is smelly?' asks Sally

Kyrie gives a sad smile. 'Yes, it seems La Lista was with her until the end. I hope it's not haunting her in the afterlife.'

'I wouldn't be surprised,' says Quin. 'The good woman arrives at the pearly gates and the Almighty Father says, "Ah, good, you're here. The shitter needs cleaning."'

'We are condemned to a Sisyphean list,' says Freycinet.

'A what?' asks Quin.

'Sisyphus,' explains Mary, 'was a bloke from Greek mythology who pushed a rock to the top of a hill only to have it roll back down again. For eternity.'

Quin blows a raspberry and says, 'Oh, diddums.'

Bizzy takes a deep breath. 'While we're on condemnation and bunkum mythology,' she says, 'Rosanna's departure might well have brought me right undone and sent me to a wicker chair by the seaside, but she would hate that. We all know she was thrilled by our Join the Chorus rally idea. So onwards we go with the plan.'

'We're with you, Bizzy,' says Mary.

'I'm going to make you all administrators of our social media accounts,' Bizzy continues. 'And Kyrie and I will wade through all the emails, they're still piling up.'

'We've had a filmmaker offer to make a little publicity piece,' says Kyrie. 'There's one from the ABC so it looks like we're getting some media attention. Wrest Point Casino want to light up purple and green *and* I had a message from an American woman who partici-pated in the New York "Strike for Equality" march in 1970. She said she is "filled with hope to see us furthering the movement after considerable distraction and disenchantment".'

'Goodness,' says Sally. 'Can we live up to expectations?'

'Are you too scared to change the world?' asks Mary.

'Well I might be a bit too fucken pregnant with triplets, just sayin',' says Quin.

Bizzy gives the chair in front of her a whack and says, 'Come on, my women, the horse has bolted. We're nearing seventy thousand followers, there's no going back now.'

'It is time,' says Avni.

'It's high time,' says Mary.

'You're right,' says Quin. 'It's high-as-a-fucken-kite time.'

'Do you agree, Rosanna?' asks Irene.

They listen as the fairy bells chime in the wishing-well garden.

𝄢

On the day of Rosanna Kalbfel's funeral, November decides to furlough the glorious spring in favour of a quick-tempered rampage complete with cold, gusts, showers and impenetrable grey. From the windows of the funeral home in North Hobart, Bizzy silently thanks the sky for not being blue. She thanks the walls for being beige and the celebrant's voice for being dull and Eleanor for wearing a sensible black dress. *Nothing*, she thinks, *is allowed to try cheering me up today.*

When she directs the choir through Rosanna's requested 'Ave Maria' and Avni's 'Mountaineer', she does not encourage her choristers to smile, and when the whistling wind outside drowns out the bridge in the second song, she is bitterly glad.

There is no coffin. Rosanna's wishes were for a swift cremation. Bizzy is cross with the idea. In the blow-away day without a visual presence, Rosanna is just so terribly nowhere.

The wind comes uninvited to the wake as well, which is held at the Kalbfels' home. It follows the mourners inside, worries the tablecloths and carries off aquamarine flowers from the drifts of ixia in vases by the door. Through the window, the dolerite columns of Rosanna's beloved mountain loom closer than usual, its fluted skirts a gloomy gun-metal grey. Bizzy gives it a sombre nod. All around, the trees thrash and roar, like furious spectators at a losing game. Rosanna's children hand out antipasti and thin, wobbly smiles.

'Bizzy?' says a wiry, black-eyed man of middle age. 'I am Rosanna's brother, Matteo.'

'Yes,' says Bizzy. 'Hello.'

'Thank you for your friendships of Rosanna, and for the singings,' he says in his viscous Italian accent. 'We are very grateful.'

'You are all very stupid over there in L'Aquila,' Bizzy says. 'Your parents have too much God to have room for a daughter, and *you*, you sent her away. Do any of you know that you have missed out on the most precious of humans? A treasure, the rarest gemstone of all. Remember that next time you feed your goats.' She looks up at Matteo's dark, perturbed eyebrows and adds, 'She loved you, though, very much. And of course I'm eternally grateful to you and to God for pushing her here and situating her in our lives.'

Matteo smiles and says, 'Thank you,' and Bizzy decides that he hasn't understood much of what she has said, until he adds, 'We are very stupid indeed,' and then 'My mother's god has done nothing to take away the pains of losing a daughter she never had.' They look at the shadowy organ pipes together for a short while before he adds, 'I am very glad she had a mountain.'

Freycinet plays her violin at the wake, and baby Bella toddles over with her arms open to Bizzy, but the dark mood is satisfyingly preserved when Bizzy gets into her Honda and leaves the wake for home. She makes the mistake of diverting into a shop for a bottle of Hellfire Gin and a scoop of black olives, where she is met with a sight that cheers her right down to her very toes. Racketing in the wind is a wire display stand holding the latest issue of *Woman* magazine. Something about it catches Bizzy's eye. She pauses, reads the headline, HE'S A FRAUD! WE HAVE THE PHOTOS TO PROVE IT. Above the text is an inset photo of Paul Bellavance pointing a ferocious finger into the face of his distressed wife.

Bizzy tips her beaming face up into the buffeting clouds and whispers, 'Rosanna, what the devil are you doing up there, you cheeky thing?'

𝄡

Stepping Stone Number 67, from *La Lista* by R.K.:
Keep music in your life. Play it, make it, sing it, dance to it, seek it out, turn it up, share it. It is a potent memory trigger, powerful motivator and healer. Use it to decorate your hours, even if it's just a muted pattern in the background.

Chapter 28
Out of the Shadows

A day later, deep into the evening, Freycinet is in the study transcribing property inspection voice memos and collating valuation data. It's work she has neglected for days, and the mind-numb of it has been a welcome escape from the recent carousel of events. But she is tired, and bored, and her eyes stray to the day's issue of *The Mercury* newspaper, open to the headline KNIGHT IN SHINING ARMOUR TAKES A FALL.

It is about the tenth time Freycinet has read this headline. She is aware that protagonists in films never dwell on their triumphs; they move coolly onto the next thing, striding bravely from the explosion without looking back. But it has been so long since Freycinet has felt the thrill of success, and she is jumpy with this one – pleased, but not certain the assignment is closed. Her instincts are still searching, glancing over her shoulder. She reads on.

Tasmanian Labor MP, former Australian Rules football star and vocal women's advocate Paul Bellavance has been asked to hand in his resignation after shock revelations he allegedly subjected his wife and a former partner to psychological abuse.

A widely circulated women's magazine has published disturbing photographs showing Bellavance in a pose of what appears to be aggression and intimidation during an altercation with his wife, Valentina. The pictures, which depict a distraught Mrs Bellavance and her husband in the kitchen of their Battery Point mansion, were taken without permission by a cleaner hired by Mrs Bellavance. They were allegedly mailed to the magazine's editor anonymously, along with other incriminating claims, including a statement from a former female colleague who told the magazine, 'I'm not surprised. In my experience, Paul Bellavance is a callous, egotistical man. His advocacy for women is a front. He's a fraud.'

The magazine also published a decades-old letter written by an alleged former partner of Mr Bellavance's, claiming controlling and belittling behaviour on his part, which led to extensive psychological damage and a chronic eating disorder. Mr Bellavance refutes the authenticity of the letter, which is signed by 'B', denies knowledge of the author and says the claims are 'baseless'.

The photographs are now the subject of a breach of privacy complaint filed by both Valentina and Paul Bellavance, as well as a libel suit brought against the magazine. The identity of the cleaner is unknown and the *Mercury*'s attempts to locate her have been unsuccessful.

'My wife and I have been violated,' Mr Bellavance said in a public statement. 'We were in our own home, the pictures have been taken out of context. My wife is in agreement that this is a misrepresentation of the truth and extremely distressing to us and our daughter.'

Mr Bellavance, who was recently assigned the Women's Affairs portfolio and has been outspoken in his support for victims of sexual crime, went on to condemn the 'irresponsible, reckless and ruinous reportage of tabloid media' as 'a complete disgrace'.

The opposition, as well as factions of the Liberal Party, have called for Mr Bellavance to resign, citing adherence to the Government's Safe at Home criminal justice response measures. Since the article's publication, domestic violence hotlines throughout the state have recorded a spike in calls.

Mrs Bellavance has made no direct statement.

'Poor bloke,' says Gil from behind Freycinet.

She jumps, puts the paper aside and manages to smile at the piece of chocolate Gil places on the desk in front of her.

He kisses the top of her head. 'Thought you might need a sugar hit with your transcripts.'

'Thank you. Yes, I do, as a matter of fact.' She pops the square of chocolate in her mouth and hopes that Gil won't engage further with the newspaper.

'The *Mercury* shouldn't even be printing that stuff,' he says. 'They're just as bad as that trash magazine.'

Freycinet sighs. 'Well, they kind of have to address the elephant in the room,' she says. 'He's like Tassie's biggest celeb. And now everyone's feeling uncomfortable.' She looks at the grainy zoomed-in photo of Bellavance, his face puckered into a ferocious warning. Valentina, in a second photo, seems tiny, her hands curled at her neck, her eyes closed. 'He certainly looks terrifying there.'

'He's in his own home!'

'And that makes intimidation okay?'

'No, I'm just saying we don't know anything about it. We weren't there.'

Frey turns back to her work.

'And the other claims are anonymous,' Gil continues, 'so that's saying something, isn't it? Can't even put their names to their accusations. That magazine probably made most of it up. That's what those tabloids do, it's criminal. Bloody hell, Paul's a good guy, but men can't do anything these days. Everyone's out to get us.'

'Only if they do the wrong thing.' Freycinet doesn't need to look at him to know that the words will hit between the eyes.

'Of course you make this about us,' says Gil. 'I'm doing my best here, Frey. I'm wearing the punishments you're dishing out. Are you ever going to forgive me? Do you think you could try?'

Now Freycinet does turn. She looks squarely into his face and notices again the strange, pulled shininess of it. It reminds her how often she has avoided looking at him lately. She searches his eyes and finds some love in them. Pain and love. The flood of relief is so strong it leaves her exhausted.

'Okay,' she says, standing and leaning into his arms. 'Okay.'

𝄢

Freycinet receives a group text message from Bizzy early the following morning. *Dearest Choristers*, it says. *I know it's only Monday but I'm calling an emergency meeting today. Midday at Laetare. Just if you're free and want to discuss things re: PB! Sorry for late notice, no obligations. Irene, Mary will collect you at 11.30 – wear clothes. BIZZY XOX.*

Everyone except Kyrie turns up. Freycinet almost made excuses on account of her ongoing jumpiness but was in the end too curious to stay away. She takes Acorn with her, partly as an escape recourse and partly because she is still looking over her shoulder and a dog is an extra pair of eyes.

There is a discernible buzz at Laetare Gardens before Freycinet even opens the door and hears the exclamations within.

'Knight in shining armour takes a fall!' Mary is shouting triumphantly.

Freycinet almost turns away again, but Acorn, homing in on the scent of Penelope, drags her onwards.

'Ah, perfect,' says Bizzy when she sees Freycinet and Acorn. 'You own the building, you can bring a whole menagerie if you like.'

'The business owns the building,' says Frey, watching as Acorn and Penelope sniff one another. Penelope returns to her place beside Eleanor with her nose in the air while Acorn puts his head on his paws and stares at her adoringly, his tail a flag of hope.

'Don't go there, dude,' says Mary. 'That dog will break your heart. She's one cold sausage.'

'Look at her,' says Sally. 'She'll roll those funny little eyes at him in a minute.'

'We were just speculating, Freycinet,' Bizzy says, 'about what brilliant personage might have laid our beloved Small Smellypants bare for the pickings.'

'Of course it's Rosanna mischiefing about in the ether,' says Irene. 'How else can you explain the timing?'

'I hope so,' says Mary. 'I can't bear the idea of her missing out on this.'

Freycinet observes a certain poise in Bizzy's already very good posture, and an uncharacteristic smugness in her smile. *She has news*, Freycinet thinks.

'I have news,' says Bizzy.

'I don't know if I can take any more,' says Avni, fanning her face.

'It's not bad news,' Bizzy says. 'I think it's good.'

'Hurry up, then,' says Quin. 'I've got to get this lot back to work.' She presses her hands to her belly.

'So,' says Bizzy. 'Two things. First, I have had a phone call from Mr Bellavance himself. He thinks that we are behind those photos, and the anonymous scoop posted to the magazine.'

'Is that good news?' asks Avni. 'Won't he find a way to ruin us?'

'No, I don't think he will,' Bizzy says. 'He'll need to keep his nose squeaky, *squeaky* clean. He can't be putting a wrong foot anywhere near groups representing women.'

'Why would he think it was us?' asks Sally. 'Grasping for scapegoats?'

'Well,' says Bizzy, 'specifically, he thinks it's Eleanor.'

She looks at Eleanor, who fidgets with the edge of her batik-printed muumuu, shuffles her feet and says, 'Right.'

'He suggested that you, as his cleaner, organised some sort of booby trap, in the form of an elderly European woman named Freida. He reckons Freida is a new choir member.'

Eleanor frowns.

Freycinet strokes Acorn's head firmly enough to drag his attention away from Penelope.

Eleanor thinks for a moment. Freycinet catches a tiny glance her way.

'Don't feel you will render us complicit by telling us,' says Bizzy. 'We already are.'

'I *want* to be complicit in this loony-tunes brilliance,' says Mary.

Eleanor glances at Freycinet again, this time for a moment longer, before she says. 'Yep, I organised Brenda.'

'Freida,' corrects Bizzy.

'Yes. Freida.' Eleanor shifts uncomfortably, squinting a little in the face of more questions.

'Thank you, Eleanor,' says Freycinet. 'For not giving me away. But it was me. I asked Eleanor whether I could take over her cleaning day, and then I sent in Freida.'

Bizzy tilts her head at Freycinet. 'And Freida is . . .?'

'An honorary member of the choir,' says Mary, 'or should be.'

'Freida,' says Freycinet, 'is a friend of mine. She has a lot of experience in . . . photography.'

'Is she a pap?' asks Quin.

'Sort of,' says Freycinet.

'Go Freycinet,' says Quin. 'And Freida.'

'Well,' says Bizzy, looking at Freycinet with slightly narrowed eyes. 'Could you please thank her for us, Freycinet? And tell her that the Angry Women's Choir has significantly more followers since this exposé. It's evidently churned up more anger and general what-the-fuckery. Also that many of those followers have written to herald her actions as brave and important.' Bizzy leaves her eyes on Freycinet's face. 'They've coined catchphrases in her honour: "Go the Cleaner" and "Come Clean, Bellavance", et cetera.'

Freycinet has to fight not to look away. 'I'll tell her, but she won't accept accolades. She's very no-fuss.'

Mary laughs. 'The vigilante cleaner.'

Bizzy's eyes remain on Frey.

'I'm worried for his wife,' says Avni. 'I mean, I think well done, Freycinet. But what if he gets even more fired up?'

'Hmm,' says Sally. 'And we need to ask Kyrie what our legal position is if we're implicated.'

'We just can't let anyone find out,' says Quin. 'Choir code of silence.'

'On the contrary,' says Bizzy. 'I think we should claim responsibility.'

'What?' Sally replies. 'No way.'

'I don't want to go back to jail,' says Eleanor.

'Hear me out,' Bizzy says, holding up a black-nail-polish-tipped hand. 'This is the other news: there are more Paul Bellavance complainants coming out of the woodwork.'

'What?' says Mary.

Avni gasps.

'Why are we surprised?' asks Quin.

'Two people have messaged me saying that they are former girl-friends of Paul Bellavance and have endured his foul, controlling treatment. Several more have said that they know of other incidents and/or narcissistic ways.'

'You fucken beauty!' says Quin.

'So,' Bizzy continues, 'if we rightfully claim responsibility for this initial exposing of the beast, then it can only garner more support, encourage others to speak up, turn the conversation into a movement, and the choir—'

'Into a goddamn chorus,' says Mary. 'I can hear a soundtrack to a revolution on the distant breeze.'

They look at Avni, who is furiously writing in her songs book.

𝄢

Bizzy closes the meeting once she has everyone's understanding and consensus that culpability for the Paul Bellavance revelations will be claimed by the Angry Women's Choir. It doesn't take long. The atmosphere in the room is willing.

Mary is singing lines from Beyonce's 'Hold Up' as she leaves.

Freycinet lingers outside as Bizzy locks up, letting Acorn sniff things for longer than she usually would.

'See you tomorrow Laetare, love,' Bizzy says to the door. 'Happy rejoicements while I'm gone.' She smiles at Freycinet. 'I'll thank you every day for saving this dear old brute of a building.'

Freycinet smiles back.

'While I've got you,' Bizzy says, 'I've been contacted by an artist who's been very inspired by the Join the Chorus campaign and has designed some posters for the Angry Women's Choir. A whole series of them, showing Angry Women in various situations. She sent through an example and, my stars, she has something special. She makes anger really beautiful and sad and inspiring and sort of muscular. I'm inclined to say yes, but I wanted to clear it with you in particular.'

'Skye Killinger?' asks Freycinet.

'Yes,' says Bizzy soberly. 'That'd be her.'

Freycinet puts her hand on Acorn's head, feeling the warmth of him. He looks up at her with worried eyes. 'It's okay with me,' Freycinet says. 'Her work is good.'

'Thank you. Splendid, I'll arrange the printing.' Bizzy puts the hall keys in her music bag.

Freycinet continues to loiter.

Bizzy inspects the silence a moment, then whispers, 'Do you want to talk to me about your life as a spy, Freycinet? Freida?'

Freycinet puts her hand on Acorn's head and says, 'No.'

'Well, all right,' says Bizzy. 'We'll just stand here and enjoy the scenery, then.' She closes her eyes and breathes the air. 'Ah, the sweet smell of burning patriarchy.'

Freycinet clears her throat. 'In the world of intelligence,' she says carefully, 'there's such a thing as a "legend". It's a very sophisticated cover made up of entirely artificial life circumstances. The deepest cover. Occasionally a legend is sustained for extended periods. Some sleeper agents build their legend for years. They can be effective enough to condition the operative, inure them to certain ways of being. Sometimes it just becomes them.'

'Right then,' says Bizzy. 'So you are a sleeper agent, living in deep cover, within an assigned legend.'

'I think so.'

Bizzy laughs. 'You and generations of women.'

Frey thinks for moment. 'Yes. But I'm lucky because I found you and Rosanna and the choir, and you helped me see that there's still the other me. The one I keep in the shadows. And she's my own territory, a place where I can go.'

Bizzy nods. 'You don't want to welcome her out of the shadows, invite her to tea? I for one would be very pleased to meet her. She seems like she has a bit of go in her.'

Freycinet smiles. 'No, thank you.'

'Fair enough,' says Bizzy, and then after a pause adds, 'I have one of those. A shadow me. Unlike yours, mine wants me to give her pretty things, sit her under a tree on a warm night and have a fecking rest.'

'She sounds nice,' says Freycinet. 'I'd like to meet her too.'

'Ah, not just now,' Bizzy says with a sigh. 'There's so much to do. It looks like she'll need to stay in the shadows for a while yet.'

B

Friday, 29 November 2019, 8.50 p.m.

OH MY GOD.

'Even while I'm exercising I'm planning the next kilojoule burn. I've banned celery. I really like hummus. I know I'm too light, I just can't see it, can't actually feel it.'

That's what 'B' said in the letter they published in the magazine. She also wrote this: 'I'm sorry I always said, "I'm fine."' Fuck. I think that's me. I can't think past the next kilojoule burn. I feel lucky to have so much dancing so I can burn energy. I only really eat celery and capsicum. Some food feels like torture. Am I in trouble? I think I'm in trouble. I think my brain has already rewired itself. I don't even get hungry anymore.

I am such an idiot. What am I doing? Am I trying to be thin so that Harry will regret ditching me? So that the ADI will want me? What happened to 'B'? Is she okay?

Oh my God. I'm so sorry, me. I'm an idiot.

. . .

I've been feeding you with myths and lies
Now you're shrunken down to half your size.

. . .

I hate myself for doing this to me. In the mirror I don't look skinny, and I don't feel skinny. In the mirror I am scowling at myself like I want to kill me. I could kill me.

10 days until showcase. I think I need to dance with the truth.

𝄡

Stepping Stone Number 207, from *La Lista* by R.K.:
Put cut flowers outside at night so they are out of the stuffy house and can breathe. They will last much longer.

Chapter 29

The Dancer

Grace looks up at the Wrest Point Casino tower as Gil drives his family towards it along Sandy Bay Road. She has seen it countless times in her life and for the first time realises that it looks a bit like a dalek from *Dr Who*. Recent days and their introspections have had a lot of familiar things changing shape, revealing different angles. Two days before, she scrolled through seven images of Harry Fenton with a glowing, athletic girl from Launceston, and decided that his face isn't quite as handsome as she'd thought.

'It's Tasmania's tallest building,' says Lily, following Grace's gaze.

'Seventy-four metres,' says Roger from the front passenger seat.

Pathetic thinks Grace. She imagines it exploding into a ball of fire. The tower's lights turn purple as they watch.

'Ooh,' says Lily.

The tower turns green.

'Are those colours for the Angry Women's Choir, Mum?' asks Lily.

'Yep,' says Freycinet.

'God, they're everywhere all of a sudden, those angry women,' says Gil.

'Maybe men should stop being dicks then,' says Grace.

In the seat beside her, Freycinet emits a small guffaw.

'Piss off,' says Tom from the very back of the car.

'The Wrest Point Tower doesn't have a front or a back,' says Roger. 'It's just pure geometry.'

The Derwent Dance Academy End-of-Year Showcase is held every year in the Tasman Room at the Wrest Point Casino. It features every dance class, from toddlers to seniors, hip hop to classical, soloists to duos to ensembles. The school's Dancer of the Year performs their solo last, and is featured prominently in the grand finale. No one is surprised that Grace Barnes is 2019 Dancer of the Year.

'Grace is called the Derwent Star,' says Lily, when they're out of the car and under the quilted ceiling of Wrest Point's foyer. Frey can see that Lily is a bit proud but mostly beside herself with envy. 'It says so on the trophy. You're the Derwent Star, Grace.'

'Sounds like a dodgy cruise ship,' says Roger.

'Grandpa,' scolds Lily. 'It's an honour. I won't be the Derwent Star because my legs are too stumpy.'

Grace looks at the swirly casino carpet and wishes Lily would shut up.

'Is it just me or are these call times getting earlier and earlier?' asks Freycinet, looking at her watch. 'It's two hours before the show.'

'The Derwent Star gets to have her hair and makeup done by a professional lady,' says Lily somewhat grumpily.

Gil presses a hand to the small of Frey's back and says, 'I'll take you for a romantic dinner.'

'Perfect,' says Tom. 'Grandpa and I can go to the bar for beers.'

'I'll get you a shandy,' says Roger.

'We'll go to the buffet,' says Frey. 'There's a dessert bar, Tom.'

'Aw, but I want the dessert bar,' Lily whines.

'Suck it, Silly-Lily,' says Tom.

'Piss off, Tomarse.'

'Okay, can you two at least pretend to like each other, please?' Frey hisses, giving Grace a kiss as they arrive at the stage door. 'Chookas, darling,' she says. 'Have a great show. We're so proud.'

'Thanks,' Grace says.

Frey looks at her. 'Are you nervous?'

'She doesn't get nervous,' says Gil. 'Do you, Star?'

'I think she might be,' says Freycinet.

They inspect Grace.

Grace, who is indeed very nervous and isn't sure what to do with such an unfamiliar emotion, says, 'Go away, I'm fine.' The words echo around her and shimmer off the chandeliers. *I'm fine. I'm fine. I'm fine.* 'I'm just, I don't know . . .'

'Bored,' says Lily. 'She's bored of Derwent showcases. She's done about eleventy of them. She wants to blow this popsicle stand and go to the Australian Dance Institute in Sydney. Liam said that Harriet said there are ADI people here to watch us. If I wasn't wearing a *brown* tutu, they might notice me.'

Freycinet is still watching her older daughter.

Grace hunches her shoulders to protect her soul.

'Oh, Lily,' says a woman nearby. 'It's dusky pink, I keep telling you.'

They look up to see Teagan Wiley walking towards them, dressed in layers of chiffon and sparkles. She wrinkles her nose in a cheeky smile that makes Grace cringe. 'I thought it was about time the costume manager got to wear her own version of the tutu.'

'You look spectacular,' says Gil.

'Thank you,' Teagan replies. 'You're looking pretty good yourself.' She pats her face with both hands. 'It's good to see a man taking care of his appearance for once.'

Gil makes a small, awkward sound; one-quarter laugh, three-quarters discomfort.

Holy shit, thinks Grace. *Dad's had work.*

She inspects her father's shiny forehead, then watches Roger's substantial eyebrows rise and furrow. She tries not to laugh.

'Hello, Derwent Star,' Teagan says to Grace. 'I can't wait to see what costume you've been hiding up your sleeve. Oh, and Freycinet, look at your Angry Women go! This very tower, lit up purple and green. And there's a huge Angry Women book display at the library: all books about women's grievances. Gawd, there's a lot of pent-up complainers out there. *So* lucky you didn't recruit Paul Bellavance as an ambassador – what a comedown that's been. And what a boon for AWC, it's really ramped up their little campaign, hasn't it? But you have to feel sorry for him.'

'Why?' Grace asks.

'Well, it was a different time back then, wasn't it, when he supposedly "emotionally abused" women.' Teagan's cheeky smile fades as Grace keeps her expression neutral. She turns to Frey for help. 'And poor Valentina. She's gone to ground. I can only imagine how she must be feeling. I doubt she'll even be here tonight to watch Esperance dance.'

Freycinet nods.

'The caps blow off where the yeast ferments too long,' says Roger.

Teagan looks confused, then rummages for a change of subject. 'I saw an Angry Women's Choir poster in the library yesterday. That woman in the piles of laundry, good Lord, that's me. Well, it's all of us, isn't it? Her face! Genius marketing to get Skye Killinger on the case. What a talent. She a good friend of yours?'

'No,' says Freycinet. 'I don't know her, actually.'

'So you must work with her, Gil? I saw you talking to her at the museum the other day. I took my Year Sixes for the dinosaur show. You were in the café. Oh!' Teagan claps a hand over her mouth. 'Have I ruined a surprise? God, me and my motormouth. Forget I said anything, but just saying, a Skye Killinger–commissioned portrait is *the best gift idea*. If I wasn't on a teacher's wage I'd do the same.'

Grace shifts impatiently. 'We should go in, Lily.' This woman's voice is jangling with her nerves. She looks at her mother, whose hands are grasping to give Lily well wishes, her face clouded with something else.

'Yes!' Frey says loudly. 'Go, go, go. See you on the stage. Give it your best, Lily, we're proud of you too.' She kisses Lily and waves with such wide-eyed animation it looks like a warning. Grace shudders and checks behind her for a sinister presence.

𝄢

The sinister presence stays with Freycinet, Gil, Roger and Tom and has buffet dinner with them. It stares at Freycinet throughout, kicks her under the table, makes Gil knock his beer over and has definitely piqued Roger's attention.

'You eating?' he asks Freycinet, scrutinising her over his glasses.

'Yeah, Mum,' says Tom over his second piece of steak. 'You've only been to the buffet once.'

'I'm actually not very hungry after all,' Frey says.

'You have to be,' says Tom. 'These roast potatoes are awesome.'

Freycinet blesses the straightforward priorities of a seventeen-year-old boy. He and his potatoes are oblivious to the sinister presence.

Frey has not been able to meet Gil's eyes, and her words to him have been stripped down to bare essentials. Bits of the sinister presence seem to have got into her food and are now swelling in her stomach, making her queasy. She doesn't dare examine her thoughts.

Tom chats about his music and his mobile DJ business idea. 'I used a DJ name generator and it came up with "DJ Please" which is kind of lame but also weirdly cool.'

Freycinet is grateful to him for his banter. 'I like it,' she says. 'It's polite.'

Tom rolls his eyes. 'No DJ wants to be polite, Mum.'

'Make it a point of difference, then.'

'Yeah, and get asked to spin at old people's parties.' Tom laughs. After another mouthful he says, 'This will be my last Derwent showcase. I'll be an adult next year and you're not dragging me to another one. Not even with a buffet bribe.'

A pulse of painful love almost makes Frey gasp. *My little boy.*

Gil has fallen silent.

'Tom,' Roger says eventually, clapping a hand on the boy's shoulder, 'I'm taking you to the bar.'

'Cool,' says Tom, trying not to appear excited.

Frey can feel Roger's hard look as they leave.

The sinister presence and all that is unsaid takes up the vacant spaces at the table, slings a cold arm over Freycinet's shoulder and forces her hand. She looks at Gil. He looks back at her, closes his eyes for a brief moment, swallows nothing.

'You love her,' Freycinet says, her voice measured and calm.

His eyes stay on hers, unwavering and filling with tears. He nods, tries to speak, clears his throat. The pain in his face is clear even through the frozen muscles.

'Don't,' says Frey. 'Please don't.'

But he does. 'Sorry,' he says. 'I'm so sorry.'

And it's his sorry that sends Freycinet out of her seat, through the doors of the restaurant and into the tilting world outside.

𝄢

As Grace's solo performance draws near, she is no longer feeling her nerves and has stopped hearing the music as it guides its dancers onstage. She has tuned out the periodic applause from the audience, the occasional cheer. She does not smell the dressing-room scent of hairspray and trepidation. She does not taste the stage smoke or see the lights, nor the hesitant smiles of peers. Instead she is focusing everything on trusting her body, letting it take her to the places it knows better than her mind, away from those duplicitous thoughts. Dance is trust. She has learnt this over and over again. Trust in the body, in the space, in the audience, in the choreography. Trust yourself to be vulnerable. *I can do this*, she tells herself as she stands alone in the gaffer-taped patterns of backstage. *This is my creation, my music, my body.* But she has wondered, during these last few weeks of intense rehearsal, what happens to trust when a mind has turned on its body. What happens to vulnerability when it is the heart of the peril?

She is not wondering this now, but keeping herself intensely in the moment, smelling nothing, tasting nothing, feeling everything. She breathes, she knows she is ready. And when she hears her Derwent Star cue, she takes her place in the centre of the dark stage, curled into the foetal position.

I was not listening
You have been singing out,
Little voice ringing out.

She follows her own voice as it rings through the theatre speakers, unassisted by beat or instruments or harmony. She responds to its confessions, its apology and its love.

I've been living lies and breathing smoke
I gave all your time and love to ghosts.

About three-quarters of the way through her dance, Grace begins to feel disconnected from her body, shifting upwards, to the ceiling, then higher still, as though the roof has come off the building. She is looking down on the huge room with its audience, all eyes on the fragile being on the stage.

She gasps. *Is that me? Is that really me?* she wonders. But there is only the night sky to hear, and it is so full of silent nothing. She gazes down, can't believe how tiny she looks, how sick. She reads the terrifying words that are being spoken with her body and a mountain-air coldness envelops her. She looks up to the stars and asks them, *Is that me?* They twinkle at her dumbly, while a tiny slip of moon offers to close the parentheses, put an end to some aside.

And then Grace falls. Down, down, down, until she is on the stage again. The ceiling is back, the audience is transfixed, but there is something wrong. It takes her a minute to realise what it is. Her heartbeat. She can't feel her heartbeat. She reaches her limbs into the final gestures, watches her fingers take their place in the detail and grasp at the air as if catching her bared soul before it slips away. In the dance's final pose, she rests her head on her arm and closes her eyes.

𝄢

In the audience, Freycinet has been sitting with Gil's contrition on one side, Roger's questions on the other and her own grief weighing heavily on her lap. She was dismayed when the MC marked Grace's solo, because it meant there was precious little time before the showcase would be over and the houselights would come up on the glaring question: what comes next? What happens to love when it has nowhere to go? She's not sure her brave face can take any more wear. In the dim theatre stalls, she has taken it off.

But when the lights came up on Grace, centre stage in a neat curve on the floor, and then the fresh-water stream of her voice had rippled into the silence, Frey had been instantly wrenched from the mumble of her lurching thoughts. She watched her daughter unfurl from the bundle on the stage floor. A haunting gasp had arisen from the audience, swallowing up Freycinet's own intake of breath. Grace was wearing a sleeveless grey crop top and black lycra bikini bottoms and all her pale skin stretched over bones.

All of your whispering
Long after midnight
Was lost in the half light.

Who is this girl? Freycinet had wondered. *She is not my daughter, she is something else. Who is taking care of her?* Frey looked away, at Gil, at Tom and Roger, all of them apparently mesmerised. Or horrified. *Do they know who this is?* For a slippery moment Frey thought she might run. To the stage? To Grace? From the room? But then she looked again at the girl who is dancing with words and no beat and Frey was mesmerised too.

Now I see your silence, your fading breath
Please don't take us away, don't slow your step
We have to stay for all the things they never told us
And they have to pay for all the fables they sold us.

The movements harmonised with the words; there was a voice in her tiny limbs. She sang with her hands and cried with her feet, was alive with distortion and sick with quiet, roaring energy. So very sick. *Grace.*

The dancer performed a series of precise pirouettes, a perfect leap, an effortless glide. The softness of her fingers, the heartbreaking curve of an arm had brought a sob to Frey's throat. She talked it down.

Everything we do is because we can't fly.

Grace closed the performance with a slow lowering of her body, folding in on herself, her face to her arm. There were four seconds of luminous silence before the audience burst into applause, taking to their feet and cheering.

And now, Freycinet is still trying to find her breath, still trying to disentangle awe from pride and horror from fear.

'That was incredible,' someone near Freycinet says. 'Hard to watch but impossible to look away.'

But Frey isn't listening. On the stage, Grace hasn't moved.

'Grace?' Freycinet clutches Roger's arm.

'She's forgotten to bow,' says Tom with a tense laugh.

'Grace!'

Someone yelps, someone else exclaims crossly as Frey lunges over seats in a direct line for the stage. She reaches the delicate drift of limbs before anyone else has registered that anything, everything, is wrong.

𝄐

Stepping Stone Number 99, from _La Lista_ by R.K.:
If you are feeling extremely nervous, try telling yourself you are excited instead. Sometimes it is easier to re-channel existing adrenaline into a positive force rather than trying to calm it down. Your brain does not need suppression, but re-direction. Guide it from a place of threat to a place of opportunity.

Chapter 30
Purple Flour Bombs

In the hospital waiting room, Roger is the first to speak.

'Lily,' he says, 'I really liked your dance routine. Five stars from me.'

Lily leans against her grandfather and bursts into tears.

Freycinet, who has fewer words than Roger, leans in to comfort Lily with a kiss. She touches her spray-stiffened hair and looks at her bejewelled, pink-brown tutu, her bright lipstick, and wonders at the ridiculous pantomime of everything.

Tom walks to the drinks machine and inserts some coins, presses some buttons. A bottle of lemonade tilts forward, lodges itself against the glass and stays there.

'What?' says Tom. 'No way.' He gives the machine a nudge, presses some more buttons, grunts and returns to his seat.

'Design fault,' says Roger.

Freycinet walks to the machine, puts her shoulder to it and shoves it backwards against the wall, then lets it fall forward with a bang. The lemonade, a bottle of water and an iced tea fall into the bottom shelf. Freycinet pushes open the flap, takes them out and gives them all to Tom.

'Thanks,' Tom says, staring at his mother in surprise. He offers the iced tea to Lily, who shakes her head. He holds out the lemonade but she refuses that too.

'I know that Grace has the anorexia nervosa,' Lily says into Roger's jumper. 'I have known for a while and I should have done something.' Her face scrunches, black tears fall from her mascaraed eyes. 'I told her to eat but I should have told you, Mum, and then you could have told her to eat, and Dad, and Grandpa and Tom could have bullied her about being that skinny and she wouldn't be in there dying.'

'She's not dying,' says Gil, his voice barely above a whisper.

'Harriet's sister has it and she's been dying for ages.'

'I didn't know she was as skinny as that,' says Tom. 'I mean, when did that happen?'

'They hide it,' says Lily. 'Lots of clothes. Grace wears baggy stuff, even to dancing.'

Tom nods. 'If we go near the bathroom when she's in there, she goes off her head.'

'I should have known, though,' says Frey. 'I'm her mother. I knew she was overdoing the exercise and overly conscious of what she ate. But what kind of mother doesn't notice this? And I'm always going on about how much I hate my bum. That's not good role modelling.' Her hands begin to shake.

'At least you don't get shit injected into your face,' says Tom, with a pointed look at Gil. 'Your face doesn't even look like your face, Dad.'

'I know, okay,' Gil says. 'I was told . . . it doesn't matter. I won't do it again.'

In the silence that follows, Roger says, 'Well, we all have design faults.'

They sit in the humming quiet until the swinging doors open to a male doctor with a serious expression.

Freycinet is on her feet.

'She's okay for the moment,' the doctor says, and the relief is so potent it nearly takes Frey's legs out from under her. She sways.

The doctor continues, his voice firm. His hand gestures suggest he has no time for disobliging family members. His job is to protect his patient.

My job is to protect my children, thinks Frey.

'She's conscious,' the doctor says, 'she's monitored. You can see her in a while, someone will come and get you. But not all at once, please. Two at a time. We really need to be extremely gentle with her. She's very, very sick. You must understand that these next few days are critical, is that clear? I know this is distressing for you but no questions, no drama, okay?'

Gil's eyes flick to Freycinet for barely an instant before they all agree.

𝄢

Frey and Gil enter Grace's hospital room gingerly, as though they hurt all over. (They do.) The small room is bright white, even with the curtains drawn. Grace is lying on her back, with her upper body slightly raised. There is a tube attached to her nose with tape, a translucent green oxygen mask over her mouth and a bag of intravenous fluid dripping into her arm. The skin on her temples is as white as the walls and Frey can't look too hard in case she sees right through it to the bones beneath. Her eyes are closed and Frey is glad of this; she has time to change the horrified arrangement of her face.

Gil speaks first. 'Gracie? Grace?'

The eyes open, focus on the ceiling, refocus on Frey's arranged face, then Gil's.

'Hi, sweetheart.' He moves to the bed, picks up her hand.

Frey takes the other side, the other hand. It's weighty and cold. She has a memory flash of Rosanna's dying hands.

Grace murmurs something but it's too muffled by the mask for Frey to understand.

'What was that, darling?' Frey asks.

Grace roughly pulls the mask aside and says, 'It was bad, wasn't it? My performance. Did it scare everyone?'

'No, darling,' says Frey. 'It was extraordinary. Exquisite.'

'It was amazing,' Gil says.

Frey nods. 'You danced a whole story, you reached everyone in the room. I'll never get over how beautiful it was.'

Grace closes her eyes again. 'I guess I didn't impress the ADI people, what with dying in the final pose and all.' She looks at Frey. 'My heart stopped, didn't it.'

Frey bites her lip, whispers, 'Not for long.'

'Your mum got you going again, Grace,' says Gil. 'She had the full CPR thing down pat.'

Frey detects a weak smile sent her way from Gil, but she can't look at it directly.

'Sorry,' says Grace. 'I'm sorry. I'm such an idiot.'

'No,' says Frey.

'I know I'm sick, I know I've been so, so bad to myself. I know I look like a skeleton. They told me I will die if I don't care for myself more. And I do care for myself, I do. But I hate this feeding tube, it feels like it's the thing killing me. And then I hate myself for thinking that. And it seems like I don't deserve to like myself and then I start all over again.' Grace begins to cry. 'The wiring in my head is all wrong.'

Gil puts a hand on her forehead. 'Hey.'

'I know,' says Frey. 'It's a disease and it's playing tricks on you.'

'You don't know,' says Grace, looking back at the ceiling. 'You. Can't. Possibly. Know.'

The fury in her voice puts a sting of tears in Frey's eyes. She imagines cracks appearing in the fractured pieces of her heart.

'Honey,' Gil says, 'for the moment you just need to rest, okay? Rest.' He replaces the oxygen mask and strokes Grace's hair.

Frey watches his hands and imagines them stroking Skye's hair, holding Skye's pretty face. Her skin crawls and she has to fight a rising urge to scream.

𝄢

Frey is unsure how many days have passed by the time a bouquet of lilies is brought into Grace's hospital room by a smiling nurse's aide. Frey whispers thanks, glances at Grace asleep in the bed and breathes the scent of Christmas. The envelope attached to the flowers bears the names 'Grace and Freycinet' so she opens it. Inside is a card made of sheet music and a folded letter. The card is signed 'with love and healing kisses from the Angry Women's Choir'. Frey smiles and opens the letter.

Dear Freycinet and Grace (it says, in flamboyant handwriting),

Bizzy here. Grace, I met you once in a carpark stairwell. I thought you were extravagantly beautiful then, so just imagine what I think now that I have seen you dance! Yes, I was at the Wrest Point Tasman Room, there with my friends Mary and Kyrie. Kyrie took me for my birthday, to see Serra Kalbfel dance; she is Kyrie's granddaughter. What a proper birthday joy it was.

Freycinet pauses, imagining Mary with her opinions, Bizzy with her gumption and Kyrie with her kindness, witnessing the catastrophe of Grace's poor body, the failings of a mother. She takes a breath and reads on.

We were all very affected by your performance, Grace, and distressed to see you unwell. We hope that you are finding your way to the recovery road. But aside from that, we all agreed that we are extremely privileged to have been there. Every once in a while, Grace, something opens the door to all the things we forget to see. Usually art or nature does this, sometimes the actions of a person and never (in my experience, at any rate) religion. They are the things that can tell us what there is beyond the limited fields of human perception. The possible.

We watched a girl who can dance with silence. An a cappella orchestra. And she opened the door.

Until we see these things, we will not wonder about whether night time has a scent, or whether Thursday morning has a colour and what Sunday afternoon might be thinking. We might not consider what the paintings say about us when we leave the gallery or what sounds are made by the curve of the earth. We mightn't ever look for the colour of someone's soul or listen for the sound of a heart when it sings.

But now that I have seen you dance I have had another wondrous, precious glimpse of what else might be. For that, I thank you, and beseech you to take care, bring strength back to yourself as best you can. Let people help you to do that. This is very important, Grace, because you have a gift, and a key.

Freycinet, we have a couple of our usual West Moonah Women's Choir gigs and then we're breaking for Christmas. So get yourself strong and come back to us in the new year, it'll be all about the Angry Women's Choir then and we'll need our best energy. We will be meeting on Monday the thirtieth so as to avoid New Year's Eve. Come if you can, but worry not if you can't.

Sending a chorus of love to you both,

Bizzy Nancarrow

Frey stares at a bowl of grapes next to Grace's bed in order not to cry, but the tears fall anyway.

'Mum?'

Frey sniffs, wipes her eyes and smiles. Grace is awake. She glances from Frey's face to the bowl of grapes and back again.

'You got some more flowers,' says Frey. 'Christmas lilies. They smell like holidays.'

'Christmas is going be awesome this year, hey,' Grace says, rolling her eyes. She hauls herself up in the bed. 'Who are they from?'

'They're from the choir.' Frey slips the letter into the card and puts both beside Grace on the bed.

'Um, okay,' says Grace warily.

Frey leaves the room to find a vase. When she returns, the letter is open on the bed and Grace is lying down again, her back to the door. Frey looks at the shoulder bones of her daughter and tries to conceive how they could possibly be the same fluent limbs that had captured that theatre and carried everyone away.

𝄢

There's a Christmas tree in the sitting room when Frey brings Grace home on Christmas Eve, after sixteen days at the hospital. It is lop-sided and sparsely decorated but Lily says proudly, 'We went and got a real one this year. To cheer us up.'

'It's beautiful,' says Frey. 'Thank you.'

'I found it up on Mount Nelson,' says Tom.

Gil smiles. 'He *stole* it from up on Mount Nelson.'

'And I made lunch!' says Lily. 'So everyone has to come to the kitchen.'

Gil glances nervously at Grace. 'Lily, like I said, Grace doesn't want us all hovering around her with food.'

'It's okay,' says Grace.

'Come here, Lily,' says Frey, sitting on the couch next to Grace. 'We should all sit down and talk about this.'

'About Grace having an eating disorder that makes you want to have total control over everything so you dump all your friends and hide away from your family?' asks Lily.

'Can we just have some nice family time *not* talking about this?' asks Grace.

Gil nods. 'Yes, it's the holidays, the sun is shining. It's Christmas Eve. I'll pour us a drink.'

'I'll have a drink, thank you,' says Frey. 'But we're talking about this.' She gives Gil a look. He stays quiet and heads for the drinks cabinet.

'Lily,' Frey says, 'you know you don't have to be responsible for Grace, or make her eat. She's getting professional help and Dad and I will support her. She knows what has to be done.'

'Yeah, but this is what happens,' says Lily. 'She will *say* she knows what she has to do but she won't be doing them really properly, and she will say she doesn't think she's fat but she thinks she's fat and you will think she's, like, getting better because she's all talking about it and stuff, but she's not getting better, and then she will have to go to hospital and nearly die again. Or maybe even die. That's what happens.' Lily's shoulders rise with her eyebrows to indicate that she's 'just telling it like it is'.

'I don't think I'm fat,' says Grace. 'I can't be a dancer and be fat, can I.'

'Can anyone smell burning pants?' says Lily.

'Piss off,' says Grace.

'Okay, okay,' says Gil, returning with a glass of wine for Frey.

Lily's voice is fluting upwards. 'And I don't think you can, like, tell me not to do things to make her better because I'm going to do them anyway, aren't I? I'll have to ask her if she wants my cheese stick, and tell her off for too much exercise. And leave her notes that say I think she's beautiful and stuff. And that she can't fade away because she's, like, the best dancer in the whole world, I think.' They are all alarmed to see that in the midst of Lily's swagger come enormous tears. Patches of pink appear on her cheeks and neck.

'I'll be okay, Lily,' says Grace.

'Well, hurry up, then,' shouts Lily, standing up from her chair. 'Hurry up and tell us you're saying lies so that you can start doing the truth. Harriet's sister made everyone think she was getting better and she never, never was and now all the years are gone and Harriet hates her a bit and it's really, really bad.'

Grace crosses her arms.

Tom says, 'Jesus, Lily.'

'And I think,' Lily continues, her voice wobbling now, 'that if you disappear then maybe no one will believe that you were real and I won't even know who I want to be.' Lily puts both hands over her face and sobs, then runs from the room. Seconds later a door slams.

'So that went well,' says Gil, with a glance at Frey.

'Why are you looking at me?' Frey asks. 'I was doing what the psychologist recommended.'

'And I *recommended* that we do this *with* the psychologist, which was her other *recommendation*, remember?'

'I think we can at least try managing this at home, together,' says Frey. 'Outside the hospital. Grace isn't comfortable there.'

'Oh, and what other management strategies shall we try?' Gil says. 'Shall we throw purple flour bombs? Bring down the patriarchy?'

Freycinet is suddenly hot. Her hands splay on her thighs, then press, as though they might save her from toppling. They don't. She looks straight into Gil's eyes and says, 'Go fuck yourself.'

'I'm out,' says Tom, standing up from his seat and leaving the room in one fluid motion.

Frey's hand covers her mouth. 'Oh my God. I'm sorry, I shouldn't have said that.'

'Okay, okay, we're all stressed,' says Gil with a sigh. 'Here's what we do: we all take some time out to *calm down*.' He raises his eyebrows in the direction of his wife. 'And then we book an urgent appointment with the psychologist who is trained to deal with these things.'

Frey nods. She doesn't trust herself to speak because the words 'calm down' have brought the heat back to her face.

Gil stands. He is wearing his cycling gear. Freycinet wonders whether the padding in the shorts could protect his testicles from a furious kick.

𝄢

By ten o'clock that evening, everyone has gone to bed and Frey is scrolling through family photos on her laptop, giving each one a verbal caption. She is on her second bottle of wine. 'Happy family in Bali,' she says. 'Tiny baby Lily. Little cheeky Tom. Happy family at the beach. Happy family at home. Gil on his bike . . .' Here she curls her lip and blows a raspberry. 'Freycinet in the garden. Grace's first showcase . . .' She looks into the angelic features of five-year-old Grace, zooms in and touches a finger to the screen. 'I'm so sorry, darling,' she says.

Her mobile phone rings. She jumps, picks it up and frowns at it. *DAD*, it says. She answers it, listens without saying anything.

'The Girl?' Roger's voice is loud.

Freycinet smiles. Her father always shouts into phones like they are hard of hearing.

'Roger Blewes,' she says. 'Is this a bum dial?'

'What?' replies Roger.

'You never ring me. I always ring you. Why are you ringing me?'

'Where's your twenty?'

'Home.'

'Grace home too?'

'Yep. Sorry, I should have called you. It's just been so much fun here and stuff.'

'Are you drinking?'

Frey raises her glass of wine and laughs. 'Oops, yep, blown. Are you on counter-surveillance?'

'I'm calling to see if Grace got home all right.'

'She's okay. Exfiltration success. She's asleep. Tom reckons she was doing star jumps in her room so she's pissed off about having to leave her door open. It's a long, twisty fucking road ahead, evidently, Dad.'

'Hmm,' says Roger.

'Are you all right?'

'Always. Are you, The Girl?'

'Oh, brilliant. Everything's just fabulous.' Frey has another sip of wine.

'Give me the sit rep.'

'Sick daughter with no self-belief and uncertain future. Confused son. Anxious dog. Terrified second daughter.'

'And you and Gil?'

'Just as terrified. Can't think.'

Roger shifts his emphasis. 'You *and* Gil?'

Frey pauses. 'Future operations unconfirmed.'

'Hmm,' says Roger. 'You did good the other night, The Girl. You saved her life.'

'The ambulance was quick.'

'You saved her life.'

'Thanks, Dad.'

'Do your thing, Freycinet. It'll be all right.'

'You know me. I blend in. Going grey as we speak.'

'Bye.'

'Bye, Dad, love you. See you tomorrow.'

'Ten-four, ditto, out.'

Frey listens for his hang-up, gulps her wine and gasps.

'Shit,' she says. 'He called me Freycinet.'

She laughs, glances over at the close-up picture of Grace. She puts the glass down, flops into the couch with her laptop and, clicking onto Instagram, resumes her running caption game as she scrolls through the school-holiday lives of other people. 'Fakers, knobs, aww sweet dog, wanker, way too much filler, nice dress . . .'

A picture of the West Moonah Women's Choir appears. They are singing carols at St David's Park. The scene makes Frey feel sad. The choir seems to Frey very far away. She clicks to the AWC Instagram account. A very young, beaming Bizzy Nancarrow scrolls onto the feed, alongside a woman with her head thrown back in laughter. The gaudy tint of the blue sky and the pink of a mountain range at their backs give the picture a nostalgic, golden-age feel. The caption reads, 'Our founder and choir director Bizzy Nancarrow with her beloved late mother, Winifred at Lake Pedder in 1972. Two incorrigible, remarkable women who stood up with voices raised and continue to lead by example. #angrywomenschoir #jointhechorus #AWC'

'Join the chorus,' Frey whispers. She scrolls back up to the top of the AWC Instagram page. 'One hundred and forty-nine thousand followers, wowee.' She swigs from her glass, hums a few lines of 'Amazing Grace', then clicks on a folder in the corner of her computer's desktop labelled 'Ernest Hemingway'.

The pictures of Gil and Skye appear. Frey scrolls through them. 'Oh, that's a great shot, love that angle,' she says in a slurred cockney accent. 'Nice, nice, have you two considered a career in film? You'd be great in, I don't know, *Homewrecker*, directed by U. R. Acunt.'

Frey snorts with laughter, tops up her wine glass and uploads one of the photos to the AWC Facebook page.

'I think such genuine performances deserve all the publicity they can get, don't you?

'I once was lost, but now am found,' she sings as she adds this caption: *That one time when you spent twenty years being a loyal wife and then he roots someone else. #standupandsingout #angrywomenschoir #jointhechorus #takethatmotherfucker.*

'Was blind, now I see.' Frey hits send, chuckles, sets down her laptop and says, 'One great big purple flour bomb. Take that, motherfucker.'

𝄢

She is woken on Christmas morning by Lily, who crouches beside the couch, pats Frey's shoulder and whispers, 'Mum. Mum? Dad's having sex with a woman on Facebook.'

𝄡

Stepping Stone Number 271, from *La Lista* by R.K.:

You will never know everything. You will never even know very much. None of us do. There is so much beyond the scope of our understanding. Who is to say that gods exist or don't? Who really knows what happens after death? Don't laugh at the ideas of others. And remain uncertain of things, because with uncertainty comes questioning and listening and thinking and conversation. Those who hold absolute certainty at all times are dangerous dickheads.

Chapter 31
On the Yuletide

On Christmas Day, with the year almost behind them and the next looming larger than might be comfortable, several members of the choir find themselves in various states of unrest.

Eleanor has joined the Christmas Day family service at St Matthew's and is discovering what jealousy feels like. She finds herself glaring at the smiling, cosied families and their genuine season's greetings, annoyed with the parishioners taking up Father Mac's time, jealous of God. She's had to cross herself and ask forgiveness four times before the service has even begun.

Penelope is at home feeling unsure whether life can be quite the same since she found a chicken sandwich at the Carols for Carers event the day before.

𝄡

Sally annoys herself by feeling pleased when her mother-in-law, Mrs Eyreton, praises her glazed ham. Later, Sally has to endure protracted complaints regarding (in no particular order) pavlova, Gen Z, sunshine, tinsel, smeary wine glasses, dogs, television, nuts, superannuation and brandy butter. After lunch, Sally feigns a headache and retires to her bedroom, where she offers sizeable commissions (using some of her superannuation) to St Michael's Collegiate School for girls for some prominent wall space and a mural, Francesca Jewellery for an AWC bracelet and an IT specialist for a feminism coaching app. With that, she feels a surge of Christmas cheer and is happy to return to the living room for carols on the telly. (Mrs Eyreton likes carols, but only if they were written before the war.)

𝄢

Irene is lying in bed, her head resting on Harvey's chest.

'Ah, Harv,' she says. 'I always love our Christmas morning. It's like a touch more sparkle comes in on the yuletide.'

Harvey laughs. 'Or it could be all the tinsel,' he says.

'Or the thought of my roast potatoes. Speaking of such, I've got to get them on.' Irene hops out of bed and pulls on her dressing gown. 'If I parboil them now I can leave them to sit while I score the pork.' She puts on her slippers and turns back to the bed. 'And I won't forget your gravy, Harvey.'

But Harvey isn't there.

Irene frowns. 'You batty old cow,' she says to herself. Looking back at the empty pillow, she says, 'Could have sworn you weren't dead.' She pats her body, as if testing to see whether she actually exists, sighs, and says, 'Well, the doggies are going to love their Christmas dinner.'

𝄢

Quinella is halfway up the local council's Christmas tree at Mawson Place on Hobart's waterfront when Mary arrives and shouts, 'Quin! Get down immediately, you idiot pregnant person. That's my job.'

'Where've you been?' Quin shouts from her perch.

'I had to be taken for a drive in Mum's Christmas present – a Bentley, for fuck's sake.'

'A what?'

'Never mind. This looks perfect, Quin.'

'I know, I've been here since seven. Couldn't fucken sleep anyway with this lot dub-stepping on my bladder.' Quin lowers herself down and together they admire the newly decorated tree. The classic reds, greens and silvers applied by Council have been almost completely covered with purple tinsel, fluorescent green baubles and AWC logoed flags.

'Merry Fucken Christmas, Hobart,' says Quin. 'Happy birthday, Baby Jesus.'

'Well done, crazy woman,' says Mary. 'You rest for a bit, I'll take phase two.'

'No rest for the wicked,' says Quin.

In another hour they have poured (one-hundred-per-cent compostable) glitter all over the paved area surrounding the tree, erected a sign saying, 'RETHINK CONVENTION, RE-EXAMINE THE CANON, REWRITE THE CAROLS' and set out sheet music for 'The Twelve Days of Christmas' with updated lyrics written exclusively for the AWC by a collective of local poets, musicians and writers.

'I'm having a moment,' says Mary, putting a hand to her head. 'Is this really happening? Has the choir really started all this?'

'Oh dear,' says Quin. 'I'm having a moment too.'

Mary, struck by Quin's sentence structure lacking its usual swearword, turns to look. Quin is staring down at her feet, where a small patch of liquid is spreading into the glitter.

'Did you wet yourself?' asks Mary.

'No!' says Quin. 'That's me fucken waters, they've broken. Trust a pack of bloody men to come along early and ruin the fun.'

B

Kyrie has opted out of Christmas. Jonathon has taken the children to the coast, and the thought of the empty house by the mountain with its Rosanna-shaped hollow is too much for her. She has packed a turkey sandwich, a notebook and a pen into her handbag and gone visiting the residents of Glenview, a nursing home near Moonah. One of them, a balding woman in her nineties named Bett, tells Kyrie, 'Every year I'd get together fifty little presents for each member of the family. Sometimes it might just be a pretty button or a bracelet I'd made from she-oak. But there was always fifty pressies for everyone, not a one less. I wound up with six children so there were a lot of pressies in them last years. They're all busy today. I'm sure one or two of them will drop by with a tin of travel sweets or something.' Kyrie photographs Bett for the AWC Instagram page.

B

Bizzy has declined invitations from Avni, Sally and Ferris and settled on a quiet day working on a new #jointhechorus Very Cross Stitch design for the Angry Women's Choir. However, she finds her peace frequently interrupted by the pings and chimes of various social media alerts. She switches her phone to silent without investigating, but by lunchtime her curiosity has got the better of her. She takes her phone to the table with a bowl of pea and ham soup and opens the AWC Facebook page.

'Jesus, Mary and Joseph's knob,' she says.

There is a queue of 718 follower posts awaiting moderation.

'What on earth . . .?'

She reads the first, which says in shouty uppercase letters, *THAT ONE TIME MY HUSBAND SPENT OUR SAVINGS ON AN OLD AC/DC TOUR BUS THAT DOESN'T WORK.*

Bizzy reads on.

That time my fella bought me a set of steak knives for Xmas. I'm vegetarian.

My bloke won't do anything about his stinking breath.

My husband hasn't remembered my birthday since 2003.

THAT ONE TIME MY DAD KNOCKED MY MUM OUT, THEN PAWNED HER JEWELLRY.

Bizzy notices that all the comments end with the same four hashtags. *#takethatmotherfucker, #standupandsingout, #angrywomen-schoir* and *#jointhechorus.*

'What the devil is going on here?' Bizzy asks herself. She swipes to Instagram and brings up the AWC account. 'Feck me,' she says, standing up so quickly her chair falls backwards onto the floor. 'Four hundred and seventy-seven thousand followers.'

𝄢

Christmas lunch in the Barnes household is a particularly tense affair. Having deleted the Facebook post from the AWC page just as soon as her wits (hangover and fuzzy recollections) allowed, Frey has spent the last few hours dividing her time between deleting reposted screenshots of the explicit photo, ignoring calls from Bizzy, answering questions from the children, avoiding her livid husband and trying to hold everything together.

Christmas Day reaches peak tension just as Roger pops his Christmas cracker and says, 'What did the snowman say to the other snowman? I smell carrots.'

No one but Frey gives him a laugh, and hers is verging on hysterical. She stops it short because it hurts her ears. The silence rings with it.

'Okay,' she says, looking at Grace, who is nudging buttery peas around her plate with her fork. 'Okay. Here's the thing. I suspected that Gil, that your dad, was having an . . . had fallen in love with someone else. And then I was able to confirm the fact. I mean, I could see that he was indeed involved with someone else. And I've been . . .' She closes her eyes for a moment, concentrates on her breathing. 'I've been struggling somewhat.'

'Frey,' says Gil.

'No.' Frey holds up a hand. 'I'm going to do this. Let me speak.' She stands up from the table, rubs her face, leans into the tension. It holds her up. 'I haven't known what to do. This has been a dilemma for quite a while. Do I preserve my family? Do I have a tantrum? Do I let the man I love, my children's father, do I let him go, let him grasp what looks very much like his happiness? Or do I pretend I don't know anything and hope it just goes away?' She sits back down. 'I couldn't work it out. And then I got a bit drunk, and apparently I went for the tantrum. I posted the picture. I'm so sorry.'

'You said you didn't know who posted it!' Lily cries. 'You lied, Mum.'

'Yes,' says Freycinet. 'Yes, I did. I lied. And the other thing I did . . .' She takes a breath, looks at Grace again. 'I read your diary.'

Grace gapes at her.

'I found it and I read it. A few times. I was worried about you. I couldn't see you clearly, so I read it and I learnt a little bit about what you were thinking. I should have known you were sick but I thought it was more about your commitment to dancing and, well, I didn't end up seeing you at all . . .'

Grace shoves her plate across the table, glares at Frey.

'I'm sorry.' Frey looks around the table. Roger's disapproval, Lily's confusion, Tom's repulsion, Grace's steady indignation. 'I'm very, very sorry.'

'What the fuck?' says Tom. 'This is so insane.'

Frey can't reach her amygdala. She can't focus on any breathing methods that might deliver instant calm. She finds herself standing again, watches her hands as they rise.

'I'm so very sorry, please believe that.' She looks at Gil. His face is flushed with fury.

'We were dealing with it quietly, with dignity,' he says. 'This is that bloody choir's fault.'

'What, that you had an affair?' Frey says.

'You read Grace's diary, Mum?' says Lily.

'Everyone – *everyone* – is talking about that photo,' says Tom. 'My friends have seen it.'

'Oh my God, bro,' Grace says to Tom. 'This is a picture of Dad having *sex* with some woman who is not our mother.' She looks at Frey. 'And no one says "root", Mum.' Grace stands and walks out of the room.

'Everything is wrong,' shouts Lily. 'And now you've given Grace the perfect excuse not to eat her lunch.' She is out of her chair and running with her sobs after Grace.

'Yeah, Merry frigging Christmas,' says Tom. He takes a thick slice of ham and a bread roll, then follows his sisters.

'I'm going for a walk,' says Gil. He throws his napkin on the table, whistles for Acorn. The two of them leave the room.

Frey watches Acorn follow Gil and resists the urge to call for him to stay. Acorn, not Gil. She puts a hand over her eyes.

'Right,' says Roger. 'Not your best use of tradecraft, The Girl.' He sighs, reaches for the silver serving tongs. 'Shouldn't waste those spuds.'

𝄒

Message from Quinella Doyle, sent via text to multiple recipients, 26 December 2019.

Well, bugger me, Mary and I had three babies in the early hours of this morning. Everyone thinks we're lezzos – it's fucken hilarious. I wish I was, I could do without any more dicks in my life but now I have three tiny ones to look after. Freddie Mercury Doyle, George Michael Doyle and Stevie Wonder Doyle, named after the three fellas who I think have the best pipes in the world. (I didn't really keep the surnames as middle names. Mary talked me out of it so youse stuck-up molls can keep your fancy pants on.) Anyway, Freddie, George and Stevie sounds good to me. They came seven weeks early so they're fucken small. We'll be staying put for a bit but I'll tell you when you can visit. Sing on, you excellent women. I'm having a fucken sleep.

    P. S. I'm pretty glad they came out the sun roof and not out of my vag. That labour business sucks balls.

    P. P. S. Morphine is the fucking best. So is Mary.

    P. P. P. S. Can someone duck down to St David's Park and tell Petal? She'll be wondering why I'm not dropping her sandwiches down.

𝄡

Stepping Stone Number 202, from *La Lista* by R.K.:
Don't turn Christmas into a chance to show off your skills. Put the kindergarten angels made of cotton balls on the tree, gift the wonky gingerbread men, choose the scraggly tree, sing the carols badly. No one wants a Christmas tradition of untouchable perfection.

Chapter 32

Cri-de-Coeur

On Monday the thirtieth of December, Bizzy stands before the choir for their last rehearsal of the year. She breathes the familiar, comforting smell of Laetare: lavender carpet cleaner layered with perishing plastic, smoke and the stale excitement of long-gone guests. She smiles at her choristers and says, 'I have Christmas presents for you all.' From a carton at her feet she pulls a stack of green T-shirts with purple trim, unfolds one to reveal the words 'The Angry Women's Choir' printed in white on the front in a simple, serif font. On the back is a phrase of music notation containing an alto clef and the words #jointhechorus.

Mary claps her hands. 'Bring it on! Shit's getting real now.'

'Why an alto clef, Bizzy?' asks Kyrie.

'It was the graphic designer's idea,' Bizzy replies. 'The alto clef represents the lesser known voices, the overlooked pitches.'

'I love that,' says Avni.

There is a buzz of excitement as they all pull on a T-shirt, then line up, making their choir rows extra straight.

Bizzy feels breathless. The choir in their T-shirts look suddenly like something locomotive and unstoppable.

'There's more,' she says, rummaging in a second carton, then holding up a deck of cards.

'Our small acts of rebellion!' says Sally with a gleeful laugh. 'I've been looking forward to these.'

Bizzy draws out a card and explains, 'On the back of the card is Rosanna's haiku: *All the women sing, their chorus so thunderous, the world must tune in*. And on the front is, yes, a small act of rebellion for the everyday feminist.' She flips the card over and reads, '"Wear something that someone told you looks ridiculous." "Make people smile, make them talk, disrupt their expectations."'

'Ha,' says Sally. 'Eleanor has that covered.'

They look at Eleanor, who is wearing a man's business suit and a tiara. She gives a little bow.

'Is there one in there about posting photographs of your husband shagging his mistress?' asks Sally.

'No,' says Bizzy.

'Is Freycinet coming today?' Kyrie asks.

'I hope so,' says Bizzy.

'Well, I hope not,' says Sally. 'I feel very annoyed with her, frankly.'

But Freycinet is suddenly very much there, bursting through the door in an untidy fluster of greasy hair and wrung-out shame and 'Oh my God, I'm so sorry. I was drunk and I posted that picture and I tried to fix it but it just kept being reposted in threads all over the place and I couldn't keep up and I know that I should have called to explain, Bizzy, but everything's such a mess and I feel terrible that I used your platform to throw my husband's infidelity back in his face.' She stops talking, looks at the women in their T-shirts and feels an ache of distance.

'You were trusted as an administrator, Freycinet,' says Sally, 'and you hijacked our hashtag for your own ends.'

'I know, and I'm sorry.'

'No sorries, Freycinet,' says Bizzy. 'Yet again, you've found a way to increase our volume. Not in the way I might have hoped, but there we are.'

'It is kind of grubby, though,' Sally says. 'I'm especially uncomfortable about the involvement of Skye Killinger, given all she's doing for us.'

'Exactly,' says Frey. 'That was particularly poor form. But she did shag my husband.'

'It's created a bit of a whinge fest,' Mary continues. 'The post I put up about Quin's babies barely registered among the grievances.'

Frey gasps. 'Quin's had her babies?'

Sally scoffs.

'But people are really feeling the permission to chime in,' says Bizzy. 'It's like a nationwide Furies session. Think of the tension release.'

'How's your husband responding?' asks Mary.

'Oh, you know,' says Frey. 'He's over the moon with his new fan base. Signing autographs, choosing an agent.' She slumps onto a chair. 'He's incensed. Moved to a hotel, keeps saying I need help. The kids despise both of us. Happy days.'

'Waa,' says Sally.

'Okay, Sally,' says Bizzy. 'That'll do.'

'We've always stood for things that matter, Bizzy,' protests Sally. 'And now we're attracting petty stories about someone's husband's halitosis. We're meant to be re-enchanting feminism, not collecting the dirty laundry of the white middle class.'

Bizzy takes a breath. 'But don't forget that the AWC and #jointhechorus has also been bringing lots of good to people's attention. Lobby groups preparing for the next federal election, women being heard from all walks of life, young children questioning the status quo, carers being seen, kindness rewarded. Despite the recent lowering of tone, I still think Freycinet has given people permission to call out the little things that perpetuate dominion. She certainly showed me a whole new world of domesticated, pre-enlightened women. And don't forget that without her, Paul Bellavance would still be poncing about dishing up oppression willy-nilly, *and* we'd still be singing vanilla pudding songs at nursing homes. I mean, at this rate we'll be a household name.'

'Okay, wait right there,' Freycinet says, holding up her hands, 'why am I suddenly feeling that my life has been co-opted to drive your latest crusade?'

'You're the one posting the pictures,' Mary points out.

'But before that,' says Freycinet, looking at Bizzy. 'Did you use me to spark up your waning energy? This "fire" of yours you always go on about?'

'Now, hang on a moment . . .' says Sally.

'It's okay,' says Bizzy. 'Let her speak.'

'Oh "let her speak",' mimics Freycinet in a perfect Irish accent. 'Let her speak, let her stand, let her be seen, let her be believed, let her ignore her kids and fuck over her life if it means I can rediscover my inner fire and as a bonus become a *household name.*'

The room falls silent. All eyes are on this new presence with her fury turned all in.

Freycinet drops the accent, lowers her voice, but her hands are clenched and her mouth is drawn up hard. 'The liniment girl. She rubs the pain from your knees just as sure as she ruins your world, doesn't she, Bizzy. You are tribal feminists, as coercive and potentially oppressive as your enemies. Can't you see that? You're in the business of brainwashing, too. I believed in the Angry Women's Choir while my daughter was wasting away. I was infatuated, loved you all to distraction. I didn't see what was happening right under my nose until my daughter died before my eyes.' Frey looks from Bizzy to Kyrie and back again. 'Grace's heart stopped, you know. On that stage. You saw it too. And now surely you can see that I can't stay here. I'm needed at home.'

'But your children need you here,' says Mary. 'They need us all here. Do they want a helicopter mother or a better world?'

'Oh my God!' shouts Freycinet. 'Find something else to fixate on! I don't see any of you campaigning against the issues in your own lives, it's all about what's wrong with my life.' She waves a hand at Eleanor. 'Sort out the justice system,' she shouts. 'Help single parents, like Quin. Or hit someone else with your stupid cars, suck them into your vortex to be socially engineered by your neo-communist wokery.'

'We attend to all degrees of oppression, in all its forms,' says Bizzy quietly.

'Shut up, Freycinet,' says Mary. 'You're just making excuses so you can preserve your privilege.'

Freycinet turns on Mary. 'No, I'm preserving myself. And my family.'

'Okay, but we didn't turn your husband into a cheating cockhead,' says Mary. 'Just saying.'

'You really know nothing about me,' Frey says. 'Nothing at all.'

'Ha, no kidding,' says Mary. 'You're so stitched up it's a wonder you can speak.'

'Thank you,' says Bizzy loudly, 'for your cri-de-coeur, Freycinet. I will have a good think over your words and use them wisely. Of course you don't have to stay. Our demands on your time are clearly too much. We will never stop making a home for you, but if you want to leave, none of us will stand in your way.'

'You bet we won't,' says Mary. 'Plenty of other helping hands. Skye Killinger's contribution, for instance, has been frigging cosmic – like, infinitely valuable to the cause.'

'That's enough from you, Mary,' says Bizzy, looking at Frey, who is standing stock still, all the past weeks etched into her face. *Sleeper agent in peril*, Bizzy wants to say but doesn't.

From somewhere way too close, a deafening siren shrieks, followed by a loudspeaker-distorted voice bellowing, 'Clear the premises immediately, this is a construction site. I repeat, clear the premises immediately!'

Eleanor is first to the window. Bizzy can't hear what she says but her actions indicate the presence of something amusing outside. There is eye rolling and a 'get a load of this' head jerk.

The rest of the choir cluster at the window, hands covering ears as the dreadful siren impales the air again. Only Frey remains were she is, her stillness redolent with, *Oh, what now?*

Bizzy is inclined to agree as she peers over Mary's shoulder to see Paul Bellavance standing alone on the footpath, wearing earmuffs and cranking a hand-operated siren.

'Ha!' shouts Sally. 'He's finally lost it.'

'What's he going to do?' shouts Mary. 'Declare war?'

Bizzy watches as Paul picks up a loudspeaker and booms, 'Evacuate the building immediately. I know you're in there.'

'Yeah, you can see us at the window, fuckwit,' says Mary.

Bizzy, who finds the sight not at all amusing but very unsettling, marches out the door waving her hands. 'What are you doing making all that racket?' she shouts, but Bellavance has taken up the siren again and is cranking its racket in her direction.

She stands back, holding her ears. The rest of the choir trail outside after her and only when all eight of them (and a very perturbed dachshund) gather on the patchy Laetare lawn does Bellavance cease his din.

'Shite in a bucket, man,' says Bizzy. 'What are you playing at? You'll have woken the dead.'

'Let's hope not, because your mother sounds like a piece of work,' says Paul with a sneer.

Bizzy makes a lunge for him but Sally holds her back.

'Ooh,' he says. 'The witches are coming.'

Bizzy sends him a daggery stare.

'Take a day off, dickhead,' says Mary. 'Go hose out your bins or something.'

'Oh, sorry ladies,' he says with exaggerated charm. 'How disrespectful of me to so rudely interrupt the inner workings of the esteemed Angry Women's Choir. You must be so proud of the brouhaha you're stirring up. And Bizzy Nancarrow, that shade of black is particularly becoming for the hair of a grand high witch.'

'What's the story with the siren?' asks Eleanor. 'You scared my dog.'

Bellavance turns on her. 'I'm sure it's used to fear, living with a murderess and all.' He lurches forward suddenly and barks in Eleanor's face.

Eleanor doesn't flinch. Penelope growls.

'One of us,' announces Sally with a glance at Irene, 'has a heart condition and must not be put into a state of disturbance.'

'Too late,' says Bellavance. 'You're already severely disturbed.'

'May the cat eat you,' says Bizzy, 'and may the devil eat the cat.'

'What did you mean by "construction site"?' asks Kyrie.

'Oh, did I say, "construction site"?' Bellavance sends Kyrie a horrible smile. 'I should have said "demolition site".' He pulls a two-way radio from his pocket and says into it, 'Truck is a go, over.'

'Wilco,' says a crackly voice from the other end.

'I know how much you lot love a bit of action,' he says.

Freycinet approaches him and declares, 'This is not your building.'

'Jeez, Mrs Barnes,' says Bellavance, surveying Frey's un-made-up face, her thrown-together clothing. 'You've let yourself go.'

A large truck turns into the street. In its dual cab are men wearing high-vis hazmat suits and hard hats.

Freycinet snatches the two-way from Bellavance and says, 'Break, break, this is the owner of the building speaking. There will be no demolition today, do you copy?'

The truck slows to a stop. Bellavance grabs for the two-way but Freycinet is too quick for him. 'Turn around immediately,' she says. *'Do you copy?'*

The passenger in the front of the truck rolls down his window and puts out a questioning arm. Bellavance raises his loudspeaker and shouts, 'Proceed with stage one, proceed with stage one.'

The truck rolls forward again. The men alight, five of them in total. They separate out into teams. 'We'll check for occupancy,' shouts one. 'Roger that, we'll barrier up,' says another.

'This building is riddled with asbestos,' says Sally. 'You need a whole procedural plan with full vicinity involvement.'

'We're on it, thank you, Doctor,' says Bellavance. He takes a two-way radio from one of the high-vis men and says, 'Haz truck and water, please, over.'

'Copy that,' says a voice.

Within minutes the men have ushered the choir behind a series of bossy orange bollards while a second truck appears, complete with hoses and face masks. 'A mask for all of you,' says Bellavance. 'Because I'd hate for you to miss this.'

'I'm calling the police,' says Freycinet. 'This is my property.'

'Negative, Mrs Barnes,' he says, taking up the two-way again. 'Let's rumble, Golf Bravo, Tango Bravo,' he says with a smile.

There comes a low growling sound, increasing in volume before a monstrous yellow machine appears from the driveway at the top of the street. Two figures wearing gasmasks are at the helm.

The women stare.

'Holy fairy, mother of God,' says Bizzy.

'Jesus Christ,' says Eleanor.

The machine, a giant excavator wielding a set of long-armed jaws, hurtles along the street and jerks itself towards Laetare Gardens.

'No, no, no,' says Bizzy. 'You can't . . .'

But her words are drowned out by the proximity of the excavator. She leaps over the bollards, attempting to put herself between the building and the machine, but two large men drag her back.

'Get your hands off her,' screams Mary, pulling at one of the men. He pushes her back roughly, sending her to the ground. From behind him, Irene sends a stinging kick directly to his groin. He doubles over, shouts in pain. Bizzy wrenches herself free and makes a run for it.

'Police, please,' Freycinet says into her phone.

Bellavance starts up his siren again.

'What was that?' shouts Frey into her phone.

Eleanor, Kyrie, Sally and Irene follow Bizzy across the capeweed lawn. They hold hands and form a line in front of Laetare's entrance. Mary stands, takes a moment to shove the ball-broken construction worker to his knees, then stands at the end of the line and begins to film with her phone. 'We will not be moved,' she shouts.

Bellavance beckons the excavator forward. It answers with a menacing rev.

Freycinet gives up on her phone, shoves it in her pocket and shouts, 'Hey, Paul, here's your radio.' She throws the two-way straight at his crotch with amazing force. It lands right on target.

'Fuuuck!' he shouts, joining the construction worker in the pose of pain.

Bizzy watches in astonishment as Freycinet launches herself into the cab of the excavator and wrestles the driver out of his seat, dragging him, head-locked, down the steps and onto the ground, where she holds his masked face at the jaw.

'This is not an authorised demolition!' she shouts through clenched teeth as the driver writhes and grunts under her hands. 'And there are lives at stake.'

'Let him go!' roars a voice behind her. 'Frey, let him go.'

Bizzy sees Freycinet freeze momentarily, then turn towards the voice and watch as the excavator's passenger leaps down from his seat and takes off his mask.

'Gil?' says Freycinet. She turns back to the body in her grip and pulls the mask from his face.

'Tom,' she says. It's a small cry on the wind; it hurts Bizzy's heart.

The boy scrambles out of her reach. 'What the hell, Mum?'

'What are you doing?' Freycinet asks as the high-vis men close in on her.

Tom looks confused. 'I thought it would be fun. Dad said . . . I didn't know it would be this big . . .'

'The police are on their way,' Paul Bellavance blares through his loudspeaker to the line of choristers. 'Assault and civil disobedience will not be tolerated. This man is working to progress development of *his* building in this dying commercial precinct. I suggest you let him get on.' He nods at Gil, who sends Freycinet a defiant stare and hauls himself into the excavator's driver's seat.

Tom sits panting on the kerb, glancing warily at his mother as she is apprehended by the men.

A police siren wails in the distance.

𝄡

Bizzy – along with her choristers – is being bundled into a police paddy wagon when she witnesses the first fracturing of Laetare Gardens. The jaws pummel into the building just above the front door. The wall buckles under the clash of brick, mortar and steel.

'Please, please, no,' says Bizzy. 'Don't do this.'

Next to her, Kyrie takes her hand and squeezes. Irene takes the other. 'Surely they can't,' Avni sobs.

But on the next catastrophic hit, the worn face of the building caves in. Its wonky pine trees startle and panic in the reverberating crash. Bizzy whimpers.

Like a deranged conductor, Paul Bellavance waves his arms rapturously, accentuating his terrible soundtrack. As the paddy wagon drives away, he smiles at Bizzy and delivers her a sweeping bow.

𝄡

Stepping Stone Number 144, from *La Lista* by R.K.:
To get the fire burning brightly without having to go out gathering kindling on a cold, dark evening, try these alternatives: corn chips, potato chips, pretzels, lint from the dryer stuffed in a cardboard toilet roll, dried citrus peel, old egg cartons.

Chapter 33

Bamboozles

Two weeks later, Bizzy is lying underneath a weighted blanket on a bed of cushions in a makeshift cubby made from chairs, the clothes horse and the contents of her linen cupboard. She has Tim Hecker's 'Dungeoneering' playing at moderate volume and is listening for nothing in the drone.

She remains there when the doorbell rings, and when it rings again. She sinks a little deeper into her pillows when it rings a third time. She has become quite the expert at ignoring the doorbell (and the phone) in the last fourteen days.

There is blessed silence for about ten minutes before she hears Ferris's voice, quite close.

'I helped her with the cubby,' he is saying. 'But I wish I hadn't, because she won't come out. Cubbies are only fun for about a day.'

Bizzy listens to some clattering, the sound of someone groaning, a yelp. *Kyrie?* she thinks. She peeks out through one of her air vents.

It is Kyrie, performing the final manoeuvres of a clamber through the window.

'Godsake, Bizzy,' she mutters. 'The things I do for you.'

Ferris is already in the room. He has spotted Bizzy through her blanket flap and he kneels down, rests on his elbows and whispers to her eye, 'Sorry, Bizzy Nancarrow, but I need some extra help to get you out and your friend was here dinging the bell, so I let her in my window.'

'It's my window,' Bizzy whispers back.

'Bizzy?' says Kyrie, lifting the blanket a little more. As her eyes adjust to the dim light within Bizzy's nest, she sighs. 'Oh, Bizzy,' she says. 'Tell me where it hurts.'

'Everywhere,' says Bizzy, turning away from the light.

'I have some things that might help soothe the pain,' says Kyrie.

'Please let it be whiskey,' says Bizzy. Her voice is muffled within the cubby.

'It's better than whiskey,' says Kyrie.

Bizzy listens to some rummaging, a beep and then a female reporter saying, 'This is the moment that two high-profile Hobart businessmen oversaw the demolition of the headquarters of the Angry Women's Choir. Eight members of the venerated choir, a rising voice for women throughout the world, were ambushed by disgraced politician Paul Bellavance and property developer Gilbert Barnes in late December, then forced to witness the destruction of their beloved Laetare Gardens.

'The West Moonah Women's Choir, now more widely known as the Angry Women's Choir, had a long-term rental arrangement dating back to the 1980s. An arrangement that came to a crashing end when the building was cordoned off and demolished without warning. Much of the process was captured on video by an AWC member.

'Spokespeople for women's groups everywhere are calling this a declaration of war by privileged white male supremacists desperate to maintain the status quo. The groups say they will step up to fight this war, but on their terms, without violence and with all the vigour and determination, mischief and intelligence of this remarkable women's choir.'

Bizzy remains silent in the cubby.

'We're at over a million followers now, Bizzy.'

'Noo!' howls Bizzy.

'People are offering us new venues, free of charge,' says Kyrie triumphantly. 'Women are wearing AWC T-shirts as far away as Sweden, and Lady Gaga has ordered a Small Acts of Rebellion pack. Rumours are rife that the choir is an outpost of the enigmatic Illuminati, a small antipodean prophet group heralding a new world order. The Chancellor of Germany has praised the choir and called her women to alms. That's A-L-M-S as in care not A-R-M-S as in weapons. Imaginations are sparked, Bizzy. Laetare did not fall in vain.' Kyrie pauses, but there is no response from the cubby so she continues. 'And locally there's a whole outpouring of love for Laetare. People are saying that despite its lack of aesthetic reasoning, it's a true cultural icon. Everyone and their daughter's friend had their school formals there. Bizzy?'

'I've been thinking,' Bizzy says finally. 'What Freycinet said, about us being brainwashers . . . I think she could be right. Perhaps we've been bamboozled for so long that all our bamboozles are filled with bamboozles. I probably *am* a bamboozle.'

'You're not a bamboozle,' says Kyrie.

'I think I am,' Bizzy says. 'And a parasite. Freycinet was right about that. The disappointment in her face when I first saw her made me feel a little more alive.'

'You just can't think straight right now,' Kyrie says. 'Too much trauma. But I'm telling you, you're on the right side of enlightenment, Bizzy. Your anger is good anger. Let it roar. Paul Bellavance and Gil Barnes should have started a bonfire in you.'

The doorbell rings again. Bizzy draws back from her makeshift air vent.

'I'll get it,' says Ferris, hurrying out.

'Don't!' shouts Bizzy, but Ferris is already opening the door. There is chatter, some bustle and the sound of something trundling along the hallway.

'This is the next surprise,' says Kyrie. There is a touch more caution in her voice.

'Bizzy,' says Ferris, his voice loud with amazement. 'There are three weenie babies!'

Quin comes into the room with two babies lying in a pram and one strapped to her front. She eyes the cubby suspiciously and says, 'Bizzy, don't you turn me away, it takes hours to get these little arseholes out and about.'

There's some rustling from inside the cubby, but otherwise, silence.

'Right, then,' says Quin, lifting one of the babies out of his pram. 'Incoming.' She looks at Ferris, who removes some clothes pegs to open the cubby door. Quin places the baby on a pillow inside. 'That there's Stevie. Wait.' She peers down at the baby on her front and says, 'George. That's George.'

There is some more rustling, some gurgling from George, but nothing from Bizzy.

'She's feeling altogether overwhelmed,' whispers Kyrie.

'She's in a bamboozle,' says Ferris. He tilts his head at Quin and says, 'Did you push all three of those little babies out your dajina?'

There is a snort from inside the cubby.

'Ah, a little laugh,' says Kyrie.

Baby George whimpers.

'George wants out,' says Bizzy.

'He'll be right,' says Quin. 'Leave him there.'

'I want out too,' Bizzy says. 'Of the choir.'

'You what?' Quin sits beside the cubby door.

'I can't do it anymore. It's been a long time coming. My energy was waning well before Rosanna died and Laetare got smashed. Freycinet was right – I was using her to stoke my stupid fire, keep me moving. But it was false fire, I think, like those ridiculous glowing fake logs. I'm stepping aside.'

'They work well, in my experience,' says Kyrie. 'The heat is real.'

Quin guffaws. 'Jesus Christ, there's no stepping aside, not for any of us. But you can take a break, I reckon, Bizzy. Because we might be the steering committee but there are allied fucken tanks every-where, and they're calling their own shots. Whether we want a rally on February twenty-nine or not, we've bloody got one. And we can show up in our best voice or look like complete twats – you choose.'

George begins to cry. Bizzy collects him up and emerges partway from the tent, holding him out to his mother. Kyrie intercepts and takes the baby, cooing softly.

'That flushed her out,' says Quin. She looks at Bizzy. 'Fizzy Wheelbarrow, don't abandon us. Look at me in my darkest hour, surrounded by blokes. Sorry, Ferris.'

'Ferris is one of the good ones,' says Bizzy. 'And your three are very sweet. Thank you for bringing them.' She looks up at Kyrie holding the baby with expert hands. 'Do you think,' she continues, 'that me and all the babies I never had have done enough?'

'Um . . .' says Quin.

'Maybe all the pretty flowers that Winifred and I never grew have *done enough*.' She gives a huge, shoulder-lifting sigh. 'All those quiet moments I didn't take, all the lips I didn't kiss and the moonlit walks I didn't go on and the little buttons I didn't sew onto little cardigans and the sitting about I never did and the memories I never made . . . perhaps it's all done quite enough, thank you.'

'You could just have a holiday,' says Kyrie. 'Take a break. There are still a few weeks before February.'

'Yes, I could take a holiday,' says Bizzy, rubbing her forehead. 'But you see, I'll just take myself along. And there *is* no time, actually. I'm a little bit more ancient every day. My bras are creaky and my knickers need two pegs to hang them on the line and everything feels that little bit more hardscrabble. I have thus far chosen mad hair and battlegrounds and Cyndi Lauper, and now I choose rest. When I'm ready I might choose to sit quietly under a tree. If I happen to die there from inactivity well, what a nice way to go.' Bizzy disappears back into the cubby, drawing the blanket closed behind her.

'Well, okay,' says Kyrie. 'That's okay. But I'm coming back through that window every day until you're ready to sit under the trees. And I have one more thing for you.'

There is a groan from the cubby.

From a shopping bag, Kyrie extracts a small marble-lidded urn. 'It's a little bit of Rosanna. She had her ashes divided into eight of these. One for each of her children, one for Jonathon, one for her brother Matteo, one for the mountain and one for the choir.' Kyrie sets the little urn down beside the silent cubby. 'This one is the choir's. As our director, it needs to stay with you. She's right here with you, Bizzy.'

'And,' says Quin, 'she'll nag the crap out of you until you cheer the fuck up.'

𝄡

Stepping Stone Number 31, from *La Lista* by R.K.:
Putting yourself in an enclosed, warm squashy place and asking to be alone is almost always okay. Self-care is a form of warfare.

Chapter 34
Reasons Not To Die

Sunday, 19 January 2020, 9.30 p.m.

So here's how shit everything is:

1. Mum posts a photo of Dad boning a famous artist
    called Skye Killinger. Everyone in the world sees it.
    I hear the words 'Barnes banging on the backdoor' in
    the library.

2. Dad shits the bed, blames the Angry Women's Choir
    for Mum going full rogue and demolishes their building
    alongside sketchy-as-fuck Paul Bellavance.

3. Mum breaks Paul Bellavance's balls and rugby tackles Tom
    like she's the goddamn Black Widow.

4. The whole world hates on Dad all over again.

5. Mum cleans the whole house like some sort of crazed
    domestic demon.

6. Dad moves out. Not with Skye. He says she ditched him.

7. I hear Tom crying in his room so I try to be nice to him and
    he tells me to fuck off.

8. Skye Killinger's AWC posters are EVERYWHERE. They
    give me the creeps and everyone says how amazing they are,

which I can tell sends Mum crazy. (They really are
full-blown amazing. I like the name Skye.)

9. I eat a tub of yoghurt and it feels like rising dough under my
   skin. I do two full barre workouts back to back to stop the
   stupid dough feeling, then I hate myself again. I can't win.

10. I get a letter from the Australian Dance Institute saying they
    will not consider me until I have a clean bill of health. How
    can I have that when my brain is a scribble and there's rising
    dough under my skin every time I eat something?

And if you're reading this MUM – yep, everything is SHIT.

Grace smells Lily's strawberry lip balm before she knows she's in the
room.

'Jesus, Lily!' she says, sitting up on her bed and turning to see her
sister. 'You're as bad as Mum, sneaking around me like that.'

'Sorry, I thought you might have been asleep. I wasn't sure.' Lily
is wearing a tutu with a chunky-knit cardigan and Blundstone boots.
'Were you masturbating?' she asks.

'What? No, Lily. I was writing in my diary.'

'Oh. Have you hidden it in a new place so Mum can't read it
anymore?'

'Yes.' She looks at Lily's ensemble of clothes and says, 'You look
groovy today.'

'I know.' Lily opens her cardigan to reveal an Angry Women's
Choir T-shirt.

'Wow, don't let Mum see you in that.'

'I won't. She's all like'—Lily puts her hands to her forehead and
imitates her mother—'"I don't want to talk about the choir anymore,
okay, Lily?"'

Grace smiles. Rolls her eyes.

'Mum says that Dad knocked down the building because he
thinks the AWC was bad for her and that he did it for us.'

'Right,' says Grace.

'Is that what you think?'

'I think that I don't want to talk about the choir either, really.'

'Why not?'

'Because everybody else is.'

'Well, I'm going to the rally. So are all my friends. We all have T-shirts. My friend Greer, she's the smartest person in my class, she says she wants to start her own Angry Women's Brigade. And our music teacher is helping us write a song for the choir. There is a lot happening, Gracie. You need to get better and get around it.'

Grace turns back to her diary.

Lily hops up on the end of the bed. 'Anyway, I've brought you some other new reasons not to die.' She doesn't wait for encouragement, or for Grace to protest. 'Number one, the corner shop is selling little pots with plants in them that eat flies. Actually eat flies! Do you know about plants that eat flies?'

'Mmmhmm.'

'Number two, I grew into your first practice tutu and your Acro shoes and you need to see me dance in them.'

'Hold up, don't do Acro,' says Grace. 'That's how I ended up with a twangy shoulder. Focus on Classical and Lyrical and maybe Jazz. If you want to . . .'

'If I want to be like you?'

Grace is silent.

'Number three, this girl I know at dance, her name's Ilaria, she said her sister said that everyone's really worried about you and I said they shouldn't worry because you ate some tuna and you are going to be better just as—'

Grace turns to look at Lily. 'Lily, *don't* talk about me to anyone, okay? Not to anyone. I don't want them to know stuff about this. I hate that. And they're not worried about me. They're happy I'm out of the way. Promise you'll keep your mouth shut from now on?'

'Okay. Sorry, Gracie.'

Grace sees that Lily has put on glittery eye shadow and that there are matching tears in her eyes.

'But Ilaria says Serra *is* worried about you. She's not happy you're out of the way.'

Grace lies back on the pillows.

'Their mum died from cancer in her lungs.' Lily wipes her eyes. Sparkly eye shadow comes off onto her hand. 'Ilaria says she's a ghost now, like, a nice ghost that helps her with stuff. She has some of her ashes in a jar.'

'That's creepy.'

'I think it's nice.' Lily sniffs. 'Our mum's creepy. Like, she's putting way too much attention on us all the time. She keeps asking me if she can help me with my homework and she tried to talk to Tom about cricket. Do you think it's better to have a ghost mum or a creepy weirdo mum?'

'I think probably a creepy weirdo mum.' Grace stretches out her leg so that her foot rests against Lily's. 'What's the number four reason not to die?'

Lily pulls out a deck of AWC cards with a flourish. 'I got these cool Angry Women's Choir cards.' Lily holds one up and reads from it. 'They are Small Acts of Rebellion and they're going to "change the world and disrupt current distorted presumptions and values".'

'How?' asks Grace, semi-interested now.

'This one says, "Eat a humungous sandwich so that you can build muscles to carry lots of signs to the AWC rally."'

'It does not.'

Grace snatches the bright green card from Lily's hand and reads it aloud. '"Wear something that someone told you looks ridiculous. Make people smile, make them talk, disrupt their expectations." Ha, cool, you've got that nailed today.'

'And have a look at this one.' Lily hands over a bright purple card. 'The purple ones are the really goady ones, but good goady, not gross.'

Grace reads aloud. '"Set up a childcare space at the offices of your local member." Wow, good idea, I guess.'

'But you should stick with the green ones.' Lily hands the fourth card to Grace. It says, simply, 'Rest'.

𝄡

Grace does rest. She doesn't eat much for the next day or two – just enough to satisfy her mother's anxious eyes – but she doesn't exercise either. She mostly stays in her room with Acorn, her diary, her phone and Bizzy's letter. All of it helps to drown out the persistent whisper on her shoulder that tells her to get off her fat arse, to do better, be better, to weigh herself, to eat nothing.

We watched a girl who can dance with silence. An a cappella orchestra. And she opened the door.

Grace picks up her laptop and spends the next hour down a rabbit hole with the members of the West Moonah Women's Choir – with Mary and her research papers, Eleanor and her criminal record, Quin and her criminal record, Rosanna and her death notices, Bizzy and Winifred and their adventures. When she's done, Grace picks up her diary, her pen and makes patterns on the page with words.

murderess

SexY

SWEET spinSTER

trouble-maker

BITTER

JUnkIE Pretty
potty-mouthed

FEISTY
media-whores

DEMENTED

> *angry LESBIANs*

BOSSy

>> *privileged*

> *lead astray*

DEAD hysterical

She stops playing with letters and writes a few sentences, an odd little poem to herself.

Maybe I do have the key.

Maybe the first step is inside me.

Better to dance and not die

Anything is possible, look how eggs can fly.

Grace sighs heavily. 'Words and words and words,' she mutters. She opens the window to the golden afternoon, hears Lily laughing with a friend in the garden.

She writes, *These women are more than words; they are deeds and good and seeing and kindness. They are answers and maybe they could be change.* She closes her diary and heads downstairs for dinner.

𝄢

Frey is out buying groceries when she sees the fifth poster in the Skye Killinger Angry Women's Choir series. It is pinned to the side of the soft-drink fridge and it stops Frey in her tracks. It features a woman standing in a kitchen, surrounded by the detritus of the everyday. There is a curtained window behind her and a half-peeled apple in her hand. The face is almost translucent with distress, to the point that Frey is looking through it for the source of the pain. The eyes are filled with tears and directed upwards in search of something that clearly isn't there. On the table, a small bowl is filled with olives, and next to it, a plate is bright with yellow grapefruit.

'Oh,' says Frey. It's involuntary, and drawn out like a groan. She leans a hand against the fridge to steady herself.

'Crikey,' says a woman behind her. 'Someone's fair cracked her heart in two, that's for certain.'

Frey remains still as the woman peers at the text written plainly below the picture: *The Angry Women's Choir. Town Hall, 29 February 2020. #jointhechorus*

'Right,' says the woman. 'Best get along to that. I've been on the warpath ever since my husband left me for a motorbike.' She laughs.

Frey returns a mild laugh noise, but doesn't turn around, because she doesn't want the woman to see that the face in the poster is her own. Freycinet. Unmistakable and startlingly real, like a version of herself that outdoes the original; out-hurts her.

She abandons the groceries, walks home steeped in the anguish she has seen in the poster. The full brunt of betrayal causes a pain that defies tears, changes the shapes of trees and the sounds of birds around her, makes her want to run. *How does she do that with a paint-brush?* she thinks. *And is that some kind of apology?*

The artist's previous AWC posters – hyperreal depictions of wistful, home-sickened, empty-eyed or furious women in domestic situations – have appeared in poster form all over Tasmania. Academics, pop-culture commentators, the general public and teens have described the works as 'devastatingly quotidian', 'heartbreaking', 'eye-opening' and 'totally shook' respectively. Skye Killinger's reputation in the world of art investment is growing and her commission requests have been suspended indefinitely owing to 'a backlog of enquiries'. Frey knows because she has spent an unreasonable amount of time examining Skye's website.

There are three more posters at bus stops along the walk home, and four people wearing the distinctive AWC T-shirts. One of them is an elderly man.

Later, when her pain keeps her moving, she takes Acorn to the dog park and overhears a woman say to her friend, 'Get the Angry

Women's Choir on to it. They'll sort the prick out.' The friend laughs and sings the chorus of 'The Liniment Girl'.

Leaving the dog park, Frey finds herself looking over her shoulder at intervals, as though the music might follow her home.

𝄢

That afternoon, while helping Lily cover schoolbooks, Frey knows once and for all that she really has lost her mind to her trauma, and that the music has indeed followed her home.

The windows are open – all of them, because the day is one of Tasmania's rare hot ones. Properly hot, high thirties and dry. The air is hazy from bushfires turning parts of mainland Australia into disaster zones and sending their ash across Bass Strait on the northerly wind. The usual suburban holiday sounds are not as clear as they might be without the haze, but the occasional distant child, dog or lawnmower cuts through.

Lily is gluing a picture of a horse to the front of her new atlas when a pristine voice reverberates through the garden.

'Why do you think all our sisters are breaking their teeth?'

Lily gasps, looks for a long moment at the atlas in her hands, then up at Frey, who has turned very still. The voice rings out again.

'Clenching our jaws as they hide all their flaws and ignore all their dreams.'

Frey looks out the window and up, as though the exquisite sound is visible in the smoky sky.

'Oh come on,' she says.

'Why are we giving our time and our hearts for a song? Removing hard wires will hurt when they've been there so long.'

'Mum?' says Lily.

But Frey is walking through the open door to the garden terrace. From there she can see seven faces looking up at her. Avni is standing at the front of the group with a microphone in her hand and close behind her are the other choristers. Quin is gently rocking a large pram.

Frey's first sensation is one of relief. *Thank God you're here*, she thinks. *My friends.* This is followed closely by prickles of irritation – with herself, for becoming emotionally dependent on these women, and with them, for reminding her she has no actual friends.

The rest of the choir join Avni in simple, soft harmony.

'All the doors, they are shut, all my corners are cut.

The windows might shine, but I can't see the sky.'

'It's the choir!' says Lily. 'The Angry Women's Choir!'

Frey glances at Lily's awestruck face and sees that she is talking to Grace, who has come out to the terrace too. Above them, Tom opens the window of his bedroom.

'Don't talk pretty anymore. Stop believing folklore.

Ask your questions, don't ignore

this unease, this malaise, cold wash cycle of days.

That the life you are living, the self that you're giving,

will leave you with nothing to say.'

Frey looks at the ground, unable to stay focused on the eyes below, all of which are on her. Above, the birds seem to have fallen quiet. She imagines them being lulled to sleep, wonders if the babies in the pram are sleeping too. She concentrates on these wonderings until the song draws to its abrupt end, the final phrase, *'leave you with nothing . . .'* left hanging in the silence that follows, haunting Frey's ears.

Lily claps, then cheers, then says, 'That was ah-mazing.' She points at each woman and says, 'Avni, Mary, Kyrie, Sally, Irene, Eleanor and Quinella. And Penelope,' she adds, waving to the little dog at Eleanor's feet. 'Where's Bizzy?'

Kyrie smiles up at Lily and says, 'You know our names!'

'Yeah,' says Lily. 'Everyone knows your names. I am a huge fan. Your voice is, like, absolutely the amazingest, Avni.'

'The most amazing,' corrects Grace with a smile. Frey is surprised to see that the smile is shy. She has never encountered a shy version of Grace before.

'Thank you, Lily,' says Avni.

'Freycinet,' calls Irene, 'Avni wrote you a song about broken teeth because you suggested she write a song about broken teeth.'

'Thanks, Avni,' says Frey. 'Like Lily said, it's amazing.'

'How are your teeth these days?' asks Mary.

'Fine, thank you,' says Frey, and the word 'fine' joins the 'nothing' in the blurry air.

'Could we have a chat, please, Freycinet?' asks Kyrie. 'It's very important.'

'No,' says Frey. 'Thank you for the song, but no.' She turns away and heads indoors.

'Bizzy's lost her shit,' shouts Quin.

Frey pauses.

'After Rosanna fucken died on us and Laetare got poleaxed by that toolbag of assorted tosspot flogs, your departure is the fucken straw that broke the warhorse's back. She's fully cooked in the brainbox.'

'Sorry, Lily and Grace,' says Kyrie. 'You'd think Quinella would clean up her language now that she's a mother of three.'

'There are far worse words than "fuck",' says Quin.

'Like "slut",' says Lily.

'Anyway,' says Sally, 'do you think we could come inside? This air is not good for our lungs and goodness knows we're going to need them.'

Frey hesitates.

'Yes, of course you can come in,' says Lily. 'I'll get everyone a drink.'

The women climb the steps to the terrace, helping Quin lift her pram up.

'Ooh, so cute,' says Lily when she sees the babies.

'I promise we'll only stay a minute,' says Kyrie, putting a hand briefly on Frey's arm. Frey lets Lily take over, then follows them in.

'Freycinet,' says Mary, 'we have a situation. This AWC rally has got wildly bigger than we expected. And we don't have our iconic leader at the bridle. Without her, there's every chance it could all get away from us, and then we'll just look like—'

'Fuckwits,' says Quin.

'It's all happened a bit fast, really,' says Sally.

Mary snorts. 'Sal, we're talking thousands of years of oppression. Indoctrination that runs so deep it's reached Middle Earth. How can you say it's moving too fast?'

'True that,' says Irene.

Frey looks at Lily, who is moving her gaze from speaker to speaker with rapt attention.

'So Frey,' says Kyrie, 'Bizzy's calling herself a parasite, preying on people to better her cause. She believed what you said back there on demolition day. We think it would really help her if you would come and join us again.'

'I can't,' says Frey. 'I really can't.'

'Why not?' asks Eleanor.

Frey glances at Grace. 'I . . . I just don't want to. I can't even sing.'

'You can play the violin, though,' says Lily.

'Yeah,' says Irene. 'You can play the violin.'

'Even if it's just at the rally, so Bizzy can see you there,' says Kyrie.

'We're a fucken measly choir just the seven of us,' says Quin.

'Please, Frey?' says Avni.

'No,' says Frey, annoyed now. 'Look, this is as much an ambush as the one Paul and Gil conducted at Laetare Gardens.'

'Except we have music and they had a demolition crew,' Mary says.

'I'm sorry. I'm out.'

'But you care about us, Freycinet,' says Eleanor. 'I know what care feels like and I saw it in you back there at Laetare.'

'Yeah, you went full-scale ninja there for a moment,' says Mary. 'There were ballbags breaking all over the place.'

'They made balls tender for a reason,' says Irene.

Kyrie nods. 'You really didn't want Laetare to go, did you, Frey?'

Frey doesn't reply.

'And there's another thing,' says Kyrie, pulling something from her pocket. 'Rosanna told me that if ever Bizzy's fire burns too low, we should find a "flying man called Charlie" and give him this.' Kyrie opens her hand to reveal Bizzy's circular brown pendant. 'Rosanna said that you'd be the best one to work that one out.'

Frey frowns at the brown disc and sees that at its centre is a tiny circle of white.

'I know it's vague,' Kyrie adds. 'Rosanna wouldn't elaborate. She loved a riddle.'

'Bizzy never took that thing off,' Quin says, 'So we think this Charlie's an old flame. Which is weird because for years I assumed she was a gold-star closet lezzy.'

'We think this Charlie is the reason Bizzy gets so into the blues sometimes,' says Avni.

'Every couple of years,' says Mary, 'she makes us sing "Good Morning Heartache" by Billie Holiday. Like, ad nauseum. Bloody depressing.'

Kyrie's expression beseeches Frey. 'Please, Freycinet. It's all we've got. Bizzy's pretty bad.'

'She's talking about a retirement village up the coast,' says Sally. 'Says it sounds restful.'

'Bizzy Nancarrow can't retire!' cries Lily.

'Mum,' says Grace. All eyes in the room turn to her. Frey's land first. Grace's blue eyes look clearer than they have for a while. 'If you won't join the choir, can I?'

'What?' says Frey.

'And me!' shouts Lily.

'I mean,' Grace continues, looking at Kyrie, 'when I'm better – and I will be better – I would love to sing for you. Or dance for you, or whatever. Help bring Bizzy back. I've been reading about her and she's one of the most inspiring people, like, ever, Mum. She can't move to a retirement village.'

Frey watches the light dance in Grace's eyes and feels a softening of the heavy coldness in her stomach.

'Well, the thing is,' Kyrie says, 'we'd love to have you, Grace. And you, Lily. But we can only take minors if they have a guardian present at all times.' Her eyes on Frey are shifty.

'You just made that up,' Frey says.

'Yes,' says Kyrie, with barely traceable uncertainty. 'But I'm a lawyer and now that's . . . our law.'

'Yep,' says Mary. 'Adult themes, occasional coarse language, violence, drug references. Parental guidance mandatory.'

'I thought you were against helicopter parenting,' says Frey. 'And it's still no. I can't go there again. I tackled my own son to the ground. I could have really hurt him.'

'Yeah, that was fierce as fuck,' says Quin.

'I wasn't hurt, though.' Everyone turns to see Tom standing in the doorway of the kitchen. 'Hey,' he says, 'I'm one of the tosspot flogs from the toolbag.'

'Hi there,' says Quin.

Tom shifts uncomfortably. The boy in his seventeen years is outpacing the man. 'I'm really sorry about your building. I didn't know . . .' He pauses, swallows, looks awkwardly at Avni. 'That was pretty cool, that song you wrote. And your voice – wow.'

'Thanks,' says Avni.

'You could do, like, a pumped version of that with, like, some crunchy beats and maybe a rap bridge. Could be something different, for a choir. You know, surprising.'

Avni laughs. 'I like the sound of that.'

'Yeah, well if you like, I could help arrange stuff. Doesn't have to be all up tempo. Mum plays a mean string ballad.' Tom looks at Kyrie. 'It could be my sorry, you know.'

'That's the perfect sorry, Tom,' says Kyrie.

'He's good,' says Lily. 'He helped me record my song. It's called "Small Act of Rebellion".'

'Well, that's settled, then. You're all in,' says Mary. 'Frey, you'll have to just come along and sit up the back or something.'

'Freycinet,' says Freycinet.

'Nup,' says Mary. 'You're Frey until you stand onstage with us.'

Frey sighs, covers her eyes for a moment, then says, 'Only if I can be there with my violin, not my voice.'

'Your violin can be your voice,' says Kyrie. 'We don't all sing with our vocal cords.'

'I sing with my heart these days,' says Eleanor.

'And sometimes I sing with my'—Quin farts loudly—'arsehole. Sorry.'

'Quin!' says Kyrie.

Lily squeals with laughter.

'I said sorry! It's those stupid vitamins Sally makes me take, I swear.'

Frey looks at Grace's lit-up face, at Tom trying not to laugh, and finds herself laughing too.

'Ah,' says Mary, 'nothing like breaking wind to break the tension in the room.'

'And in my guts,' says Quin. The two of them guffaw together.

'Okay, enough!' says Kyrie. 'Come on, choir. See you tomorrow, Freycinet?'

Frey is still laughing. 'Tomorrow?' she asks.

'Tomorrow's Tuesday. We're meeting at the Moonah Arts Centre, usual time.' She places the stone disc on the kitchen table and adds, 'See you, Grace and Lily there.'

B

Stepping Stone Number 251 from *La Lista* by R.K.:
Don't cover schoolbooks, it's a huge waste of time, bad for the
environment, and feeds primary school and parental insecurities.
Plastic sticky wrap is evil.

Chapter 35

Save Our Baking

Bizzy has discovered afternoon napping. She has been vaguely aware of it as common practice, but always looked down her nose at the idea as something other people do, the ones closed off to the urgency of the present and the potential of daylight. But a little snooze in the sunny patch in her sitting room is a delight she has begun to relish. A gin and tonic at lunchtime enhances the experience, adding a certain drifty weightlessness to the moments before she slips into sleep.

The members of the choir have been doing their best to disrupt her newfound pleasure, popping in at various times with AWC reports.

'You should see what the filmmakers have done so far with their mini-doco,' declares Mary as Bizzy sits in her garden doing cross-stitch. 'They got a kick-arse film editor to put it together, an animator and a post-production sound engineer. It's nearly finished and I can't wait for you to see it. I even inspired the shit out of myself.'

Bizzy breathes deeply, closes her eyes and says, 'Wonderful,' in the long, drawn-out manner of someone emerging from a meditation.

'We've got our performance songs ready, including some new ideas you won't want to miss out on! We'd love your input on the new arrangements. Avni's great but she's so timid.'

Bizzy doesn't reply.

'We have permission to close Macquarie Street, like they do on Anzac Day.' Mary makes a cartoon trumpet noise and laughs.

Bizzy doesn't.

'The mural outside the girls' school is done. Want to come and see it, Bizzy? It's all of us, singing. Very stylised but I think I can tell who's who. Come on, I'll take you.'

'No, thank you,' says Bizzy. It's a phrase she has repeated many times in recent days, another new habit she is rather enjoying.

'And Freycinet—'

'Please,' Bizzy interrupts. 'Mary, I love you, but I need you to stop talking. I'm staying very firmly in my moments, thank you. A break from rushing headlong into the future.'

Mary pauses, then mutters, possibly to herself, 'There's no time like the future.'

Bizzy gives an aggrieved sigh, so Mary opts for a more innocuous conversation point.

'What are you stitching?' she asks.

Bizzy holds up her almost complete work. In perfectly stitched shades of pink it says 'Home Sweet Home'.

Mary gapes at it, then says, 'Are you on drugs?'

𝄐

Roger is in the yard outside his block of flats, leaning over an enormous, upturned baby pram when Frey pulls up.

'Nice wheels, Dad,' she calls from the car window. 'Anything you need to tell me?'

He glances up at her and says, 'Nope.'

Frey gets out of the car, hoists herself up onto the narrow top rail of the fence and walks the length of it before turning, loping back and then springing off, landing lightly at Roger's side.

Without looking up from his work he says, 'What, no salto backward double flip dismount from The Girl?'

'Not feeling it today. Whose pram?'

'It was out for big rubbish collection. Three punctured tyres are evidently too hard to fix.'

'That's criminal, it's in perfect condition.' Frey watches him work. 'I have a friend with triplets who might need another pram.'

'Quin.'

'You know Quin?'

'Yep.'

'How?'

'Gracie introduced me to her.' He starts to whistle a tune.

'Right. So you could give it to her.'

'Nah, I won't give it to her.' He whistles on.

'Right then,' says Frey. 'Okay.'

'I'll keep it here for when I look after Stevie, Freddie and George.'

Freycinet laughs.

'What's funny?' asks Roger.

'You're serious?'

'Yep. Quin has to go to uni. And she has some ruddy mad-women's rally to sing at next week.' He side-eyes Frey and chuckles. 'I'm here, I have time. Why not?' He takes up his tune again.

Frey wraps her arms around Roger and gives him a squeeze, breathes in the seaside, motor-oil smell of him and says, 'You're the best, Dad.'

'Enough of that, make yourself useful.' He hands her a shifter.

When the pram is back on all four new tyres and Roger is satisfied with its motion, Frey pulls Bizzy's stone pendant from her pocket and asks, 'Do you know what this is, Dad?'

Roger peers at the disc on Frey's palm, picks it up and inspects it closer. 'I'm about sure it's a Pedder penny,' he says, and Frey is struck by the awe in his voice.

'A Pedder penny, as in Lake Pedder?'

'Yep. People found them at the bottom of the lake before it was drowned. That should probably be in the museum.' He watches as Frey pulls her phone from her other pocket and starts flicking at the screen. 'You putting your tradecraft to better use these days, The Girl?'

'Yep,' she says. On the Angry Women's Choir Instagram page, she scrolls to the shot of Bizzy and Winifred Nancarrow at Lake Pedder in 1972. Two women, a vibrant sky, a mountain range. No others present.

'Thanks, Dad. Knew you'd know.'

He hands her back the penny and says, 'Right you are.'

On the drive from Roger's flat to the State Library, Frey realises that the tune he'd been whistling was the chorus of Avni's song 'Broken Teeth'.

𝄡

A day and a pile of microfiche cards later, Freycinet and Acorn drive out of Hobart and turn west along the Derwent River. They travel for almost an hour to where the river bronzes and narrows and falls in rapids over shallows. On a piece of highway that leaves the river, Frey turns right onto a dirt road marked by a letter box and an aged sign that only just says, *Herondale*. The road takes them down a gentle slope and through closely mown orchards of well-uniformed apricot trees, some of them carrying bright, soft fruit. After a right-hand bend, the road emerges from the trees to reveal the river again, and beside it a rambling house that looks like it could be built of sandstone, weatherboard and roses.

She pulls up at a circular lawn, at the centre of which is a small child holding a dribbling hose and covered from head to toe in mud.

'Hello,' says Frey when she gets out of the car.

The child, with eyes stark white and blue against the mud, studies Freycinet for a long moment, then says, 'Are you here to rescue me?'

Frey decides that the child is a little girl, about six, though it's hard to tell through the mud. She has shoulder-length hair, is wearing only underpants and her facial expression is obscured by mud. 'Do you need me to rescue you?' Frey asks.

'Yes please,' says the child.

'What from?'

'The baddie.'

Frey detects a wobble in the girl's voice and her heart quickens. 'Where's the baddie?'

'I don't know. He was chasing me but I rolled in the dirt and hid with the chooks. He might be chasing Granny now. She was in the kitchen doing her jam.'

'Okay, what's your name?' Frey takes her phone from her pocket and checks for coverage. Emergency calls only.

'Gloria. Can you help us, please?'

'Do you know this man, Gloria?'

Gloria nods gravely. A tear falls from one of her bright blue eyes and trails through the mud on her cheek.

'It's okay. You can stay with me now and let's see what we can do for Granny. Can you show me where the kitchen is?'

Gloria shakes her head fearfully.

'What's the baddie like?'

'Really really bad.'

'Is he big?'

Gloria nods.

'Bigger than me?'

'Yes. With a giant red scary face that sometimes does growls.' She pulls a face that reveals her small, white teeth. 'I don't want to go in there. He'll catch me. Please don't let him catch me.'

'Okay, we won't go in, but I'd like you to stay with me, and we can maybe look in the kitchen window to check on Granny?'

Gloria nods, puts her hose carefully on the ground and takes Frey's hand. They walk through a gate set into a high hawthorn hedge and into a pretty, brick-paved courtyard filled with raised beds of vegetables and herbs.

'There's the kitchen in there,' Gloria says, pointing at a wide, paned window that is slightly ajar.

'Stay close to me,' Freycinet whispers, and leads Gloria to the window.

Inside is precisely the sort of kitchen Frey had been expecting of this bucolic place, all blue china and antique timbers. On a huge stove stand four steaming pots, and on a long table are cooling racks filled with biscuits, but the room is empty of people. Quietly, Freycinet leads Gloria to a side door which is open but covered by a screen that looks sure to have shrieking hinges.

Freycinet kneels in front of Gloria and whispers, 'In a second I'm going to open the screen door, and go in, okay, Gloria? Can you hold the door open for me? And when I'm in, I want you to stand just inside the doorway and shout, "Granny!" and then quickly, quickly come back outside, let the door slam and stand right here.' She presses her hand against the exterior wall of the house, just beside the door. 'Right up against the wall, very still okay?'

Gloria nods, her eyes wide with fear.

'And if you need to, use my phone to call triple zero – zero, zero, zero, all right?'

Gloria takes the phone and nods again.

'Okay.' Freycinet takes off the low-heeled shoes she's wearing, keeps one in her hand, nods at Gloria and opens the door. As expected, the door sends out a long, almost tuneful squeak. Frey walks into the entrance hall, which is filled with the glorious smell of stewing apricots and freshly baked biscuits. Behind her, Gloria stands inside the doorway and shouts, 'Granny?' then ducks back outside and lets the door bang behind her.

Freycinet pads further into the house, stands beside a staircase and listens. Aside from the sound of bubbling coming from the kitchen stove, all is very, very quiet.

Frey moves from there to the kitchen, taking small steps. From somewhere else in the house, she hears the creak of a floorboard. She waits.

The next sound comes in a rush, thunderous footsteps from above, two sets of them at least. They pummel across the ceiling and down the stairs. A distressed woman's voice calls out, 'Gloria, he's coming! Gloria?'

Frey slips in behind the kitchen door, watches a small, grey-haired woman scuttle past, then leaps out to catch the woman's pursuer neatly around the waist in a swift rugby tackle that brings him hard up against the lath-and-plaster of the opposite wall. He grunts as Freycinet slips him into a head-lock and shouts, 'Gloria! I have him. Call the three zeros and ask for the police!'

'No!' This cry comes from the grey-haired woman. 'Who are you and why are you in my kitchen?'

Freycinet tries to order her thoughts, just as Gloria skids past them all, grabs a biscuit from the cooling rack and yells, 'Gloria gets the treasure!'

Freycinet watches in astonishment as Gloria chomps happily into the biscuit, wiggling her hips in a victory dance.

Frey turns to the grey-haired woman and says, 'So, you're not in trouble?'

'No,' says Granny. 'Not until it comes to that bundle of trouble there,' she points at Gloria. 'Please unhand my husband. He's harmless.'

Frey lets go of the wiry man in her grip. He grunts again and hurries shakily to lean himself against the kitchen table.

'I'm sorry,' Frey says. 'Gloria told me you were a . . . a baddie. An intruder. I thought—'

'Oh he is the baddie,' says Granny. 'In our game of Save Our Baking. He threatens to take the lot, Alice and I have to protect the biscuits.'

'Alice?' asks Frey.

'That's Alice.' Granny points to Gloria. 'Gloria's her game name. Save Our Baking has evolved a complex set of rules. We stay in character, you know. Sometimes Gloria opts for camouflage because if Grandpa catches her, she loses her protective powers.' Granny wipes the air with her hand. 'We're ridiculous. Always have been. Alice, love, dip yourself in the river and scrub off, you're not fit for the kitchen.' Granny tips her head at Freycinet. 'Oh my dear, you look so upset. Can I get you some tea?'

Grandpa clears his throat and says, 'And you might like a biscuit.'

₿

Twenty minutes later, Freycinet feels that she has found three new friends: Alice, Rhonda and Charlie Herondale. Alice is their youngest grandchild, staying over while her home-schooling parents take her siblings hiking on the Overland Track.

'We school her imagination,' says Rhonda with a chuckle.

'You should probably be on the stage,' says Freycinet to Alice. 'You were extremely convincing as poor hunted Gloria.'

Alice, having returned shining from the river, is revealed to have a cheeky, freckled face. She smiles up at Freycinet and says, 'You're quite brave, aren't you.'

'Yes,' agrees Charlie. 'The baddie was no match for you, Freycinet.'

'I'm sure I must have hurt you,' Frey says. 'I'm very sorry.'

'Not at all,' says Charlie. 'You'd be handy to have around in the event of an intruder.'

'He's a wiry old thing,' says Rhonda, 'tough as a bullock.'

'I'm the intruder,' Frey says. 'Turning up here, on your gorgeous farm.' She briefly entertains the idea of telling them that she'd like a job and some shelter, please, in this parallel riverside world. *There are so many worlds we never see*, she thinks, then clears her throat. 'I was hoping to talk to you, Charlie, about my friend, Bizzy Nancarrow.'

Charlie nods, as though he's been expecting the question. He smiles fondly.

Frey glances at Rhonda, wondering whether she should have conducted this conversation in private.

But Rhonda's face is alight. 'Bizzy Nancarrow!' she says. 'I was hoping she'd pop into our lives one day. Oh, Charlie, and now she has.' Rhonda looks at Freycinet with an earnest expression. 'Bizzy was Charlie's first love. And vice versa, I believe. They fell in love at Lake Pedder, just before it was swamped. He was a pilot, she was an activist, can you think of anything more fairy-tale?'

'And now she's a superhero,' says Alice. 'She makes things better for people. I want to be like Bizzy Nancarrow.'

'I've joined her chorus,' says Rhonda, 'though I sing like an old crow. Our local bowls club are getting the bus to the rally on Saturday.'

'Is she well?' asks Charlie.

'She's, um . . .' Freycinet says, 'she's a bit under the weather, actually.'

Freycinet explains the series of events that caused Bizzy to take refuge under a weighted blanket. Rhonda punctuates the speech with a series of dismayed sounds, tuts and sighs.

Afterwards, Charlie says, 'She was never as fervent as her mother, I didn't think. Has the sort of nature that could do with a bit of solitary. Some time to watch the birds.'

'That may be, Charlie, love,' says Rhonda, 'but she can't miss the rally, it's the pinnacle of her life's work, the whole world is watching. She can rest after the rally. The blooming birds aren't going anywhere.'

'The shorebirds are,' Alice points out. 'Because climate change.'

'I agree she should be at her rally,' says Charlie. 'But I can't help. I haven't seen her in about fifty years.'

'She might have dreamed about you all these years,' says Rhonda. 'Could be waiting for you to come back to her and tell her you took to your apricot farm and stepped out of her way for her career of activism.' Rhonda clasps her hands together. 'The fairy story doesn't have an ending, Charlie.' She smiles at Frey. 'We need an ending.'

'What, you want me to sweep her back into my arms?' asks Charlie.

'Don't be daft,' says Rhonda with a chuckle. 'I'd fight her to the death.'

'Well, I don't know how you think I can get her there on Saturday,' Charlie says.

'I do,' says Rhonda.

𝄡

Stepping Stone Number 7, from *La Lista* by R.K.:
Exercise your imaginations, every day, more than once a day. Unplug yourself from external stories and make up your own. Let your brain have its own adventures. Make them silly, make them wild. Tell them to your friends, tell them to yourself, tell them to the lost. You never know what magic they could make.

Chapter 36
Out in the Woo-Hoo

Tasmania brings its purest, most concentrated light to the twenty-ninth of February 2020, the day of the Angry Women's Choir rally. Bizzy wakes and blinks out into the dewy early hours, a dawn washed clean. Waiting. She wonders with a fizz of irritation what it's waiting for. *Stay in the moment*, she tells the day.

After breakfast, she decides, on her own terms and in her own time, that she will have a little potter in the garden. She takes the bit of Rosanna in the marble urn with her and kneels on the lawn to pull weeds from the choked-up rose bed. 'Roses,' she tells the urn, 'don't like competition.'

She imagines Rosanna's reply: 'The poor delicate princesses, can't share their bed with the commons.'

Bizzy leaves the urn on the lawn and waters the lemon tree.

There, her mother's voice pops into her head. *'Story horse?'*

This is an Irishwoman's way of saying, 'What are you doing?'

'I'm just having a piddle about,' says Bizzy. 'Out from the worries.'

Winifred's voice comes again. *'Look at the state of you.'*

'Well, it's better than you, Mammy.'

'Barely that.'

Bizzy looks over at the urn and rolls her eyes. 'Rosanna,' she says, 'meet Winifred. Winifred, Rosanna. No doubt you've already met and are getting along like houses on fire.'

'Who're you talking to?'

Bizzy jumps. Ferris's seven-year-old voice isn't loud but it's very near, though she can't see him. 'Feck and Joseph, Ferris, you'll give a girl a heart attack, you will. Where are you?' She peers at the fence.

'Up here.'

Bizzy looks upwards into the magnolia tree and sees a foot, then a face smiling down from the highest branches. 'What the? Get your arse down from there, you don't have wings. And you'll break your head if you fall!' She puts a hand to her clamouring heart and is amazed at the breadth of her concern for this little boy.

'I won't fall, Bizzy,' calls Ferris. 'I've been up here heaps.'

'You what? Wait, this here is my tree, and I say no to climbing up it.' She swallows, adopts a gentler tone. 'Come here to me, Ferris. Now.'

'It's really cool up here. I saw the postman's bald patch the other day.'

'Could you just come down a little bit? You're making me feel bilious.'

'I'll come down a little bit if you come up a little bit. We can meet in the middle.'

'What? No, absolutely not. I'm an old woman, don't be an idiot. I mean it, Ferris.'

'I'm staying up here, then, if you don't come up. I mean it, Bizzy.'

Bizzy stares up at him, wonders whether to call his mother. He grins down at her. 'Instead of piddling about under trees, you should sit in one.'

'Good grief,' she mutters.

'It's really easy,' Ferris calls. 'There's a bit you can put your foot on. Look around the other side.'

Bizzy circles the tree and sees that at about her hip height there is indeed a stout branch, with a slightly flattened part in the middle, as though Ferris's foot, or the feet of children before, have made a step of it.

'Hurry up!'

And somewhere in the distant carries of the golden afternoon, Bizzy thinks she hears Winifred laugh.

'Oh, for crying out loud.' Bizzy holds her breath, lifts a foot onto the flat part of the branch and hoists herself up into the tree. 'There,' she says with a grunt as she shuffles onto the lowest branch and wraps an arm firmly around the tree's trunk.

'I'll come down one branch,' calls Ferris. 'And you come up one.'

'I'm not coming up any more. I'm in the blinking tree, that was the arrangement.'

There is silence from above. Bizzy dares not look up in case she loses her balance.

'I'll come down three if you come up one.'

Bizzy peeks upwards and sees that the branch above her is fatter than the one she is on, and that it cradles a newly opened magnolia flower. 'Ferris, you bugger,' she mutters, manoeuvring herself into a position from which she can clamber onto the next branch. She swings her body up, then lies facedown across the cool wood.

There is a rustling from above which is Ferris being nimble and seven. In under twenty seconds he says, 'You don't look very brave, Bizzy.'

'I'm not,' Bizzy says to the cool wood under her cheek.

'I thought Bizzy Nancarrow was very brave.' Ferris seems to be saying this to the tree.

'What made you think that?' calls Bizzy.

'Mum says you are very brave. Also, you have brave hair.'

'I think I make my hair look brave because I'm not,' she says, mostly to herself.

There is some silence into which the tree offers up some agreeable leafy sounds.

Ferris moves down another branch. His voice is close now. 'Sit up so you can properly feel being in a tree. It doesn't feel like being on the ground.'

Bizzy catches a waft of magnolia scent, and decides to be as brave as her hair. She pushes herself slowly into a sitting position.

'See, Bizzy, see!' Ferris bounces on his branch in excitement. 'You're being in a treee, with meee!'

Bizzy tenses and grabs at leaves. 'Hey there,' she says. 'Wind your neck in, you're wobbling us.' But her branch holds steady.

'Okay. Let's sit quietly.' Ferris sits quietly.

Bizzy puts her face in the flower for comfort. The scent transports her to something long ago, something with Winifred in it, with adventure and surety. She touches the petals, their texture like the finest kid leather.

Ferris continues his sitting quietly, then reaches down and pats the very top of Bizzy's head. The tiny fluttering touch makes her want to cry. 'I've never been good with a height,' she says quietly.

'We're not up a very big height,' Ferris says.

'High enough.'

They are quiet for a bit longer before Bizzy says, 'Being in a tree is nice.'

'I told you.'

'Even without wings.'

They sit quietly together. Eventually, Ferris says, 'You'll have to get down soon, though, Bizzy. For your Angry Women's rally day.'

'Ah, I'm not going, Ferris. They don't need me there. All the "sisters in alms" are taking care of it.'

'My mum's going,' says Ferris. 'She told Dad that he needs to stay home and be a father today, and that he needs to wash the bedsheets and do painting with me and make the dinner. I had to show him how to work the washing machine.'

'Good on your mum.'

'Dad is nicer because of you, Bizzy.'

Bizzy feels a sting in her eyes. 'Ah, get off the stage,' she says.

They listen to the drone of a distant aircraft.

'Who were you talking to before?' Ferris asks.

'My mam.'

'Is she a ghost? I want to see a ghost.'

'I suppose she is, sort of. But I've never seen her. I just feel that she's near sometimes.'

'Like your friend in the ashes.' He glances down at the urn on the grass below.

'Yes, like my friend in the ashes.'

'They're out in the woo-hoo.'

'Yes,' says Bizzy. 'The woo-hoo.'

'Doesn't your friend in the ashes want to go to the rally?'

There is silence while Bizzy remembers with a pang what Kyrie had said when she gave her the urn: *These are for the choir.*

The drone grows louder.

Ferris leans out from his branch, craning to see the sky.

Bizzy gasps. 'Mind yourself, Ferris.'

But Ferris leans out further, points a grubby finger upwards and says, 'Bizzy Nancarrow, look at that! Sky-writing!'

Bizzy peers cautiously up through the magnolia leaves to see that a loop-de-loop of bright white vapour has formed letters against the electric blue sky.

'A-W-C,' Ferris spells out. 'The Angry Women's Choir! The whole world will be able to see that, Bizzy!'

Bizzy closes her eyes, feels dizzy and opens them again. She reaches for the Pedder penny around her neck and then remembers that it's not there. She feels dizzy again, so she clutches at the tree and leans back just a little to watch a tiny dot of a plane return to make the shape of an alto clef.

Bizzy isn't sure how much time passes as they sit there, she and
the little boy, in the magnolia tree, but she spends some of it on a
faraway pink beach, watched by a meeting of mountains, in the arms
of a man with tannin eyes.

'What's Pedder?' asks Ferris, jolting Bizzy from her daydream.

She is so startled she has to hug the tree again to save her from
falling out. *Did I speak aloud?* she thinks. *Or is this boy some sort of
seer?* She dares a glance up at him. He is looking out of the tree, to
another part of the sky, where the words *RESTORE PEDDER* drift
above the cityscape.

'Winifred and Rosanna,' she says, 'you cheeky old cows. You have
a hand in this I'll warrant, out there in the woo-hoo.'

$$\text{B}$$

By noon, around fifteen thousand sisters in alms have taken their
Saturday to the Hobart streets and filled them with care and colour
(mostly green and purple), music and voices, courage and hope.
Everyone from women's auxiliaries and school bodies, mothers'
groups, church groups, corporates, a huge cohort of LGBTQI+
activists, children's sporting clubs, First Nations communities, carers'
unions, extended families and individuals are there to watch the
premiere public performance of the Angry Women's Choir and to
join the chorus.

Several pockets of anti-AWC protesters shout a variety of threats,
obscenities or oppressive views from the far right, but they are
drowned out by the lending of voices to the cause. Every media outlet
in Tasmania, and some from mainland Australia, are present too.

'Wouldn't Governor Macquarie and his fellow patriarchs
fair shit in their coffins to see this,' says Mary, looking out from
the Town Hall steps over the sea of people that has inundated
Macquarie Street.

'Never mind those doinks,' says Quin. '*I'm* shitting myself. Haven't been this scared since I got stuck on the roof at TCA Oval during the AC/DC concert.'

'You think you're scared,' says Kyrie. 'Look at Avni – she looks like she might actually die of fright.'

They look. Avni's face is grey with fear. She is wringing her hands and saying, 'I'll be okay, I'll be okay, it'll be okay, don't panic,' until it threatens to panic everyone. Except Irene, who says, 'Happy birthday, Kyrie, love.'

'Irene,' says Kyrie patiently, 'it's not my birthday.'

'What's all this then?' Irene asks.

'AWC rally day.'

'Ah,' says Irene. 'Of course it is. Where's Bizzy?'

'Oh Lord, I wish she was here,' says Avni.

'Damn you, Bizzy,' whispers Kyrie. She turns to Freycinet. 'We know our songs inside out and I'm confident it will be fine. But, to be honest, I feel like we're missing something. Not just Bizzy or Rosanna, but that bit of extra that these original songs deserve.'

'It's a bit late to be worried about that, Kyrie,' Freycinet says. 'We'll just have to make do with fine.'

'You all right, Sal?' asks Mary.

Sally is unusually quiet. 'Hmm,' she says. 'Yes. Just unsettled, you know. There's a bit of talk about this coronavirus thing, that's all. It'll be okay, don't mind me. Just wash your hands thoroughly when you get home.'

'Just nerves tuning into our anxieties,' says Mary. 'I've got a nasty Icarus feeling, and the sun is so low in the sky.'

'Lucky Sally's a burns specialist,' says Eleanor.

Freycinet, standing beside Sally with her violin, also feels wholly unsettled. Lily is so utterly full of self-importance there's a chance she might topple with it. Tom, having been given the responsibility of operating the sound desk and audio engineering, is a bit too puffed

up and full of Tom for Frey's liking. And Grace has been overconfi-
dent with breakfast, had toast with her bravado, and now appears on
the brink of an anxiety attack.

What are we doing? Frey thinks. *Out here with these lunatics.* She
looks at the choir, restless and anxious, some in AWC T-shirts and
some not, because no one has remembered to set a dress code. And
the crowd, as Frey scans across its vastness, is seething with impracti-
cal optimism and embarrassing eccentricity.

'Freycinet!' someone calls from the crowd. Freycinet looks down
and spots Petra, standing a little way back from the steps, smiling up
at her. Beside her, Petra's son, Liam, waves at Lily and a little further
along, Teagan holds up a placard that says 'Derwent Dance Academy
#jointhechorus'. Beside her stands a woman with dark sunglasses
and shiny bobbed hair. Valentina Bellavance. Her arm is linked with
her daughter's.

Freycinet smiles at them. She looks back out across the crowd
and sees expression and freedom. Happiness. No mindless crazies or
fruitless hope. *Look out from the shadows, Freycinet*, she tells herself.
It's amazing what worlds you'll see.

'Girls,' Freycinet says, 'the whole dance academy is here. There's
Esperance, look.' She turns to Grace, who is now seated on the top
step, out of sight from the crowd.

'Great,' Grace says, gulping down deep breaths. 'I think I'll go
stand with them.'

'No, darling, you're singing with us.'

'I can't. Mum, I feel like shit.'

'You're not fat,' says Lily.

'I know that! Shut up, Lily,' Grace shouts.

'You're not fat, Grace,' Lily says again.

'Lily,' warns Freycinet.

'You're not fat,' says Lily again, brushing off Freycinet's reaching
hand. 'You're NOT FAT.'

'Well, I feel it, okay?' shouts Grace. 'I feel it. And I can't do this today.'

'But it's your song,' says Freycinet. She watches Grace hurry unsteadily down the stairs and crouch beside a stone column at the bottom of the steps. A pinch of pain sends Freycinet's gaze to the sky. Up there, the contrailed sky-words billow and slant with the breeze: *AWC*.

Freycinet watches the alto clef as it moves, thinks of Charlie and Rhonda and Alice, with their kind hearts. She thinks of Bizzy and her weary heart, Rosanna and her stopped heart. She puts a hand over her own broken one.

Don't feel sad, she tells herself. *Don't feel regret or guilt or shame. Just feel the anger.* She pictures the coloured stones on the table at Rosanna's house, concentrates on one stone, imagines it red, makes it grow and names it fury. *I can't sing*, she thinks, *but I can show*. She looks down at Grace, whose body is still tiny enough to make her beautiful face and the strain in her eyes seem huge.

The violin in Frey's hands, by contrast, seems sure of itself, shiny with belonging. Freycinet hopes she can make it sing a note that might sound at least a little like Rosanna. She looks over at the choir. 'Quin,' she says. 'Quin?'

Quin looks over at her. Frey beckons, leans in and says, 'I've had an idea.'

𝄡

At the foot of the steps, Grace speaks to the trembles in her hands and the wobble in her knees. The tangible things. Plants can eat flies and souls can have colour and night-time has a scent. I can dance with silence and music can be seen. She looks at the sky. People can fly and write courage with clouds. She turns to the cold, persistent voice on her shoulder, hardens her resolve and says, *You are not real and I am not fat. I cannot feel breakfast under my skin. You and Harry Fenton and all the other fuckwit douchecanoes who mistreat vulnerable people need to be shown that they can't win.*

'Grace? Are you okay?'

Grace turns to see Serra Kalbfel leaning down towards her, then sitting next to her on the ground. She puts a hand on Grace's knee, as though it's not repulsive and ghastly and part of a nasty skeleton. Grace looks at it, the hand, and says, 'I'm going to be. But I just want to watch and listen from here.'

'Mind if I watch from here too?'

'That'd be good.'

Lily suddenly plonks herself between Grace and the stone column and says, 'Mum said I have to sit here with you.'

'Lily, no,' says Grace. 'This is your dream come true, singing with the choir, get back up there.'

Lily, her expression still grumpy, shrugs and says, 'Well, my bigger dream is to perform with you, so . . .' She rests her head on Grace's shoulder and says, 'I'm an AWC member now, I can sing with them anytime, but you – you'll be away on Broadway soon.'

Grace gives her a shove, but is pleased when she leans back into her. Her little body is soft and warm. Grace returns the lean, smiles at Serra and thinks, *We have to stay for all the things they never told us.*

Together they watch Sally speak her Welcome to Country to a listening crowd, while First Nations women, Sally's Aunties, move through metal pails they feed with green eucalyptus leaves. Scented smoke streams into the air.

Grace breathes the smell of Australia and feels grateful for the welcome. She looks over at Serra and sees that she is clasping a small marble urn to her chest as she listens to Sally's words. 'Always was, always will be,' Grace sees Serra chant with Sally and the rest of the crowd as Sally leaves the stage.

Mary is at the microphone next. 'And here is another truth,' she says after the applause has receded and she has left a long, dignified silence. 'All women and those who identify as female come from a place of oppression. And I'm hoping that's why you're here. To claim back your right to be more than a body, more than a person who does kind, helpful stuff for nothing and looks pretty all the time. To show up, to speak up, to wake up. And if you're a bloke, or you identify as a bloke, maybe you're here in solidarity, or to learn a thing or two. To all of you, thank you for being here and thank you for raising your voice and joining the chorus, we hope you enjoy these songs from the Angry Women's Choir!'

The roar from the crowd is so deafening it takes the tremble from Grace's hands and drowns out the voice on her shoulder. Amid the thunderous whoops, she gets a bit of peace.

Kyrie takes centre stage, gives a smile to the crowd before turning her back on them. She sends a nod to Tom in the sound tent, then raises her hands.

𝄢

Stepping Stone Number 30, from *La Lista* by R.K.:
Look at the trees more than you look at screens. You'll find so much more in the trees. The souls of the lost might be there. See those branches waving at you? Look at that bird over there too. Listen to it sing. This kind of listening lets your soul breathe. It's *abbiocco* for the mind. (There is no English translation for *abbiocco*, it means eating-induced tiredness.)

Stepping Stone Number 27, from *La Lista* by R.K.:
Listen to the stories of First Nations peoples. Listen hard. Those stories hold the key to survival.

Chapter 37

Kintsugi

Bizzy Nancarrow has taken Rosanna's ashes with considerable urgency towards the city. On her short walk from home she forces herself to admit that she is also following the sky-writing. *What are you doing, you complete ninny?* she asks herself. *Running into your lover's long-lost arms? Looking for excuses from a first love who never turned up to give back my heart?*

'He's not even there, you eejit,' she says. 'He's in the sky. If it's even him.'

She almost turns back but is stopped in her tracks at the top of Davey Street. A great mass of people, many of them wearing AWC T-shirts and carrying signs, have swamped the wide road and are already chanting, 'Join the chorus, join the chorus.'

One of the placards reads, '"What we cannot imagine cannot come into being" – bell hooks', while another shouts, 'TAKE THAT, MOTHERFUCKERS'.

Bizzy jostles through in a daze of shocked awe. At the mural outside the girls' school, she touches her painted image – a statuesque woman with bright orange hair standing on a Lux soap box, music notes marching out from her hands.

'That's my girl,' she hears her mother say, so close to her ear that she jumps. Winifred's voice comes again. 'Let's not dilly-dally.'

She follows Winnie through the thickening crowd onto Macquarie Street and slips into a spot in the middle of the street, directly in front of the Town Hall. It is here that she decides she has come because everyone else has. This thing that she dreamed up and kicked off, everyone has run with it and joined in.

'This is your business,' Winnie says to her left.

And on her other side, Rosanna says, 'You have to be here to mind it.'

Bizzy peeks out at the stage from behind a cluster of women and watches as the choir gathers and bustles into position. Her director's eye takes over. *They're not centred*, she thinks. *They are unfocused and nervy. Irene looks properly out of it.* Part of her wants to run to them, take up the baton, be their guide. Another part of her wants to see what they can do without her.

Come on now, she thinks. *Do me proud.*

She looks up for the letters in the sky, but they have shifted into shapeless fleeces of white on blue. Watching over the city is kunanyi, Mount Wellington. The mountain, come to the meeting. Bizzy smiles at it, slips a hand into her shoulder bag and squeezes the small marble urn within. *Winnie and Rosanna press in close.*

Bizzy recognises the stillness of the choir just before they sing. Kyrie, her silver hair shining in the sunlight, is perfectly poised. Bizzy holds her breath. *Start the show with a bang*, she thinks.

And they do. Bizzy jumps when a drum burst hits the speakers. Flam, kick-drum, high-hat, kick-drum, snare. Then before she knows it, Freycinet launches in with her fiddle and the choir are *boop-boop*ing a harmonised intro to a song she doesn't recognise. Or does she? Only when Avni takes the first verse does the song register. 'The Liniment Girl'. Bizzy laughs, covers her mouth, and rolls her eyes. 'You smart-arse windbags,' she says.

'She'll raise you from the steps,
And rub the liniment
Into your weary knees.
She'll take your chalky hands,
And strike up the band
Put whiskey in your tea.'

Avni is nervous, Bizzy can tell, but the choir echoes her words and overlaps in cheeky waves, in an arrangement that is anything but serious.

You're the Angry Women's Choir, thinks Bizzy. *Where's your fecking anger?*

As if by way of response, the pre-chorus turns darker, the harmonies lower.

'Can you feel, can you feel the fire burn?
Can you see, can you see the overturn
Of the tables you laid with such careful concern?'

And the chorus pares right back to Eleanor, who turns to face the crowd and gives them her muscular contralto.

'Oh, the liniment girl.
Oh, she'll ruin your world.
She'll turn things upside down
She'll turn kings into clowns
And she'll give, she will give you the sun.
All the stars and their sky and the sun.
And she will teach us to sing
and it won't take much
It will take – everything.'

Bizzy doesn't notice tears on her cheeks until the choir reaches the bridge and Quin takes the tail end of it and flips it into a furious rap.

'You're so once-bitten that you're tripping on the slightest pejorative,
Calling seven shots of tequila restorative,
The Herald Sun *informative.*

You like to take your newsreel light, with extra short-sight
Where the cat makes it home and the neighbours had a fight.
Don't be a princess in a tower
A fading flower
While the pop-star devours all the soul.
Keep your broken heart where it can see,
Because it's shot through with gold, it's motherfucking kintsugi.'

Bizzy cries out with amazed glee, then listens as Avni repeats the chorus twice more. The final note is delivered by Kyrie. No drums, no harmony, just a single, perfect note one octave up. It makes Bizzy glance upwards to check for a G-sharp written on the sky. There isn't one, of course, and the cursive cloud writing has drifted into nothing on the breeze. Winnie and Rosanna cheer wildly, clasp Bizzy's hands and squeeze them as the choir begins a rendition of Sam Cooke's rousing 'A Change is Gonna Come'.

'Everyone's here,' Bizzy says, squeezing them back. 'Everyone. Even the long-lost, the vanished, the missed and the dead.'

$$\text{I\kern-0.2emB}$$

But Harry Fenton is not there. He's on the couch watching cricket with his father and having the rules aggressively explained to him for the fifty-eighth time. By two o'clock, neither of them can understand why they haven't been brought their lunch, until they find a note on the fridge that says, *'Get your own, you arsewipes, I'm off to join the ANGRY WOMEN's chorus. If you're really hungry, you could #eatmydust.'*

$$\text{I\kern-0.2emB}$$

Paul Bellavance is not there. He is drunk, sitting on an uncomfortable designer couch in an overpriced apartment, eating takeaway and swearing at the television. Occasionally he gets up and does his swearing at the laundry, because he can't work the washing machine and he has run out of undies.

𝄢

Gil Barnes is not there either. He's on his bike, working up a sweat on his way up Cascade Road in Fern Tree. He is just passing a modest house in the corner of a sloping, rocky yard when a sign on the fence catches his eye and upsets his balance. He jerks to a halt, holds himself upright against the fence and stares at the sign. Freycinet, with her eyes cast upwards, a half-peeled apple in her hand, stands in an orderly kitchen with the disarray of her everything explicit in her face.

'Holy shit,' Gil says, because the painting is a battle cry he can hear. Two voices – subject and artist – shout at him from their painting, an alliance of fury and pain. It is deafening. The pierce of it would crease his face if his muscles weren't paralysed.

He rests his forehead on his arm. As he does so, a beautiful palomino horse gallops towards him from the paddock nearby. It shrieks out a sudden neigh. Gil jumps in alarm, wobbles and topples onto the verge, his shoulder clashing painfully with a piece of embedded rock.

𝄢

The choir's third song is a ferocious rendition of Cyndi Lauper's 'Girls Just Wanna Have Fun', which turns the rally into a four-minute, all-encompassing dance party. After that, the choristers retreat indoors for a short break while Mary remains at the microphone to thank the many sponsors, contributors and supporters for the day.

It is at this point that Freycinet's heart begins to pound in her chest. There's no talking it down. She is aware that when the choir returns to the steps, she will be cementing herself in history as a widely documented member of the Angry Women's Choir. No denials, no hiding it away. *Are you watching, Bizzy?* she wonders. *Are you watching, Rosanna? And Grace, please, please be watching.*

As the choir returns to their places, Frey is relieved to see that Grace is still there, at the foot of the steps, Lily at her side. But she can't dwell on that for long at all because a sudden, unsettling hush has descended on the crowd. This lingers, the hush, for several excruciating minutes before someone calls out a wolf whistle, triggering a sweeping cheer and the delighted shout, 'They're in the frigging nude!'

It's true. They are in the frigging nude. Apart from purple-and-green armbands, they wear nothing else, not a stitch.

'This special once-in-a-lifetime performance,' says Freycinet, trying to speak over her heartbeat whilst not clenching her bottom cheeks, 'is dedicated to our beloved friends and sisters, from Hobart to Honduras, Launceston to L'Aquila, Devonport to Devon, Freycinet to Finland and all the places in between. Our costumes are designed especially for those who are yet to find the opportunity, the resources, the good health, the courage, the clear sight or the freedom to see how truly wondrous and beautiful and deserving they are.'

The stunned crowd begins to clap. More whistles and cheers rise up as the applause crescendos.

'Fucken hell,' says Quin to Mary out one side of her smile. 'We've really lost the fucken plot now.'

'This better be worth it,' says Sally.

'The crowd are on board,' says Mary, taking Quin's hand. 'Look at them.'

Quin looks out at the heaving, smiling crowd and says, 'Yeah, it's like the fabric of society's had a good wash and a cup of fucken Cuddly.'

Kyrie clasps the hand of Eleanor, who is rigid with goodness knows what unfamiliar emotion.

Sally takes Irene's hand, leans in and says, 'How's your heart?'

'Well,' says Irene, 'if this doesn't get a rise out of it then I might as well be dead.'

Freycinet puts her hands up to call for silence. 'I must also add that we are performing an original song with kind permission from the songwriter, Grace Barnes. With thanks and sisterhood to her, with our best wishes, our imperfect selves and our love. And just to quickly introduce you to the members of the choir, my dear friends . . .'

Serra is clapping her hands and laughing. She gasps and turns to Grace. 'Oh my God, look at them! Oh my God. And they're going to sing your song.'

'Grace!' shouts Lily. 'They're going to sing your song in the rudie nudie.'

Grace spends a solid ten seconds studying the scene on the stage before she says, 'Okay.'

'Grace!' shouts Lily again. 'They're in the buck naked. This is GOAT!'

'Yeah!' yells Serra. 'It's like performance art.' She frowns. 'What's GOAT?'

'Greatest of all time,' says Grace, looking up at her mother as she lifts her violin to her chin and sends Grace a wink. 'This is the greatest of all time.'

𝄢

Bizzy, standing warm between the exhilaration of Winnie and Rosanna, looks at the mismatched bodies at the top of the Town Hall steps with a sense of triumph mixed with pride. There is also a dull ache, which she identifies as envy, but this, she also recognises, is an automatic response. Missing out hurts when you've never been on the sidelines of anything.

'Look what they can do without us,' she whispers to Winnie and Rosanna amid the swell of music and cheer, and the thought contains no regret.

The haunting song rises and falls through the streets of Hobart, onto television screens and live feeds throughout the country and into the ears of four generations. When it's over, the final harmony leads straight into a thunderous roar from the crowd.

Bizzy closes her eyes and imagines that the clamorous sound is holding her up. She straightens into her singer's posture, raises her left arm, points to the sky and says, *Thank you, Charlie Herondale, for bringing me along, but off you fuck now. I'm ready for some alone time.*

'Self-care is warfare,' Rosanna reminds her.

On the stage, the choristers are smiling, glowing, resplendent with naked skin, their arms raised in the Angry Women's Choir salute. Palpable in the air that swirls around their pointed fingers, is the adrenaline of sisterhood, music and rage.

Bizzy looks at Freycinet, her arm raised higher than anyone else's, her beautiful face alight. *Perhaps*, Bizzy thinks to herself, *it's not always a terrible thing to ruin someone's life.* But her thoughts snap away from Freycinet in a rush because in the soprano section, at the end of the choir's front row, Irene sways, smiles up beyond the crowd and into the sky, then falls like a sack of taters into Sally's arms.

Bizzy is running for the stage before she has time to think.

𝄡

Freycinet sees Bizzy's frantic face coming at them from the crowd before she notices the choir clustering around the fallen Irene. She stands unmoving for a few seconds, part of her marvelling at the sight of the women, skin to skin, gathering themselves against disaster, blocking the sight of Irene's dire moments from public view. She knows they are dire, the moments. After the very recent experience with Grace, the look of a stopped heart is fresh in her mind. She moves closer, joins the cluster, puts her hands on Irene along with all the others.

Bizzy closes in, falls to her knees at Irene's side. 'Oh, my dearest,' she says. 'Your poor, sweet heart.'

They watch Irene's blanking face, her moving mouth.

'Don't try to speak, Irene,' Sally calls above the now chanting crowd. 'We've got you.'

But Irene does speak, the words clear on her lips and just audible on the air. 'I'm coming, Harvey,' she says. 'I'll be there in a blink.' Then she puts a surprisingly firm grip onto Sally's hand and says, 'Don't spoil it, just listen! Oh, it's the lovely sound of the end.'

At the foot of the steps and for miles into the streets, the seething river of faces puts its call on the wind: 'Join the chorus! Join the chorus! Join the chorus!' The mountain leans in to listen and the people begin to dance.

$$\mathbb{B}$$

Stepping Stone Number 276, from *La Lista* by R.K.:
Fabric softener, when mixed with water and put into a spray canister, can be used to tame knotty, coarse or wild hair. Just spray liberally, comb then wash as usual with shampoo and conditioner. (NB Wild hair is the best hair.)

Chapter 38
Awake Now

'Grace's Song'

I was not listening
You have been singing out,
Little voice ringing out.
All of your whispering
Long after midnight
Was lost in the half light.

I've been living lies and breathing smoke
I gave all your time and love to ghosts
But I, I am awake now
And I will not be told
Who, what, where, with and how
You and I should be
We were blind, now I see.

I was not watching.
I was not seeing you,

Never believing you.
I have been blocking
Your perfect arabesque
Look away, pass the test.

I've been feeding you with myths and lies
Now you're shrunken down to half your size.
But I, I am awake now
And I will not be told
Who, what, where, with and how
You and I should be
We were blind, now I
See your silence, your fading breath
Please don't take us away, don't slow your step
We have to stay for all the things they never told us
And they have to pay for all the fables they sold us
So stay,
Bring it home.

𝄢

29 February 2020

Dear Freycinet,

I read somewhere that if you write a letter on a leap year's extra day, it will be received with an open heart.

I need to apologise. I remind women often not to be too ready with apologies, but ah well, I have one, and here it is: Indeed I did take you and your circumstances and use them to fuel my guttering fire. For that I am sorry. I was terrified of the fall into doing nothing; it was like a deadly precipice before me. A forbidden place. My mother, who rarely did nothing, died doing just that. Far too soon. Perhaps I was worried that if I paused too long, I might expire too. But by natural inclination as it turns out, I like a bit of a sit-about. I don't like giddy heights. I favoured stitching over marching. I just didn't listen to my shadow self all that much. This is not an excuse for my parasitic behaviour, but I am hoping it might help you to understand.

Also, I would like to thank you for using your espionage powers to find Charlie. He was always a treasure I carried with me, until he started to feel a little bit like regret. For a moment on rally day I thought perhaps he might be coming back to claim me. When Kyrie told me that he is happily married and spawning generations of good people, I was completely relieved. Where would I put a man in my life when I'm just discovering self-care and solitude? I always thought mindfulness was for eejits but oh how wonderful is sitting watching the white light inside you? Mine flickers sometimes, but by crikey it's there.

I don't think you needed true espionage to find him, did you? I could have tracked him down myself years ago. He was always going to be settled and reliably home. Turns out I never needed that sort of love.

Also, congratulations on the rally. You were all wonderful but it was an especial thrill to see you at the centre of it all. The sleeper agent is awake, I see.

Irene would be thrilled with her final exit. In her birthday suit and all. Rosanna and Winnie will be hearing all about it.

And anyway, so I lied about the leap year thing, but I still hope you will receive this in the spirit with which it is sent. With love.

From Byzantine Nancarrow.

𝄢

Stepping Stone Number 42, from *La Lista* by R.K.:
Write letters. Actual pen-and-paper, put-in-the-post letters. Then you might receive one back and what a delight receiving a hand-written letter is.

Chapter 39

Jazz Roots

Friday, 22 May 2020, 4.30 p.m.

I can't believe it. It's just incredible to think that a small choir
from little old Tasmania has made such an impact! All the other
people who jumped on the Angry Women train with their 'take
that, motherfucker' messages and their 'awake now' hashtags
and their reasons to join the chorus. People are saying that
the Angry Women's Choir has made enormous steps forward
in the women's movement simply by singing out and waking
everybody up a bit more. Heaps of other #jointhechorus rallies
were held on the same day all over the world, which is amazing.
None of them have had the impact of ours here in Tasmania.
What with the nudity and Irene dying and all.

There's been a bit of backlash about the nudity, from people
who can't handle it and say it's 'disgraceful' and 'indecent'.
But the choir's been brilliant about it. Kyrie made a statement
saying that, 'Body negativity is indecent. So is blaming women's
clothing (or lack thereof) for men losing control.' The Prime
Minister made a statement saying that we are 'an extraordinary
choir, displaying indiscriminate kindness, courage and creativity,

providing a platform and a voice to women everywhere who might otherwise be silenced or ignored'.

Nice.

On the down side, OF COURSE a stupid pandemic silences the women, just as their voices are breaking through. What comes after pestilence? A plague of locusts? Flood?

The coronavirus has shut down EVERYTHING. Choirs are apparently really risky because of all the singing and droplet spray and so on. So we haven't even been able to get together. We all meet online, though, and we still sing. So that's something. But it's just not the same. Nothing's the same, really.

The West Moonah Women's Choir has more than doubled in size. We have twelve new members, including an ARIA-Award-winning singer from Hobart, a beat-boxing grandmother from Hamilton, a drummer from Risdon and a rapper who makes the weekly trip from Burnie. And there's me, Lily, Serra and Ilaria. And Mum. Mum's still right into the choir. She plays her violin mostly. She says it helps her be civil to Dad.

He's moved into a house a few streets away. He's doing his best to stay alert, too. Lily's especially good at calling out what she's labelled 'knob-shiner behaviour'. It drives Dad and Tom crazy but it's fun to watch. Tom's okay. He's been mixing up stuff for the choir to sing. I think he has a massive unrequited crush on Avni, which is doing him good. He did an Irene Hawke memorial mix and a Rosanna Kalbfel dedication, which was pretty cool.

Bizzy hasn't come back to direct the choir. She says she won't. She hasn't even joined the Zoom choir. Mum said she's okay, though. She's having some time off. Everyone's trying to work out how to entice her back. Tom and I have an idea that we're working on. Lockdown at least makes you think outside the box.

It's nice to write in this diary again. I haven't for a while, mainly because I have a therapy journal as part of my treatment. I have to document all my irrational thoughts, and then rationalise them, give myself a slap in the face and get on with being normal. I had SO MANY irrational thoughts that I was writing flat out. And sometimes it all got too hard and I'd pretend the irrational was rational because honestly, surrendering to this disease was so much easier than fighting it, and the relief felt a bit like happiness.

I'm not having so many irrational thoughts now. I'm way more alert to them and often I can stop them before they even come. A lot like women waking up to all the shit treatment they used to accept as normal. I've put on enough weight to be allowed to dance again. I'm doing a bit, seeing whether my body trusts me. Sometimes it does but singing is less scary for now. Singing feels like healing.

Seriously, scientists should be working out how to use women's anger to generate power. Mum said that Bizzy worried about it burning down the world, but it just lights the world up. Tasmania, the island run on hydropower, brings a new infinite resource to the energy game. Ha.

𝄡

By the end of 2020, Bizzy Nancarrow's hair – after being all the colours of the rainbow over forty years – has returned to its natural colour: pale brown, shot through with grey. She is still in her small, eccentric house, still surrounded by whimsy and colour and life. But the house is not anxious anymore, not wondering which version of Bizzy will arrive home and how best to receive her. There is always music playing lightly, with Bizzy singing along. The magnolia tree has been fertilised to strengthen its bones, and the books on the bookcase are being read.

Bizzy has decided that only for particularly consequential causes and wholehearted concerns will she revisit her activist heritage.

Today, she is having one of those moments, out on Hobart's River Derwent in a borrowed kayak, one of a small flotilla paddling purposefully towards the Tasman Bridge. Bizzy lets herself fall behind the others, pausing to take in the light composure of floating, the shine of the water beneath dramatic clouds and streaks of sun.

'Um, hi, Bizzy?'

Bizzy turns to see a single kayak approaching, occupied by a young woman in a cap. Her first thought is, *What a beauty.* Her second is, *That's Grace Barnes.*

'Grace!' says Bizzy. 'My dear, it's lovely to see you. Really lovely. There's a healthy young woman where a bag of bones used to be.'

Grace laughs. 'Thanks. I'm getting there, slowly. More good days than bad.'

'And how's your gorgeous mother?' asks Bizzy.

'She's well.' Grace laughs. 'Still in the choir. And she got a job.'

'So I heard,' says Bizzy. 'Doing what exactly?'

'Stuff for the government,' Grace says. 'Data processing or something. She says it's too boring to explain.'

Bizzy sees a glint of knowing in Grace's smile and has to look away before she returns it with the same.

'Come along, then,' Bizzy says, paddling on towards the bridge.

'Here we go!' shouts one of the other kayakers as Bizzy and Grace catch up. They look upwards to the bridge as a banner is released, unfurling to reveal the words, *RESTORE LAKE PEDDER.*

Grace watches as Bizzy pulls out a bundle of red cylinders. 'Distress flares,' she explains. 'Our wilderness is in distress. Would you like one?'

'Sure,' says Grace.

On three, the group of kayakers release the daytime ends of their flares. Bright orange smoke hisses out, fluorescent against the dull

grey sky. A cluster of people high on the bridge send out a corres-
ponding chant of, 'Restore Lake Pedder, restore Lake Pedder.'

'Nice of you to come out and add a person to our number, Grace,'
says Bizzy.

'To be honest,' says Grace, 'I came out to talk to you specifically.
I hope you don't mind.'

'Right,' says Bizzy, her heart sinking. 'If you've been sent to bring
me back to the choir, it's a no, I'm sorry.'

'It's just an idea I've been working on,' says Grace shyly.

'How did you know I'd be here?' asks Bizzy.

'Well, I didn't, really. But Mum told me you probably would be.
She always seems to know where to find things.'

'Ah, yes,' says Bizzy, 'that she does.'

They paddle on in silence for a bit until they reach a large disc of
sunlight beneath the loom of the Tasman Bridge.

'According to sailors,' Bizzy says, 'it's dangerous to share ideas
while sitting in God's rays on the surface of the sea.'

Grace laughs and says, 'You made that up.'

'All right, so. Out with it and hurry up, we have a lake to restore.'

They sit in the patch of bright and Grace speaks.

'Well,' she says, 'during lockdown I was doing a lot of reading
and heaps of researching about some of the Angry Women's Brigades
around the world, as well as learning more about the choir.' Grace
laughs nervously. 'Sorry if it seems a bit stalky, Bizzy, but I read
about you and your amazing mum. Then I found Eleanor's case and
how she killed her horrible husband. And everyone's told me about
Rosanna. And Quin told me about her difficult background. Avni
told me about coming here when she was so little from Iran after her
father was killed for believing in unity and peace. And, you know,
all these stories could be complete tragedies, couldn't they? Including my story. But the choir is totally the opposite of misery, it's all
about laughter and friends and healing. I mean, for instance, I don't

think I'd be anywhere near close to recovery without the choir. And then there are all these amazing, creative people all over the world who want to support us, do something to help women's places in the world, keep everyone's eyes open. So'—Grace closes her eyes for the crux of the idea—'I think we should put together a musical theatre show.'

Bizzy says nothing. She feels exhausted all over again.

'The thing is,' Grace continues, 'there are at least thirteen art forms that make up a musical theatre show, and you have – *we* have – a whole army of people who want to lend their expertise and imagination to this. And a zillion others who only have to buy tickets to support us, then sit and watch.'

Bizzy looks at the water, where Grace's enthusiasm is sending waves sloshing against her kayak. 'Grace,' she says, 'you might be on to something, but the truth is, I was petering out just as your mother was flung in amongst us. Then, Rosanna took more life out of me when she died, and then poor old hideous Laetare got banjaxed and the harrow from all that was just too much. And anyways, we all saw – the whole world saw – what the choir can achieve without me. You have my blessing, if that's what you're after, but count me out.'

'But Bizzy,' says Grace, 'you're so central to the story. There's a really good libretto in there. I can't write it, but someone amazing will want to. And we already have many of the songs. Avni wrote her head off during lockdown.'

'She's a folk singer,' says Bizzy. 'Her songs are quiet and beautiful but there's nothing musical theatre about them.'

'Well, maybe musical theatre is a bit too musical theatre for its own good. And Avni will have producers helping, experts. My brother Tom's an amateur but he's done some good things with Avni's songs already. And other composers will jump at the chance if we pitch it well. There is nothing more powerful and enchanting than a well-developed musical theatre show.'

'You'll never raise the funds. It'll take millions to polish up our motley lot.'

'But we could try. The other choristers are keen.'

'As I said, sure, look it, go bananas. I'll do you up a cross-stitch for your promotions but other than that, it's a hard no from me. I'm sorry, my love, but I'm just getting to know a quiet life, and loving the shit out of it, to be frank. Thank you, though.' Bizzy turns her kayak away just as a cloud obscures the sun and takes the disc of light with it.

'I really believe,' Grace says, 'that this musical is what we need, Bizzy. It's a powerful re-enchantment tool, a way to show people what is possible outside the fields of human perception! We have to keep telling women's stories, we have to rewrite the myths. People are getting sick because they're meant to love a world that makes them feel like shit. I nearly died from patriarchy and now I'll die on this musical hill if I have to.'

'Sweet Jesus alive,' says Bizzy, paddling back to face Grace again. 'Look at you and your performance! Did you include dramaturgy on your list of musical theatre requirements? Because I'm looking at quite the practitioner if you need her.'

'Mostly we need you, Bizzy,' replies Grace. 'We won't do it without you. Say yes.'

A car horn toots from the bridge, then another. Two abseilers are lowering themselves down from the parapet towards a large flat barge at sea level, a banner held between them. '*RECOVER THE ENCHANTED BEACH, SAVE LAKE PEDDER,*' it shouts as it unfolds.

'Can this musical show have some jazz in it?' asks Bizzy after a long moment. 'Winifred loved her jazz, and I've had a proper yearning lately to return to my jazz roots.'

Grace smiles. 'Of course.' She paddles closer to Bizzy. 'And Bizzy. I should warn you that my sister, Lily, is kind of obsessed about this too. She's written a death metal song.'

Bizzy laughs. 'I'll give it a listen,' she says. 'Everything deserves that.' She laughs again, louder and Grace hears for the first time that wonderful, boots-up guffaw.

'And one more thing, if we're to go into production,' says Grace. 'I can't stand sad endings.'

'Nor can I,' says Bizzy. 'Not one bit.'

𝄢

On the Western shore, standing on the jetty just near the Hobart Regatta grounds are Freycinet, Tom, Lily and Roger. Their eyes are narrowed against the sharp Derwent air as they study the distant cluster of kayaks out by the bridge.

'A hundred bucks she has Bizzy convinced already,' says Tom.

'I hope she's talked about me and my song,' says Lily, who sits then swings her legs above the polished pewter of the river.

'I hope we get some other blokes on board if her musical idea gets going,' Tom says. 'I'm doing my best to understand women better but wow . . .'

'There are two things you need to know about women and you'll be all set,' says Roger. They wait as he pauses for effect. 'She can eat your chips, but you can't eat hers. Also, mark in your diary when her hormones are on the rise and set down eggshells for yourself. Hormones are a great, powerful mystery and you'd do well to do the washing up for them.'

They all smile in amazement at the length of Roger's speech.

He smiles back. 'Put that in your sample machine and set it on loop.'

'Right, thanks, Grandpa,' says Tom. 'And what if they all get their gear off again?'

'Oof,' says Roger, glancing up at the nearby cenotaph. 'Best we forget.'

'Can we go and get some chips?' asks Lily. 'There's a kiosk up at the bike track.'

'Yes,' says Freycinet, who is still watching the kayaks.

'My shout,' says Roger.

They head back along the jetty, leaving Freycinet with her thoughts. She imagines Grace's musical idea hovering above the dotted kayaks, folding and shapeshifting with the clouds, and her wishes. She imagines a world filled with ideas like this: people dancing like musical notes on the loose, leaders who are not hard in the face or rigid with ego, hours slowed by patience into silken ticks and golden tocks. She pictures tree-filled green space for delicious shudders of deja vu and roll-about, belly-ache laughter. And streets where all the weekday suited people in their coffee-aftershave air stop and give up their very best wishes for the sake of a stranger's day. She sees a place where tickboxery is set aside to watch the moon rising over the horse shed and people take a moment and use it to say, 'I like your hat.' She imagines a future where stones of excessive guilt can be removed, buried in high traffic areas and pummelled into fossils that might one day be dug up and placed in museums alongside other ancient relics. And she dreams up a world in which company towns with their Capability Brown gardens can be torn down, muddled in with ramshackle souls and turned into cathedrals; where nasty flare-ups of uncaring can be soothed away with scented oil and washed down the plughole or sent to don aprons and clean the windows and wipe down the bench tops.

Freycinet returns her gaze to the water and the now. The drift of kayaks is moving towards her as a streak of sun breaks through the clouds, changing the colour of the bay and all the ideas whirling above it. And there with the mountain, the river, the sky and her shadow, she waits.

Stepping Stone Number 1, from *La Lista* by R.K.:
Be kind be kind be kind be kind be kind be kind be kind be kind be kind, including to yourself. It makes you feel good, every time.

Epilogue

ANGRY WOMEN FACE THE MUSIC

Review by M.A.B., 18 February 2025

Five years ago this month, Tasmania's famed Angry Women's Choir faced incredible triumph, shocking tragedy and huge disappointment, all in the space of a few days. They had just completed their #jointhechorus rally, the culmination of their consciousness-raising efforts and quite possibly the beginning of a revolution. A revolution that couldn't quite get off the ground.

Choir member Irene Hawke didn't rise from the ground either. She died of sudden heart failure at the close of the choir's famed naked performance, and is immortalised now by a Skye Killinger bronze sculpture at the foot of the Town Hall steps, just metres from where she died.

The choir's activities and their momentous support base gave them a global audience and a place in the history books of feminism and civil rights.

Throughout 2020 (and onwards), COVID-19 galumphed across the world in all its evil, green-crowned glory, striking indiscriminately at humankind. Well, it seemed indiscriminate at the time. With glaring hindsight, it is obvious that this calamity hit the marginalised, the poor, the elderly, the sick and the care workers hardest of all. And it brought feminism back to its aching knees. Paid childcare was no longer an option, and so the work of caring for children was for the most part taken on by mothers or grandmothers. Meanwhile, the invisible 'second shift' wasn't going anywhere, nor was the emotional labour given over to most women. The gender pay gap yawned, wide and exhausted. Domestic violence statistics soared. It all drew a clear picture of what had always been said: that women are not being seen.

Later that same year, on Wednesday, 4 November at around two p.m. Australian Eastern Daylight Time, just as the United States broke the daily case record of one hundred thousand new patients infected, I lay on the lawn in my garden and tried to stop panic engulfing me. Inside, on the television, America was turning red while a gloating orange troll yawped victory from his podium. I had spent that catastrophic year clinging to silver linings, turning over leaves, counting blessings, sowing optimism in our veggie patch. But the orange troll and his idea of great turned the future very dark and the blessings were impossible to see. For two hours or so, I cried for the people the troll would persecute or ignore or scorn or abuse. I cried for the people that would die because of him. I cried for the damage it would do to our planet, our progress, our causes, our care. And I raged against the permissions given to locker room boys and their minions to be complete, pussy-grabbing cockheads.

Pretty soon, America started turning blue again, thank all the goodness. And I picked myself up, wiped my tears and put on my high-vis Angry Women's Choir T-shirt. I thought about the AWC and all the other choirs across the world, maligned for their potentially deadly saliva spray and silenced or sent to cyberspace to commune as best they could on glitching screens.

The Angry Women's Choir, it seems, was doing some thinking too. Because soon after the US election, they reinvented themselves as a series of new iterations. First as a sort of pre-production development think tank, then officially as the Angry Women's Production Company, and now as a full-scale theatre production called *The Angry Women's Choir*.

This musical theatre piece, to which I was irresistibly drawn, previewed this week for its world premiere at Hobart's own Theatre Royal. And it is nothing short of a triumph. Famed librettist Georgia von Metz and lyricist and trans activist Pandoria Eleganza have weaved together the extraordinary and the ordinary using the stories of the choir's core members with an astonishing rhythm that would have its own beat even if you took away the music.

But the music! Based on original compositions from the choir's own Avni Sasani, it is a rhapsodic fanfare of genres drawing from (but not limited to) the amateur choir's longtime influences. These including riot grrrl, activist rock and eighties pop. Add side serves of hymn, murder ballad, jazz, panto and metal and you have a production that will surprise you at every turn, give you goosebumps and regale you with revelation.

The Tasmanian production stars many of the choristers themselves. The choir's former longtime director, Bizzy Nancarrow, says this was a deliberate decision, made to pay homage to the choir's amateur values. But aside from the odd wobble (which I swear were deliberately placed for endearment) these performances are first rate. World class, in some cases. And given that the production has attracted a professional-standard production crew, from set and lighting to sound and costume, nothing has a chance to appear even slightly amateur. The show has already been picked up in the US, Off Broadway, and I would hope that Grace Barnes would be selected to play herself. She was flawless.

A breathtakingly gifted triple threat. Her mother, Freycinet Barnes, played her violin with the orchestra and was brought to life onstage by beloved Australian musical theatre star Lucinda Smith.

Story-wise, there is plenty of grief to justify tissues, but none of it is unresolved. All the characters, all the artists, all the songs have given form to their grief, they dig it out, hold it up, cry with it, poke fun at it and laugh with it. They share it, they dance it, they play it and they sing the shit out of it. And it strikes me, as the curtain falls, that when Irene Hawke's weak heart gave itself to women's liberty, she might have just been living more than ever before.

Five brilliant stars from me. And now I need to go and lie firmly on my lawn before this theatre high takes me flying clean away.

Author's Note

The Angry Women's Choir is a work of fiction. The West Moonah Women's Choir, to the best of my knowledge, has never existed. The choristers and their director depicted in this book definitely haven't existed.

Laetare Gardens Function Centre was a popular venue for Hobart schools to host their dinner dances and formals in the eighties and nineties. It was demolished in 2009 and rebuilt as Laetare Court, independent residences and community housing for people with an acquired brain injury.

Many of the events and settings that backdrop the choir are drawn from truth. Some dates have been altered to fit the narrative.

The Bon Secours Mother and Baby Home in Ireland was a real place with a dark history.

Tasmania is a real place with patches of very dark history.

Please contact the Butterfly Foundation on 1800 334 673 for help with issues surrounding disordered eating.

Please contact White Ribbon Australia on 1800 737 732 for help if you have suffered domestic violence or sexual assault.

Please contact No to Violence's Men's Referral Service on 1300 766 491 if you feel you are a risk to others in your home.

For these or any other personal crises, contact Lifeline on 13 11 14.

Acknowledgements

This novel was written on unceded country of the muwinina and paredarerme peoples of the South-East Nation of lutruwita/ Trouwunna (Tasmania). I pay my respects to all palawa elders past, present and emerging and acknowledge their ancient culture and deep knowledge of their lands. They are our first storytellers.

𝄡

I sent the full catastrophe of this novel in its first draft to two remarkable people before I showed anyone else: Fiona Inglis, my literary agent, and Ali Watts, my publisher. I am grateful to both for seeing the potential in my enormous, firey polemic and for not running away from those burning pages.

Fiona, thank you for continuing to champion my work, for taking my needy phone calls and playing the long game with me.

Ali, I'm so lucky to have you and your patience, diplomacy, realism and clarity so enthusiastically on my team.

Genevieve Buzo, editor extraordinaire, thank you for hanging out with me in the track-changes columns and for being gentle, thoughtful and clever therein.

Debbie McGowan, thank you for your tireless enthusiasm, your good humour, and for brandishing my book all over the island with such vigour.

To others at Penguin Random House – publicist Bella Arnott-Hoare, marketer Kelly Jenkins, proofreader and continuity genius Pamela Dunne, production manager Ben Fairclough and audio producer Veronica Eze – thank you for knowing what you're doing and doing it so well.

Christa Moffitt at Christabella Designs, thank you for making my book cover go POP!

Midland Typesetters, golly it's a pleasure to see how you magically turn a mess of pages into a book and remind me in the midst of brutal edits that I'm an actual author.

Thank you to my stage partner in crime, choir director and music producer Jude Elliot, who has somehow never stopped believing in me despite my limited vocal range and my snowflakey self-belief.

Nick Storr, you got me through the audiobook recording with your skill, patience and good humour. *Grazie mille amico mio.*

To my wonderful singers, Jude Elliot, Sarah Parsons, Nicole Farrow, Amelia Howell, Gabriella Vavoulas and Robyn Lawrence-Vick, thank you for lending me your beautiful voices and bringing the music of *The Angry Women's Choir* to life.

Thank you as always to my quieter chorus members, those who provide harmony, inspiration and accompaniment for my work without asking for any spotlight: Maggie Mackellar, Emily Warner and Fiona Blackwood.

To Sarah Sentilles, whose gentle, profound wisdoms have challenged and changed my writing for the better and reminded me that choosing art over washing is a powerful political act.

To the others on my writing raft – Bronwyn Birdsall, Jessie Cole and Carolyn Fraser – thank you for being such premium-quality floaties. Annie Keely, thank you for your kind words and early encouragement. I love sitting around those cave fires with you.

Dick Friend, thank you for the Pedder inspirations and for sending funny emails when writing didn't feel very funny.

Thank you to readers and booksellers. Oh, how the world needs you.

To my monthly newsletter readers, thank goodness for you keeping my writing muscles limber in between edits. You're the real reasons to be cheerful when it comes that project.

Kate and Dick Warner (Mum and Dad), thank you for being such enthusiastic early readers and even earlier influencers on my work. Dad! You finally got through one of my books. Sorry (not sorry) about That Scene.

Ed, Bess and Lucie, thank you, my darlings, for putting up with my distracted absent-mindedness, which can so unexpectedly turn into me wanting to know all your beliefs, everything you're thinking and whether you want to come beach-combing. Thank you for driving me bonkers enough to write novels, and for making me laugh even when I'm angry. I'm so glad our children are funny.

Finally, Dickie – thank you for being the dependable one who gets the milk out of the cows. I love you even when you're rampaging about with the broom.

Meg XX

About the author

Meg Bignell grew up in a sprawling garden on the banks of the Derwent River in Tasmania's Derwent Valley. She now lives with her husband and three children on a dairy farm at Bream Creek on the east coast of Tasmania. She is the author of *The Sparkle Pages* and *Welcome to Nowhere River.*

www.megbignell.com.au

Discover a
new favourite

Visit **penguin.com.au/readmore**